THE
BONE
PALACE

AMANDA
DOWNUM

ORBIT

First published in Great Britain in 2010 by Orbit

A CIP catalogue record for this book
is available from the British Library.

ISBN 978-1-84149-815-7

Printed and bound in Great Britain by CPI Mackays, Chatham ME5 8TD

Papers used by Orbit are natural, renewable and recyclable
products sourced from well-managed forests and certified
in accordance with the rules of the Forest Stewardship Council.

Mixed Sources
Product group from well-managed
forests and other controlled sources
www.fsc.org Cert no. SGS-COC-004081
© 1996 Forest Stewardship Council

Orbit
An imprint of
Little, Brown Book Group
100 Victoria Embankment
London EC4Y 0DY

An Hachette UK Company
www.hachette.co.uk

www.orbitbooks.net

To Sarah, Sonya, and Liz,
my muses for all things classical,
and to Steven, for not getting a
third-book divorce

I am weary of days and hours,
Blown buds of barren flowers,
Desires and dreams and powers
And everything but sleep.

> Algernon Charles Swinburne
> —"The Garden of Proserpine"

Love is a many splintered thing
> The Sisters of Mercy

> —"Ribbons"

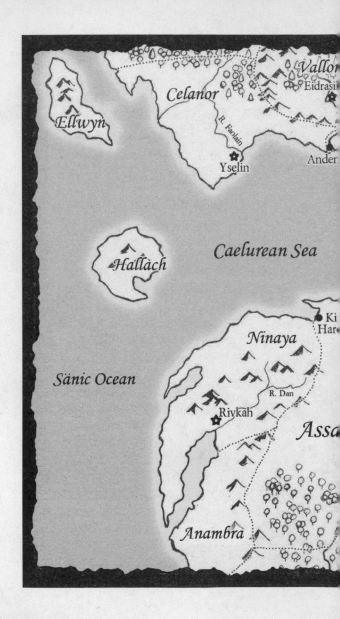

PART I

Crepuscule

PROLOGUE

496 Ab Urbe Condita (1228 Sal Emperaturi)
Three years ago

Death was no stranger in Erisín. The city named for the saint of death and built on the bones of its founders had known its share of suffering, but the pestilence that struck that summer was enough to horrify even the priests of Erishal. The plague had come from the south, borne on a merchant ship that slipped through a lax quarantine. It spread now through the bites of fleas and midges, so that any drone of wings or sudden itch meant terror. Hundreds dead throughout the city, temples and hospitals become mass tombs, and in the slums they dispensed with the proper rites altogether and stacked the infected dead like cordwood.

Not even the palace was safe.

The queen no longer trembled. She lay still now in the wide curtained bed, only the shallow rise and fall of her breast and her fluttering lashes to show that she lived. Sweat soaked her linen shift, matted her long black hair. Brown skin flushed gold with jaundice and the whites of her half-open eyes were yellow and bloodshot.

The room stank of sick sweat and vomit, the cloying sourness of old blood. Shutters and curtains blocked the windows despite the summer heat, and lamps trickled dark malodorous smoke. Meant to keep insects at bay, but it served with men as well. Sane ones, at least.

Kirilos Orfion, spymaster of Selafai and the king's own mage, sank into a chair and wiped his brow with a sodden cloth. A cup of tea sat on the table beside him—long cold, but it eased the ache in his throat, if not the ache in his bones. His hands shook, sloshing brown fluid over the rim. Sunken, shaken, sweating—he must look as though the fever burned in him too.

Boots rang heavy in the hall outside. Mathiros keeping vigil. The king hadn't slept since his wife took ill, save in fitful snatches beside her bed. Kiril had finally sent their son to rest with a whispered spell, but it was all he could do to keep Mathiros from the room. It was all he could do to keep death from the room. He rarely wasted energy on regret and might-have-beens, but now he wished for the healing skill he'd abandoned so many years ago. In his decades of service to the Crown he had known worry and fear and even the sharp edge of panic, but never this sick helplessness.

Kiril felt Isyllt waiting beyond the door as well, tasted her own fatigue and worry. Ten years as master and apprentice and two as lovers had left their magic inextricably twined—even now she reached for him, a soft *otherwise* touch, but he drew away, tightening his mind against her. She would only exhaust herself trying to comfort him and that would serve nothing. If he burned himself out here, the city would need all the mages it had left.

The fever might not be the work of spirits as the superstitious claimed, but so much suffering still attracted them. The mirrors in the room were draped with black silk, the windows warded with salt and silver, but even now something skittered over the shutters, larger than an insect. Those mages who weren't tending the sick spent the nights hunting newly fledged demons.

He stood, wincing as his joints creaked, and limped toward the bed. "Lychandra." His voice broke on her name, hoarse and ugly.

Bruised lids opened and golden-brown eyes met his. Lucid now, at least, delirium fled. No wonder people thought the plague demon-born, when victims died bloody and raving.

Her lips cracked as she smiled. "You're as stubborn as Mathiros." Her voice was soft and ragged. "Find someone else to save—it won't be me."

He pressed a cup of willow bark tea to her mouth. She coughed around the swallow and bloody saliva flecked her lips. The physicians had shaken their heads when she first vomited black blood, said she was beyond their skill. She was likely beyond his, too, but he had to try.

Kiril sucked in a deep breath and tried to clear his mind. The magic answered slowly, scraping like broken glass in his veins. A cool draft whipped through the room, fluttering the bed hangings and rattling the shutters. Lychandra sighed as it breathed over her skin, respite from the fever's heat. Kiril laid a hand on her brow and she gasped.

His vision blurred and he saw with *otherwise* eyes—illness hung on her like a pall, swirled dark and yellow-green as bile inside her. Contagion flared like an asp's hood as his magic lapped over the queen's skin; it had feasted and grown fat in three days, while Kiril had only worn himself dry. His power broke, splintering ice needles inside his chest. He fell to his knees beside the bed, jarring bones even through thick carpets.

Lychandra turned her head and pink saliva dripped onto the sweat-stained pillow. "Kirilos—" Her long brown hand touched his, burning his numb fingers. "No more. You'll only hurt yourself. Please, let me see my husband."

He nodded, climbing shakily to his feet. Hard to breathe around the pain in his chest. He'd seen this woman a glowing bride, listened to her curse in childbirth. He hadn't thought to stand her deathwatch, too. Pins and needles stung his hand as he opened the door.

The king's face only made it worse—skin ashen, eyes black pits under his brows. Mathiros read defeat in Kiril's expression and let out a sound neither sob nor howl. He shouldered the sorcerer aside as he rushed to his wife.

Isyllt followed the king into the room and stepped into Kiril's arms. She cupped his face in white hands and kissed him, the familiar scent of her hair filling his nose. Her grey eyes were shadowed and dark with worry; he winced from his reflection there. So tired. So old.

"You have to rest," she said. "You'll kill yourself this way."

He would die, sooner or later. Sooner every year. Leave her grieving beside his bed like Mathiros beside Lychandra. He lowered her hands away from his face. She was too young to be a widow—certainly too young to be his.

He might have told her so, but he couldn't get enough breath. His chest ached like a bruise.

"Kiril." Mathiros's voice cracked on his name. "Is there nothing— Anything—" Tears soaked his beard, splashed his wife's hand. Kiril wanted to cringe at the pain in his eyes. "You can't do this!"

Whether he spoke to Kiril or Lychandra or Erishal herself, the sorcerer couldn't say. His palms slicked with cold sweat and Isyllt's hand tightened on his.

Lychandra's eyes sagged and she whispered to her husband. His name turned into a cough and she gagged, turning her head to vomit. Mathiros flinched; the liquid that soaked the side of the bed was watery, clotted with blood dark as soil or tea dregs. Her organs were failing, and no skill or magic could undo the damage now.

The king knotted his fist in the gauzy curtains as if he meant to rip them from the bed. "Kiril, please!"

Kiril closed his eyes. Mathiros hadn't pleaded with him, with anyone, since he was a child. He'd never been able to say no to the boy.

The queen hitched and shuddered, twisting stained linen. Isyllt gasped—she felt it too, the icy presence filling the room. The black diamond rings they both wore began to spark and glow. Kiril's vision darkened. Mathiros screamed his wife's name.

Kiril reached, scraping himself raw, and threw every bit of strength against the shadow. For an instant it balked, mantling over the room. He couldn't breathe, could feel nothing but that black chill.

The ice inside his chest broke and stabbed him through the heart.

His legs folded. The shadow crested over him, crashed

down. Mathiros screamed. Isyllt screamed. The floor rushed up to meet him. Old debts come due at last.

The shadow retreated; it would take Kiril with it, and at last he might rest. Isyllt's face lingered behind his eyes—no surprise that death would wear her countenance. But she called his name, invoked it, held him inside his pain-riddled flesh. Over the roar in his ears he heard his king's wailing grief. He might only have imagined Erishal's mocking laughter.

Darkness stole over him, dark and blessed silence.

The bells tolled an hour before dusk, slow and solemn and irrevocable.

In her chambers in the Gallery of Pearls, Savedra Seve-ros sank onto the edge of the bed and pressed her face into her hands. Her eyes ached, though she had no tears—it wasn't her grief, but the weight of it still crushed her. It would crush the whole palace; the queen was well loved.

Had been.

"I should go to him." Her voice snagged and broke halfway. Maybe it was her grief after all. Lychandra had always been kind to her son's impolitic mistress, more than Savedra could have hoped for. "If he'll see me."

She had been the prince's lover for six months, for-mally installed in the Gallery for three, but it still felt unreal that she might walk the palace corridors and visit Nikos whenever she wished. Even now. Especially now.

It was almost a relief, if only to leave her room. The windows were shuttered and draped and warded, the air close and cloying with smoke and incense. With no sun-light for days, too many candles had smudged the ceil-ing and curtains and left the taste of wax and char on her tongue with every breath. The ashes of prayers streaked her shrine, but no saint had answered, not Sarai or Alia or even owl-winged Erishal. Or rather, Erishal had answered, but not as Savedra had begged.

"He'll see you," her mother said, sipping her tea. No amount of death or chaos could shake Nadesda Severos' flawless deportment. It made her seem colder than she was, but it was reassuring. A familiar comfort. "He needs you now more than ever."

Savedra frowned, letting her hands fall. Her hair hung in kinks and tangles around her face and she didn't need a mirror to know how bruised her eyes must be, how dull her complexion. Nothing she could do for it now—it was madness to uncover the mirror with so many demons about, and she'd sent her maids away days ago.

That her parents had stayed in the city, let alone come to visit her in the palace, was testament to either pride or love. Or both, she conceded. There was room for both. And ambition, of course—that the Severoi stayed when other great houses fled the Octagon Court would be marked. Especially now, as the city's horror became the kingdom's grief.

"This is an important time for you and the prince," her father said, leaning over Nadesda's chair. "With Lychandra gone, it will be you he turns to more and more."

Ambition again. Her fists clenched in her already-wrinkled muslin gown. She'd been grateful, at first, that her parents hadn't repudiated her when she became Nikos's mistress. It might have been easier if they had.

She touched the pearls at her throat—the mark of her station. Her fingers tensed against the cool slickness and for an instant she thought of ripping them away, scattering them across the room. "I'll never be queen, Father, not for all your scheming." Her voice was calm when she would rather scream; her mother's child, after all. "Can't you at least feign a little sorrow? Or tact?"

Sevastian's lean brown face creased in a frown. A familiar expression—she'd have the same lines on her brow in ten years. Or sooner. Her mother's smooth olive skin and silken hair were not to be hers.

"I don't have to feign sorrow, Vedra," he said, crossing his arms over his chest. "Lychandra was a good woman, a good queen. She'll be missed. Saints know she made Mathiros bearable. But sorrow doesn't negate practicality. You may not be queen, but consort isn't beyond your reach. There's precedent enough for that."

Savedra pried her fingers from the pearls and touched instead the telltale bulge above them. The joke of her birth, that kept the rank of queen forever from her as surely as politics did. If only that were as easy to rip away as a necklace. "There will be a queen. The betrothal is already set and Lychandra's death won't dissolve it. And even if this foreign princess doesn't make Nikos set me aside, I'll still be nothing more than another pearl. Sorrow doesn't negate practicality."

Nadesda raised a hand when her husband would have spoken. "Enough. This is a time for tact as well as sorrow. Vastian, leave us. I'll help Vedra dress." Her teacup didn't clink against the saucer, but her veils spoke in a dry rasp of lace and netting as she rose.

Her father gave them both a sardonic little bow and retreated to the antechamber. Savedra found a comb on her dresser while her mother opened the wardrobe to inspect her gowns. Sandalwood teeth caught in snarls and she fought the urge to tear them free. The sharp pain in her scalp grounded her.

"Why do you bother, Mother? I won't be queen, and I'll give you no Severos heir or cat's paw bastard. Why keep including me in your schemes?"

Nadesda pulled out Savedra's white mourning dress— a year out of style—and turned, sinking onto the bed next to her daughter. She wore eucalyptus oil to keep insects away, and the sharp minty smell clashed with the more familiar perfume clinging in the folds of her skirts.

"My love for you has nothing to do with the children you can't bear, or the marriages you might make." Her manicured hand closed over Savedra's and she smiled. "I've always been grateful to have a daughter, even if it took us a few years to discover it." The smile fell away. "But my love and loyalty to the house demand I take all of those things into account. As a mother I want you to be happy with your prince, but as archa I have other well-beings to consider too."

Savedra continued combing for a moment, then gave up and twisted her hair into a thick knot at her nape. No one whose opinion she valued would care what she looked like right now. "Just remember, schemes that hurt Nikos will hurt me as well."

"None of us can stop the world from hurting those we love. The best we can do is be there to ease the pain." Her mother draped the white silk across Savedra's lap and went to the bathroom; water gurgled, and she returned with a damp cloth. "So wash your face and go to your prince. You could have made worse choices, even if he is an Alexios."

Savedra couldn't help but smile at the approbation— the strongest an archa of House Severos might ever grant their ancient rival. "Mother, can't you leave us out of your machinations?"

Nadesda rarely frowned, but her beautiful face stilled with sadness. "Even if I could, others won't. I can only promise to spare you any suffering that I can, and to keep you innocent of anything that might compromise you."

Savedra wanted to argue. Wanted to scream. But she was too tired, too empty. More than anything she simply wanted to go to Nikos. Her hands tightened on the washcloth till water dripped onto the dress in her lap. She'd need a new one made, anyway. The palace would be awash in white for a year.

"Thank you," she said at last. Then she began to scrub away the clinging smoke, and the ghosts of tears she hadn't yet shed.

CHAPTER 1

499 AUC

In the Sepulcher, death smelled like roses.

Sachets of petals and braziers of incense lined the marble halls and scented oil lamps burned throughout the long vault, twining ribbons of rose and jasmine and myrrh through the chill air. Meant to drown the smell of blood and rot that crept from the corpse-racks in the walls, but death couldn't be undone so easily. The raw copper scent of recent violence teased past the sweetness, creeping into Isyllt Iskaldur's sinuses as she studied the dead woman on the slab.

Blue-tinged lips parted slightly, expressionless in death, but the slash across her throat grinned, baring red meat and pale flashes of bone. Barely enough blood in her to settle—some clotted like rust in brass-blonde hair, pasted damp-frizzed tendrils to her cheeks. Lines down her ribs showed where corset stays had pressed into flesh.

Her clothing, cut away by competent, uncaring attendants, was shelved in an oubliette of an evidence room upstairs.

Isyllt crossed her arms beneath her breasts and shivered in her long black coat. "Where did you find her?" Her breath trailed away in a shimmering plume; spells of cold etched the stones.

"In the Garden," Khelséa Shar said, "in an alley just after dusk." The police inspector lounged against the wall between corpse-drawers, a short, dark woman in the garish orange coat of the Vigiles Urbani. Frescoed vines and leaves swirled behind her—the builders had tried to make the room cheery, but no amount of paint or plaster could disguise the death that steeped these stones. "She was cold and stiff when we got there."

Isyllt frowned at the dead woman, brushed a finger against a lock of yellow hair. A prostitute, then, most likely. A foreigner too, from the coloring—Vallish like Isyllt, perhaps, or Rosian. Refugees from Ashke Ros crowded tenements and shantytowns in the inner city, and more and more turned to the Garden for work.

Isyllt pressed gently on the woman's jaw and it opened to reveal nearly a full set of tea-stained teeth. Her elbows were still stiff, knees immobile. Rigor had only just begun to fade. "A day dead?"

"That's our guess. It was raining when we found her, and she was soaked, but there were hardly any insects. The alley is visible from the street—she couldn't have lain there all day."

"So dumped. Why call me?" The Garden was the Vigils' jurisdiction, unless the Crown was somehow involved, or the crime was beyond the city police. And while pride insisted that the Vigils' necromancers weren't as well trained as the Arcanostoi or Crown Investigators, Isyllt knew they were perfectly competent. She bent over the white stone table, examining the wound. The knife had nicked bone. The killer was strong and sure-handed—left-handed. "What can I tell you about this that you don't already know?"

"Look at her thighs."

The woman's legs tapered from flaring hips to gently muscled calves and delicate ankles. No spider veins or calluses on her feet—chipped gold paint decorated her toenails. Flesh once soft and supple felt closer to wax under Isyllt's careful fingers. Death whispered over her hand, lapped catlike at her skin. The cabochon black diamond on her right hand flickered fitfully, ghostlight sparking in its crystalline depths.

She ran a gentle hand between the woman's thighs, tracing the same path as a dozen customers, a dozen lovers. But this time there was no response, no passion real or feigned. Only stiffening muscles and cold flesh.

No wounds, no bruises. No sign of rape. No violation but that of the blade.

"What am I—" She paused. On the inside of the left leg, near the crease of the groin, she touched a narrow ridge of scar tissue. More than one. She pressed against stiff flesh to get a better look. Old marks, healed and scarred long ago. Teeth marks. She found the same marks on the other leg, some only recently scabbed.

Very sharp teeth. Isyllt knew what such bites felt like.

"Do you think this had anything to do with her death?" She kept looking, but found no fresh wounds.

"Maybe." Khelséa reached into an inside pocket of her coat and pulled out a folded piece of silk. "But this is why I called you."

Isyllt stretched across the dead woman and took the cloth; something small and hard was hidden in its folds. She recognized the shape of a ring before she finished unwrapping it.

A heavy band of gold, skillfully wrought, set with a sapphire the size of a woman's thumbnail. A rampant griffin etched the stone, tiny but detailed. A master's work. A royal work.

"Where was this?" A knot colder than the room drew tight in her stomach.

"Sewn inside her camisole, clumsy new stitches. Her purse was missing."

A royal signet in a dead whore's clothes. Isyllt blew a sharp breath through her nose. "How many know?"

"Only me and my autopsist." Khelséa snorted. "You think I'd wave something like this in front of the constables?"

Isyllt stared at the ring. A woman's ring, but no woman alive had the right to wear it. She looked down at the body. A sliver of blue iris showed beneath half-closed lids, already milky. "What was her name?"

"Forsythia."

Not a real name—at least she hoped it wasn't. Not many mothers branded their daughters with a prostitute's name at birth.

Isyllt dipped a finger into the gaping wound, licked off coagulated blood and fluids. Khelséa grimaced theatrically, but the inspector's nerves and stomach were hard to upset.

Cold jellied blood, bittersweet and thin with rainwater. No trace of illness or taint, nothing deadly save for the quantity spilled. The taste coated Isyllt's tongue.

"Forsythia. Are you there?"

No answer, not even a shiver. Her power could raise the corpse off its cold table and dance it around the room, but no ghost lingered to answer her questions. She sighed. "They never stay when you need them to. She might be wherever she was killed, though." She nibbled the last speck of blood from under her fingernail.

Gently she pushed back Forsythia's kohl-smeared eyelids. *Rain,* she wondered briefly, looking at the ashen streaks, *or did you have time for tears?* Her reflection stared back from death-pearled eyes. She rested her fingers on the woman's temples, thumbs on her cheekbones; the black leather glove on her left hand was stark against pale skin. The woman's soul was gone, but memories still lingered in her eyes.

Isyllt hoped for the killer's face, but instead she found a sunset. Clouds glowed rose and carnelian as the sun sank behind the ragged rooftops of Oldtown, and a flock of birds etched black silhouettes against the sky. The last thing she saw was those jeweled clouds fading into dusk, then a sudden pressure of hands and darkness. Much too quick for death, even as quick a death as this must have been.

Isyllt sighed and looked away, the colors of memory fading into the white and green of the mortuary. "She was grabbed off the street, somewhere in Oldtown. Maybe the Garden." Death must have come not long afterward; she hoped the woman hadn't suffered much. "What else do you know?"

"Nothing. There was nothing but rain in the alley, and no one saw anything." Khelséa rolled her eyes. "No one ever sees anything." She pushed away from the wall, shaking back her long black braids. "Do you have any magic tricks for me?"

"Nothing flashy." Isyllt turned toward the back of the room, where tables and benches were set up for students and investigators. "Bring me gloves and surgical spirits, please. And a dissection plate."

The inspector opened a cabinet against the wall and removed thin cotton examiner's gloves, a bottle, and a well-scrubbed tin tray. "What are you doing?"

"Testing for contagion. Someone touched this before she did." She sat down, stripping off her left glove. The hand beneath was scarred and claw-curled, corpse-white after two and a half years bandaged or gloved; she was mostly comfortable with only seven working fingers by now. She scrubbed her hands with cold spirits, then wiped down the tray and tugged on the white gloves. The ring was already contaminated, of course, but every little bit helped. It was much easier to test for transference—be it of skin, hair, blood, or energy—with a suspect at hand, but she could also tune the ring to react to the presence of anyone who had handled it recently, and even to seek them out at close range.

Closing her eyes against the bitter sharpness of alcohol fumes, she touched the ring lightly. Tendrils of magic wrapped around the gold, resonated through the stone. Mages used sapphires and other such gems to hold energy—the cut and clarity of this one made it ideal for storing spells.

The taste of the spirits crept over her tongue, stinging her palate as it sharpened the spell. Alcohol, like her magic, was clean of living things, anathema to disease and crawling necrophages. Against its stark sterility, any contagion should shine clear.

Isyllt opened her eyes and leaned back, wrinkling her

nose at the mingled stink of spirits and roses and death. Witchlight glimmered and faded in the sapphire's depths. "There. Let's test it." She stripped off the cotton gloves and touched the ring with her bare hand. The light flared again briefly at the familiar skin, and the spell shivered in her head. She let the essence of the alcohol erase the contamination, and it stilled again.

"Now you," she said, holding the ring out to Khel-séa. Another shiver and flare at the inspector's touch, and again she let the memory of it vanish. Now the stone should react only to whoever had held it before Forsythia. She found a spare silver chain in the exorcist's kit in her pocket and slid the ring under her shirt. It settled cold against her sternum, warming slowly between cloth and skin.

"Do you need anything else?" Khelséa asked. "You look tired." Her tone changed with that last—a friend's concern instead of a detective's.

Isyllt ran a hand over her face. "I haven't had any sleep." She'd been happier than was healthy when the inspector's message had summoned her into the night— murder was better than being alone after midnight with a dark mood.

Khelséa's raised eyebrow must have worked wonders with guilty criminals.

"It's nothing." When the eyebrow didn't lower, she finally conceded: "The usual thing."

The other woman's lips compressed. "Kiril."

Over the past fifteen years Kiril Orfion had been her mentor, her friend, and briefly her lover; Isyllt was still glad she wasn't the one to say his name. "What else? He's been withdrawn lately, secretive. More than usual," she added to Khelséa's wry snort. Every time she thought she was finished with grief over their broken relationship, something stirred the embers. "I worry."

Sympathy shone in Khelséa's long leonine eyes, but her voice was light. "You need a distraction. A vacation."

Isyllt laughed. "My last vacation ended badly." She flexed her left hand. Two and a half years ago she'd been sent to stir rebellion in the distant port city of Symir. The mission had ended in murder, chaos, and the near-destruction of the city—a success, as far as the Crown was concerned. "Work is distraction enough. I'll go to the Garden next."

"Do you want company? Or backup?"

"No. I'd rather tread lightly. More Vigils will only attract attention."

Khelséa snorted and tugged her orange coat straight. At least her dark skin let her wear the Vigils' distinctive shade well. "What's one more death in Oldtown, after all?"

"Eight for an obol." Their boots echoed in unison as they started for the stairs, leaving the dead woman on her slab.

Outside, the night smelled of cold rain and wet stone, and cobbles glistened under the streetlamps. Isyllt's breath frosted as she sighed—the wet chill of late autumn was still more pleasant than the unnatural dry cold of the vaults.

Inkstone was a quiet neighborhood after midnight, scribes and bureaucrats long safe in bed. Shadows draped the columned façade of the Sepulcher, and the twin bulk of the Justiciary across the plaza. Isyllt felt the unblinking granite stares of the owl-winged gargoyles on the roof as she descended the broad steps. Sentinels of the Other-world. A carriage waited in the street, the driver half-dozing, horses snorting restlessly.

"Speaking of distractions," Khelséa said with a grin, "I saw your minstrel friend in the Garden tonight. Maybe I should take him in for questioning."

Isyllt snorted. "Is that the only way you can start a conversation with a man?"

"Better than calling them from their tombs." The inspector unlatched the carriage door and held it open. "Let me know what you find. I'm sure it will be interesting."

Isyllt smiled. "This job always is." She pulled herself into the carriage and Khelséa shut the door. The horses' hooves clattered against the cobbles as they carried her across the city.

The driver stopped one street from the Garden and Isyllt climbed down. She pressed a tarnished silver obol into his hand and a whisper of forgetfulness into his mind.

The ring swayed heavy against her chest as she walked. A treat for the gossips and rumormongers, certainly, but she doubted the scandal would grow teeth. The king had been campaigning in the north since spring, and the crown prince had enough to keep him busy without visiting—or murdering—prostitutes. This was likely an old ring stolen or lost, fallen into careless hands.

She just needed to convince herself of that.

Nights in Elysia—or Oldtown, as it was more often called—weren't quiet, especially in the Garden; music spilled from taverns, voices raised in song and anger and drunken confusion. Hooves and carriage wheels clattered against stone and visitors and residents still walked the streets. Some looking for fun, others going home after late shifts. Isyllt remembered the rhythms, though she'd lived elsewhere for fifteen years.

With Forsythia's empty eyes fresh in her mind, she noticed the differences too. More pale faces in the crowds, fair hair flashing beneath caps and scarves. When she listened to the voices instead of letting them wash over her, she heard the curious mix of clipped, heavy words and musical trills that marked Rosian, much more prominent than the usual Assari or Skarrish curses. The smell of cabbage and beets wafted from vendors' carts and drifted from open windows—Cabbage Town was the vulgar name for the refugee neighborhood otherwise known as Little Kiva. Fifteen years ago, the sounds and scents and flavors had been Vallish.

Her parents settled in Oldtown when she was seven, fleeing civil war in Vallorn. Not quite the slums, but as much as refugees could afford. When plague killed them four years later, Isyllt had drifted into the tenements and rookeries of Birthgrave, where an obol would buy you more than eight murders on any given night and orange-coats vanished at sundown. The majority of bodies dragged from the southern river gate came from Birthgrave. After surviving nearly five years there, she'd hardly balked at necromancy and the "good service" of a Crown Investigator.

Climbing roses covered the Garden's crumbling walls, worming into moss-eaten mortar. The scent of the last autumn blossoms reminded her of the Sepulcher, but it was better than the usual street stink. Light glowed through windows and leaked under doors; lamps burned on street corners. Since the Rose Council formed over a century ago, the Garden had been a safe haven for those who lived and worked within its walls. It was safer to be a whore in a Garden brothel than a shopkeeper in Harrowgate. Most nights, anyway. The flowers here had thorns, if customers presumed too far.

The reek of death hit her when she turned the corner onto the Street of Thistles. Not a real smell, not blood and bowel, but a tingle of *otherwise* senses, a chill down her back. But not as strong as it would have been if someone had died here.

News had spread; the street was too quiet for the hour. Isyllt followed the unscent to a narrow alley cordoned by orange ribbons. Her skin crawled as she faced the dark mouth. The night weighed inside her head: violence, death, and more.

Intention. Plans, cold and cruel. Isyllt's ring chilled.

She walked into the shadow of the alley, boots splashing in puddles, coatskirts slapping around her ankles. The air smelled of wet stone, and even her mage-trained eyes saw nothing but black. Still no trace of the woman's ghost. Usually the young and violently killed were more likely to linger. Saints knew Birthgrave was crawling with specters, more than the exorcists could ever lay.

She worked her tongue against the roof of her mouth, recalling the taste of Forsythia's blood. She whispered a word, not quite hoping for a response.

Nothing. Wherever the woman had bled out, it wasn't here.

Isyllt let out an annoyed breath and turned around. And froze. Beyond the alley mouth stretched a familiar skyline. Sunset colors were long faded, only the stain of streetlamps against the low clouds to outline the buildings, but the angles were the same. Forsythia had stood here when she was kidnapped, and been returned after death.

At least the murderer was tidy.

A soft footstep scraped the stones behind her, followed by a quick intake of breath. "Come out," Isyllt called as she spun. Witchlight licked her fingers, curled into a ball and hovered over her palm. Eerie opalescent light rose along the walls.

Another hesitant footstep, but the lurker didn't bolt. "Come out," she said again. "I won't hurt you."

Several heartbeats later, a girl stepped around the corner. Twelve or thirteen, Isyllt guessed, skinny and tousled. Her eyes widened as she saw the spellfire. "Sorcerer." Her voice fluttered like a ragged-winged sparrow as she dipped a curtsy. She looked closer at Isyllt's black ring, and her eyes widened more. "Necromancer."

So much for not attracting attention; she should have worn another glove. "What's your name?"

"Dahlia."

Isyllt's lips twisted. The girl was too young to work the Garden—some mothers were willing to brand their daughters. "You should be careful where you lurk, Dahlia, or we might be picking up your petals in another few hours."

The girl blanched, iridescent shadows rippling over her face as she ducked her head. "Do you know who did it?"

"Not yet. Did you know Forsythia?"

Dahlia nodded.

"Who else knew her well?"

Thin shoulders rose in a shrug. "Mekaran knows her. Mekaran knows everyone."

Isyllt gestured toward the street. "Let's go."

*   *   *

The Briar Patch lay just a few blocks down the Street of Thistles. A popular tavern, and open for at least another hour, but tonight lanterns dripped honeyed light onto empty tables. The clientele, never fond of Vigils, must have scattered when the constables came questioning. Now the sole musician played only for himself, a softer tune than boisterous Garden crowds usually asked for. Isyllt smiled.

"Go find Mekaran," she told Dahlia, closing the door behind them. The cold night breeze cut through smoky spice-thick air. As the girl scurried for the kitchen, Isyllt turned toward the minstrel sitting on the dais.

His head was bowed over his kithara, but he watched her approach through dark lashes, fingers caressing strings and rich polished rosewood. Small hands for a musician, but clever. A smile creased one corner of his neat beard.

She pulled a coin from her pocket and dropped it in his bowl. Metal rang against wood.

"Slow night?" she asked as the song finished.

"Police are bad for business."

"So is murder."

He leaned down and kissed her. "Murder is your business. You're cold." He packed the instrument carefully and stepped off the stage. One arm snaked around her waist and pulled her close. Isyllt let herself lean into his warmth for a moment, inhaling the smoky herbal scent of his hair.

"But why this murder?" he asked. "Wasn't it just a slasher?" Dark eyes met hers—earnest, honest eyes.

Isyllt chuckled. "What do you know, Ciaran? Don't make me torture you."

"I thought you were working."

The kitchen door swung open and Isyllt disengaged herself. Dahlia emerged, followed by a tall man wearing an apron over the remains of brightly colored drag. He wiped flour off his hands and nodded a circumspect greeting.

Isyllt knew Mekaran Narkissos by reputation, though they'd never been introduced. He'd been Daffodil once, before he retired to run the tavern. Now he sang in flamboyant peacock shows, and fed and housed the Garden's denizens.

"I'm Mekaran. And you…" Shrewd eyes studied Isyllt, and she could all but see him marking things off a list— white skin, black diamond, ruined hand. "You must be the Lady Iskaldur. You're here with the marigolds." The street slang for the orange-coated police was even less flattering when spoken by a former prostitute.

Isyllt fought a grimace; she should have spent more time studying illusion. "I'm not here at all, actually. But I would like to talk to you."

Mekaran nodded slowly and gestured to a booth. "Sit down. Dahlia, bring us tea, please." He glanced at Isyllt again. "And something to eat." The girl bobbed her head and hurried toward the kitchen.

Isyllt raised an eyebrow. "Sheltering the girl?" She shed her coat and slid into the booth, resisting the urge to prop her elbows on the worn wooden table. She doubted she'd see her bed before dawn. Ciaran sat beside her, his thigh a line of warmth against hers.

Mekaran snorted, a silver ring in his nostril flashing. "Shelter a whore's child? But yes, there are some things she doesn't need to hear about."

Isyllt met his dark grey eyes, still lined with kohl and

glittering powder. "Things like slashers, or things like Forsythia's clientele? The ones with sharp teeth."

Mekaran cocked his head, birdlike. His hair was plumage, short and tousled and washed with pink and orange dyes that caught the light in sunset shades. No pretty cagebird, not with his height and muscle and weight of bone—more like an Assari terror bird.

"Not clients." He leaned forward. "Forsythia didn't bleed for money. But she had...a lover." His mouth twisted on the word.

Isyllt raised an eyebrow. "The jealous sort?"

He shrugged. "I don't know. She didn't bring him round to meet her friends. She never would have told me, but I saw the marks one day in the bath." Dark eyebrows rose. "Is that why the Crown is interested in a whore's death?"

Isyllt lifted a cautionary finger. "The Crown isn't interested." She thought for a heartbeat, then unbuttoned the high collar of her blouse. "I have a more personal curiosity." She tugged the cloth aside to reveal a double crescent of white scar tissue where her left shoulder met her neck. You could never escape gossip, but sometimes you could misdirect it. When the innkeeper's eyes had widened and narrowed again, she redid the buttons. "Did she say this lover's name?"

"No." Mekaran picked at a notch in the table with one painted nail. "But...Syth had been nervous for the past decad. Jumping at shadows. She took fewer clients, stayed in more often. She never told me why." He looked down at his broad, olive-skinned hands. "I didn't see her last night, or today. She might have been on her way here—"

He fell silent as Dahlia returned from the kitchen, a tray carefully balanced in both hands. In better light, Isyllt saw the girl's worn and patched clothes, her peeling shoes and tattered stockings. Not starvation-thin, but whittled lean and lanky. As she drew closer, the smell of black tea and honey made Isyllt's stomach rumble.

Ciaran raised heavy brows at the sound. "You should take better care of yourself, or you'll end up on the other side of the mirror yourself." He poked her ribs where they jutted under her shirt. His fingers trailed down to the sharp angle of her hip and lingered there.

Isyllt devoured three nut and honey pastries; after the second she couldn't taste the dead woman's blood any longer. Black peppered tea burned some of the death-chill from her flesh, eased the fatigue dragging at her eyes. Mekaran watched her eat and smiled when the plate was clean.

"Is there anything else you need tonight? I'll listen around here."

"Did you know Forsythia's name?"

He frowned. "No," he said slowly. "She was a refugee, I think. She didn't like to talk about the past."

An omission, if not a lie, but Isyllt didn't feel like bullying him. She licked honey off her fingers. "If you hear anything at all"—she included Dahlia with a glance—"come to me, not the Vigils. Quietly." She counted out coins, several times the price of tea and cakes; she'd need to start a new expense tally when she got home.

Mekaran nodded, unasked questions in his eyes. "You should come here more often—as a friend of Ciaran's, at least. The Crown ought to keep its agents better fed." He gathered Dahlia—and the money—and steered the girl back to the kitchens.

Ciaran's hand slipped round Isyllt's waist again.

"You're still cold. Come to my room and warm up." His voice was smoke and wine, rich and dark. She shivered.

"Not tonight," she said with a smile. "I'm working." She took a last sip of tea, spices burning the roof of her mouth.

His brow creased in a frown. "You're not going underground alone?" He'd known her for nearly sixteen years, and knew the sort of stupid things she was likely to do.

"Not now," she promised. She bumped his hip until he moved aside. With a sigh she collected her coat, leather heavy in her arms. "First I pay a visit to the palace."

The fastest way to the new palace was past the old. Nearly everyone was willing to sacrifice time to avoid it, but Isyllt tipped the coachman well enough to overcome his misgivings. She drew the curtains back in the cab as they passed. The night was already morbid; what was a little more gloom?

A wall had been built decades ago to contain the ruin—thick grey stone, tall and topped with warded iron—but the towers and domes were visible above it. White sandstone shone soft and ghostly in the cloud-tattered moonlight. By day the grime and decay of centuries were visible, but the night washed it clean as bones. The horses didn't care about the view. Already they sped into a bone-jarring canter. Over the creak and rattle of wheels and springs Isyllt heard the driver curse.

By Isyllt's standards it was a mild night. The breeze over the ruin only made her nape prickle and her ring itch. On bad days proximity to the palace would set a mage to retching, or leave their head throbbing for hours. And that was after decades of wind and sun and clean rain to ease the taint—she couldn't imagine what it must have been like two centuries ago.

No one was entirely certain what had happened in the original palace. Everyone who had been in the throne room died—instantly, some legends told it, others slowly and terribly, but either theory was only conjecture. That they died was certainly true, and nearly everyone else in the palace as well, save those lucky few who escaped the maelstrom of furious magic and summoned spirits. Over the decades, the story had been built and layered and embossed to a tragedy worthy of a thousand stages.

The events leading up to the disaster were well-documented, or as well as two-hundred-year-old sources could be trusted. Tsetsilya Konstantin, cousin and purported lover of the crown prince, died from a fall down a flight of tower stairs. The prince, Ioanis Korinthes, fled the palace that night in a rage and returned several days later, no less wrathful and with a handful of sorcerers at his back. Who exactly might have pushed Tsetsilya—if pushed she was—and what words were spoken between Ioanis and his father, Demos II, could only be speculated. Ioanis's involvement with a proscribed sect of spirit worshipers was also speculation.

However it came to pass, the barriers between the mortal world and the reflected world were ripped violently asunder, and a vortex of magic and hungry spirits emerged. Incursions into the palace days later found bodies charred, eviscerated, flayed, sucked to empty husks, and deliquescing in foul puddles. Intact corpses had already been possessed, as well as any survivors who hadn't escaped quickly enough.

All the mages in the Arcanost couldn't undo the damage, nor salvage the palace, though they held the city together through the terror. Demons prowled the streets even by daylight, and untrained mages and mediums went mad or catatonic. Magic fouled the air and water, and those too close to the epicenter contracted bizarre maladies. The once wealthy neighborhoods around the palace were deserted in weeks, never to regain their glory. House Korinthes never reclaimed the throne, and lost the rest of its power within a generation. Isola Alexios, a general at the time of the Hecatomb, had used the unrest to ease her way to power, and her family to the Octagon Court.

The city was never the same, but at least it went on, and learned to thrive all over again.

They turned off Desolation Circle, and Isyllt pulled the curtain shut. History was good for perspective—after a disaster like the Hecatomb, a dead prostitute and stolen ring and her own heartache hardly seemed so much.

The new palace, called the Azure Palace for its blue domes, was everything the old palace was not—colorful, sprawling, lush with gardens and orchards. Removed from the decay at the city's heart.

The guards wasted no time when a disheveled sorcerer knocked at the door on the wrong side of morning, but escorted Isyllt inside. The prince's page, a boy about Dahlia's age who stared at her as if she might sprout wings and snatch him through the closest mirror, led her to a book- and map-lined study and ran to fetch his master.

Isyllt draped her coat over a chair and sank onto the soft upholstery with a weary sigh. Her eyes and neck ached, and she felt the cold and damp more keenly in her left hand. Her hair slipped free of its pins, trailing dark strands over her shoulders. She stared at the toes of her boots, wincing at the muddy prints she left on the expensive Iskari carpet. The air leaking through the shutters smelled of rain and roses and conjured the taste of blood into her mouth once more. She grimaced—death and decay might be her specialty, but she didn't always like to be reminded.

A few moments later she heard footsteps and the door opened. She caught a glimpse of the page's wide dark eyes peering around the corner, and then the crown prince of Selafai entered the room, a tea tray balanced on one hand.

Isyllt rose and bowed, the ring bouncing against her chest as she straightened; the spell was quiescent. Nikos Alexios came to her barefoot, wearing a hastily tied brocade robe over loose silk pajama trousers. Sleep still tousled his black curls and stubble darkened his jaw. He blinked at her, disconcertment comical on his handsome face—no one wanted to be awakened before dawn by a necromancer.

He shoved papers across the polished mahogany desk and set down the tray. "Lady Iskaldur. To what do I owe this unexpected visit?" He sat, and she followed suit.

She had known the prince for years, since she first became apprenticed to the king's own sorcerer and spymaster; they were nearly of an age. Though never close, he greeted her at balls and social functions, and she and Kiril had dined with Nikos and his mistress—and later with his wife—from time to time. He looked so much like his dead mother, from his brown Archipelagan skin to his long-lashed golden brown eyes. Those eyes were wary as he regarded her now.

She took the cup of tea he offered, letting it warm her hands. An unlooked-for honor, to be served by the prince, but she knew it was nothing but habit, his ongoing efforts to be nothing like his father. His pleasantness and approachability weren't a lie, precisely, but he did nothing without reason.

"I'm afraid I need to ask your whereabouts last night, and earlier this evening."

He paused in the midst of spooning honey into his tea, then relaxed a little when she smiled. "Last night I was at the Orpheum Tharymis with Thea Jsutien and her husband. *The Rain Queen* is worth seeing, by the way, though their tenor was only adequate. Tonight I stayed in, hiding from my lovely harpy of a wife." He made a wry face as he wiped up a stray drop of honey, and the gold marriage ring in his left nostril flashed. "Kistos saw me, and my guards, but of course they'd lie for me." He offered her a smile in return. "Why? What might I have been doing?"

"Murdering a woman in the Garden."

He leaned back in his chair. "Why me?"

She set down her untasted tea and pulled the chain from beneath her shirt. "Not you in particular—anyone who could have put their hands on this."

He sucked in a breath as gold and sapphire glittered in the light. A nearly identical ring sat on his right hand. "That was my mother's."

Just the answer she'd feared. "You're sure?" She held it out. "It couldn't be some older ring that was lost?"

The spell tingled in her head as he touched the band, so faint she barely felt it. Nothing like its reaction to her or Khelséa. But if it was his mother's ring, he might have touched it a hundred times.

He ran a finger along the gold; he had his mother's long sandalwood hands. Many still felt the queen's loss keenly after three years, but Isyllt suspected her grief was more selfish than most.

"I'm sure," Nikos said. "This should be in her tomb."

Isyllt's aching eyes sagged shut. "Shall we go and pay our respects, Your Highness?"

She finished her cooling tea while the prince dressed, but all she tasted was bitterness and blood. Tomb robbers. The queen's tomb. Hadn't Lychandra's death been painful enough, that they were forced to relive it now? Kiril might never have set her aside if not for that day. He would still be at the king's side, at least, if not hers.

What would Kiril do when he learned of this? She could only thank the saints that Mathiros was in Ashke Ros and not here to receive the news. He was too sensitive to any mention of his wife—the desecration of her crypt would drive him into a rage.

Dawn bruised the eastern sky as they crossed the grounds and the palace came alive around them, servants starting their day and guard shifts changing. Today was an owl day, at least, auspicious for piety and offerings to the dead. Though most people preferred to save their piety for well after daybreak. Nikos fidgeted with his embroidered sleeves, finally shoving his hands into his coat pockets.

Crickets chirped in the garden as they followed the mossy flagstone path to the temple, and trees and banners rustled in the breeze. The air held the fragrance of the season's last blossoms; soon the cold rain of autumn would turn sharp and bitter and give way to frost.

The domed temple rose over the trees, white marble

ethereal in the grey light. The same Sindhaïn architecture as the dead palace, and the comparison made her shiver—maybe she shouldn't have ridden past it after all. The temple doors stood always open, symbolic sanctuary and hospitality, but in truth every inch of the place was warded, and the comings and goings of the pious carefully watched. Old magic sighed in Isyllt's ears as she crossed the tiled threshold.

Colored glass lanterns hung from the vaulted ceiling, scattering prisms of blue and green across the walls. An acolyte bowed to Nikos as the prince paused to collect a dish of incense and a lamp.

A hundred broad stairs led down into the catacombs, worn shallow from a century and a half of feet. Frescoes watched with stony eyes, saints and spirits and long-dead kings, darkened by passing hands.

The air chilled as Isyllt and Nikos descended, thickened with dust and incense. Their footsteps echoed down the passageway no matter how lightly they tried to tread. Witchlights burned at intervals, set into recesses in the walls. The shadows they cast were eerier than darkness might have been.

They passed sealed doors and open ones, shelves of sarcophagi set into the walls. Kings and queens so old Isyllt didn't know their names. Many were empty, the intended occupants long turned to dust beneath the old palace, but a few coffins had been salvaged and relocated. Such catacombs riddled Erisín, though the tombs outside the palace were smaller, plainer affairs, and the temples closed their crypts except on holy days.

Some newer coffins were made of glass, to show off the preservation spells cast on their occupants. A flashy macabre custom, but it kept second-rate necromancers in business. Isyllt studied the dusty glass with amusement; Nikos kept his eyes on the hall ahead.

Finally they came to the Alexios family crypt and Nikos pulled out an iron key from a cord around his neck. The lock clicked and the heavy door opened soundlessly into darkness. Nikos paused to light his lamp, but Isyllt had already summoned witchlight. The pale glow sent their shadows crawling across the floor and up the walls, but did nothing to dispel the cold.

These sarcophagi were all stone—the Alexioi tended to conservatism. Nikos' mother, the newest death, rested on a marble plinth in the center of the room. The likeness carved upon the stone lid was very good. Lychandra hadn't worn that look of peace when she died, but by the time the body had been prepared she was serene. Isyllt had cleaned the queen's corpse herself and cast the first of the preservation spells while Kiril recovered.

A smell distracted her from memories, the sharp scent of lightning. "Someone's been here. It reeks of magic."

Nikos sniffed and stifled a sneeze at the dust. He set aside his lamp and incense and crouched beside the chests piled around the plinth to inspect the locks. "Broken." He made a face as though he wanted to spit. "Kistos could do a better job with a hair pin." He stared down at the velvet-lined bottom of a gilded box. "All her jewels..."

"They weren't given as alms?"

He shook his head wearily. "Father couldn't bear the thought of seeing them again on some other woman's breast. How did thieves get in here?"

Isyllt laid a hand on the door and frowned. "The spell may have been tampered with. It wouldn't be hard, for a witch worth her salt and silver." There—a faint discord in the gentle hum of the spell. "Someone broke and reset it." She turned toward the sarcophagus, trailed her fingers over the dead queen's face. "This one is intact." She couldn't stop the upswell of pride; they'd be hard pressed to undo Kiril's work. Even weakened as he had been after the plague, he was still the most powerful sorcerer in Erisín.

Nikos sighed, relief on his face. At least his mother's body had been spared. And the city might be spared the sight of the thieves' entrails hung from the city walls, when Mathiros found out about this.

"How did they get in and out of the catacombs to begin with?" the prince said. "I'd like to think the priests would have noticed someone so burdened with stolen goods."

"They might have found a way in from the city's tombs, though that would mean a lot of digging and crawling in the dark—" Her nostrils flared again. Dust, magic, the fragrant sandalwood Nikos had brought. And under that, something musky, bittersweet, like anise and autumn leaves. Like snakes. Isyllt's brow creased in a frown. "Do you smell that?"

Nikos moved closer, inhaling sharply. "What is it?"

"Vampires."

CHAPTER 2

An hour before dawn the Diadachon Garden was fragrant with rain and roses and the tang of wet grass, and bread from the kitchens when the wind shifted just so. Fountains splashed softly and a palace cat sang love songs to a would-be paramour somewhere in the distance. A quiet hour—the staff were either already at their chores or clinging to last scraps of sleep, the nightshift guards trying not to drowse as they waited for their replacements.

Savedra had nearly given up on the assassin.

Her mother's note had arrived this morning, coded in one of the Severoi's many private ciphers: Someone meant to spill Alexioi blood tonight. Nadesda's warnings had never been wrong before, but Savedra's feet were soaked and toes numb, she ached from the cold and from standing motionless for what felt like hours, and she was a hair's breadth from not caring who was murdered if it meant she'd be asleep before sunrise.

The same argument she always had with herself circled in the back of her mind. Nikos had his own people to do this—trained, competent people. The royal guard had decades of experience keeping kings and princes alive, and were successful more often than not. But none of them had the archa of House Severos whispering in their ears.

When the vines twining the wall finally rustled—barely audible over the breeze and falling water—she drew up with a start. Shock burned her cheeks and tingled in the tips of her fingers as her hand closed over her dagger.

Savedra pressed deeper into the shadows of her hiding place in the columned arcade and peered into the garden. The glow of distant lamps glimmered in the fountains, traced the tops of the walls and neatly pruned trees. Even with her eyes adapted to the night, she barely saw the thicker darkness creeping past the trellised walls.

At least it hadn't been a false alarm.

A familiar welter of emotion followed: shock, doubt— what if it was a mistake this time, what if this one were innocent—and then the cold rage that someone dared to threaten those she loved. When a hooded man climbed into the royal gardens in the dead of night, the odds of an innocent assignation were poor.

Soft shoes moved from grass to flagstones with only the faintest scuff to betray their wearer. The man was good; Savedra would have to be better. She knew his path— down the arcade and up the stairs, to the glass-paned double doors that led to the prince's suite. Or the other set that led to the princess's. And if it were the latter, the little voice that sounded like her mother asked, why did she not merely stand aside and let the deed be done? She would be there to comfort Nikos in the morning, after all.

She moved before she had to answer the question, anger and excitement loosening stiff limbs. On the other side of the arcade, a soldier moved slower and louder. The assassin spun, blade gleaming, and gave Savedra his back.

Too easy.

The impact jolted her arm. The blade slowed on leather, quickened through flesh, then struck bone with a scrape that set her teeth on edge. She braced as the assassin's weight leaned back against her. She might regret being born a man every time she had a gown fitted, but it meant she was stronger than she looked.

The killer cursed softly, quiet even in death, and tried to pull free. One gloved hand groped backward. Savedra twisted the knife.

Lanterns bloomed in the shadows to blind her and swords rattled. Then Captain Denaris was there, knocking the man's weapon away, pulling him off Savedra, a soft stream of profanity fit to rust steel hissing from her lips.

"Alive! Alive, damn it! Why is that so bloody difficult?"

"He's no more threat now," Savedra said as the man gurgled and bled onto the stones. The words came out ragged; her chest ached. She wasn't sure how long she'd been holding her breath.

"And no more use."

"I'll find out who sent him." Her vision swam with orange blossoms. She started to rub her watering eyes and stopped just in time.

The captain snorted but didn't argue. It had taken years—and several dead assassins—for her to trust the prince's mistress, but now that she did, she never pried into Savedra's sources.

Savedra turned away from the soon-to-be corpse, reaction setting in now that action had ended. She had only been sick the first time, but she always shook after. Her right hand clenched, blood cooling sticky on her fingers. The raw metallic smell filled her nose and she stumbled to the fountain to wash her hands.

Denaris followed, boots swishing against wet grass. Lantern light picked out strands of grey in her dark hair, showed the pity in her lean and whittled face. "You could have people to do this for you. You should have them. You'd serve him better—"

Savedra shook her head, the weight of her hair tugging sharp against pins. It was an old argument. "I'm no spymaster. And if I have to do this, better my hands be stained for it." She pulled the hands in question out of icy water and scrubbed them on her skirt.

"Nikos needs a spymaster more than he needs a mistress."

"Lord Orfion—"

"Isn't here." Cold and implacable as a blade. "And likely won't return."

"And whose fault is that?" Savedra folded her arms tight across her stomach, as if she could stop it churning so easily.

The captain shrugged, mouth twisting eloquently, but didn't speak. Not quite treason, to call the king a fool, but hardly politic either. "Fault or no, it's true. Lord Orfion needs a successor as surely as any king."

"Then let him name one, Kat. I haven't the stomach for it."

Denaris glared, but didn't belabor what they both knew—Orfion had named a successor, and the king had ignored him and chosen his own replacement. And taken that replacement with him to Ashke Ros, leaving Nikos to get by as best he could with lesser agents.

"May I go?" Savedra asked. "I'd like some sleep before sunrise." Not a lie, but no matter how much she wanted rest, she knew none would come this morning.

The captain shook her head, but let the matter drop. "Go. We'll mop up here and search the corpse."

Savedra turned toward the narrow servants' hall that led out of the garden. She had a key to Nikos' rooms, but not the heart to go to him like this. She paused, sodden slippers squelching on the lawn. "What will you tell him?"

"I always tell him when you give us warning. I don't have to tell him you were here."

"Thank you." The smell of blood and roses followed her as she left the garden.

Her footsteps carried through the silent polished halls of the Gallery of Pearls—she was the only pearl in residence. Portraits of long-dead men and women watched disinterestedly from the walls, but the Gallery had stood nearly empty for most of recent history. Supposedly Naomi II had filled every room in the old palace's gallery with her concubines, but since the Azure Palace was built the monarchs had been more restrained. Sometimes councilors brought their mistresses here in the summer, but the other women offered mainly awkward silences and ill-concealed stares around Savedra. At least the portraits didn't whisper.

She didn't bother pulling back the covers, but fell limp across the bed, staring at the shadowed canopy as dawnlight brightened through the curtains, waiting for her nerves to settle and her shaking to still. When they finally did, she rose to bathe and dress and face the rest of the day.

The lawns were still wet hours later and the sky hung dull and heavy, thwarting most morning pursuits or driving them indoors. And so Savedra found herself in the Queen's Solar with Nikos's wife.

When Lychandra Alexios lived, the room had been filled with couches and tables and expensive carpets, a place for comfort and quiet conversation. After she died, the furniture had gone into storage and dust had dulled the tall windows and skylights. Only last year had the king given his son's wife leave to refurnish it.

If he expected her to turn it into anything other than a private practice yard, he never said so. Not that anyone who knew Ashlin would expect otherwise.

Steel rang and echoed as the princess and her sparring partner drove each other back and forth. Breath rasped, and boots scuffed and thumped on stone. Today they used western longswords, straight functional blades without the Selafaïn fondness for curve and ornament. Still beautiful, Savedra supposed, though she preferred her weapons more subtle. Her hand wanted to clench around the memory of a dagger and she adjusted the drape of her forest-green skirts over the bench instead.

Metallic light trickled through the windows, robbing the pink and yellow granite tiles of their warmth. Thick clouds dragged past overhead, pregnant with unshed rain. Savedra regretted the image as soon as it came to her and looked down again. She studied the flash of steel, the fighters' footwork, the play of muscle under sweat-sheened skin—anything but Ashlin's face or waist.

The princess's stomach was lean as ever under her leather vest, she decided after several moments of carefully not looking. The last pregnancy had progressed far enough to show, but that softness was gone now. Muscle corded in Ashlin's arms as she lunged and parried, and sweat darkened her linen shirt and pasted stray wisps of short candle-flame hair to her cheeks and brow. In the light of day Savedra's fears seemed ridiculous—Ashlin could more than handle any assassin.

Warrior princess. Barbarian. One-day queen of Selafai. And by some joke of the saints, Savedra's friend instead of bitter rival. A friend she would kill to protect.

As a friend, she should convince the princess to rest. No one else dared—no one wanted the edge of Ashlin's tongue, especially Nikos. But the last miscarriage had been harder than the princess would admit, and Savedra had been the one to stroke her hair, to clean away the blood and pretend she never saw the tears. For all the years she'd wished to be born a woman in flesh as well as mind, some things she didn't envy.

A footstep in the doorway drew her head up. The grey light wasn't kind to Nikos—his sandalwood skin looked sickly and shadows smudged his eyes. Even his usual flamboyant clothing was subdued to shades of black and emerald. He hadn't been in his rooms when she'd first knocked, far earlier than he normally rose, and Kistos had only shaken his head with the pained look that meant he'd been told not to speak of something. Nikos tried to school his face now, but she caught the tightness at the corners of his mouth. His lips quirked as he watched Ashlin.

He stopped behind Savedra's bench and brushed a quick caress across her shoulder. "Have breakfast with me. I need to talk to you."

Had Denaris told him about the assassin already? Usually she waited till lunch, if the would-be killer was already dead.

Once Savedra might have thought it a point scored, that he came to her and not his wife for counsel, but she had long since given up scorekeeping. Now loyalty and friendship pricked and tugged her with every conflict.

"Alone?" she asked, arching her eyebrows.

Before he answered, the sky opened with a sigh and rain rattled against the windows. The clash of steel died. Out of the corner of her eye, Savedra saw Ashlin frozen in place and scowling, her opponent's sword brushing her belt buckle.

The guard, one of Ashlin's personal retinue, said something joking in Celanoran and stepped back with a bow. She repeated the word, still frowning, and turned away to sheathe her blade. The soldier, well-used to her temper, caught Savedra's eye and quirked an eloquent brow. One corner of her mouth curled wryly in response.

Ashlin crossed the room in long strides, rain-shadows rippling across her flushed skin. From her expression, Savedra guessed she wanted to chide Nikos for costing her the match. But that would mean admitting that he could distract her.

"My Lady," he said with a shallow bow. "As I was just asking Vedra, would you join us for breakfast?"

Her scowl transformed into an entirely different frown as she sniffed herself. "I need a bath more than food."

Savedra thought he would drop the matter now that courtesy was satisfied, but he surprised her. "You can have both in my rooms. I think you'll like to hear this story."

Nikos' suite was in its usual disarray: clothing draped over bed and chairs, tables littered with books and notes and the glitter of whatever cunning or lovely things had caught his eye this decad. The city called him the Peacock Prince—for his sartorial extravagance as well as the company he kept—but Savedra thought him more a magpie. He'd spent so many years studiously not being his father that it had become ingrained. The door that led to Ashlin's adjoining suite was shut—Savedra didn't want to know if she was locking it this decad.

Savedra helped herself to a cup of steaming coffee while servants laid out breakfast. She'd begun tasting his food as a warning to her mother; that habit too had become ingrained. It had its benefits, though—the new Assari empress was freer with trade than her predecessor, but coffee beans were still costly. Water gurgled in the pipes as Ashlin drew herself a bath, drowning the gentler susurrus of the rain.

Then Nikos began to recount his expedition to the royal crypts, and food and bath water and coffee alike cooled untouched.

"Vampires?" Ashlin perched on the edge of a velvet-cushioned chair, one boot still on, the other hanging forgotten in her hand.

Nikos nodded and ran a weary hand through his hair. "They live below the city, in catacombs underneath the sewers."

The boot slipped from the princess's fingers and thumped to the floor. "I thought those were only stories."

"It was an arrangement made with an ancient Severos king," Savedra said. That agreement was part of the family histories her mother had taught her. Those not often found in public records. She sipped her coffee and winced at the lukewarm bitterness; if only it tasted as wonderful as it smelled. Nikos refreshed her cup from the carafe before he poured his own. "The vrykoloi agreed to stay in the catacombs and be ... discreet."

"Like murdering women in alleys?" Ashlin asked, eyebrows climbing. She brushed sweat-stiffened hair off her forehead absently.

"Of course. It would be indiscreet to kill them on the street, after all."

The princess snorted and tugged off her other boot, letting it fall beside its mate. "What are you going to do?"

Nikos shook his head and stared at his cup. "I don't know. I—" His voice lowered. "I can't let Father find out."

A chill snaked down Savedra's back. Another fine line between discretion and treason. But he was right; Mathiros's wrath was an ugly thing. He vented his grief and bitterness by campaigning in Ashke Ros, fighting the Ordozh raiders who pillaged there. That was madness and folly enough—no one wanted to bring the folly home.

"You'll have to work quickly," Ashlin said, with a soldier's practicality. "The campaigning season is already over."

"Not that quickly." The flavor of Nikos's frown changed. "There's been a delay." He flicked a fingernail against a folded parchment half-buried on the table.

"What now?" said Savedra. The king had promised his council a short campaign when he led troops to aid the Rosians in the spring, but one thing or another had delayed their return since late summer.

"An armistice."

That sent Ashlin's eyebrows winging toward her hair. "With the Ordozh?" The raiding horsemen were feared like demons by any country that shared their border, and no one had managed to treat with their warlords in decades.

"They have a new *khayan*." The foreign word slid smoothly off his tongue—for all his magpie mind, he knew how to pay attention. "An emperor of sorts. Father fought him." His mouth twisted wryly at his father's diplomacy. "This emperor is willing to have peace for a year, but he wants Father to be present for negotiations. The Council will complain, of course, but a treaty with the Ordozh is enough to give them pause. But we still need to find Mother's jewelry soon, and deal with these tomb-robbers."

Ashlin turned, unlacing her vest and peeling off her sweat-stained blouse on the way to the bathroom. She left the door ajar, and Savedra glimpsed the peach-pale curve of her back as Ashlin dropped her shirt. "I want to fight the Ordozh emperor," she called over her shoulder. "Lacking that, I want to see a vampire. Your demons sound much more interesting than ours back home."

Nikos rolled his eyes. "Your desire is my duty, Your Radiance." Splashing drowned Ashlin's retort. She swore in Celanoran, anyway.

One of their rare moments of easygoing humor. Savedra's throat closed. Neither of them tried to shut her out, but they didn't need to. Fate had done that well enough.

She stood, shaking her skirts with a practiced fillip, and poured the rest of her cooling coffee back into the pot.

"Where are you going?" Nikos asked.

She leaned in to kiss his cheek, sliding deftly away when he tried to pull her close. "To visit my mother."

Savedra and Nikos' relationship might not be the most impolitic the Azure Palace had ever seen, but she was hard pressed to think of many others. Their houses had been bitter rivals for decades, ever since Thanos Alexios led the rebellion that overthrew the last of the Severoi kings. Not that Ioris Severos had been what anyone would call a good ruler, but that hardly mattered to the family. The last thing the Alexioi and their allies wanted was a Severos worming her way near the throne, especially the daughter of Nadesda, an archa known for her ruthlessness and wide-flung web of influence. Since Savedra moved into the palace she had narrowly avoided three poisoning attempts. Had she been able to bear Nikos any bastards she would be dead by now, no matter how careful she was or how powerful her mother.

Instead she was hijra; the third sex, in old Sindhaïn— men born in women's bodies, women born as men, and the androgynes who were neither or both. The hijra veiled themselves with ritual and mysticism, keeping mostly to their temple in the Garden. The curious paid to see the faces of their priestesses, and paid more for their prophecies and their bodies. So Savedra's rivals called her freak and whore—never mind that she had never taken the mark of the order—and made cruel jokes where Nikos couldn't hear, but she would never be queen or mother to a usurper, and so wasn't a permanent threat.

Savedra tried to let the hiss and splash of rain and wet streets drown her thoughts as the carriage bore her to the Octagon Court, but it was no use. Murder and sleeplessness left her maudlin, and the weather didn't help. The grey veil, autumn was called, for the storms that swept down from the mountains; the same name was given to the listlessness and depression that took some people when the light and warmth vanished.

She had the use of Nikos' coach, but it was simpler

and quieter to pass the gate and hire one of the dozen that always waited to carry visitors and courtiers to and fro. The ride was short—less than half an hour before the horses stopped under the covered walk of Phoenix House and the driver scrambled to help her out. His quick appreciative glance might well have been as much for her cloak as for her face, but he didn't hesitate over the polite *milady*. Her bolstered pride earned him a gracious tip, and she nearly laughed at herself.

Eight houses brooded at one another from eight sides of the court, and at the tall bronze statue of Embria Selaphaïs that stood in the center. Severos, Alexios, Konstantin, Aravind, Jsutien, Hadrian, Petreus, and Ctesiphon. Eight houses, eight families, constantly squabbling and backstabbing over land and position and trade, a web of enmities and alliances that shifted every year with deaths and births and marriages. The rain turned all the houses into glowering grey hulks, but windows in only six glowed against the gloom. The Petreoi had retired to their estates in Nemea last month to elect a new archon, and the Ctesiphon house had stood empty since the family's head had plotted against King Nikolaos twenty-eight years ago—the attempt had cost him his life, and his house their archonate and all holdings in the city for thirty years.

The carriage rattled away and Savedra turned back to Phoenix House, her heels tapping on wet flagstones as she climbed the steps. Two guards in black and silver livery bowed and held the door for her, and a maid appeared in the foyer to take her damp cloak.

"Is my mother in?" she asked as she shrugged off heavy velvet folds. Blue silk lining flashed in the lamplight.

"The archa is in the library, milady, with Lord Varis."

"A private conversation?"

The woman shrugged one soft shoulder. "No more than usual."

Meaning that no one had spelled the room to silence, then, and Nadesda wouldn't mind an interruption. "Will you have tea sent up, please, and something to eat?"

"Of course, milady."

The smell of Phoenix House settled over her, the unique blend of stone and polish, wax and oil, the inhabitants' favorite meals and pets and perfumes that time had ingrained into the walls. The scents of the palace were familiar now, and she still remembered those of Evharis, the estate in Arachne where she was born, but they had never been so comforting. Phoenix House had awed her as a child, with its shadows and stillness and secrets, treasure troves in gabled attics; now it was simply home.

The library drapes were pulled against the chill, and firelight and low lamps lit the room, gilding dark wood and silver sconces and warming the deep colors of the carpets and wall hangings. Nadesda and Varis sat near the hearth, a tea tray on a table between them. Nadesda glowed darkly in bronze brocade, regal as a queen in her high-backed chair. Her beauty was undimmed at fifty-three; another reassuring constant in Savedra's life.

"Savedra, darling." Varis stood when she entered and held out a hand.

"Uncle Varis." She hadn't realized until she smiled just how unhappy her morning had been.

He was actually her mother's cousin, but he'd been a familiar and cheering presence as she'd grown up. He'd soothed her adolescent awkwardness with shopping expeditions and visits from his tailors, and taught her to bury the gangly teenaged boy she despised under careful cosmetics and deportment. And, on rare occasions when she'd thought she would go mad, with subtle illusion charms. He had taken her away from the palace on Nikos' wedding night and gotten her thoroughly drunk.

He took her hand, jeweled rings pressing against her skin. His cheeks creased with a smile that always looked like a smirk, no matter how sincere. He resembled none of her closer relatives, being slight and bird-boned, with startling pale eyes and translucent skin. He'd begun losing his hair before she was born, and made up for it by shaving his head; it set off the delicacy of his features. Malachite powder glittered on his eyelids, and he smelled of lime and lilac and white musk when she kissed his cheek.

He wore black, which meant he must have come from the Arcanost—sober colors were his only concession to Archlight's dour ideas on fashion. Nothing else about the sculpture of layered velvet and leather that was his coat was reserved. Not that combining chartreuse and fuchsia was the worst of his scandals by far.

"You look tired, my dear," he said as Savedra bent to kiss her mother. "Is that Alexios pet of yours keeping you up?"

"I keep him up, Uncle. I wouldn't be much of a mistress if I didn't."

"Did you ever try that Iskari massage oil I recommended? I've had—"

"Varis." Nadesda's quiet reproving tone had worked on children and archons for thirty years. "Pretend for a moment that you have the decency not to corrupt my children. Or at least the tact not to do it while I'm in the room."

"You know I was never any good at acting, Desda. A pity too—imagine Uncle Tselios's reaction if I'd run off and joined the Orpheum Rhodon."

"Hah!" Nadesda's bright laugh was one of the rare unschooled expressions that no one outside of House Severos had ever seen. Garnets and marcasites glittered as she shook her head. "Too bad you never did. We didn't outrage the old bastard nearly enough before he died."

"Maybe it's not too late. I could find a necromancer to summon him back."

Nadesda reached for her teacup and stopped when she realized it was empty. "Sit down, Vedra. What's the matter?"

Savedra drew up a chair and sat, envying as always her mother's perfect posture. She ought to wear more corsets. "Can't you guess?"

One eyebrow rose. "Something to do with the note I sent you?"

With perfect timing, a diffident knock fell on the door and a maid slipped in with a new tea tray. While she laid out the dishes, Savedra wondered if she ought to talk to her mother in private. Varis disdained politics, being more concerned with debauchery and thaumaturgy, but she didn't precisely trust any member of her family with secrets. But, she decided, this was safe enough as far as intrigues went. He already knew about her arrangement with Nadesda.

When the maid had left and everyone had fresh tea— and Savedra had devoured a scone with undignified haste—Varis snapped his fingers. The orange padparad-scha sapphire on his right hand sparkled with the motion and a hush filled the room like water, drowning the hiss of rain and crackle of the fire. Theatrics, for all he pretended not to be an actor. Any Severos could invoke the silence—the spell was bound into a marble ornament on the hearth—but there was no point in wasting a mage if you had one at hand.

After the silence deepened and scone and tea settled warm in her stomach, Savedra set her cup down. "Who sent the assassin, Mother?"

Varis's eyebrows climbed. Nadesda cocked her head, tendrils of steam drifting around her face. "Who has the most to gain from the princess's death?"

Savedra snorted. "We do, of course."

One manicured nail clicked against her teacup. "Ah, but that's not true, is it?"

"Can't we skip the lessons?" But Nadesda only waited expectantly. "Fine. Even if Ashlin died and Nikos married me, I would never be queen or produce an heir. The best we could hope for would be another Severos adopted, and the other houses would fight that with all their breath." Her forehead creased as she contemplated it more. "But other houses have marriageable daughters." *Real daughters,* she didn't say. Murder left her bitter as well as maudlin. "Daughters already slighted by Mathiros's choice of a foreign bride for his son." She tapped thumb against fingers as she counted the daughters in question. "Ginevra Jsutien, Radha Aravind, and Althaia Hadrian being the most obvious of those."

"Your first example was the best," Nadesda said. "Ginevra Jsutien was the favorite of at least four houses, and her aunt knew it. Of course, I'm sure Thea is much too clever to involve herself with assassins, or to leave any links behind if she did."

"Thea." Savedra shook her head. "That silver-tongued bitch." She couldn't stop the thread of admiration that crept into the words. "She went to the theater with Nikos just the other day. And she's attending the boating party at the palace on Polyhymnis."

"If the princess goes with them," said Varis, "tell her not to stand too close to the rail."

"What will you do?" Nadesda asked.

Savedra shrugged, not quite keeping the anger from the gesture. "The same thing I always do. Wait. Watch. Stop them." Ever and always, the unceasing vigilance—tasting food, staring at shadows, studying every gift and visitor who came too close. It wasn't what she'd imagined when she and Nikos had exchanged their first too-long glance across a crowded room nearly five years ago. "I should have been a whore after all."

She only saw it because she was looking: the tightening around Nadesda's eyes, the heartbeat-quick compression of painted lips. A mother's pain beneath an archa's poise.

Varis's response was less controlled—his jaw clenched, and his pale eyes darkened with anger—but gone just as quickly. "Of course you shouldn't have," he said, voice carefully light. "That would be boring." He tugged at his high sculpted collar. "Never let them forget you."

Tea dragged into lunch, and then an hour spent gossiping about court and family, until Nadesda excused herself for an appointment and Varis became distracted by a conversation with the gardener about western herblore. Savedra took her chance to slip out quietly and return to the library. The assassin was only half her reason for visiting. Many volumes of Severos history weren't stored in

Phoenix House, but secreted in vaults in remote properties or in the family library at Evharis. She wished she had those at hand, but there was no subtle way to visit them. For now the Phoenix Codex would have to satisfy her curiosity about the vrykoloi.

So of course it didn't. An hour passed as she turned page after page with careful gloved fingers, squinting at the cramped scholarly hand. The book spoke in detail of the reign of Darius II Severos, including his dealings— in circumspect, politic language—with the vrykoloi, but of the vampires themselves she found little besides footnotes: Sovay's *Mathematics and Thaumaturgy*, Anektra's *Principia Demonica*, a monograph about blood magic by a Phaedra Severos published in 463. She pulled the Anektra off the shelf, risking a sprained wrist, but the handspan-thick volume was too daunting to open.

"Don't tell me you've finally decided to study magic."

Savedra started, cracking her elbow on the table and cursing. The silence on the room had faded, but Varis could still come and go unheard.

"It would make an old degenerate so proud."

She snorted. This was a conversation they'd had a dozen times. The only way Varis had ever tried to shape her life was by encouraging her to take up sorcery, to test the fabled mysticism of the hijra. It was, to her knowledge, the only way she'd ever disappointed him; she had neither the desire nor aptitude for magic, and even less desire to remind people of the marks she didn't wear.

"Not today, Uncle." She shut the Phoenix Codex with a soft *whump* and stripped off the library's cotton gloves.

Beneath his paints and powders, Varis looked tired. The skin around his eyes was delicate as crepe, the lines there deeper when he smiled. He had been gone from the city for much of the past year, and distant and withdrawn about his trips. Scandal was his specialty, but secrets ran in their blood.

"What do you know about vampires?" she asked, thinking of secrets.

He stilled for an instant, then plucked imaginary lint off one sleeve. "Not much, I'm afraid. Why the interest?"

Savedra smiled, carefully bright. "Some of the courtiers have started reading those awful penny dreadfuls. I hoped I could find something in here to impress them with."

"Ah. Sadly, no. No one knows much about the vrykoloi, except perhaps a few who know better than to speak of it. A proper treatise or examination would make the Arcanost scholars' teeth ache with envy, but none of them have the guts to go underground." He waved one perfectly manicured black-nailed hand. "No one likes to get their hands dirty anymore."

"Pity." Savedra rose, shaking out her skirts, and reshelved the books. "I'll have to settle for knowing looks and sly silences, I suppose."

"Clever girl." He tugged his collar straight again. "And now that your mother is gone, you can tell me about that massage oil."

Savedra laughed and let herself be distracted, but a warning chill had settled in her stomach. That he lied only stung a little—she was used to her family—but that he lied now unnerved her.

What *did* he know about vampires?

CHAPTER 3

Kiril had given up many of his duties over the last three years, but he couldn't prove it by the paperwork. A single lamp burned on his desk, spilling yellow light across stacked ledgers and rolled parchment and drifts of loose paper. Legal forms scribed in triplicate and foreign news and hand-scrawled notes in private ciphers. Agents who reported directly to the king still sent him copies of their reports, and he had plenty of contacts who communicated only with him. His slow slide from favor had done nothing to lessen the tide. Fallings out might be counterfeited, after all, or damaged friendships mended.

There was nothing false in his split from Mathiros, nor did it hold any hope of reconciliation. He had seen to that himself.

He glared at the two latest missives; the words blurred less than an armspan away. Lamps were bad for his eyes, the physicians swore to him, but he made no move to draw back the curtains. The day outside was rain-washed and gloomy, the autumn afternoon already dull as dusk. Neither did he reach for the spectacles folded on the corner of the wide rosewood desk. Instead he called witchlight, harsh and white.

The simplest of spells, it should have been effortless. Instead he felt the drain of it all the way to his bones. But it was much easier to read by.

The first letter was a report from the front. The king had not seen fit to send it to him, nor had the mage who took Kiril's place at the king's side, but the scribe was an old friend. For such a foolish enterprise, Mathiros had acquitted himself well enough. An armistice with the Ordozh, and only two hundred Selafaïn dead to show for it. That number might be lower had Kiril been at the front, and it might not.

Which rankles more, old man? he thought wryly, rubbing the bridge of his nose against an incipient headache. *That he needs you and ignores you, or that he doesn't need you at all?*

But among the dead were forty mages, and that wasn't a number to be shrugged aside. Kristof Vargas, Kiril's replacement and former student, was a talented sorcerer but still cocky with advancement. Selafai didn't have scores of battle mages to spare.

That rankled most of all. That Kiril had been set aside after long service he might forgive, but for a decade he had groomed Isyllt Iskaldur to be his successor, and Mathiros had ignored her as he ignored all of Kiril's advice these days.

Leaving her in the city to stumble over tomb robbers, and secrets he couldn't confide to her.

He banished the witchlight and touched both notes to the coals in the brazier, breathing in the acrid smoke of

burnt parchment. The warmth eased the pain in his hands
more than he cared to admit. His joints had begun to ache
even before his heart failed three years ago, and the rheu-
matism had worsened with every winter since. Now even
his magic couldn't distract him from the pain.

It would pass. He'd endured worse.

When the last corner of parchment blackened and fell
to ash, Kiril wiped the soot from his hands and rose, leaning against his chair. He didn't need strength or magic to
deal with tomb-robbing vampires, only wits and caution.

He snuffed the lamp and prepared to lie to someone he
loved.

Rain hissed and tapped against the rooftops of Calderon Court, streaming past the warped panes of the great
octagonal window in Isyllt's living room and rinsing the
city into a grey blur. The streetlights weren't lit till true
dusk, but lamps and candles flickered in other windows,
bleeding pale and gold through the gloom. Isyllt's stomach felt as cold and watery as the glass.

Her left palm ached against her teacup. During the chaos
in Symir a would-be assassin had put a knife through
her hand to steal her ring. She'd reclaimed the diamond,
but all the skill of the Arcanostoi surgeons hadn't been
enough to save her hand. Foretelling the weather was a
paltry compensation. She swirled her tea, watching leaves
twist and spiral through the dregs. A pity she couldn't
foretell anything else.

Hours remained till sunset—only a formality, with the
sky the color of old pewter, but one to be observed nonetheless. She set the teacup aside and wished for something
stronger. The thought of the catacombs sent a not entirely

unpleasant chill up her back, and she rubbed the scar on her shoulder. She had known of the vrykoloi since she first became an investigator, but only met one two years ago, after she'd come home from Symir. The meeting hadn't begun well, but they had sorted things out since.

Her wards shivered a moment before a soft knock fell on her door. Her magic recognized the man outside and rubbed against him in friendly greeting, even as she tensed. Isyllt forced her hands to relax as she opened the door and smiled up at her master.

Once he would have kissed her cheek; once she would have kissed his mouth. Now they settled for a brief clasp of hands, and she felt the starkness of bone through skin. His short beard was finally more white than dark auburn, his hair even paler. Students had called him "the Old Man" since his thirties, but it had never seemed like the truth before. Shadowed black eyes met hers and he smiled wryly.

"I know," Kiril said, shrugging out of his dripping oil-cloak and hanging it on a peg. "Any day now I'll be leaning on a stick and complaining about the stairs."

"Don't be silly." Beneath the clinging scent of rain, he smelled of incense and herbs, orris and olibanum and resinous dragon's blood, and under that the lightning tang of magic. Sharp and sweet and comforting—she still wanted to lean into it whenever he was near.

She also wanted to shake him; it shouldn't take tomb-robbing demons to bring him to her door. It had been more than a decad since she'd spoken to him, and all their visits in the past several months had been strained and brief. After fifteen years, she wanted to tell him, she could tell the difference between honest distraction and willful avoidance.

Instead she ushered him in and moved to stir the fire and pour wine. After fifteen years she also knew how impossible it was to pry things from him that he didn't want to share. His footsteps creaked unevenly across the floorboards; she wondered when he'd begun to limp. Fabric rustled as he sank into a chair near the great window.

Isyllt handed him a glass—a cunningly wrought cage cup, one of a pair he'd given her for a long-ago saint day— and sat down in the other worn and much-mended chair. Her apartments had been new and richly furnished fifty years ago, but nicks and scuffs had accumulated over a succession of government employees, and Isyllt was more apt to spend her salary on clothes and expensive wine than new furniture. Decades of pacing feet had worn the patterns from the rugs, and the smoke of lamps and candles darkened the high beams.

"What do you think of this?" Kiril asked, his voice carefully bland.

"I don't know." Leather creaked as she crossed her legs. "I don't know what the girl had to do with the robbery, or why she was killed, or who even amongst demons would be mad or foolish enough to do something like this." She sipped her wine, rolling tannin and warm spices across her tongue. "If Mathiros hears of this . . ."

Kiril's mouth hooked down. "He'll storm the catacombs with flame and silver and hang the charred bones from the walls. Yes." He tasted the wine and nodded approval. "Which would be madness in its turn—the vrykoloi would certainly retaliate. But he isn't rational where Lychandra is concerned."

He stared out the window; the light died by inches and thunder growled in the distance. The gloom washed his face grey, filled the hollows of his cheeks and eyes with shadows. Isyllt couldn't remember the first time her breath had caught when she looked at him too long, but it had never stopped since. Her hand tightened on her cup till the filigreed silver cage bit her palm.

The ache of memory wasn't enough to distract her from his frown, or the faint movement of his fingers against the arm of the chair. "What is it?" she asked. "You know something."

"It's nothing," he said after a pause. At least he had the grace to look rueful when he lied to her. She pushed the fleeting sting aside—there had always been things he couldn't tell her. A hazard of their work. "Investigate as you see fit. If we can find those responsible and return what was stolen, perhaps Mathiros need never learn of this." His frown deepened. Did it pain him to hide things from the king he'd served so long? Isyllt didn't think he would have kept secrets three years ago. Three years ago he could have swayed the king from any foolish vengeance. But maybe there had always been secrets between Kiril and Mathiros too. "Perhaps Aphra and Tenebris know something."

She nearly smiled. Many in Erisín avoided even the word *vrykoloi*, for fear of attracting unwanted attention—Kiril named their elders as he might old friends.

He turned back to her and the firelight picked out glints of garnet in his hair, lined the weary creases on his face. "You're not going alone, are you?"

"I'm taking Ciaran. He knows his way around the sewers." The musician's days of fencing and sneak-thievery might be over, but he hadn't forgotten them any more than she'd forgotten hers. Elysia branded its children deep.

Kiril's eyebrows rose. "You and he are still close, then?"

She chuckled. She'd had other relationships over the years, before and after Kiril, but of all her lovers in Erisín, she only spoke to him and Ciaran. "I'm not made of rosewood and strings—it will never be serious. I trust him at my back." *But not like I trust you.* She washed the thought away with a swallow of wine.

He nodded and raised his own cup. "That's good. You need more people you can trust around you. Perhaps you should consider taking an apprentice of your own."

Her smile felt brittle. "I don't need to worry about that yet, do I?" Was his health the secret he was keeping? He had never truly recovered from the attack he suffered after the queen's death, but she hadn't imagined things had worsened so much.

He stared into the ruby-black depths of his glass and the spiderweb lines around his eyes deepened. Isyllt wanted to soothe them away, along with the bruised shadows on his eyelids and the weariness that showed in every line of his lean frame. But all her magic was useless for that. No healing for either of them, only death.

Kiril looked up and smiled, and lied again. "You're right. Let's solve this mystery first. We have plenty of time to worry about other things."

She smiled back, and tried to make herself believe it.

As the sun sank behind its vault of clouds, Isyllt sat on the foot of Ciaran's narrow bed and waited for him to finish fussing with his clothes. The little room—practically compact was the kindest description—smelled of baking and spices from the kitchens below and all the familiar scents that clung in his clothes and hair: orange-and-clove wood polish, pine oil, and the rich musk of his skin. Charms hung in the windows, cords of dried leaves and shining beads; she didn't recognize the foreign magics, and Ciaran never told the same story twice when she asked.

He wore dark colors tonight, snug lines that wouldn't trip him up in narrow places, none of his usual flamboyance. Isyllt was dressed much the same—plain leather trousers and a short jacket—but chains of opals and amethysts clattered faintly when she moved, a wealth of gems wrapped around her throat. A peace gift for the vrykoloi, who valued beauty and things of the earth.

Ciaran gave his boots a final stamp and pulled on his coat, double-checking all the weapons secreted about him. Isyllt stood, rolling her shoulders to settle the bone-and-silver kukri knife sheathed down her back, and tugged on her other glove.

"Will the Crown reimburse me for my time?" Ciaran asked as he braided his long dark hair.

"I'll add it to my expense account."

He leaned in to kiss her; his mouth tasted of mint and cumin. "For luck," he said with a wink.

Ciaran might never swear devotion to her, but he was warm and pleasant company. Friends for sixteen years, lovers on and off for many of those—sometimes his company was almost pleasant enough to make her forget the loneliness of the last three years.

"In that case—" She pulled him back and kissed him again.

They entered the city's cloacae through an old service door built into the Garden's wall, rain splashing the cobbles around them and running cold fingers through Isyllt's upswept hair. Rust clogged the lock, but the key Khelséa had given her finally clicked. Hinges shrieked as the metal door swung open and the effluvium of the tunnels wafted around them. Ciaran's long nose wrinkled.

"Are you certain this is wise?"

She grinned. "No. That's why you came with me."

Darkness swallowed them as the door swung shut. Isyllt's witchlight glistened on damp walls and slime-slick stairs leading under the city. The roar of water echoed through the stairwell as they descended. Sewage ran in open channels, while cleaner water sluiced through great pipes on its way to taps and fountains.

They followed the narrow walkway beside the canal, breathing shallowly against the stench. The rain helped, pouring down from gutters, sweeping the city's waste toward the river Dis. The ledges on either side were perhaps a man's height across, and the canal thrice that width, spanned by narrow stone arches every few dozen yards. Water churned black and frothing an armspan from their feet. Its noise was deafening—they would never hear anyone approaching.

Not that the vrykoloi would make a sound if they didn't want to. But for all that some Erisinians hung charms against vampires and told bloody and improbable stories, there had been no real trouble between the humans and the underdwellers for generations. The ancient Severoi kings—generally thought of as sorcerous and too tolerant of demons—had brokered a truce, granting the vampires freedom in the undercity in exchange for the safety of the citizens. Or at least only discreet murders. Ghosts and demons and ordinary human killers were much more common a threat in the city.

So why rob a royal crypt? Impossible to imagine it

would go unnoticed, or that the Crown wouldn't take action. She hoped the vrykoloi's opinion of the truce hadn't changed.

They climbed a rusty ladder down to the next level of sewers. Isyllt had no idea how far the tunnels truly sprawled. Generations of kings and city councils had added to them, and most maps conflicted. Every so often a new sewer line or enlarged crypt would open into a strange tunnel that no one could account for. Hopefully the vrykoloi or other mystery diggers knew what they were about, and sections of the city wouldn't collapse into the ground one day.

The din of water faded as they climbed lower and the tunnel walls roughened. Moisture dripped from the ceilings, splashing in puddles and echoing along low corridors. The air grew heavy with moss and rust and stone, a cloying taste over Isyllt's tongue. The weight of earth around them was enough to silence even Ciaran, and she strained her ears for any sound of company. The conjured light bobbed at her shoulder, threw their shadows wild and flickering against the walls.

Kiril had showed her this way years ago, while they crawled through the tunnels in search of other quarry. In the days when they worked together, wading through death to the knees. The vrykoloi must surely have heard them coming by now—

She never heard a sound, even as a white shape stepped out of the darkness in front of them. Breath hissed between her teeth and her boots scraped stone as she stumbled back, right hand reaching over her shoulder. Behind her, Ciaran cursed softly.

Witchlight glittered in wide yellow eyes, glistened on

ivory fangs bared in a grin. Animal teeth in a mockery of a human face. Batlike ears hung with gold and silver hoops pricked forward under cobweb hair.

"Spider." A whisper, but too loud in this place. She dropped her hand. The ring hung quiescent against her sternum and she held her breath against a relieved sigh.

"Hello, little witch." He straightened, his head nearly brushing the ceiling—a creature of sharp angles and spindle-thin limbs, attenuated to the point of grotesquerie. "I thought I heard your heartbeat." He bowed with marionette grace. "What brings you to my doorstep?" His eyes flickered briefly over Ciaran and returned to her.

The scars on her left shoulder tingled. Spider still carried silver burns from their first meeting as well. "I need to speak with your elders."

He cocked one white brow. "Really? Do you come on your own business, necromancer, or your Crown's?"

Her smile felt tight. "Somewhere in between. It's important."

He moved between eye-blinks, between heartbeats. She never saw him stir, and then he had closed two yards to stand beside her, stooping till his face was near hers. Not yellow like an animal's, his eyes, but brilliant and crystalline as brimstone. His nostrils flared. "Your heart is beating very fast."

Isyllt tilted her head and smiled, breathing in his unnerving aroma of decaying leaves and anise, old blood and older earth. "You do have that effect on me."

Fangs flashed with his laugh. "Would you like to see my scars?"

"Maybe some other night. I want to see the elders before dawn."

Spider sighed—an affectation, since she was certain he didn't need breath—and stepped back. "Oh, very well. Your companion—"

"Comes with me," Isyllt said. She was willing to risk both their lives on Ciaran's discretion. He'd use anything as fodder for a song, but could usually be convinced to change the important bits.

Spider nodded. "Then follow me, witch. I'll take you down."

In another flickering movement he vanished down the tunnel. Ciaran's hand closed on Isyllt's elbow, and she wasn't sure whom he meant to reassure.

Spider led them deeper into the earth, through narrow twisting crawlspaces that she and Ciaran cursed and struggled their way through. The walls glistened with moisture, sparked with flecks of crystal. She was thoroughly lost before long; only the vrykoloi's goodwill would see them safely out again. The silver knife weighed heavy on her back.

Finally the cramped corridor opened, only to end abruptly in a black pit. Isyllt sent her witchlight dancing over the precipice, but its glow couldn't reach the bottom.

"Watch your step," Spider said, laying a cold hand on her arm.

"Do we fly down from here?"

His eyes glittered. "Almost."

And before she could reply, he scooped her into his arms and leapt over the edge.

Isyllt didn't scream, mostly because she didn't have enough breath. A dizzying rush of air, then the jolt of landing. Spider's long legs absorbed most of the impact, but the force still rippled through her hard enough to crack her teeth together. Her control slipped and the light went out.

She couldn't breathe. Spider's arms, impossibly strong for their gauntness, cradled her against his chest. Her heart tripped against her ribs and her stomach thought it was still falling. Colors swam in front of her as her eyes strained against the black and the taste of blood filled her mouth; she'd bitten her lip.

Spider's breath wafted cold against her cheek. "I remember what you taste like." His tongue, long and rough as a cat's, brushed her mouth and she shuddered.

Then he was gone. Wavering on her feet, she called the light again in time to see him scurrying up the rock, nimble as his namesake. He returned a moment later carrying Ciaran.

"Don't worry," he said as he deposited the minstrel. "That's nearly the hardest part."

The light flickered treacherously across the floor, but couldn't touch the walls or ceiling. No matter how softly Isyllt stepped, the scuff of boot-soles on stone carried through the wide empty space. Sweat chilled beneath her jacket.

Ciaran took her arm again as they followed the vampire, making a show of helping her over the uneven ground. "Why did I come with you, again?"

"Because you love me. And because I'm going to pay you."

"As long as I had a good reason." His fingers tightened on her sleeve, warm through the leather.

The sloping cavern floor ended at wide stone doors. Skulls embedded in white rock grinned madly in the capering light. Human and otherwise, some so foreign Isyllt had no idea what their original owners might have looked like. The gates of the vampires' ossuary palace, through which very few mortals had ever returned alive.

Spider turned. "Douse your light, little witch. Some of my brethren have more delicate eyes than I."

She swallowed and felt Ciaran's tension through his fingers. The opalescent light died and darkness rushed over them, so thick she could taste it. The door opened with a soft scrape and dank air gusted out, fragrant with stone and the snake musky sweetness of the vrykoloi. Like walking into an animal's den, but so much worse; goose pimples stung her skin.

Spider's long fingers claimed her right hand and glove leather slipped against sweat-greased flesh. "Follow me."

Death breathed over her as they walked, whispered in her head; her ring spat diamond sparks. Ghostlights glimmered in the darkness, pinpoints of blue and green. Not enough to see by, but they gave her an idea of the great size of the chamber. The floor was slick underfoot now, smooth as polished flagstones. Water dripped in the distance, a slow plink into a pool that scattered echoes through the black.

They weren't alone. Isyllt felt eyes on them, felt whispering voices too faint to hear. Surrounded. Ciaran held her crippled hand tight enough to ache, and her right was trapped in Spider's. She wouldn't reach her knife in time if they were attacked. Sweat trickled down her back, soaking her linen camisole. Her heart beat strong and fast in her throat.

Isyllt smiled, baring her teeth to the dark. Somewhere in the shadows, laughter answered.

Spider paused for a moment, squeezing her hand when

she drew breath to speak. Then he turned. "Lady Tenebris will see you, but your friend waits here."

Isyllt's left hand tightened awkwardly on Ciaran's. "Don't worry, little witch," the vampire said, amusement coloring his voice. "You're our guests here. Perhaps the bard will sing for us—we seldom host musicians."

"Far be it from me to refuse an audience," Ciaran said. His voice was calm, despite his trembling hands. "I'd be honored."

Isyllt brushed his arm in reassurance before Spider's hand closed on her elbow and pulled her forward again.

He led her down a flight of shallow steps. The air grew closer around her, dust tickling her nose. The smell of snakes and old blood grew stronger and she fought a sneeze. Her shoulder brushed a doorway as he steered her to the right and she felt the closeness of walls.

"There's a chair in front of you," he said. "The Lady will join you soon."

Isyllt moved carefully forward until her knees bumped stone. A bench, strewn with pillows of threadbare velvet and soft-worn brocade. The stone leeched warmth from her flesh as she sat. She tugged off her right glove, shaking her hand dry. Her breath was harsh and loud in the stillness.

An icy draft heralded the vrykola's arrival, a *presence* that made the hair on Isyllt's nape prickle. She rose and bowed low, grateful not to stumble or crack her head on anything.

Tenebris's laugh crawled over her skin, cold and slick as oil. "You sit so bravely in the dark." A match crackled and orange-gold light blossomed, brilliant enough to make Isyllt's eyes water. A candle flame quickened and acrid blue smoke coiled through the air. "Is that better?"

"Yes, Lady. Thank you." Isyllt blinked back moisture and reached for the chain around her neck. The room was smaller than she'd imagined after the vastness of the hall outside, low-ceilinged and narrow. Tattered hangings draped the walls, and a broken chair crouched in the far corner. "My master sends his greetings, and gifts." Gems slithered into her palm, warm from her skin. Amethysts glowed in the candlelight and opals spat iridescent fire.

"Lovely," Tenebris murmured. Shadows trailed her like gossamer, fluttering from her gaunt limbs. Isyllt couldn't see her features, save for a faint glitter of eyes and the flash of teeth when she spoke.

Aphra and Tenebris were old, the oldest of the vrykoloi as far as Kiril knew, and they were even less human than Spider. Arcanost scholars knew very little about the origins of the vrykoloi, and even scientific curiosity and prestige weren't enough for most to brave the undercity. Isyllt wondered if she could scavenge the beginnings of a monograph from this audience.

Tenebris spilled the jewels from palm to palm in a shimmering stream. "Send my regards to Lord Orfion. It is a pity we don't speak as we once did, but the years weigh heavy."

Isyllt looked at her hands to hide her frown.

"Aphra won't join us tonight," the vrykola said, turning away. Her shadow-draperies fluttered farther from the light. "She sleeps much lately, and is not easily roused. What is it that we can do for you, necromancer?"

Isyllt swallowed, her throat dry. "Some of your people have taken up tomb robbing, Lady."

Tenebris paused. Or more aptly, she *stilled*. For a

heartbeat Isyllt had no sense that anything else was in the room with her. "Tomb robbing?"

"The royal crypts, no less. The late queen's jewelry was stolen."

One gaunt hand waved, shedding darkness like a flame shedding smoke. "Which queen is that, child? I fear I've lost track."

"Lychandra, wife to Mathiros Alexios, who still reigns."

"Alexios. Pity the Severoi aren't still on the throne. Or the Korinthes—I remember them. What makes you think vrykoloi were responsible for this theft?"

"I smelled them, Lady. It's not a scent easily counterfeited."

Tenebris chuckled again. "No, I imagine it is not." Silence filled the room again, wrapping them in cold coils.

"The king hasn't heard of this yet," Isyllt finally said, "but when he does he'll be...angry. His temper is easily ignited, especially where his wife is concerned."

"I fear I cannot help you. Aphra and I would never countenance such a thing, but there are those who stray from the fold, who don't follow the order of the catacombs. I can claim no responsibility for these rabble, nor hope to chastise them to any effect."

Isyllt swallowed again. "My master and I would keep this from the king, if possible, but to do that we must recover what was stolen. Is there nothing you can do to help us?"

Tenebris sighed, a sound like slow-pouring water. "I shall inquire. Perhaps one of the young ones has seen something, heard something." She melted from one shadow to another and stood beside Isyllt; the candle didn't flicker in her passage. "I smell your blood. It's... distracting."

Isyllt pressed her tongue against her sore lip; the taste of metal filled her mouth. Her shoulders tightened and tingled. Tenebris's hand brushed her cheek, silk-wrapped bones like the sticks of a lady's fan.

Then she was gone, back on the far side of the room. "It's better when we sleep. Sleep is soothing, dulls these appetites." She glided toward the door. "It would be best if you returned to the upper world, necromancer. Investigate as you will. Perhaps Spider can help you—he is still young and curious, and doesn't yet feel the pull of earth. He was fond of the last mage who braved the underground, too." Her voice chilled. "If you find these rabble who threaten our peace, dispose of them as you see fit."

With that, Isyllt was alone.

Biting back another frown, she called witchlight as she left the room, trailing it behind her so she wasn't blind. Bones glimmered against grey stone, intricate swirls of phalanges and vertebrae bleached slick and pale as cream, ribs curving like buttresses along the ceiling. The death-sense of the place dizzied her; her ring was a band of ice.

She might have lost herself in the twisting ossuary corridors, but she heard the familiar sound of Ciaran's voice. His smoky baritone led her back to the broad stairs and into the main hall. A smile tugged her lips as she recognized the ballad—of course Ciaran would sing love songs to vampires.

Her tiny light glittered on walls inlaid with gems and bone. A cathedral, all soaring columns and statued alcoves. She wanted to stop and gawk, but forced herself to keep walking, eyes on Ciaran.

He sat on a bench against the wall, surrounded by his deathly audience. A few of them fled at her light, melting into the shadows or skittering up the walls like insects, but most remained, giving her no more than a passing glance. She waited till he finished the last verse and silence filled the vaulted room once more. Eerie eyes glittered, reflecting opalescent flame. No tears, but the rapt expressions on bone-pale faces were just as eloquent.

Ciaran smiled as she approached, his face alight. He loved an audience, no matter how unusual. "Sound carries beautifully in here. It would make a marvelous concert hall."

"You should discuss that with Lady Tenebris the next time we visit. But I'm afraid we need to leave now." She glanced at the gathered crowd, but recognized none of the faces. "Where's Spider?"

"Here," the vampire said, appearing at her elbow. "I'll escort you up."

The vampires stared at Ciaran as he stood and straightened his coat, their eyes hungry. He bowed with a flourish as graceful as any he might offer a crowd at the Briar Patch, or an orpheum. A slender arm reached out of the shadows, almost shyly, and pressed something into his hand. Isyllt caught his sleeve and pulled him away before anyone demanded an encore.

When the tall stone doors shut behind, Isyllt finally let out a sigh. The back of her neck still prickled furiously and her muscles were strung tight as kithara strings.

Spider smiled crookedly. "How was your meeting?"

She kept walking. "Trying," she said at last, voice low. "She doesn't care about any of this. It's not just our skins—" a vague upward gesture encompassed the city above them "—I'm trying to save, you know."

"I know." Spider took her arm with casual grace. "That's what happens to the very old ones. They grow torpid, dull. All they want to do is sleep, the rest of the world be damned."

"She said you might help me."

He nodded, pale hair drifting like cobwebs around his face. "I will, little witch, I will." The doors vanished into shadow behind them and soon the light lapped at the cliff wall they'd descended. "I'll listen in the dark and see what I find."

She glanced at him out of the corner of her eye. "And how is it that you know what to listen for?"

He grinned. "I'm very good at listening in the dark."

"Who was the other mage Tenebris mentioned, who you were so fond of?"

"Another sorceress, years ago. Decades, it must be. She wanted to learn our secrets, and even managed to charm one or two out of us. She's dead now, I fear."

He turned at the wall instead of hauling them back up the way they'd come as Isyllt expected. "There's an easier way back." He led them to a narrow door in the rock, where a stair twisted up into shadow.

Isyllt raised her eyebrows. "You couldn't have brought us down this way?"

"It's not as much fun." He bent close, till she could smell his coppery poison-sweet breath. "I'll find you when I have something to report." He bowed over her hand and pressed a cold kiss against her knuckles. "The stair will take you back to the bottom of your sewers. Don't use it again without permission."

Before she could speak he was gone, leaving only a lingering chill in her flesh.

The stair was narrow and low, with only room for one at a time to pass. The steep uneven stairs were worn shallow in the centers, and Isyllt wondered how long the vrykoloi had passed this way in the silent dark.

Ciaran went first, the light bobbing ahead of him. Darkness crawled up the stairs in their wake, whispering against Isyllt's back. Her skin still tingled with the aftermath of nerves. A liability, Kiril called her craving for danger, but he understood it. They waded in death, drank it and swallowed it whole; sometimes it was good to be reminded that they still lived, and wanted to go on living.

"What did the vrykola give you?" she asked Ciaran as they climbed.

He paused to fish in his trouser pocket and pulled out a coin. Gold, crusted along the edge with a dark grime Isyllt didn't care to identify. The profile stamped on the face wasn't one she recognized. Ciaran peered at it for a moment, then laughed.

"It's a chrysaor." The winged boar that had been the crest of House Korinthes. "She tipped me with two-hundred-year-old gold."

As her pulse slowed she felt the long walk down. Her legs burned and her breath ached in her lungs. By the time they reached the top of the stairs even so small a magic as the witchlight drained her strength, and fatigue laid a heavy yoke across her shoulders.

The reek of the sewers struck them as the stones swung open, thick and fetid after the smell of rock and earth. The door closed silently behind them, blending seamlessly into the rough wall of the tunnel.

Ciaran sighed, the sound nearly lost in the rush of water. "I need a drink. Come back to the Briar with me— the Crown's treat."

Isyllt chuckled. Dust and mud itched on her face and

scalp and she craved a hot bath, but wine and pleasant company might suffice. "I think the Crown can afford a bottle or two—"

She broke off as the sapphire began to pulse against her chest and the sharpness of surgical spirits cut through the sewer reek. That and the intake of Ciaran's breath were all the warning she had.

Weight hit her from behind, driving her to the floor and scoring her palms on stone as she caught herself. Cold hands held her, pinning her arms and clamping her jaw. Much too strong. Ciaran shouted.

Steely fingers yanked her head to the side, ripped at her collar. She twisted, but couldn't break free, tensed against the strike—

Needles through her skin, sinking into flesh where neck met shoulder. Razor teeth, jaws like a vise. She screamed once, short and sharp. Only a moment till the poison started to work.

Her knife gouged her spine as the vampire's weight pressed her down; she couldn't reach the dagger in her boot. But blades had never been her weapon of choice. The witchlight exploded, from candle wisp to blazing star, a burst of light and searing cold.

Someone shrieked. Teeth ripped out of her shoulder, blood gushing. Isyllt pushed to her feet, dragging the kukri free of her ruined jacket. The silver blade shattered the light, threw back shards of brilliance. Tears streamed down her cheeks and she didn't see the vampire's rush in time to dodge it.

He caught her low in the stomach, driving the air from her lungs and lifting her off the floor. She stabbed wild and clumsy as they both became airborne.

The water hit her like a wall. Frothing current buffeted them, grabbed her leather clothes and pulled her down. The vampire sank with her, their limbs tangled together. Grit and debris rushed past them, stinging Isyllt's eyes. Rank, sour water flooded her mouth and she tried not to gag. She shoved left-handed against the vampire's face, slicing her glove open on a fang. His hand caught her right wrist and forced the blade away. Her back bumped the bottom of the canal, scraping along slime-slick stone as the water bore them on. Her shoulder burned; her lungs burned.

Burned. Burning. A gentle warmth coursing through her veins, soothing aching flesh and taking the pain away...

The venom of a vampire's bite, working its way into her blood. The poison that calmed their prey, rendered them quiet and pliable while the vrykoloi drank their life away. She'd felt it before with Spider, as sweet and strong as poppy wine once it took hold.

The vampire's grip numbed her arm—her strength was nothing against his. But she wasn't alone.

Her diamond flared. Leather cracked and peeled and flaked away, and the spectral glow lit up the water as trapped ghosts answered her call. Their terrible chill seared her bones.

The vampire recoiled from the light, face hidden behind writhing dark hair. His hold loosened and Isyllt swung her knife. Clumsy, hampered by wet leather and wounded shoulder, but the blade sliced along his stomach. Black blood clouded the water, shredding and dissolving in the flow. She thought her lungs would burst as she kicked upward.

She gasped as she broke the surface, lungs screaming. Her right arm was numb to the elbow; she could barely feel the knife hilt against her hand. Her clothing dragged her down, threatened to pull her under again.

A hand closed on hers and lifted her out of the sewer. She gasped in pain as she fell onto stone, scraping her knuckles as she tried to keep hold of her weapon. The witchlight was gone, drowned in the morass of her pain and panic.

"Saints, you reek." Spider's voice. She struggled to her knees, raising the knife. "Put that down, witch."

"Who—" She gulped another breath. Her stomach roiled. "Who was that?"

"I believe that was the rabble Tenebris mentioned."

Starbursts of color swam in front of her eyes. She felt warm, though she couldn't stop shivering. Heat trickled down her shoulder. Calling another light was an effort, and the flame sputtered and wept incandescent sparks. "Where's Ciaran?"

Spider shielded his eyes with one long hand and pointed down the tunnel. "Back there. He's in better shape than you."

With trembling fingers she unbuckled her torn jacket and peeled it off. Her blood was nearly black in the eerie glow. The pain made her bite her already tender lip, but it wasn't as bad as it should be. The poison would take hours to work out of her body. Languorous warmth lapped inside her head, promising peace if she would only close her eyes....

She shook her head, the pain in her neck holding lethargy at bay. Her stomach cramped and she retched, spitting fetid water and the remains of her lunch over the stones. She scrubbed a hand over her mouth and tried to control the nausea. Spider's mouth quirked, but he wisely remained silent.

When her head stopped spinning she took the vampire's proffered hand and leaned on his arm. The current had carried her farther than she'd realized. "What happened to the one who attacked me? I doubt I killed him." A situation she would remedy if she had another chance. Her boots squelched with every step, water shifting between her toes.

Spider shrugged. "The water took him. I'll try to find his trail once you and your friend are safely gone."

She glanced up at him, eyes narrowing. "How did you know to come back?"

"I caught Azarné following you. I thought she meant you harm."

"Azarné?"

"Her." He pointed to a slender shape crouching beside Ciaran.

The light spilled over a delicate face half-hidden under elf-locked black hair. The vrykola who'd given Ciaran the coin. Eyes wide and gold as an owl's stared up at Isyllt. "I wouldn't have hurt you." Her voice was soft and husky and accented. "I only wanted more music."

Isyllt knelt by Ciaran and brought the light closer. Blood trickled down one side of his face, but his eyes were clear. He wrinkled his nose at the reek that clung to her. "Are you all right?" she asked.

He nodded carefully. "A bit bruised, but whole. The lovely lady intervened before things became unpleasant." He picked up Azarné's small bronze hand and kissed her knuckles. She blinked, hair sliding over her face.

"It was Myca," the vrykola said. "He didn't stay to fight me." Her tiny mouth twisted with distaste.

Spider frowned. "Who attacked Isyllt?"

Azarné shrugged. "I didn't see. They were already in the water."

Ciaran stood, wiping at the blood on his face. Only a little cut on his scalp, Isyllt thought, but she wanted to inspect it in better light. Her own bleeding had slowed, but she was already dizzy. Her head pounded and the witchlight sputtered with every throb. The sapphire was silent once more.

"Let's get you home," Spider said, glancing down the dark tunnel.

CHAPTER 4

Dawn stole past the windows as Isyllt and Ciaran soaked in her wide wooden tub, and candle-shadows danced across the high-beamed ceiling. Cooling water lapped over her breasts, thick with myrrh and poppy oils; Ciaran's chest was warm and solid behind her, his clever hands lulling her as he stroked her uninjured shoulder. She'd drained one tub-full already, flushing grime and filth back to the sewers where they belonged. The wet bandage stung the wound, but vrykoloi bites healed fast, and her magic would kill any infection that tried to grow in her flesh.

Ciaran's lips on her nape startled her awake as the world greyed around the edges. "You'll drown if you're not careful." He nudged her until she sighed and pushed herself to her feet. Tendrils of hair clung to her skin as she rose, like ink bleeding from a brush.

"I should try to find their trail while the sun is up," she said as he helped her out of the tub and wrapped her in a towel. His touch sent warmth and gooseflesh rippling down her skin in turns; the poison's effects lingered.

"You should sleep, or you'll pass out anyway." He steered her toward the bedroom, leaving a trail of wet footprints behind them.

Heavy curtains covered the windows in her room and the hearth was cold. She climbed into the high draperied bed, heedless of wet sheets. Big enough for two, like the tub, but she most often slept alone. When she couldn't find an excuse not to sleep at all.

Ciaran lay down beside her, wrapping a feather quilt around them. "Will you rest now, or do I have to sing you to sleep?"

Isyllt brushed light fingers over his face, tracing the bruise purpling on his brow. "I nearly got you hurt tonight." Or worse. "I'm sorry."

He caught her hand and kissed her fingertips. "If I was afraid of harm, I certainly wouldn't keep company with you." She felt his smile. "You can send my payment round to the Briar." He kissed the hollow of her wrist, humming softly. "Are you going to sleep now?"

She smiled and twined her fingers through his curling damp hair. "Not if you keep doing that."

He hummed another bar, trailing his lips up her arm to her collarbone. His mouth brushed the uninjured side of her throat and she tilted her head back, ignoring the pain. Her fingers tightened in his hair, her left hand sliding down his back.

She stiffened as her wards tingled. Ciaran chuckled, and she sighed and rolled out of bed, securing her slipping towel. Her stomach tightened as she recognized Kiril, and all the warmth Ciaran's touch had conjured drained away in a rush.

"What are you doing about at this hour?" she asked as she opened the door, trying to keep her voice light. Her fingers clenched in nubby linen.

Kiril blinked down at her and frowned. He touched her shoulder, brushing the edge of the bandage. "What happened?"

"An unfriendly vampire." The smell of herbs and magic dizzied her and she leaned into his touch before she could stop herself.

His brows pulled together and he cupped her cheek with one calloused palm. "Are you all right?"

"I will be." She covered his hand with her crippled one. "They escaped, but I'll try to pick up the trail after I've rested a bit." His pulse beat against her skin and she tightened her grip on the towel. "It was them. The tomb-robbers. But I didn't see their faces."

"We'll find them." He turned his hand to catch hers, tracing his thumb over the web of scars she wore like a lace glove. "I won't let you get hurt again."

That made her laugh, despite the tightness in her stomach. "I get myself hurt. I learned from the best."

He smiled ruefully. "True." His eyes flickered toward the bedroom and the smile twisted. "I'm glad you have someone to look after you."

"Kiril—" His name caught in her throat.

He squeezed her hand. "I know. I made my choices—I have no business regretting them now."

"You can always unmake them."

He laid a finger on her lips. "I'm sorry. I only came to see that you were all right, and to hear what you'd learned." His face darkened as he touched the bandage again. "We'll find the ones who did this." He brushed a damp strand of hair out of her face and kissed her forehead. "But first, rest."

He turned and left before she could speak.

Tears burned her aching eyes as Isyllt stumbled back to the bedroom. Ciaran pulled her close, stroking her tangled hair while she cried.

"Enough foolish grief for any tragedy," she whispered against his shoulder.

He rocked her gently and sang her lullabies until she finally slept.

The sun crested the line of the eastern mountains as Kiril left Isyllt's apartment, chasing away the blue softness of dawn and spilling long shadows across the ground. Fog coiled thick as milk in the streets, slowly unraveling in the light. Smoke drifted across the sky and temple bells tolled the start of morning rites, rousing faithful and faithless alike. The narrow arch of the rear entrance framed the sloping streets and sun-gilt spires, windows sparkling bright as gems. The beauty of the city at daybreak still caught in his throat sometimes, even after so many years. Much the way his hand ached with the memory of Isyllt's cheek.

For all the familiar morning clatter, this corner of Archlight was too quiet for the hour. Besides the sorcerers who had ridden north with the king, there were always students who chose the uncertainty of a soldier's life to the certainty of a scholar's poverty. How many of those two hundred dead might have taken classes when they returned?

He should never have let Isyllt go underground. Which was ridiculous—besides the fact that she was well-trained and knew all the dangers, asking her not to take a risk would only make her more determined to do so. Telling her not to do her job would raise a dozen questions, each sharper than the last. And he had long forfeited the right to ask her to stay out of harm's way for his sake.

Old fool. And more folly, his resolve still wavered every time he saw her. Three years of nothing but mentor and pupil, as they should have stayed from the beginning. Three years, and she still asked him to unmake his choice. He breathed deep, trying to banish the smell of her hair with the stink of the streets.

He had put her in danger from the very beginning, of course, from the moment he recruited her. Trained her and used her and sent her out to kill or be killed. His loyalty to the king had demanded it, and he never hesitated. She knew the price of the game, he'd told himself, she accepted it. But after the last assignment cost her a hand, and his own relationship with the king grew strained and bitter, he had sworn to himself that he wouldn't see her hurt that way again.

And now his secrets had nearly killed her once more.

He shook such worthless thoughts aside, focusing on the strain in his muscles instead, the creak of his knees as he climbed the winding staircased streets; regrets were useless. His chest burned by the time he reached his house on the far side of the quarter, but it was only the pain of tired lungs, not his traitorous heart. He'd owned the house for years, but only taken up residence the past spring, after the last disagreement with the king finally sealed the rift that had been growing for three years. Mathiros had never forgiven him for Lychandra's death, for his failure to do the impossible. More bitter still were all the impossible things he had managed that the king had no knowledge of.

Leaves drifted across the broad steps, scarlet and gold against pale stone. They crunched like bone underfoot, clung to the hem of his cloak. Lucky that he'd always been lax about calling servants in, fonder of privacy than swept walks or polished banisters. Careless intrusion now would end badly. A raven perched on the carven lintel, watching him with one coldly curious eye.

The entry hall was dark, drapes and shutters drawn, but Kiril conjured no light as he climbed the curving marble stair. He knew he wasn't alone before he reached the landing. The ease with which Phaedra passed his wards made his flesh crawl. No matter how softly he walked, the demoness heard him coming.

A fire crackled in the bedchamber hearth and Phaedra lounged on a divan beside it. Her veils lay across the foot of the couch in a shimmer of bronze and ocher silk, and black curls spilled around her shoulders. It was such a meticulously artless arrangement that amusement overcame his irritation.

"Comfortable?" he asked, arching an eyebrow. The fire was too warm after the morning chill, but the cold pained her like an ague. He resisted the urge to throw open the shutters and heavy drapes.

"I am." She stretched slowly, and he wondered if undead limbs could stiffen. "Though you're nearly out of wine." She waved a lazy hand toward the flagon on the table; bangles chimed on her wrist.

He bowed sardonically. "Forgive me. I'm not accustomed to entertaining these days."

She looked up through eyelashes thick with kohl. "You

keep me quite entertained, Kirilos." Looking at her face was a knife between the ribs every time; he held her gaze for as many heartbeats as he could stand it.

Sorceress, demon, undead—she was treason clothed in stolen flesh. Once she had been a colleague, if never a friend. Now she was the greatest betrayal he had ever committed—of his king, his vows, the memory of those he'd loved. And perhaps most especially of his sanity. But it was his own fault she wore a stolen body; he had destroyed her own years ago.

He could tell himself that she would be in the city without his involvement, that people would still die for her schemes and he wouldn't be there to stop her. It might even be true. But no one would ever forgive him this if they knew.

He turned before she might scry any hint of emotion on his face, tossing cloak and jacket across a chair. Heat bled quickly through his fine linen shirt, but that brought no comfort. He abandoned all of his tangled thoughts but the most pertinent.

"We have a problem."

"Oh?" She sipped her wine, glancing at him over the rim of the goblet.

"Your pet vampires bungled things." He made no attempt to keep the anger from his voice as he related what Isyllt had told him about the ring and the murdered girl and the attack in the sewers. Phaedra's involvement with the vrykoloi had made him uneasy from the start, and now all his misgivings were given shape. One blood-thirsty demon was bad enough.

Phaedra frowned as she listened, a crease forming between arching black brows. Her eyebrows were much the same as those of her first face, and the prominent lines of her cheekbones. The thought unnerved him—had the resemblance always been there, or was it only a trick of memory? Her skin had been ice white then, her hair straight as a razor. He had never forgotten her face glowing with delight or pallid with anger, nor transfigured in horror as she fell. His hand clenched, as it had the day he'd let her fall.

He turned away from the chasm of memories, so sickened by them that he almost missed her words.

"Fools," she said softly. "I knew she would be trouble, but not about the ring."

He gathered his scattered wits. "What did you know?"

"About the girl. About the vrykolos's...indiscretion with her." Painted lips twisted. "I didn't know he was fool enough to give her a royal signet, or I would have searched the body."

Anger chilled him. "You killed her and didn't have the sense to do something with the corpse? Even the river would have done the work for us." He knew better than to antagonize her, but the next words slipped out anyway. "You killed an innocent girl because it was *expedient*?"

He had the satisfaction of seeing her flinch. Then she uncoiled from the couch like an asp, and her eyes sparkled bright as Iskari amber. Demon eyes. "I learned from the best, didn't I? And none of us were ever innocent. Isn't that what you told yourself—what Mathiros told himself? That I had brought it on myself? Temptress, harlot, witch."

Rusty orange skirts swirled around her ankles like a forest fire as she advanced on him, gilt thread flashing. Her perfume burned too, cinnamon and orange and bitter almonds, crawling into his nose. But her hand was cold when it closed on his jaw—no hearth was warm enough to chase the death-chill from her flesh.

"I never called you those things," he said mildly, controlling his pulse when it wanted to leap. She could break his jaw without effort, and her magic was at least a match for his own—more so in his weakened state. If anyone deserved to take his life, it was Phaedra, but he had no intention of giving it to her.

"No." Her touch melted from steel to silk, fingertips trailing down his neck, nails rasping against his beard. "No, not you. Do I tempt you now, Kirilos?"

"I have no taste for dead kisses."

She leaned in, breasts cold and yielding against his chest. "I won't be dead forever. I'll be warm again. I can make you young and strong again, too."

It was not the first time she'd offered; the prospect intrigued and repulsed him. He stepped away, carefully plucking her cold brown hand off his shirt collar. "Not if your schemes are blown before Mathiros returns. We must retrieve what was stolen. Before anyone else is hurt."

Her mouth curled. "Why aren't you with your apprentice now, if her health concerns you so?"

"She has others to tend to her."

She circled him, slow and predatory, running her fingers down his spine. "Poor Kiril. I don't understand this celibacy of yours."

"I can't imagine you often worry about sparing others pain." Or sparing herself pain, for that matter.

A knock at the door downstairs and the accompanying chime of wards spared them both. Kiril recognized the inquisitive touch of magic and released the lock with a thought, sealing it again after the door had shut.

Varis appeared a moment later, framing himself in the doorway for a beat before stepping into the room. He had always been good with entrances, Kiril thought wryly, and even better with exits. Today he wore a coat of claret velvet with silver embroidery thick on the sleeves and dove grey trousers and high boots. Restrained for him, but it was also much earlier than he usually came visiting. When he moved closer, Kiril saw fatigue shadows beneath his maquillage.

Varis cocked one penciled brow, looking pointedly from Kiril to Phaedra and back again. Garnets glittered in his ears, and white lace rose from beneath his high velvet collar to frame the line of his jaw. "This is a fraught little tableau. Am I interrupting something?"

"Nothing," Kiril said with a sigh, sinking into the chair on top of his crumpled cloak, "except the litany of our sins."

A flick of Varis's slender wrist dismissed those. His rings flashed, pigeon's blood ruby and orange sapphire, lesser emeralds and topazes, but no diamonds; Varis was one of the cleverest mages Kiril knew, but never a vinculator. "I hear sins and litanies every night, darling. Surely you have something more interesting."

Not for the first time, Kiril wished that it hadn't been Varis who'd brought Phaedra to him. If she could only have snared someone else in her schemes, someone he wouldn't miss if forced to kill. But Varis had always been fascinated by her, and just as fascinated by secrets and clever sorcery and flaunting rules. And he had his own reasons to despise the Alexioi.

Kiril recounted again everything Isyllt had told him about the investigation. He didn't mention Phaedra's involvement in the prostitute's death, though he wasn't sure exactly why—it wasn't as though Varis had innocence to preserve. He expected another flippant response, but by the time he finished Varis had paled to a sickly shade of paste.

"Saints and specters," he whispered. "So that's it. Damn." He began to pace, short measured strides scuffing against carpets and clicking on tile. "Your apprentice told the prince, and the prince told Savedra."

Kiril's spine stiffened. "Told her what, exactly?"

"I don't know. Everything, I imagine. She was asking about vampires yesterday, with much too convenient an excuse." He stopped his circuit and flung himself into another chair. Phaedra watched him with an expression somewhere between amusement and befuddlement and Kiril nearly laughed—Varis had that effect on people. The pale sorcerer sighed, rubbing a hand over his scalp. "We know entirely too many inquisitive people."

"We'll take care of it," Phaedra promised. Kiril didn't have the energy left to argue with her.

Silence fell between them, broken only by the crackling of the hearth. They were, Kiril thought, an unlikely conspiracy. Varis was known for his dissipation and excess, and despite a brief assignment at the Selafaïn embassy in Iskar over twenty years ago no one imagined he might have a political thought in his head. No one remembered or cared about the rumors that had attended his birth: his mother had held the old king's regard, and been removed from court too hastily; her marriage to her cousin Tselios had also been too hasty, especially to account for Varis's birth; Nikolaos Alexios had had the same pale blue eyes, so uncommon in Selafaïns. It could have been the makings of a terrible scandal, but had faded instead into obscurity.

It had taken more than rumor control and royal unconcern to keep Phaedra Severos quietly obscure. She had been a prominent fixture at the Arcanost, famed for her beauty and brilliance and mercurial temper. Her death, and that of her foreign noble husband, would have meant not scandal but ruin for the young Mathiros had the truth of them ever been found out. Preventing that had taken all of Kiril's resources, and the greatest magic he had ever wrought. He had been paying off the debt of it for three years now, but it had worked: no one outside this room remembered Phaedra, or had any concern about her if they did.

The way no one would remember him. History cared for kings and princes and their scandals, but spymasters were brushed quietly away with dust and pen shavings. The most effective were never known at all. As it ought to be.

"Speaking of care," Varis said, distracting Kiril from the bitter spiral of his thoughts, "we can't let you wander around dressed like that." A wave of his hand encompassed Phaedra's gown and shed veils. "You're years out of style, and unseasonal besides."

"We can't let her wander around at all," Kiril said, even as Phaedra plucked at her dress—sleeveless gauzy silk belted below her breasts—with a frown. The shade of orange should have flattered, but her brown skin was unhealthily pale, like tea with too much milk. Or dead flesh through which no blood flowed.

"Things happen," Varis replied, "as your story so clearly illustrates. It's impossible that she won't be seen eventually—we need to make sure that when she is she doesn't look like a mad vengeful ghost from one of Kolkhis's tragedies."

Kiril opened his mouth to argue—*And never mind,* he thought, *that that's exactly what she is*—but Phaedra's eyes had already widened, shining with manic light. He remembered her wild moods from her first life; death had done nothing to settle them. Some physicians thought that her particular combination of mania, black despair, and violent temper was an illness, an imbalance of humors or aethers. But if it were a physical malady, shouldn't it have died with her first body? A defect of the soul, perhaps? Or was she simply so used to being mad that it had become habit?

He set the problem aside—he had no time to write a dissertation about her, however fascinating it would be. By now she and Varis were deep in a conversation about fashion and milliners, and how one could be properly fitted without showing one's face. This was an argument he wouldn't win, and he had no strength to waste on it. He rose, wincing as his joints popped, and left them to their folly. The demon might have finished his wine, but hopefully she'd left the whiskey in the study intact.

Isyllt woke to a fire dying in the hearth and warm light edging the curtains. Ciaran's spiced-smoke scent clung to her sheets, but the bed was cold and the house echoed empty to her outstretched senses. Gone back to the Briar Patch to sing for his supper.

Supper seemed a sensible plan—rat's teeth of hunger gnawed her stomach, and her mouth was parched and aching, but inspection of her pantry found nothing but a bunch of shriveling grapes and a heel of bread gone green around the edges. She'd neglected the market again. If the landlady's daughter didn't occasionally offer to go for her, Isyllt suspected she'd starve.

Uncovering her bathroom mirror did nothing to cheer her; her hair hung in rattails around her face and dried tears crusted her lashes. Her eyes were bruised and sunken and her shoulder throbbed. Her bones felt scraped hollow. After running another bath and combing her hair with poppy oil to banish the phantom sewer-stink, she removed the bandage from her shoulder and examined the wound.

A double crescent of teeth-marks, bruised and seeping. More savage than a human could inflict, but not quite animal in shape. Her neck and shoulder were swollen, and the flesh and muscle around the bite ached more furiously than the punctures. Her cheeks were already mottling with fever as her magic fought infection. When it healed, it would be nearly identical to the scar Spider had given her.

Staring at the twin bites, an idea sparked bright enough to make her swear. She swore again as she threw the silk cover back over the mirror, and several times more as she struggled into her clothes. By the time she was dressed, the pain in her shoulder dizzied her and sunset painted low clouds gilt and cinnabar. Not enough daylight to brave the sewers, but early enough that she might still catch Khelséa at her cohort's headquarters.

Two hours later, she and the inspector sat in the Sepulcher once more. Isyllt sat, at least, perched on the table next to Forsythia while Khelséa measured both bite wounds. The dead woman was holding up well with the chill and a light preservation spell, but someone else in the racks had started to go off; Isyllt wondered if anyone who worked here could enjoy the smell of roses again.

"This is how you tread lightly?" Khelséa said, angling for better light.

Isyllt winced as calipers pressed tender flesh. "It's progress. I found the bastards, didn't I?"

"Next time try holding on." Khelséa turned away, scribbling measurements and rough sketches on a scrap of paper. "These two are definitely different. Your old scar and Forsythia's don't match, either."

"What about the new one?"

Her dark face creased in a frown. "The distension from the swelling"—at this she poked the swelling in question hard enough to make Isyllt yelp—"makes it difficult to get a clear comparison." She tapped her stick of charcoal against the paper. "But the canines seem to be the same distance apart, and the shape of the jaw is similar. I can't be certain until you've healed a bit, but they may well be from the same vampire."

"So I found Forsythia's lover. Charming." Isyllt let Khelséa replace the dressing, then tugged her shirt up again. "Which explains how she came by the ring, but not how or why—or where—she died." Her stomach growled as she slid off the table.

"No question how you'll die," Khelséa said. "If stupidity doesn't get you, starvation will."

"Misadventure, darling, misadventure. So you're buying dinner, then?"

Most of Inkstone closed at night, but a few taverns and kiosks stayed open for late-working bureaucrats. Isyllt and Khelséa sat beneath a vendor's awning with plates of olives, bread, and cheese. The air was sluggish with haze, blurring the edges of buildings and bleeding golden halos from the streetlamps.

"What next?" the inspector asked, neatly sucking the flesh off an olive.

Isyllt frowned at her food. Even chewing made her shoulder hurt. "Back to the sewers, I suppose. I have to find the bastard who bit me, and the rest of the stolen jewels."

"I hope you're taking more than a minstrel with you this time."

"Are you volunteering?"

Khelséa's eyebrows rose. "Can you think of anyone else you trust?"

Maybe Kiril was right. Maybe it was time she took an apprentice. She ripped off a piece of bread and chewed, ignoring the pain. Relishing it.

A shadow fell across the table before she had to answer. She looked up at a tall cloaked figure, face lost beneath a cowl. A stripe of light kissed one pale cheek bone as he tilted his head, and the rich taste of goat cheese turned metallic as blood on Isyllt's tongue. Her right hand clenched around the diamond's chill.

"Good evening." Spider nodded to Khelséa before turning his attention to Isyllt. "I've missed the chance to ask you to dinner, but perhaps I can buy you a drink."

Khelséa tensed, one hand vanishing beneath the table. She might not be a mage, but she had a good nose for danger. Isyllt caught her arm, feeling muscles flex as the inspector reached for her pistol. "It's all right."

The woman's dark eyes flickered from Spider to Isyllt and back again, shining with skepticism in the lamplight. "Misadventure?"

"Exactly." Isyllt stood, reaching for her purse. "I'll talk to you before I do anything stupid."

Khelséa's hand caught hers, forcing coins back into the bag. "I'm buying, remember. Next time."

Isyllt nodded, and regretted it quickly. She followed Spider down the dark and misty street, feeling Khelséa's eyes on her back until they turned a corner.

"What kind of drink did you have in mind?" she asked. She walked slowly, leisurely, but her nerves thrummed with his nearness. Their first altercation had been a misunderstanding, but he made no secret of his appetites. The truce forbade killing, but there were always people who disappeared in a city as large as Erisín. And those like Forsythia, willing to bleed for love or money.

His chuckle made her shiver. "How's your shoulder?"

"I'll live." She glanced at him from the corner of her eye. "He didn't bite as hard as you."

He laughed again and took her arm, covering her hand with his. Grey gloves hid his claws, supple as snakeskin and as cold. But only as cold as the night, not the aching chill of death. She touched his arm; it might almost have been living flesh.

"You're warm. Who did you kill tonight?"

He arched an eyebrow. "There are always willing donors. You should try it."

She rolled her eyes toward her wounded shoulder. "No thank you."

"It doesn't have to be unpleasant."

She ignored him, and felt his shoulders shake with amusement. They managed to walk comfortably together despite his gangling height. The vrykolos' magic was a subtle thing compared to human sorcery: instinctual, blood-born instead of studied. It crawled over her skin, wrapping her in his glamour. Alien, but not—as he said— unpleasant. She tried to push the thought aside. She'd slept with a demon once, but she didn't need to make a habit of it. The Arcanost didn't look fondly on those who did.

The vrykoloi were unusual among demons. Among the Arcanost's countless classifications of spirits they were *katechontoi*—possessors—and more specifically *moriens*— the possessors of the dead. But they were nothing like the shambling monstrosities that came of unburied corpses. They hungered, but with wit and intellect instead of mindless drive and animal cunning; they lived together in societies instead of warrens, and they had their own secrets and rituals that no living scholar had learned. It was nearly curiosity enough to let Isyllt forget how dangerous Spider was.

Streets wound and twisted like dark ribbons through the city's core. Elaborate stonework decorated the quarter—gargoyles crouched on roofs, their snarling faces smoothed by years of wind and rain, and lichen-skinned nymphs danced in fountains. Here and there ancient graveyards nestled snug between buildings, tombs worn nameless with time; they had stood before the city sprawled so far, and the builders had simply wrapped the streets around them. Autumn leaves dripped from trees, skittering in the breeze and piling in the gutters till feet and hooves crushed them against the stones.

They left Inkstone, winding deeper and deeper into the city's heart, where the streets were still busy so late. No one spared them a glance. Spider made no sound as he walked; if not for the strength of his arm in hers, she would have thought him no more substantial than a shadow.

She recognized the path he followed just before they turned into a dark alley mouth. Even so, her shoulder throbbed a warning as they stepped into the shadows. Spider felt her hesitation and smiled, a flash of ivory teeth.

The alley ended at an iron door set in a rough stone wall. Rust traced twisting spirals across the metal, dripped down the frame like dry blood. But for all its age, the door opened soundlessly beneath Spider's hand. A narrow stair led down, lit at the bottom by dim red light. Smoky air wafted up, redolent of poppies and wine and warm human skin. Spider stood aside, gesturing Isyllt ahead of him.

Kiril had brought her here years before on an investigation. As much to entertain her, she thought later, as for the information they found. The place had been hallowed ground once, a section of catacombs, before a demon infestation led to the burning of the temple and the tombs below. Shops had been built aboveground, but the charred tunnels below remained. Old spells whispered to her as she descended, traces of long-broken magic lingering in the stones.

The patrons called it Sanctuary now, only half joking. It was known for the quality of its wine and opium, and for the darkness of its tables. It was a haven for well-off criminals and those who played at spies. And maybe those who did more than play. Interesting things could be overheard there, if one listened carefully enough.

She stepped out of the stairwell into a long, low room. Music drifted through the air, haunting pipes and low throbbing drums, the musicians hidden behind carved sandalwood screens. Red and violet lanterns stained the smoky haze that shrouded the ceiling. Isyllt stifled a sneeze.

Spider steered her through the foyer to a velvet-curtained alcove. His hooded cloak was standard attire for this place—Isyllt's bare face and hair felt much too exposed. She kept her hands in her coat pockets, concealing the telltale stone and equally telling injury.

Dark wood paneled the booth, and the light of the single candle slid like water across its well-oiled surface. Spider shrugged back his cloak, revealing a coat of worn grey brocade. By candlelight his face was the color of yellowed bone.

A young woman appeared to take their order. If she noticed that Spider wasn't human, she gave no sign. An abundance of tact, Isyllt wondered, or were demons really so common in the city? It would have bothered her to think so once, but for the past two and a half years she'd held a steady correspondence with a demon. He sent her presents every summer.

"Have you learned anything?" Isyllt asked when the girl was gone, turning her attention back to the demon across from her. She leaned back against the cushioned seat and crossed her legs.

He waved a hand. "Have some patience, witch. Can't I enjoy your company for a moment without discussing business? It's vulgar."

Isyllt scooped a spoonful of crushed lavender and anise from a bowl on the table and poured it onto the nicked and polished boards. Dusty sweetness filled the air as she traced a sigil of silence through the powdered seeds and flowers. "A vampire lectures me on manners?" She rolled her eyes. "Besides, my company can't be that enjoyable."

He leaned forward, crystalline eyes abruptly serious.

"You've seen my home. Do you think I don't want something different now and then?" He took her hand, caressing her palm with one gloved thumb. "Do you think I don't yearn for a little warmth?" His fingers strayed to the hollow of her wrist.

She tugged her hand free. "Yes, wet and pumping from an artery."

He chuckled, low and dark. "That too."

The serving girl returned with a tray of liquor and food. Spider pressed coins into her hand and pulled the curtain shut behind her.

"Vulgar business first," Isyllt said, "or you'll feel the warmth of Mathiros's torches."

Spider sighed. "As you wish." He uncorked the bottle and a heady green scent filled the alcove. The liquor was the same murky green as the verdigris for which it was named.

Isyllt raised her narrow glass, breathing in bittersweet spices. The fumes burned her sinuses, and the first sip seared her throat with viridian fire and made her eyes prickle. The burn eased into a lingering sweetness and she sighed. "As you were saying?"

Spider turned his glass between long fingers. "What Tenebris said about rabble is true, but there's more to the matter than that." He stared at his untasted drink, strands of cobweb-fine hair drifting in front of his face. "You saw her—sluggish as a snake in winter. That's what happens to us when we age."

Isyllt took a cube of herb-veined cheese from the tray and waited. For a moment she wondered if he'd lapsed into hibernation himself.

"Aphra and Tenebris only want to sleep, and they would

gladly bury the rest of us in their tomb as well, deny us the light. This doesn't sit well with some of the young ones."

"So they stray from the fold?" She sipped verdigris, its fire filling her stomach and licking through her veins. At least Spider had good taste.

He nodded, eyes glittering yellow in the candlelight. "Some run off, commit whatever foolishness catches their fancy."

"Like mortal lovers and tomb-robbing." She split a date with one fingernail and plucked out the pit. "What do the others do?" she asked, swallowing the sticky-sweet flesh.

He turned serious again—she preferred him mocking. "Some of us want to change things."

Isyllt raised her eyebrows. "You sound like a revolutionary."

He stretched closer, folding his long body over the table. "I do."

A laugh caught in her throat and crumbled dry as dust. Her left hand curled before she could stop it, till healed fractures and silver-pinned tendon ached. She still had nightmares sometimes, though she never admitted them to anyone—dreams of the knife that stole her hand, and the blood and ash that followed.

"Let the elders sleep away the centuries," he continued. "I'm tired of hiding in the dark, away from the wind and sky, not able to walk the streets for fear of torches and silver."

Isyllt met his eyes, the impossible yellow of sulfur and buttercups. "You're serious."

"I am. I want your help."

He reached for her hand again, but she pulled back and refilled her glass instead. "Why? What could I do?"

"You have influence in the overground. You know the king."

She shook her head, and hardly felt her wounded shoulder through the warmth of alcohol in her too-thin blood. "Barely, and through unpleasant circumstances. I don't have his ear."

Spider shrugged. "You know those who do. The spirits whisper about you, you know. I'm not the only demon you've allowed to live, am I? You treat us like something more than abominations to be destroyed."

"My service to the Crown sometimes calls for strange bedfellows. But the Arcanost and the temples rule the mages of Erisín, and neither of them countenance demons."

"They might be made to learn. I want to renew the truce, on better terms."

"The truce will fall to pieces as soon as Mathiros returns."

"We'll catch the thieves, return what was stolen. Find the ones who hurt you." He took her hand again, held it tight. "We can help each other."

Verdigris scorched her throat, hitting her stomach with a burst of heat. Her voice was raw when she spoke. "Help me catch the thieves, and we'll continue this conversation." It was a lie, she told herself. She couldn't get involved for so many reasons, not the least of which were her nightmares. But she wasn't about to admit that.

He lifted her hand to his cold lips. "I knew I could count on you."

"Show me progress before you add me to your revolution."

His smile gleamed. "Don't worry. They're rabble, as Tenebris said. We'll track them down."

"Tonight? The trail is likely already cold."

"You're wounded and need rest. Tomorrow we can hunt." He tilted his head, watched her from under pale lashes. "I thought perhaps we could continue another conversation tonight."

She shivered. Her blood was spice and fire; the smoky air dizzied her. "You still want to show me your scars?"

"Among other things."

Isyllt laughed, trying to ignore the tightness in her stomach. Too much drink, too little food. Too much old grief. She should find Ciaran, find somewhere warm....

Spider raised her hand to his lips again, rough tongue flicking over one fingertip. She shuddered, but didn't pull away. A fang pierced her skin. She closed her eyes, biting her tongue to stay silent.

Spider released her. A jewel-bright drop of blood glistened on his lip. "You look sad, little witch. What's the matter?"

"Nothing." She shook her head. "History."

He unfolded himself from the seat, holding out a hand. "I'll help you forget it."

"No one can do that." She brought her palm down on the scattered charm, hard enough to sting and rattle the cups. The music and soft murmur of voices washed over them again, deafening after their absence. She pushed past him, pride and practice keeping her pace steady when she wanted to stumble.

She bumped shoulders with a cloaked patron on her way past and murmured a hasty apology. Pale blue eyes flashed in the shadow of a hood as the man glanced at her and she nearly swore; she would have to pass a gossipmonger like Varis Severos with her face uncovered.

She scrubbed away a glaze of tears when she reached the top of the stairs, cursing herself for a dozen types of fool. The damp night air was a welcome relief from the haze below. Spider caught up with her before she left the alley.

"I'm sorry," he said softly. "I didn't mean to upset you."

"It isn't your fault." When she didn't turn, his hands settled on her upper arms, cool and light. She wanted to lean into him; after a heartbeat, she did. It was foolish, worse than foolish. But his touch set her magic tingling, and maybe warm and safe weren't what she needed tonight.

She led him through her wards. She led him to her bed.

Candlelight warmed his skin to the color of old ivory; shadows pooled in the hollow of his chest, the valleys between his ribs. White ridges of scars crisscrossed his abdomen where her silver blade had opened his flesh. She remembered the blows that had caused them: two before he struck—reflex at stumbling on an unexpected demon—and the third and deepest after, to drive him off. They had managed to sort the situation out before any more became necessary.

"Dead thing," Isyllt whispered, laying a hand over his silent heart. The scholarly portion of her mind noted the lack of function in undead sex organs, which was only sensible. The rest of her was distracted by the feather-light touch of his claws.

"Necromancer." He pulled the pins from her hair and its weight slithered down her back. The smell of poppy oil mingled with serpentine musk. "A good match, I think."

She took a hairpin from him—silver, and sharp—and

pressed the tip to his breast. He made a low noise in his throat as skin popped and a dark bead of blood welled. It tasted of death and anise, bittersweet and tingling on her tongue. Spider laughed and pushed her down against the pillows.

She snuffed the candle with a thought; his skin and glittering eyes were the brightest things in the room. She closed her eyes and let the dark take her, darkness and cold and the heat of poisoned kisses.

Kiril came awake with a start, eyes sharpening against the dark as magic crackled around his fingers. A breeze stirred the drapes and a pale stripe of moonlight fell across the end of the bed, silhouetting the slender shape standing there. The shadow moved, and orange demon eyes sparked.

His breath left in a hiss and his hands clenched. "Phaedra—" He rarely spoke her name; it felt strange in his mouth.

The bed shifted under her weight. His throat closed as she settled against him. Her conflagrant perfume had faded to spice and embers; beneath that she smelled faintly of meat, and of nothing.

"I'm lonely, Kiril," she whispered. Not a seductive whisper, but a lost and childlike one. "So lonely."

Maybe it was the darkness sparing him her face, or that his defenses were still scattered from sleep. Maybe it was the need in her voice, in her fingers closing in his nightshirt. Maybe it was his own grief and guilt. His arm tightened around her.

"I know."

"I loved Ferenz. For all my foolish sins, I loved him.

He died because of me, and all the vengeance in the world won't bring him back."

There was no answer for that save the obvious. He stroked her hair instead. So alien, the press of dead flesh. Of any flesh. There had been no one else in the three years since he broke with Isyllt. She had been all bone-thin angles and clinging sea-wrack hair, sharp-nailed and biting. Phaedra was fuller, softer, stomach and breasts ripened by age and childbirth. He couldn't control a shudder, so strong he thought his flesh would crawl from his bones.

Phaedra made a choked little sound. "Is it so awful to touch me?"

"Yes. But not because . . . of what you are." He wanted her close and vulnerable if he was to stop her; he pretended that was why he let the words leave his tongue. "You are the worst thing I've ever done. Out of a lifetime of murder and lies and schemes. You are the unforgivable deed."

"Do you want my forgiveness? Are you asking for it?"

"I could never do that."

"No. You never would." She buried her head in the crook of his neck; no breath stirred his skin until she spoke. "Hold me. Please. I have bad dreams."

He didn't believe in forgiveness, or atonement. But he held the demon in his arms and stroked her hair until she grew heavy and still. And, eventually, after the moonlight had crawled away and died, he slept too.

He stands on a tower of grey stone, overlooking a dizzying drop. The hands on the crenellated stone are not his, but white and slender and ringed with gold and rubies, laced with fine scars. Black hair whips around his face; the stomach beneath heavy skirts has barely begun to round.

The dream is not his own. He knows that, even as it ensnares him. He might escape it, but perhaps he believes in penance, if not atonement.

Far below, beneath the castle walls and the sheer plunge of cliff, the Ardoş River runs cold and wild. The wind tastes of snow, and slices to the bone as it rushes down the winter-dark slopes of the Varagas Mountains. Riders approach from the south, faint with distance on the winding road. They will be here soon.

He turns, trapped in her flesh as he is trapped in her memories, to face the man standing behind them. Ferenz Darvulesti. Tall and lean and hawk-nosed, with deep-set green eyes shadowed by heavy brows. A warrior, swathed in leather and fur and mail with a sword at his hip, but his hands are gentle as they close on Kiril-and-Phaedra's arms. He speaks, but no sound accompanies the shaping of his lips. There is no sound at all, not even the wind. Only the empty and aching silence of what is past and gone.

The man kisses them twice. Once hungrily, pulling them close till cold steel links bite their flesh. And again, soft as a snowflake on the brow. A kiss of benediction, or forgiveness. Then he turns and strides down the frost-rimed steps, knuckles white around his sword hilt.

Phaedra-and-Kiril raise a hand, and a cloud of ravens bursts from a lower rooftop, fighting the wind on soundless black wings to reach them. They have their own defenses to marshal, even as Ferenz readies his soldiers below. The riders draw ever nearer; this will end soon, one way or another.

* * *

Kiril woke to dawnlight and an ache like cold iron in his chest. He could still feel the wind's bite, the press of rough lips on his mouth. The weight and softness of foreign limbs.

He needed no oneiromancy to parse the meaning of it. A true dream, a memory, bleeding out of Phaedra and into his mind. Whether she did it on purpose as punishment, or whether the pain of recollection was simply too strong to contain, he couldn't say.

He might have asked her, but the bed was empty beside him, save for the ghost of cinnamon in the wrinkled sheets and a strand of black hair wrapping his fingers like a fetter.

CHAPTER 5

Isyllt woke alone, tired and aching, to an insistent pounding on her door. A cursory inspection revealed a dark bruise scabbing on her inner thigh—a delicate nip instead of a full bite. Only a taste taken, since she was already weak. A few stray drops of blood spotted her sheets.

"Sand and saints," Khelséa said when Isyllt opened the door. "You look terrible. *More* terrible. You did something stupid, didn't you?"

"Probably." The smell of spiced meat wafted from one of several bags the inspector carried, and saliva flooded Isyllt's mouth. Her courses always left her craving meat and greens and this was many times worse.

"What did I tell you about that?"

"Believe me, you don't want to know about some of the stupid things I do."

Khelséa unpacked her bags, producing lanterns, rope, a map of the sewers, a small arsenal of weapons including an extra pistol loaded with spell-silver, and lunch.

Isyllt fell on the food, but shook her head at the proffered gun.

"I'm hopeless with them," she said around a mouthful of spiced mutton and spinach. "And magic has better aim." She stopped short of licking the last of the grease and yoghurt from the wrapping, but it was a near thing. Khelséa's eyebrows rose in eloquent disbelief, but she slipped the spare pistol into her own pocket rather than press the matter.

Isyllt washed and traded her dressing gown for leathers and boots—older, well-worn ones this time, since she wasn't about to lose another good jacket to the sewers. The high collar chafed her wounded shoulder, but she stopped herself before she numbed the bite. Some things ought not to be forgotten. Last night's souvenir, however, she was willing to ignore.

Khelséa puttered in the apartment's tiny corner kitchen when she emerged, and the air smelled of jasmine tea. Watching the other woman, Isyllt almost wished she didn't live alone. She and Kiril hadn't cohabitated since the first few days after he found her; they'd spent so much time together it hardly mattered. She hadn't had anyone else to make her tea—or to make tea for—since she was fifteen and living with three other girls in a leaking tenement attic. They were too poor most decads to afford tea, anyway.

A pity, she thought wryly as Khelséa handed her a mug, that she didn't appreciate women that way. And even if she had, the inspector's taste ran to plump and pretty and not remotely self-destructive. Her latest lover was a seamstress.

"Do the other vigils know you're misadventuring with

me?" Isyllt asked, letting the warmth of the cup soak her hands. The sun had reemerged an hour past noon, leaking like watered honey through the curtains and pooling along the dusty baseboards.

"This is my day off." Khelséa grinned, a quick flash of white. "Gemma is always telling me I need more hobbies." She leaned back in a chair and stretched her legs in front of her. "My autopsist knows—the one who saw the ring. In case we don't come back." She shrugged aside the possibility of death, and her wealth of braids—twisted into one forearm-thick plait and wrapped with brown yarn—rustled against her jacket. "Do you have a plan?"

Her surname, Shar, meant "sand" in Assari, and foreign inflections still colored her vowels. Not for the first time, Isyllt wondered how a woman from the deserts of Assar ended up working for Erisín's Vigils. One day, she resolved, she'd ply the inspector with enough wine to get an answer out of her.

"Go back to where I was attacked and track them from there, I suppose. One of them is called Myca, but I doubt that's enough to summon with." Vampires, like prostitutes, were unlikely to use their birth names. And the true names of demons were nearly impossible to determine, anyway. Binding a foreign spirit to flesh, living or dead, changed both irrevocably.

"The one who bit you?"

"No, that would be too easy." The bond of the wound coupled with even an untrue name might have been enough to use, but not only one or the other. "I'd almost rather search for Forsythia's ghost first, or for someone who knows her story."

"But—"

"Yes, but." She grimaced at the dregs of her tea. "We don't have time for that." Stolen royal goods would always take precedence over a murdered prostitute. Part of her wanted to argue, but the calendar was against her—it was already Hekate, and the rain and chill that wrapped Erisín would be snow in the north. The king and his forces were already decamping or would be very soon.

Which wasn't need for so much haste that she shouldn't talk to Kiril first. Khelséa might be better prepared than she and Ciaran had been the first time, but there were still a dozen dangers in the sewers. A dozen reasons to seek his advice. And the only reason not to was the set of his shoulders as he'd turned from her, the warmth of his hand on her skin and the chill of its absence. The foolish pain of rejection and loneliness that could still prick her to tears years later. Whenever she thought she'd finally moved past it, a touch or glance would undo her all over again. How many more years would pass before she was free of it?

"All right," she said, taking a last swallow of cold tea to rinse away the bitter taste in her mouth. The light cooled and greyed again, and they had little enough of it to waste. "Let's go."

They didn't enter through the Garden's access this time, but by one in Harrowgate that Isyllt judged to be closer to the place where she and Ciaran had been attacked. It might have been easier to track the thieves from the palace crypts, but also easier to draw attention and unwanted questions. At least the trail here was fresher.

The door shut with a metallic clang behind them and echoes scattered and sank beneath the rush of water. The sewer didn't care about day or night—its blackness was absolute. A carriage rattled overhead, and the clatter of hooves and wheels echoed painfully.

They kept careful counts of turns and branches, but the tunnels in Oldtown all looked the same and getting lost was far too easy. If Isyllt had brought any food, she might have trailed crumbs behind her like the children in cradle-stories. Not that the sewer rats needed more to eat, by the size of those who so brazenly crossed their path. A pity she couldn't talk to them and save herself some detective work.

She found the site of the attack after two wrong turns, or at least a stretch of sewer that looked promising. Isyllt drew a knife—not the kukri at her back, but a razor-honed folding blade that fit neatly in her pocket—and pricked her left wrist. A drop of blood glistened black in the pale light, and washed metal-and-seaweed over her tongue as she licked it away. Her instructors at the Arcanost would chide her for needing to draw her own blood—she was filled with it, after all—but she'd always found the spell easier with the taste of it sticky in her mouth.

With a whispered word, light blossomed on her wounded wrist and on the damp stone ledge, a pale blue no brighter than cave lichen. From the shape of the stains she could see where the vampire had first bitten her, where blood had dripped from her shoulder and later splattered as she shook him off. The trail ended with the ledge.

Now that she knew where to look, Isyllt could also see the shadow-faint outline of the secret door in the wall. She kept her eyes away; Khelséa didn't lead a cohort by being inobservant.

"This is it." The pounding water drowned her words,

and she shouted the next. "The water carried one away, and I imagine the other followed."

Khelséa gestured ahead with a flourish. "After you, Crown Investigator." Isyllt read the shape of the words instead of hearing them.

Isyllt sniffed, hoping to catch the scent of vrykoloi, but all she got was a noseful of wet shit and offal. She shook her head with a grimace and started walking.

They followed the current for several turns, but finally came to a fork where the water rushed left and right. Isyllt sent her witchlight back and forth over the ground and along both arches; peperine bricks glittered with dark flecks of magnetite and brighter mica, beautiful amidst the filth, but she saw no sign of anything having chosen one tunnel over the other. Finally she leaned back against the wall and sighed in disgust.

"Do you have a coin we can flip?" she yelled to Khelséa. Echoes bounced off slime-slick stones.

"I thought," a familiar voice said from the darkness, soft but carrying, "that you were going to wait for me."

Khelséa spun, pistol shining in her hand, and Isyllt flung out a hand before she could pull the trigger. Her heart spiked sharp in her chest. "Don't! He's—" *Safe* was definitely not the word. "Not a threat," she finished half-heartedly. "Are you, Spider?"

"Not to you or yours, necromancer." He stepped into the light and Khelséa's breath hissed through clenched teeth. In the darkness and witchfire it was hard to believe he could ever walk the streets unnoticed, glamourie or no. Gaunt and grotesque, inhuman. Demonic.

Isyllt realized that she'd never talked to Khelséa about consorting with demons, and if the inspector might ever condone it. Maybe that was a conversation to have with plenty of wine, too.

"It seemed a pity to waste the daylight," Isyllt said, stepping neatly between Khelséa and Spider. From the corner of her eye she saw the inspector lower her pistol, but not holster it. "I thought you'd be sleeping." She blushed, and gave thanks for the darkness.

He chuckled. "You've been reading the wrong sort of stories. Oh, yes," he said when she raised an eyebrow. "I follow the penny dreadfuls."

"You should write some of your own, if the others are so inaccurate."

His grin bared his fangs, and the gaps around them that let him close his jaw. Like an animal's. "I don't think your citizens would like to read the truth of us."

Isyllt snorted. "We can discuss literature later. If you want to help us, then by all means lead on."

"So impatient," Spider said. "You haven't introduced me to your companion."

Khelséa stepped forward, holstering her pistol and extending her gloved hand in one smooth motion. "Khelséa Shar." No rank or title, and Isyllt silently blessed her discretion. And from her willingness to share her name with a demon, guessed that it wasn't her birth name.

"Spider." He bowed over her hand with an exaggerated marionette grace. "Delighted to meet you."

He hadn't been so delighted to meet Ciaran. Maybe Khelséa was more to his taste. Isyllt thanked the saints that he wasn't to hers.

"Do you know which way they went?"

He studied the branching tunnel, nostrils flaring. Finally he cocked his head toward the far one. "That way, I think."

Of course it would be the side that made them cross the canal. She glared at the churning black water. Spider caught her expression and laughed. He moved faster than she could follow, a pale blur and a ghostly afterimage behind her eyelids. When she blinked again he stood on the far bank, sweeping out a mocking hand to invite them across.

"Show-off," Isyllt muttered as she backtracked to the last narrow bridge.

"You do have the most interesting friends," said Khelséa.

Another winding, branching walk followed. Isyllt had long since lost track of time, but getting out of the sewers before early autumn darkness fell seemed unlikely. Not that it mattered, if the vrykoloi truly didn't sleep. Although he'd earlier said they did.

She wondered if Spider could read her thoughts, or only knew the curious minds of mages. After a while he slowed till she walked at his shoulder; Khelséa kept watch at the rear.

"The older we grow, the more we sleep," he said softly. She shouldn't have been able to hear him over the din, but she could. "The elders nap for months at a time, or longer. But only injury drives the young ones to rest, while they're safe from the sun. Daylight is . . . tiring. Painful. Like the worst of summer and winter is to the living."

He was only trying to bribe her with information, but her curiosity was piqued all the same. "And how old are you?"

His eyes glittered with a sideways glance. "Older than you, little witch. Young enough to remember summer and winter, wind and rain."

"When you do sleep, do you dream?" She meant it to be clinical, but wistfulness crept into the words.

"Yes." He said nothing else, and soon drifted ahead again.

Of course they must, Isyllt thought. Nothing freed you from the past. Not even death.

He stopped not long after, letting Isyllt and Khelséa catch up. As they approached, the witchlight revealed rusty iron bars bound with a heavy chain.

Khelséa pulled the cloacae's skeleton key from her pocket, but it didn't turn in the lock. "Well," she said mildly. "This is problematic. I didn't think to bring a saw."

Isyllt leaned her head against the cold bars. Nothing even remotely human-sized would fit through them, unless vampires could turn to shadows like the penny bloods suggested. She remembered Tenebris, and wondered how far from the truth those stories really were.

"We could try to swim under...." She didn't try to keep the disgust from her voice.

Khelséa examined the lock. "It doesn't look like this has been opened recently. So if your vampires did come this way, how did they get through? Unless they swam." She didn't sound any more thrilled with the prospect.

"There are," Spider said after a pause, "other tunnels down here. Crawlspaces and byways that I doubt are on your maps. I imagine whoever comes this way leaves the lock intact to avoid attention."

"You imagine?" Isyllt's eyes narrowed. "Have you known all along where we were going?"

"I suspected it." He shrugged one shoulder, a disturbing articulation of bones. "You wouldn't have trusted me if I'd had too much information too soon."

"I don't trust you *now*. But if you make me swim through the sewers again when there's an easier way, I'll give a few new scars for your collection."

He laughed, like dry leaves scraping stone. "There's always an easier way." He twined two fingers through the shackle of the lock, another two through the nearest link of chain, and twisted. Link and lock groaned, and the shackle snapped free of the body with a screech. The sound echoed down the tunnel.

"Easier, but not quieter." Isyllt fought the urge to cover her aching ears. If the vrykoloi were in their den, they'd soon know someone was coming.

"We hear you mortals crawling through the tunnels no matter how softly you walk," Spider said. "Like mice in the attic, but clumsier."

He stilled abruptly, raising a hand to cut off Isyllt's reply; his ears twitched. She listened, but heard nothing but water and a distant carriage.

"Speaking of mice…" Spider's wide mouth twisted in a frown. "I hear you, too, Azarné. Come out."

For several heartbeats there was no reply. Then the tiny vrykola melted out of the shadows. She didn't move with Spider's drifting ghostly grace, but with the lazy purpose of a predator. Isyllt didn't doubt her deadliness for an instant, despite her size and delicate, almost childlike beauty. Her eyes flashed in the light like an animal's; also yellow, but a warmer, more golden shade than Spider's. Her clothes had been lace and velvet once, something lovely, but now they hung in stains and tatters.

"You're turning up quite often lately," Spider said, still frowning. "One might mistrust it."

Azarné smiled—or bared her teeth; Isyllt couldn't

be certain. Either way, fangs flashed white, incongruous behind her tiny rosehip lips. "There's much to mistrust in the catacombs these days. Thieves and schemes and strangers." Her eyes flickered over Khelséa, and Isyllt thought she saw disappointment there. Ciaran often had that effect on mortal women —why not undead ones too?

"I'm Isyllt," she said, stepping forward and holding out a hand. "And my friend is Khelséa. Fewer strangers now, at least."

Azarné stared at the outstretched hand as one might at an unexpected dead mouse. Then she reached out and clasped it briefly, cold and light, with the echo of a courtier's grace. "Manners," the vrykola said, with a sound that might have been a laugh. "I remember those, I think." She sank into a curtsy, ruined skirts pooling around her. Broken chains and jeweled pins glinted in the tangled mass of her hair. "I am Azarné, called Vaykush."

Owl, the word meant in Skarrish. She looked it, with her wide eyes and small round face. And that would explain the faded accent, though her vowels didn't sound quite like those Isyllt heard in the markets. How long since Azarné had last seen Skarra or Iskar?

"Pleased to meet you," Isyllt said, the ridiculousness of the scene nearly making her head spin. From Azarné's brief twitch of a smile, she appreciated the absurdity as well. Spider simply glowered.

"Since we've all established that we don't trust each other," Khelséa said, "shall we keep going?" She tugged the chain free of the broken lock, and the gate squealed inward.

"You're hunting Myca, aren't you," the vrykola said. "And his friends."

"Yes." Isyllt raised her eyebrows. "Do you object?"

"They tried to kill you and your musician. They would break the truce and bring the armies of daylight down on us all. I remember the last time that happened." She stripped the sleeve from one narrow forearm, baring the scar-slick ridges of old burns. "I'll help you stop them."

"As you will," was all Spider said. He turned between heartbeats and ghosted down the corridor.

Isyllt and Khelséa exchanged a glance, then resumed their hunt. Azarné drifted behind them, as silent as her namesake.

Another stretch of tunnels, these rougher than before, less traveled by sewer workers. Isyllt could feel the difference in her head—not the sharp chill of death, but a cool stillness. The absence of life, not the end of it. It might have been soothing, but her legs ached and the constant witchlight was giving her a headache.

The knowledge that she was lost did nothing to ease it. Khelséa's map was a comfort, but even that wouldn't help them if they turned into one of the uncharted tunnels. She felt like a spirit caught in a maze-trap. Better, she supposed, than being caught in a labyrinth, and circling toward one certain fate.

A rustle of parchment drew her out of her brooding. Khelséa unrolled the map and stopped to frown at it. Isyllt leaned close to look over her shoulder.

"What is it?"

"We've been going south all this time, more or less." One dark finger tapped a section of faded lines and branches, slid down the paper and stopped against a darker, wider line. "Which means we're going to hit the river soon."

"Problematic," Isyllt murmured. No architect was mad or ambitious enough to dig under the Dis; the sewers on either side were unconnected.

"I told you—" Isyllt stiffened to realize Spider was right beside them; the map crinkled in Khelséa's hands. "There are passages not on your maps."

"I hope you know what you're doing, or you'll bring the whole city down one day."

"Not on accident," Spider said with a grin. "Come on—we're almost to the crossing."

"On second thought," Khelséa muttered, "next time you can take the minstrel."

The crawlspace was as close as Spider promised, at least. A narrow crevice in the wall, barely wide enough for a man to squeeze in. It shivered in Isyllt's head as she leaned close—not human magic, but the same sort of glamour that Spider wore in the city streets. Most eyes, she suspected, would slide over it unnoticing.

"Be careful," Spider said. "The way is steep and long." He twisted sideways and vanished in a pale blur.

Isyllt and Khelséa exchanged a glance. "Well," the inspector said. "Go on."

"I'll be right behind you," Azarné added, with only the phantom of a smile.

Isyllt glared at both of them, then sent her witchlight into the fissure and followed it down.

"Steep" was an understatement. Her boots slipped and slid, and bits of rock skittered down into the darkness ahead of her. Her hands soon ached from bracing against the wall. The roar of the sewers faded, leaving the ringing in her ears and the harsh echo of her breath. Sweat ran down her back, slicked her scalp and squelched inside her gloves.

"This wasn't quite the sort of misadventure I had in mind," Khelséa muttered. A rivulet of dust and pebbles spilled from beneath her boots, rattling past Isyllt into the echoing darkness.

"Watch out," Spider called from below. "The way branches here, and you have to turn."

"Or what?" Isyllt asked, breathless.

"Or you go all the way down. It only gets steeper."

"Of course it does."

It happened in a rush: She yanked her right hand away from a particularly cruel bit of rock, just as one foot slipped in scree. Cursing, she grabbed at the wall, but her crippled hand was already cramping and her right had nothing to hold. Her stomach flipped as she skidded faster. Khelséa shouted her name.

By the wildly flickering light, she saw Spider reach for her. But undead strength was no use without a good grip. Her sleeve snagged and tore on his claws, an instant's jolt that did nothing to slow her slide.

The witchlight only dizzied her; Isyllt let it die, wrapping her arms around her head. Spilling her brains down a tunnel was all she needed—

The ground beneath her vanished. She flailed through the air with an undignified yelp, getting her feet below her in time for an awkward landing. Her knees buckled and she fell sideways, bruising her shoulder and knocking the wind from her lungs. She rolled down wet stone toward the sound of water.

Not again, she had time to think. Then her head struck something cold and unyielding, and there was nothing at all.

*   *   *

She woke with a groan. Her head throbbed and red spots swam across the blackness. Someone was calling her name, echoes scattering queerly. For a moment she couldn't tell who it was or why they wanted her so badly. Returning memory only made the pain worse. She couldn't feel her legs, and had an instant's terror of a broken spine. Then she realized that from the waist down she lay sprawled in frigid water.

"I'm here," she finally shouted, only to hiss in pain at the echoes. "I'm all right." That was likely a gross exaggeration, but at least her legs moved. And, she realized a moment later, she hadn't fallen in a sewer. The air around her smelled of stone and clean water, the bitter metallic scent of the Dis, and a subtle floral sweetness. She hadn't realized the river flowed underground....

Something brushed her leg, cold and slick and curious. She jerked leaden limbs out of the water's reach; the movement brought tears to her eyes. Her stomach churned, and she fell limp again.

"I told you to be careful," Spider chided, crouching beside her. Cold hands eased beneath her arms, pulling her out of the water. "Are you hurt?"

"Only my pride," she said. "And my head."

"How badly? The latter, I mean." His fingers were soft and careful as he touched the back of her head, but she jerked away when he found the injury. "Oh, hold still."

She did, with an effort, clenching her teeth as he examined the back of her skull. "Barely bleeding," he said at last, "but swelling. I don't remember much of mortal injuries—is your vision blurred?"

"That implies I could see in the dark to begin with." Even sitting still on solid stone dizzied her, and her ears rang worse than ever—she doubted her vision would be any better. It took much too long to call a light.

The witchlight sparked and shivered, sending mad shadows capering across the walls. Isyllt hissed at the brightness, squeezing her eyes tightly shut. Sure enough, when she opened them again, Spider was a bone-colored blur watching her with three sulfurous eyes.

He frowned. "You can't go on like this."

"Of course I can—" She broke off as she looked past him at the cavern they'd fallen into.

The cave was wide and cylindrical, stretching into shadow on either side. Black water filled the bottom, still save for scattered ripples. The walls glistened and sparked—not carved, for all their perfect arch, but oddly ridged; they seemed to ripple, like a giant sphincter contracting. Isyllt's stomach lurched at the image. Columns rose from pool to ceiling, thick and gnarled as tree trunks. The light turned rough stone into leering faces, winking eyes and gaping mouths.

She dragged her gaze away from the pillars, and froze again as she saw the floor by the water's edge. Coins, gems, and scraps of cloth lined the shore, beside carvings of wood and stone and bone. Flowers too—some brown and rotted, others almost fresh—and bowls of incense, sweet and cloying in the damp air.

Offerings.

"Isyllt!" Spider's hand fell on her shoulder and she flinched. From the concern on his face, she guessed he'd called her name more than once already. The sound skipped across the water like a stone.

"Who are they worshipping?" she murmured. Spirit worship was illegal—one of the few Assari traditions the founders of Selafai had kept when they broke away five hundred years ago. Mortal saints could be venerated, or abstracts, but turning little spirits into gods was dangerous.

The answer came to her as she stared at the columns and arch of stone overhead. What was this place, after all, but the river's own cathedral?

She had visited another river's temple once—the Mir, for which the city of Symir across the sea was named. A gentler river than the Dis, and a kinder one. A young woman Isyllt had known had sacrificed herself to the Mir to save the city, and the river had answered. She heard lately that the girl had been sainted.

She hadn't thought that anyone worshipped the Dis, but of course they did. The river carved through the very heart of Erisín, swift and black and implacable, rich with lifeblood of the dozens of corpses that fetched up against the gates each decad. Flowers and trinkets were more pleasant offerings.

She wondered which the river preferred.

"Perhaps," Spider whispered, "we shouldn't stay and find out."

In the depths of the pool the water bulged and rippled, and Isyllt remembered the cold touch in the dark. "No. Let's not."

She stood, and Spider's hand on her elbow kept her from collapsing again. They didn't run—mostly because she couldn't—but their exit was too hasty for any dignity. Clinging to Spider's neck like a child while he climbed back into the tunnel didn't help either. At least she didn't vomit, though she gave it serious thought. In the darkness below them, something heavy moved in the water and fell silent again.

Spider carried her back to the fork in the tunnel, where Khelséa and Azarné crouched. Khelséa had lit her lantern; the light hurt Isyllt's eyes, and the heat and smoke choked the narrow space. Her soaking clothes warmed from frigid to merely clammy.

"What happened?" the inspector asked.

"Only a detour."

"She struck her head," Spider said. "And probably needs to rest."

Shadows turned Khelséa's frown into an exaggerated snarl as she held the lamp closer to peer at Isyllt's eyes. "A concussion?"

"I'm fine," Isyllt snapped, raising a hand against the glare. At least she could count her fingers. "We can hardly turn back now."

"You're clumsy and slow," Azarné said softly, "weak. The others will smell your blood." She leaned forward as she spoke, eyes burning.

Isyllt grinned, though it made her skull ache all the more. "Then I'll be excellent bait, won't I?"

CHAPTER 6

Savedra had hoped that the weather might impede the scheduled party, but Polyhymnis dawned grey and dry with only a light breeze. So evening found her bathed and oiled and dressed—yards of blue velvet over a tight-bound corset, her hair ironed flat and curled again and piled high, dripping feathers and strands of bronze and ivory pearls—and picking her way carefully down the crushed gravel walk that led to the palace quay. Pale rock shone in the dying light; streetlamps hissed to life on distant hills, gold against the slate and violet dusk. The chill was only a nip now, but promised to bite deep by midnight. This would be the last outdoor party of the season.

When Mathiros returned Savedra might not enjoy her present position near the head of the procession, just behind Ashlin and Nikos. It pushed the limits of propriety and taste to bring one's mistress and one's wife to the same parties, and Nikos had already stood up to his father enough where she was concerned that she tried to avoid further confrontation. Tonight it was Ashlin who'd insisted that Savedra attend her—*suffer with me,* she said—so no one would complain within earshot.

The Canal Sarai had been dug decades ago, a wide curve of water gated and locked to slow the Dis's deadly rush. History was conflicted as to whether it was named for Saint Sarai, saint of lovers and of sighs, or Princess Sarai Aravind, who had drowned in it not long after completion. The Isle of Cormorants stood between the two waterways, crowded with trees and flowers and hedge-mazes—and gull shit, one imagined. In theory it could only be reached by the palace side, but Savedra had heard tales of enterprising thieves rigging lines across the river to steal fruit. She doubted the haul would be worth the trouble, but the risk and thrill alone might be. In any case, the island was searched thoroughly by soldiers before any barges docked there.

Today colored lanterns hung on both shores, and costly hothouse blossoms bobbed on dark water. The royal barge, the *Daphne*, dripped with more lamps and bright ribbons, and her oiled canopies rippled in the breeze. The canal looked so innocent dressed in jewels and finery, but it was as black and cold as the Dis, and just as hungry.

Nikos helped Ashlin down the step at the end of the ramp, earning him a narrow glare. A footman stood ready to assist Savedra, but before he could the princess turned and offered her a hand.

"Darling," Savedra whispered as Ashlin's calloused fingers tightened around hers, "people will talk." She could already feel the weight of stares on her back.

Ashlin's grin was more a baring of teeth. The gold ring in her nose flashed with it. "Let them."

Her life might be easier with less scandal, but Savedra couldn't help smiling back. She dipped a shallow curtsy. "As Your Highness wishes."

Nikos watched them with an expression between amusement and horror; the thought of one's wife and mistress conspiring together must be terrifying.

But she was only willing to push propriety so far, and didn't join them on the covered dais at the aft of the barge. Thea Jsutien did, and her niece, and other scions of the eight houses who presently held favor in court. Savedra had told Nikos about the assassin, but without proof it would be no use acting against the Jsutiens, even by a social slight. Better, she supposed, to keep them close, but the sight of Ginevra Jsutien glowing in blue silk and topazes was enough to sour her stomach. Behind them all, Captain Denaris was a lean brown shadow at the back of the dais.

The musicians' barge floated alongside the *Daphne*, and the night was bright with songs and voices and laughter, the air heavy with wine and perfume and the bitter-cold smell of the river. Savedra threaded her way through trestle tables laden with food and found a spot near the prow. She missed the days when she could enjoy parties, instead of watching and worrying every time anyone wandered too near the prince or princess.

They made an attractive couple, Nikos and Ashlin, if not a traditional one. He wore green-and-violet peacock finery, aglow with gold and carnelians. She wore black and forest green, slim trousers and high boots and a short jacket, with her hair slicked back to bare the strong bones of her face. Besides the nose ring, the princess wore only the golden torc that was the marriage custom of her people, and two rings—the sapphire Nikos had given her, and the ruby in white gold that marked the royal house of Celanor. If she'd worn a sword—a habit that Savedra had talked her out of—she would have looked like a foreign bodyguard, hired for show as much as skill.

Savedra leaned against the railing, Varis's caution echoing unpleasantly in her head. Ashlin at least could swim if someone tipped her over the side—Savedra imagined the weight of her skirts and pearls would bear her straight to the bottom of the canal. She refused a passing servant's offer of wine, though she badly wanted some; her imagination was morbid enough already. And though she'd never admit it, the steady sway of the barge unsettled her.

The *Daphne* drifted slowly across the water, the carven nymph at her prow gilded with lamplight. Eventually they would alight at the island, where more food and wine and music waited, and doubtless a game of hide-and-seek in the hedge, which would quickly devolve into tipsy trysts. She and Nikos had taken advantage of their share of those. Now the thought of him or Ashlin wandering off in the dark sent a chill down her back.

Soft footsteps and a hiss of silk skirts drew her attention, and she turned to find Ginevra Jsutien approaching, her gown shining in the lamplight, a wineglass sparkling in her hand. Even distracted and paranoid, it was hard not to give Ginevra one's complete attention when she crossed a room.

Thea's sister had married an Aravind, and Ginevra had inherited his copper skin and lustrous black hair. Gowned in azure and blue and yellow topazes, she shone like a flame. Savedra had to concede the merits of a match between her and Nikos; the girl had wits to go with her lovely face, not to mention Jsutien wealth and trade as a dowry.

Her dark beauty would remind the people of Lychandra, though the late queen had held the added attraction of being a nobody from the Archipelago—in truth the child of wealthy merchants and titled landholders, but that wasn't as romantic—instead of a scion of a great house. In choosing her, Mathiros had thrown over a dozen daughters of the Octagon Court, and had angered the Eight again when he betrothed Nikos to a foreign princess.

It was a minor miracle and a credit to palace security that no assassin had been successful yet.

"What are you contemplating so seriously?" Ginevra asked, her voice light and musical. Savedra felt like a clumsy rasping thing beside her. She closed her hands on her fan to keep from brushing at her own midnight skirts. Both shades were close enough to royal sapphire to be daring, but far enough to prevent scandal.

"Assassinations," she said, before she could think better of it.

"Really? I didn't think it was that boring a party yet." Savedra thought that she turned away quickly enough to hide her frown, but Ginevra's eyebrows quirked. "Either you don't like my jokes, you're angry about our dresses, or ..."

She stopped herself from snapping her fan in annoyance, but the sticks rattled softly with the effort. "Or maybe I don't find assassins amusing."

"Does anyone?"

Savedra couldn't keep from glancing at the dais, where Thea laughed at something Nikos had said. "I imagine some people do."

"Ah." Ginevra blinked. Beneath kohl-dusted lids, her eyes were a striking grey. The stones draping her collar-bones flashed with her sigh. "And so you judge me by my aunt's schemes."

The forthrightness of it startled her, and she answered in kind. "How can I not, when you benefit from them?"

"She doesn't speak of them to me, you know."

"No. You would need to be guiltless, in case she was caught." A predicament she was all too familiar with. What should have been righteous anger soured in her mouth.

"And since you're speaking to me of this and neither Thea nor I are in chains, I gather she hasn't been caught." Ginevra paused, studying the wine in her glass. "I don't want anyone harmed, even if it would see me queen."

"But you let her scheme and cling to your innocence."

"Do you think she would stop for my sensibilities, for ethics or mercy?" This time her eyebrows rose high enough to crease her brow. "Would your mother?"

Her fan snapped now, but Savedra lowered it again, conceding the point with a wry twist of her lips. "No."

"I don't want to be your enemy." And saints help her, the girl sounded as if she meant it. Sounded almost wistful.

"Your aunt will be, as long as she sends assassins after Nikos or the princess."

Ginevra turned, leaning her stomach against the rail, graceful and sad as the Lady of Laurels on the figurehead. "I had another aunt, you know."

"Yes." She could name most of the members of the great houses, including Thea's sisters. Talia, the youngest, was Ginevra's mother. Tassia, the eldest... The realiza-tion settled cold in her gut even as Ginevra spoke.

"Do you really think she died in childbirth?" She smiled wryly at Savedra's momentary discomposure. "I know I'm a coward, but I would rather Thea had some use for me."

She drained her glass and walked away, all shining hair and skirts, leaving Savedra to curse the sympathy that already spread slow as poison in her blood.

The barge docked smoothly and the laughing courtiers spilled into the manicured gardens. A new set of musicians was already in place, playing livelier tunes to invite dancing and games. Tables strained with the weight of wine and confections, and the breeze was heady with sugar and alcohol and the tang of freshly clipped grass. Colored lanterns and candles in glass bowls painted the night with red and green, blue and gold, turned trees and hedges into a phantasmagoria of color and darkness. The cold light of the waxing moon cast opposing shadows.

Nikos lingered beside Savedra while the guests waited impatiently for him to begin a dance. "What's wrong?"

She laughed too brightly. "Shall I draw you up a list?"

He traced the crease between her brows. "You'll wrinkle if you keep frowning like that."

"You sound like my mother."

"Your mother is a woman of taste and wisdom. Do you think she'd accept a seat on my council?"

That drew an honest laugh from her. "I imagine she would, if only to see the looks on the other archons' faces."

He kissed her lightly; he'd had years of practice learning not to smear paint or powder. "Forget about politics. Dance with me."

She plucked his hand off her arm with feigned indignation. "Dance with your wife, Your Highness."

He clasped the slighted hand to his breast. "As you command, my heart. But you must join me at least once tonight."

"I make no promises. Go on—your court is waiting for you."

The musicians struck up a new song as Nikos entered the circle of light that served as a dance floor and offered his hand to Ashlin with a bow. She rolled her eyes, but let him lead her into the center of the lawn. The princess rarely danced, but when she did it was with the same grace with which she wielded a sword. The guests watched them move together for an extra measure before pairing up and joining the steps.

Savedra tensed at footsteps in the grass behind her, but it was only Ginevra again. The Jsutien held another glass of wine; her eyes glittered, and Savedra wondered how many she'd already drunk.

"People will think we conspire," she said.

Ginevra hid a smile by raising her glass. "I'll say you were angry about my dress, and all we did was snipe and quarrel." She watched Nikos and Ashlin move in each other's arms, dark and bright. "Are you jealous?"

"Are you?" Savedra retorted, though the question had been honest and not biting.

The woman's shrug made it look as though her gown would slide off her shoulder, but the dress was too well sewn for that. "No. But I don't love him."

"I've always known Nikos would marry. And he could hardly marry me, could he?"

"You might be jealous of *him*. The Princess does flirt with you, after all."

Savedra shot her a startled sideways glance. "We're friends, however mad that seems. And she likes to unsettle. She doesn't like women that way." She realized how foolish that sounded as soon as the words left her mouth.

Ginevra made a noncommittal sound. And, Savedra realized, she didn't know that for a certainty. Ashlin scorned the giggling pampered doves of the court, of either sex, but Savedra had never heard her speak of lust for anyone. But the princess hadn't come virgin to the marriage bed—the tactful long betrothal was proof enough of that, for all that they had called it mourning for Lychandra. Who had Ashlin left behind in Celanor?

The flash of jewels as Ginevra shifted her weight drew Savedra from her brooding. The wine in her glass was nearly gone. "You don't wear the hijra mark."

She snapped her fan again; let watchers think they quarreled. But no one had asked her this in months, and she supposed it was due. Tactless, perhaps, but Ginevra was tipsy and curious. And, she realized with a flash of empathy, lonely. She kept her free hand from rising to her forehead, to the spot Nikos had touched, the place where the mark would be.

"Despite popular opinion, I am not precisely a whore."

"I never—" Ginevra's eyebrows rose. "Is that really what it means?"

"To bear the mark means accepting the rules of the hijra, and the hijra have joined with the Rose Council. They are their own faction within the Garden, and sell other services, but most sell themselves as well. I'm told this wasn't always so, but in recent history they have found it expedient." She let scorn flavor her voice. "So many are curious, after all, why not make them pay for it?"

She'd received her share of propositions since she came to court, and nearly all of were based on curiosity instead of honest desire, or hopes of the fabled hijra luck. She spurned them all, until Nikos.

"What do they think of you, unmarked?"

It was her turn to shrug. "Proud, I suppose, that I have a prince on my string. And annoyed that I won't join them. Disappointed." It was more than supposition, but her conversations with the Black Orchid weren't ones she liked to recollect. "Some think I'm no better than a peacock in gaudy drag, since I shun the hijra mysticism." She was always careful to keep her wardrobe subtle enough to deflect the worst of the barbs, though she envied the peacocks their stunning colors and their seeming comfort in their own skins.

"Did you ever think of joining them? Before Nikos."

"I never had to." Not precisely a lie—she smothered memories of the Black Orchid and the stifling incense-and-opium heat of the hijras' temple, and blessed the darkness that hid her burning cheeks. "My family accepted me. Most androgynes have nowhere to turn when they discover the truth of themselves." Her hand rose before she could stop it, one fingernail tracing the crease in her brow.

Ginevra made another soft sound, this one unhappy. Whether it was for the fate of the third sex or for her empty glass, Savedra wasn't sure.

Her neck prickled—not just the itch of hair and feathers, but of eyes on her back. She turned away from Ginevra as if annoyed, snapping her fan as she risked a backward glance. Only Captain Denaris, lingering in the shadows of a fig tree, and she relaxed again. But the Captain looked unhappy, more so than even Thea Jsutien's careless laughter might warrant.

The dancing continued for at least an hour. Savedra chose not to join, but Ginevra did, flouncing away with such perfect disdain that it was all Savedra could do not to laugh. The woman was a better actress than many she'd seen in an Orpheum. Natural talent, or a product of growing up under Thea's ruthless gaze?

She wanted to like Ginevra. Wanted to believe her, but she knew that was foolishness. Instead she watched her charm Nikos into a dance and didn't quite hide her glower behind her fan. Tomorrow's gossip would be entertaining. After the dance, a knot of laughing young nobles swallowed Ginevra, leaving Savedra to wonder if the loneliness she thought she'd glimpsed was only a ruse.

The dancing ended with an eruption of giggles in a lull between songs. A Konstantin girl whose name Savedra could never remember slapped Ginevra on the arm with a shriek and cried "Hart!" The other girl shrieked in turn, then gathered her skirts in her hands and fled into the black mouth of the hedge maze. The rest of the crowd laughed and clapped and began counting loudly.

Amidst the clamor, Captain Denaris materialized at Savedra's elbow. Her dark clothing and matte-painted steel were meant for skulking—the silver streaks in her tight-plaited hair were the brightest thing about her.

"I don't like this," she murmured, face creasing. "We haven't found anything, but something isn't right."

Savedra frowned in turn and nodded. Perhaps she'd been too quick to dissuade Ashlin from bearing steel. Her hair sticks were sharp enough to serve in a fight, and she carried a small blade in a garter around one calf, but neither were practical enough to reassure her. "I'll keep my eyes open," she said, all she could ever do, and moved to join the hounds.

The Isle of Cormorants' maze was nothing compared to the one at the heart of the palace grounds, but still large and winding enough to swallow the twenty-five people in attendance tonight. Some hunters snatched lanterns from their poles, and light swayed and rippled along the tops of the hedges as they ran. Which only served to make them easier to avoid, of course. Savedra kept to the shadows, pulling her skirts close to keep them from snagging on briars.

She leapt when a hand reached out of the darkness and caught her arm, taut-strung nerves singing. She had one sharpened stick out of her hair before she recognized Nikos. He froze with the tip inches from his throat.

"This would be an embarrassing way to die," he said after a heartbeat's pause.

"And an embarrassing reason to be executed." The words rasped hoarse and breathless; the pulse in her throat left little room for air. She let him lean in to kiss her, but couldn't relax into his embrace. Sticky warmth trickled down her scalp—she'd scratched herself. Good thing she hadn't poisoned the sticks.

"What's the matter?" Nikos whispered. His mouth tasted of wine. Her lip rouge wouldn't survive this kiss.

"Kat thinks something is wrong. I'm inclined to agree. I'd rather know exactly where you and Ashlin are until we leave the island."

He sighed. "I don't remember appointing you to my guard. Or Ashlin's either." But he drew back and straightened his coat. Her arms tingled where he had held her. A trio of laughing hunters staggered past them, oblivious. "Let's find our princess, then," he said when they passed, "if it will make you feel better."

She twined grateful fingers through his and drew comfort in the steady throb of his pulse. "Thank you."

She tried to return the hair stick to its proper place, but already curls pulled loose from their pins. Jewels and feathers snagged and fluttered free as they ran deeper into the maze.

They wound their way to the heart of the maze, where a marble statue of Zavarian, saint of hunters, stood amid a wide circle of hedges. A colored lantern hung beside the saint, washing the stone blue and shining on Ashlin's bright hair. Savedra's growing worry burst into sharp relief, until she saw the glitter of topazes and shimmer of blue silk beside the princess.

Savedra lunged forward, catching Ashlin's arm and hauling her away.

"Too late," the princess said with a startled laugh. "I've already won."

Ginevra's eyes narrowed. "You really think I'm a murderer, don't you?" The words were nearly lost beneath the shouts of the approaching hunters. For an instant they stood still as stone themselves beneath the saint's blind eyes. Nikos lingered at the end of the path.

"What's going on?" Ashlin asked, the flush of the chase fading from her cheeks.

It was all Savedra could do not to flinch from Ginevra's gaze. "Captain Denaris thinks something is wrong. I thought it prudent to find you."

"I outgrew my nursemaid years ago, Vedra—"

Savedra was so busy watching Ginevra that she nearly

missed the rustle of leaves and glint of metal from the far wall of the hedge. Nikos shouted, but she was already turning, knocking Ashlin to the ground.

The shot shattered the stillness before they struck the grass.

Ashlin cursed, then grunted as Savedra landed on top of her. Ginevra yelped, high and startled. Someone shrieked nearby. Savedra rolled, tangling her and Ashlin in her skirts, trying not to lose her bearings. She looked up in time to see Nikos dash for the shaking hedge, but before she could draw breath to curse his stupidity Captain Denaris had pushed him aside and lunged into the shrubbery herself, shouting for her guards.

Ashlin swore breathlessly in Celanoran, struggling out from under Savedra.

"Stay down," she hissed, elbowing the princess in the ribs. They crawled into the narrow shelter of the statue's plinth, where Ginevra crouched shaking. Blood trickled black down the girl's cheek, spotting the bodice of her gown.

"Are you hurt?" Savedra asked, fumbling with her skirts till she could reach her knife. The dagger would be no use against pistols, but it was warm and solid in her hand.

"Not badly." Ginevra touched her cheek, throat working as she swallowed. "This was flying shards, I think. The statue took the bullet for me." She smiled shakily. "I suppose this doesn't make you any more inclined to trust me."

Nikos crouched beside them, while guards circled the four of them and kept the crowd of courtiers at bay.

"He wasn't aiming at Ashlin," he said quietly. "Not even if he was an abysmally poor shot."

Savedra and Ginevra exchanged a glance. Their skirts puddled together, blue silk and blue velvet, flecked with grass and stray feathers.

"Well," Ginevra said, pulling her smile on firmly once more. "I'll let you know what colors I'm wearing before the next party."

CHAPTER 7

Despite her insistence on continuing, Isyllt knew she was slowing the others down. Her head swam, a slow nauseous spiral inside her skull, and every so often she had to pause to lean on the nearest wall or arm. She could ease pain, but her magic was useless to repair damage.

No one complained, but Khelséa and Spider exchanged frequent glances. Nothing like someone else's insanity to draw people together.

It was madness, but it was also the best of her options. If she retreated now the vrykoloi would move their hiding place, and that would cost too much time.

The way back up was less perilous, if slow and painstaking. By the time they returned to the lowest level of sewers she was caked with sweat and grime, and the ache in her legs nearly dwarfed the sharp throb in her head.

Isyllt wasn't sure when the feeling began. At first it was lost beneath the nausea and tinnitus, one more tiny unpleasantness amid the aches and bruises. If the lantern bled painful colored halos and sounds echoed queerly, that was only to be expected after a blow to the head. Then her ring began to itch—not the chill that bespoke death, but a greasy crawling sensation like she'd dipped her hand in oil. Soon after a tingle spread across her scalp and nape. Then she saw the first of the sigils traced on the walls, glowing softly to her *otherwise* sight: wards and warnings, designed to contain the twisted magic and caution intruders.

She wasn't the only one discomfited: Spider's eyes flickered back and forth and his shoulders drew up like a vulture's. Azarné's delicate jaw clenched and she fretted with her tattered skirts. Was mortal magic as alien to them as their glamourie was to her?

She'd felt this before—all students at the Arcanost were taken to the ruined palace early in their studies as an abject lesson of magic gone awry, and she'd helped set the yearly wards once or twice. You could still catch traces of it in the inner city if the wind shifted the right way. But it was milder above, faded by decades of sun and rain and clean air. Here the *wrongness* echoed from the stones.

Khelséa didn't twitch like the others, but her frown grew the farther they went, till finally she set the lantern down and crouched to consult the map. Isyllt knelt beside her and leaned close, but the ink writhed and blurred across the page and wedged splinters behind her eye sockets. She closed her eyes for an instant and would have fallen if not for her death grip on Khelséa's shoulder.

"Do you know where we are?" She didn't have to shout here; the water pipes had been diverted, lest the presence of the palace taint them.

"Near the center of Elysia." From the inspector's

pinched expression, she could have given a more precise answer.

"Can you feel it?" Isyllt asked.

"The palace?" The unhappy lines around her eyes deepened. "No. But knowing it's there is bad enough. Can you?"

She nodded. "The stones are steeped with it. Old, sour magic."

Khelséa's lips thinned. "Lovely. Is it dangerous?"

"We won't run mad or fall over dead. Probably. The wards seem to be working. But stagnant magic breeds things the way stagnant water does, and attracts little nasty spirits. And vampires, apparently." She stood carefully and pried her fingers free of the other woman's jacket.

Khelséa shook her head as she rose. "And they just kept building the city around it. Like it was a tree no one wanted to cut down."

"Even dead trees have deep roots," Azarné said. "And I can't imagine this attracting anything sane, even demons. I would chew my own limbs off to escape this feeling." She glanced at Spider and he nodded sharply in agreement. "I can only imagine that Myca and his accomplices hide here to avoid being found. Or because they have already gone mad."

"Well," Isyllt muttered, leaning against the wall. "That's something to look forward to." Her left hand scraped stone, feeling the sour magic through her glove. And the quiet strength of centuries, as well. Erisín had endured, and continued to endure. It would outlast the blight. Affection for the city warmed her, and she closed her eyes against a sudden prickling in her sinuses.

Saints and specters. Head wounds really were dangerous.

She glanced up to find two sets of yellow eyes and one of brown watching her, their expressions ranging from concern to the elaborate disinterest of a well-fed cat watching a wounded bird. How long had she been standing there?

"Come on," she said, pushing off the wall. A blink cleared the glaze from her vision. "I'd rather not breathe this in longer than I have to."

The tunnels grew quieter and quieter the nearer they drew to the ruined palace. The great copper pipes were corroded and caked with verdigris, and the sewer canals held only a low thick sludge that smelled of mud and stagnation instead of waste. Isyllt saw no rats; animals often had better sense than men. The only sound now was their footsteps and the rasp of her and Khelséa's breath.

They stopped when the tunnel split into three equally dark and unappealing branches. Isyllt and Khelséa exchanged a glance, then turned to Spider. He gave them an articulated shrug in response.

"I thought they must be lairing somewhere near the old palace, but from here I have no more clue than you. But"—his voice lowered—"if they are here, they know we're coming. I imagine we'll find them waiting for us eventually."

"So your plan is to keep going till we walk into an ambush?" Khelséa folded her arms across her chest in eloquent critique of the idea.

"It does have a certain brutal efficiency," Isyllt said wryly. "Do you have a better idea?"

"You're the sorcerer. Can't you do something clever?"

She winced at the thought; even a witchlight's worth

of concentration was daunting right now. But she was the only one who could magic a solution. She leaned against the wall and slid slowly down, careful not to bump her head.

"Spider, Azarné, give me some of your hair." She tugged her gloves off, shaking dry a film of sweat. It was hedge magic, the sort of craft children practiced and Arcanostoi disdained. But Isyllt had learned such charms from her mother, and they worked more often than not.

The vrykoloi each gave her three long strands, and she plaited dark and fair together into a slender cord nearly the length of her forearm. The hair was curiously slick against her skin, and she wondered what it would look like under magnifying lenses. "Now I need a weight."

After a pause, Azarné untangled something from her hair and handed it over; a thick gold ring set with lapis. Isyllt nodded thanks and tied it to the end of the cord, where it swayed heavily. The trick was convincing the crude pendulum to seek out vampires other than the two closest.

The answer, as it so often was, was blood. She pulled her jacket away from her wounded shoulder, wincing as she did. Amid all her new discomforts, the bite had faded into the background. Working a corner of the dressing loose, she prodded the tender flesh until blood and lymph smeared her fingertip. The physical poison was long since cleansed, but its ghost remained and that was enough for her. She slicked the ring and tugged her jacket back into place, ignoring the way Spider and Azarné's gazes had sharpened and trained on her.

She cleared her head as best she could, concentrating on the memory of the attack in the sewers, of the vampire's teeth in her neck and his chill skin against hers. When she opened her eyes again her shoulder throbbed fiercely and the ring swung in a straight and steady arc, pointing toward the right-hand tunnel.

The tunnel had been a dead end once, but now a ragged hole opened in the wall. The pendulum tugged sharply toward the blackness. A faint draft breathed through, cold and stale and dry. Its touch conjured ghostlight in the depths of Isyllt's diamond.

"Are you sure you want to do this?" Spider murmured. His nearness made the pendulum twitch. "You're in no condition for a fight."

"Your concern is touching."

"I need you alive if you're to be of any use." He squeezed her elbow as he said it. It would have reassured her, had his fingers not been cold and vising.

"You haven't earned your use of me yet."

She pulled her arm free, shoving the pendulum into her pocket and drawing her kukri. Opalescent light licked up the blade as she gave Khelséa a nod. Isyllt sucked in a deep breath and blew it out slowly, then stepped forward.

The echoes of their footsteps changed as they stepped from the narrow tunnel into a wider space. Lantern- and ghostlight brushed the curves of a high vaulted ceiling and the shadows of coffined alcoves in the walls—a great crypt. Doors led into darkness in all directions. Isyllt opened her mouth to question Spider when Azarné hissed, jerking her face upward.

She had an instant's glimpse of pale shapes clinging to the stones like insects before the vampires fell on them. Spellfire cut the air in the wake of her blade, throwing shadows wild across the walls, but the vrykolos was already out of the way. Pain blazed in her shoulder, and she knew she faced the one who'd bitten her.

She swung again, too slow and clumsy. He moved faster than she could follow, sliding under her guard and shoving her against a wall. Only dumb luck kept her from striking her head again. He cracked her hand against the stones—once, twice, and on the third blow her kukri fell from useless fingers, its light fading as it clattered to the floor. Her ring still glowed, bathing half his face in eerie blue. She heard shouts and struggles around them, but only had eyes for the demon in front of her.

"Was it you?" he hissed, fangs shining. The light lined a knife-edged nose and hollow cheeks, reflected in the depths of eyes pale and crystalline as ice and agates. Grey skin glittered dully, like flecks in unpolished stone. He smelled of snakes and earth and sweet poison. Isyllt squirmed in his grasp and kicked him in the groin, but he only snorted angrily and shook her.

"Was it you?" he demanded again, dragging her up by her collar. "Did you kill her?" Her toes scraped the floor and she could barely breathe, let alone think. His eyes distracted her, flecks of yellow floating in striated irises—her own confusion, or a predator's enchantment?

"Kill who?" she gasped.

"Forsythia!"

She clawed at his hand and annoyance cut through her fear. "Of course not. I'm trying to find her killer."

His fangs snapped inches from her face. "*Liar.* Liars and schemers all of you. She was the warmest thing I ever knew, and you slit her throat and *wasted* it!"

"I did not!" The conversation was making her headache worse, and lack of air wasn't helping. "I'm a Crown Investigator—I find the people who slit women's throats in alleys. And I find idiot tomb-robbing vrykoloi too." She clenched her throbbing right hand, letting the different pain and the press of her ring ground her.

The vampire's grip loosened, and the balls of her feet met the floor. "If you didn't kill her, who did?"

She kicked him again out of pique, beyond caring if she antagonized him. "That is *what I'm trying to find out.* Why did you rob a royal tomb?"

Confusion narrowed his strange depthless eyes. "Because—"

A sound like thunder shattered the air, pierced her ears like hot steel, and Isyllt yelped. The vampire flinched, letting her fall as he clapped his hands over the sides of his head. She felt the second gunshot, but was already deafened.

Through a haze of tears she saw Spider seize the other vampire by the neck and drag him away. She read Spider's name on his lips. Then a bone-white blur, and cold black blood sprayed across her face.

The vampire toppled, clutching at his ruined throat. The wound didn't pump as a human's would, but leaked viscous dark fluid. His lips moved, but in the flickering light Isyllt couldn't read the shape of the words. The look on his face was clear enough, though: shock and betrayal, a confused and childish hurt.

Her own confusion was enough that she didn't realize what Spider was doing until he moved again. Her throat ached; she was shouting at him to stop, but she couldn't hear her own words. The kukri flashed in his hand as it arced down and metal sparked on stone. The vampire's head rolled free, tangling his long black hair. His lips continued shaping soundless accusations while the last of his unlife oozed onto the ground.

"He was going to tell me why," Isyllt whispered, staring at the twitching body. Speaking made her cough, which made her throat ache all the more.

As she watched, the edges of the wound blackened and curled—the burn of spelled silver. Vertebrae glistened like pearls amid bloodless grey-pink meat. The corpse began to blanch even more as flesh shrank against bone; color drained away till his skin was white as ashes. Even his hair faded, paling from root to tip. When it was over he lay still, legs curled toward his chest, one arm stretching toward his missing head.

Trembling, Isyllt crawled on hands and knees to reach the corpse. The hand that had held her throat had been cold and undead, but still moving flesh. What she touched now was rough and unyielding as stone.

Spider took her arm and helped her up. Blood smeared her skin, already tacky. The lantern had gone out—the only light was the pulse of her ring. "Why?" she asked.

"I'm sorry." Again, despite the roar in her ears, she could hear him. His tone and insouciant stance were anything but sorry. "I thought he was about to eat you." He wiped the knife clean on the hem of his coat and handed it back to her.

She couldn't argue with him, not when she couldn't hear herself speak. She willed the witchlight brighter and turned to find Khelséa.

The inspector crouched beside the broken lantern and another petrified vampire. This one had not died as prettily—one silver bullet had shattered his breast and the other his skull. Azarné brooded over a third corpse like her namesake bird, her hands sticky with blood.

Khelséa looked up when Isyllt knelt beside her, her face drawn and ashen with pain. She only shook her head when Isyllt spoke, and when she pulled a hand away from one ear, a thin streak of blood glistened on her palm.

From the vaulted chamber, Azarné and Spider tracked their brethren's spoor down a narrow corridor, up a flight of half caved-in stairs to another room. Isyllt knew the den was near before they reached the top of the steps; the musk was unmistakable.

The room reminded her of the lairs of street children she'd known in Birthgrave. Of places she'd slept herself. Torn, stained mattresses and nests of blankets wedged into corners, a single lamp on a broken wooden crate. Only the smell of sour sweat and stale food was missing, and Isyllt was just as glad the vrykoloi hadn't brought their dinners here.

And as with orphan dens, the vampires had hoarded precious things, hiding them under mattresses and loose stones. But this treasure was more than polished stones or bits of glass, pennies or a sharp knife. Gold and gems sparkled and glittered under the erratic witchlight. Earrings and bracelets, chiming girdles, fabric stiff with gold bullion, slippers glowing with sequins and stones. Jeweled coffers and vials of perfume, statues of saints carved in bronze and sandalwood and alabaster.

But not all the clothing was the same size, nor all the colors those Isyllt remembered Lychandra to wear. How many tombs had been pilfered over the years?

Among the glitter of jewels, she found a long lock of

brass-blonde hair, braided and coiled and tied with silk thread. A lover's token, the kind sweethearts exchanged. Had Forsythia kept a knot of her vampire's hair in return? Isyllt wished she could have asked him, and didn't know whether to weep or curse in her frustration.

They emerged filthy and exhausted from a sewer access in Birthgrave. Not the sort of place Isyllt liked to be at midnight, but she was too tired and sore to be nervous. If anyone tried to cut their throats or purses, she would be perfectly content to let Spider eat them and throw the bodies in the river.

No one tried, though, and they staggered into a better neighborhood and finally managed to waylay a carriage. The man's eyes widened when she showed her ring, and she shoved Khelséa into the cab before he could decide to bolt. Spider ghosted inside as well, but Azarné had vanished.

The carriage deposited them at St. Alia's, Archlight's own hospital—the driver didn't wait, despite Isyllt's promise of more payment if he did. Khelséa found a physician to inspect her ruptured eardrum, but Isyllt waved away offers of assistance. The hospital was unusually full, and she wanted sleep more than anything—dying in the night of the concussion was a risk she was prepared to take.

Spider waited for her when she emerged; the building's wards were too powerful for him to easily pass. He didn't offer her his arm this time and she was just as glad, though she could have used it.

"He thought I killed Forsythia," she finally said when they reached Calderon Court. She could hear again, though her ears still rang like cathedral bells and her voice sounded queer and not her own.

Spider shrugged. "I imagine lairing there hadn't been good for his mind. Who knows what he thought, or why?" He met her eyes unblinking, but she didn't know his tells enough to find truth or deception in his face or stance. He wasn't telling her everything, though, and he'd silenced Forsythia's vampire before she could learn more. "Does it matter? You have what you sought."

It matters to Forsythia. But that would hardly sway him. Nor could she say it had been too easy, though she knew in her gut it had.

"No," she said at last, wrapping her arms around herself. She couldn't stop shivering. "It doesn't." He was a demon, with his own agenda—she couldn't let herself forget that for a few kisses.

He reached for her, but stopped at her flinch. "You should rest. I'll find you again when you've mended."

And he was gone, with only a cool draft to mark his passage. Isyllt lingered on the steps, watching the eastern sky pale. The moon had set, and false dawn glowed above the rooftops. The Dragon's fire, chasing the Hounds below the western horizon. The leader of the pack was already hidden by the city skyline.

By the time the second hound had nosed beyond view, the sky was tinged with blue and her shivering had become a teeth-rattling tremble. Lights flickered to life in nearby windows. At last she turned, unlocked the door with shaking hands, and began the slow climb to her rooms.

Spider was right: She had accomplished what she needed to. The queen's jewels were found, and would be returned to her crypt, and Mathiros need never be the wiser. The vrykoloi responsible were dead, and she had the petty satisfaction of revenge for the attack on her and

Ciaran, and more knowledge of vampires than she'd had before.

But there was a dead woman moldering on a slab without justice, and Isyllt still didn't know why any of it had happened.

Sleep claimed her as soon as she pressed her face to the pillow, but it brought neither peace nor satisfaction.

PART II

Nocturne

CHAPTER 8

On the seventeenth of Hekate, seven days after the party, a carriage left Erisín through the Aquilon Gate, on the north road to Arachne. The coach bore no colors or devices, but everyone in the palace knew it carried Savedra Severos and was bound for her family estate. Four Severoi guards rode beside it—all the archa would lend her—and an octad of hastily hired mercenaries. Excessive, some said, but everyone also knew that banditry in the countryside increased with every wave of Rosian refugees driven south.

Rumors and speculation chased each other through the court: Savedra had quarreled with the prince; she had quarreled with the princess; her famous loyalty couldn't withstand an assassin's gun pointed at her own head. Ginevra Jsutien displayed her wounded cheek with brave fragility, and was cosseted and made much of by her peers. She spoke no word against Savedra, but her silences were eloquent.

The prince saw Savedra off, though their farewells were stilted. Of the princess there was no sign; she had taken ill the day before. Maids had heard her fighting with Nikos, and rumors of another pregnancy or the unlikelihood thereof circulated with knowing glances and shaken heads.

The carriage kept a leisurely pace till the city walls shrank behind it, then the driver urged the six Medvener Bays into a gallop. The countryside rolled by, coastal scrublands giving way to brush, and the wooded hills drawing ever closer. The wind from the north was heavy with the tang of pine and graveyard cypress and the distant bite of snow.

Inside the cushioned cab, Savedra brooded. She ought to be pleased her plan had worked so well, or at least happy to see her childhood home again. Glad of a respite from court and politics. And she was, but still her thoughts spiraled down to frets and worries with every idle moment.

"Your face will set that way if you don't stop frowning. And you'll wear a hole in your skirt."

Savedra blinked and dragged her hands away from the hem she'd been picking. Ashlin lounged on the opposite side of the carriage, one booted foot drawn up on the bench. Every so often she tugged the window open, slitting her eyes against the cold wind. It had taken some argument to convince her to ride in the carriage instead of remaining with the outriders after they left the city walls, but even in confinement her mood had improved since they left the palace. Savedra had seen her smile more in the past several hours than in two months in Erisín.

The princess wore mercenary armor in patchwork black and brown, and her hair had been trimmed to a rougher shape than her usual sleek bob and dyed a dark nut-brown. The color wouldn't fool anyone who saw her pale eyelashes, but it made her green eyes all the more striking. She'd even pierced her ears again and hung them with gold and silver hoops, the wealth of a successful sell-sword. It didn't look like a disguise—more like a disguise had been stripped away to show the truth. Ashlin would never have agreed to leave the palace for her own safety, but the ruse had caught her interest, as had a trip to the library at Evharis. It wasn't an invitation an Alexios was likely to receive.

"If you mean to keep me penned in this rattling box, you could at least offer more conversation than my horse." Metal flashed with her smile; a silver stud kept the hole in her nostril open in the absence of her wedding jewelry.

"Sorry." Savedra's own smile was wry and lopsided. "You might be better off with the horse."

"My guards used to say that the only useful thing a horse couldn't do is dice. I don't suppose you have any of those on you?"

"I'm afraid not. And the bouncing wouldn't help." The ride was actually quite smooth—the coach was well sprung and the roads maintained, but the constant soft rattle made her spine ache; her ears ached from the clatter of hooves and wheels. She'd never cared for riding especially, but the sight of nothing but the dim wood-and-upholstery interior of the cab might be enough to drive her ahorse after another day. "I imagine there's a deck of cards here somewhere, though."

After a bit of searching she found one in a door pocket, along with a charcoal nub and scraps of paper smeared with old scores—the coach's last occupants had taken their tarock games seriously. The cards were worn soft at the edges, faces faded. They whispered as Savedra shuffled, a muted hiss instead of the sharp slap and crack of crisp stock. Teaching her to play for money was one of the myriad ways Varis had corrupted her as a child.

Thinking of her uncle nearly made her frown again, though she kept her face smooth this time. A visit to Evharis was only half an excuse to keep Ashlin out of harm's way; Savedra and the princess had both been with Nikos when Isyllt Iskaldur came to the palace, shaken and bruised and grey as paste, to report that Lychandra's jewelry had been recovered and the thieves dealt with. Nikos had been pleased with the timely handling of the situation, but it was clear that Isyllt was still troubled.

The idea of blood-drinking demons creeping through tombs was troubling indeed, and Savedra still wondered what knowledge of them Varis was hiding. After a quiet inquiry around Phoenix House, she'd learned that he'd been distracted lately, underslept and much more subdued than usual. It might be nothing but one of his countless affairs, but the confluence of events sent unease worming through her gut. Between family intrigues and machinations at court, she had learned to trust that sensation.

She concentrated on the blur of cards, and wondered if she could read the future from them the way some fortunetellers claimed to.

Ashlin pushed the curtain aside and tugged the window open. The cold draft pricked gooseflesh on Savedra's limbs, and cut through the scent of oiled mail and leather and warm flesh that she hardly noticed anymore. She caught a glimpse of low grey sky and hills dark with winter-brown oaks; soon the road would rise into the pine and juniper forests that skirted the mountains. When the carriage was unpleasantly cold the princess shut the window again and leaned back against her seat, blowing her tousled fringe out of her eyes.

"Should I leave my hair this way?" she asked, brushing at the dye-dulled strands.

"No," Savedra answered immediately, lifting the latch that held the narrow plank table to the wall. Hinges creaked as it lowered. "It's hideous. You have beautiful hair. What you ought to do is grow it out."

"All it does is tangle and get in my eyes."

Savedra lifted a hand to her own wild hair, bound up for travel and still frizzing free of its pins. "I have no sympathy. Anyway, you have maids to style it for you."

Ashlin frowned. "No one's brushed my hair for me since my mother died."

"Let Nikos do it—he spent long enough learning to brush mine."

The princess's frown twisted sideways. "Probably not. I might let you, though. I trust you around me with knives, after all, so why not combs?"

"Combs don't attract attention," Savedra said automatically, slapping cards onto the table, "and are just as easy to poison." One of the first attempts on her life had been a gift of poisoned combs. She was careful now to buy her own, and never from the same shop.

Ashlin's eyebrows climbed. "Is it safe to be trapped in a carriage with you?"

"Probably not. It's a good thing you have a sword." She collected her hand and winked over the cards. "Your move, Your Highness."

They stopped that night at a crossroads inn to eat and change horses and catch a few hours of sleep, rising before dawn to continue. The lieutenant Cahal took Ashlin's place in the carriage the next day, a dark-haired Celanoran who had come to Erisín with the betrothal party three years ago. Half the ostensible mercenaries riding with the coach were the princess's own guard, and the other half Captain Denaris's handpicked soldiers. The lieutenant was hawk-eyed and quiet, and a cutthroat tarock player. Savedra might have to pawn her pearls soon.

"Am I being careless with her?" Savedra asked while Cahal shuffled. She'd tried to keep her worries to herself, but the soldier's calm and obvious loyalty invited confidences.

Cards blurred from hand to hand before he answered. "I've ridden with the princess since she was sixteen," he said at last. "When she was younger, no one could have been more careless with her health than she was. That's most of why she isn't heir—too much like her mother."

Savedra had asked once why Ashlin, the firstborn, wasn't Crown Princess of Celanor; the princess had said only that a crown suited her younger brother better.

"Did you know the queen?"

He shook his head. "I was too young. She spent little time in the castle by the time I was training there. But I saw her sometimes—bright and fierce and beautiful. A wildling warrior of the old Clans. They call the castle at Yselin the Eyrie, but it was always a mew to her." He gave a rueful shrug, a soldier speaking of things that weren't his to know but everyone knew anyway. "She died in battle when Ashlin was thirteen. No king or queen or prince of Celanor had fallen so for generations, not since Dhonail and Siobhan, but Nemain wouldn't leave the defense of her clanhame to her soldiers when brigands came raiding." Another shrug. "Ashlin worshipped her, and by the time she was sixteen everyone thought she'd kill herself the same way."

He grinned wryly, black eyes glinting. "Her Highness has mellowed a great deal since then. In some ways your palace intrigue is good for her—makes her think before she rushes blindly in." He dealt a new hand. "So, no, I don't think you're being careless with her. Coddling only makes her angry, anyway." This shrug was sympathetic and long-suffering.

They passed the road sign for Arachne as afternoon shadows stretched into evening on the third day. Every other time Savedra had made the trip it had been a leisurely journey of half a decad or more, but neither she nor Ashlin were in the mood for leisure now. The carriage veered off the main road onto the narrower path that led to the Severoi's hillside estate. They were high in the hills now, near the crux of the Varagas and Sindrel mountain ranges, at the edge of the Sarken border. Miles to the west, the Herodis thundered down from the heights, surging black and icy toward Erisín and the sea.

The ride roughened as the road sloped, and by the time the horses clattered to a stop Savedra's teeth ached from clenching her jaw and sharp pains pierced through her shoulders and back. She swore like a dockhand as Cahal handed her down, and was rewarded by the amused crease of his eyes. Her left leg had fallen asleep, and stung with pins and needles as she dragged it across the cobbles.

She raised a hand against the sun, and forgot her aches and complaints as her eyes adjusted. The sun slanted across the western mountains, gilding the sharp peaks of the Varagas and blinding the windows of the house. Shadows gathered thick in the lower forests. The air tasted of pine and woodsmoke and dead leaves, and Savedra breathed deep with a sigh. She'd played in these woods with her brothers and the household children, and sulked in them during the miseries of her adolescence. Phoenix House and the Gallery of Pearls might be more a home to her these days, but Evharis would always carry a weight of memories.

Ashlin dismounted, stroking her sweating horse and drawing aside her scarf to bare wind-flushed cheeks. She shaded her eyes as she studied the hills and terraced orchards, and the wilder trees beyond. "I've missed the forests," she said quietly.

Stablehands appeared, hesitating at the sight of mercenaries. Before Savedra could identify herself the great doors swung open and the familiar gaunt form of the house steward descended the steps. Savedra smiled and stepped forward, trying in vain to shake the wrinkles from her heavy skirts. As a child she would have run to him, but dignity and her still stiff leg kept her from it now.

Iancu Sala blinked when he saw her, surprise foreign on his creased aquiline face. "Vedra!" He hurried to embrace her, stooping to do so. "I had no word you were coming. Is everything well?"

"I'm fine, Iancu. It's— It's complicated." She smiled wryly.

"Ah." He brightened, straightening his immaculate jacket. Any Severoi vassal was well versed in complications. He gestured the stablehands forward, and sent another servant to prepare rooms and extra portions for dinner. Cahal led the other riders toward the stable, while

Ashlin fell in beside Savedra. If Iancu thought a mercenary out of place in the family house, he gave no sign.

"How is the archa, and your father?" Iancu asked as he
took their cloaks. He poured an ewer of lavender-scented
water into a basin by the door and let them wash the dust
and sweat from their faces. The hall always smelled of
lavender and wood polish and wax.

"They're well. They would send greetings, if they
weren't pretending to ignore this trip." They followed him
into a parlor, where Savedra sank into a chair and nearly
moaned with pleasure at a seat that didn't move. Ashlin paced behind her, maneuvering her sword carefully
around the furniture.

Iancu's heavy brows arched, but he only moved to the
sideboard to pour plum brandy.

"Sit down," Savedra told Ashlin. "My feet ache just
watching you."

"You need to stretch too, or you'll regret it in the morning." In compromise, she leaned against the arm of a
couch, angling her sword aside.

"Excuse my manners," Savedra said, accepting a glass
from Iancu. "Iancu Sala, steward of Evharis, this is—"

A heartbeat's pause while she scrambled for a suitable
name, but Ashlin filled it by standing and bowing gracefully. "Sorcha Donelan, King's Talon and Captain of the
Royal Guard." Her lilting accent, faded after years in Erisín,
came to the fore. "At your service and that of your house."

Iancu's eyebrows climbed higher, but he returned the
bow with all due dignity. "The hospitality of Evharis is
yours, Captain. You're a long way from home."

"Farther every day, it seems. But it's my honor to escort
the Lady Savedra wherever she goes."

Savedra realized she was gaping, and took a gulp of brandy to cover it. Liquor seared her throat and sinuses and brought tears to her eyes. Ashlin sipped her own drink, lips twitching with amusement.

Iancu's dark eyes flickered as he studied them both, but it took more than aliases and disguises to dent his discretion. "Dinner will be late, I'm afraid. Many of the staff are helping with the pomegranate harvest, and we didn't expect guests."

"That's all right," Savedra said, even as the brandy lined her empty stomach with heat. "We came to use the library. May we?" Asking permission was merely a courtesy, but Nadesda had trained her in politeness as well as poisons.

"Of course," Iancu replied in kind, collecting their empty glasses and returning them to the tray.

He led them through the back of the house, pointing out useful rooms and stairs to Ashlin as they passed. It wasn't the grand tour, but still meant to impress—the route took them through the great family room, lined with paintings and statues and costly heirlooms. Ashlin made appropriately admiring noises. The rear doors opened onto the columned porch and into the gardens. The space behind the house had been carved out of the hillside, and above the high walls a dark slope of trees brooded. It unnerved some of her cousins, but Savedra had always found the forest's weight reassuring.

Beyond the garden's lavender-lined paths and trellised arches rose the library, imported red sandstone glowing incarnadine in the dying light. High windows shone amid the intricate redents. The main house was arched and columned and sprawling in classical Selafaïn tradition, but the library had been built years later as a wedding gift by an archon for his southern bride, crowned with ogival lotus-shaped towers in the ancient Sindhaïn style.

"I'm glad you've come," Iancu said as they climbed the broad red steps. "No one has visited the library in months, since Lord Varis and his friend were here. Your generation has no sense of history."

An old jibe, long become a joke, but Savedra didn't rise to it this time. "When was Uncle Varis here?" she asked instead, trying to keep the sharp interest from her voice.

"Four months ago, it must have been. At the end of Janus. He came without warning as well—clearly he has been a bad influence on you after all."

"And which *friend* did he bring?" She used the same carefully bland inflection he had.

"I don't know." He paused at the top of the steps to sort through his keys, and the playfulness drained slowly from his voice. "She was hooded and cloaked the whole time, and offered no name. We're all used to Lord Varis's assignations, of course, but this one... I didn't like her. She was a witch, I think. Not one of your Arcanost scholars, but a proper *vrajitora*. I even thought I heard a bit of the eastern mountains in her voice."

Iancu's parents had crossed the mountains from Sarkany decades ago, and not survived long after settling in Arachne. Their orphaned son had eventually been adopted by a housekeeper at Evharis and risen high in the family's confidences, but the wild lands east of the Varagas were in his blood. He'd kept Savedra up at night with stories of hungry wolves and bloodthirsty spirits and great smoldering wyrms who laired in the mountains by the Zaratan Sea. But there was no hint of exaggeration in his tone now.

Savedra's stomach chilled. "Do you remember what they looked at? I need to see it."

Iancu frowned as the brassbound door swung open. "I do. But you put me in an awkward position, milady. Lord Varis didn't swear me to secrecy, but no member of this family should ever have to. Gossip is one thing, but it isn't my place to betray a confidence, intentional or otherwise."

Savedra pressed her tongue between her teeth, biting back a hasty reply. Only her mother might blithely order Iancu in matters such as this. Even if Ashlin revealed herself, the word of an Alexios, princess or not, meant nothing to the steward of Evharis. There were already Severoi who thought Savedra a traitor to the House, though Nadesda's approbation kept their tongues in check.

The last rind of sun slipped behind the mountains, and the light cooled and greyed. Somewhere in the garden a cricket began a slow droning chirp.

"Forgive me," Iancu said, holding the door for them. "It's not my place to keep guests standing on the front step, either."

They moved past him into the cool gloom of the library. Light from the high windows cast diffuse streaks across the polished tiles. The steward took a match from a table by the door and struck it—not to ignite a lamp, but a spell. The flame died quickly, but light kindled in a glass globe set on the wall, then in another, spiraling upward one by one until their pale gold glow filled the tower. An extravagant sort of magic, and one that required renewing every month, but it meant that no candle or oil lamp ever endangered the library's collection.

Savedra was familiar with the royal palace's library, and had seen the one in the Arcanost, and knew that both collections dwarfed this one. But the sight of the shelves lining the walls never failed to impress her. A wide marble stair spiraled around the room, its landings positioned under the windows where tables and chairs might catch the best light. Pointed arches led to the smaller domes that budded from the sides of the tower—the bindery, secure vaults, and the librarian's rooms. The last librarian had retired over a year ago, half-blind and rheumatic, and the family had yet to appoint another. Iancu had taken up the duties, as he did with any left lying unfulfilled.

Savedra turned back to Iancu, who lingered by the door, obviously preparing to excuse himself. "Can you tell me this, at least? Varis was researching the vrykoloi, wasn't he? Demons and blood magic and their history in Erisín? The sorts of thing an eastern witch might be interested in."

The last was a blind strike, hastily cobbled together from Iancu's old bedtime stories; she didn't expect it to hit home. But he flinched, left hand rising in a warding gesture before he clenched it at his side again.

"I'm sure I wouldn't know," he said. "And you should be careful what you speak aloud, especially so near the mountains. But if you wish to research such things, the index is all you need." He bowed shallowly. "If you'll excuse me, I must see to your men, and to dinner. It should be ready within the hour." He hesitated for a heartbeat as he turned, then squared his shoulders and stepped into the gathering dusk. The door echoed shut behind him.

The books were missing.

Savedra and Ashlin searched for an hour before they were certain of it—not misshelved, or set aside, but gone from the building. Demonologies, treatises on blood magic, certain family histories, and those were only the most obvious. Checking the entire catalog was a task for more than two people and one evening.

Iancu returned just after the hour to call them to dinner, but when Savedra explained the problem he immediately joined the search. Books were not removed from the library, not even by archons, and none had been stolen in living memory. Another hour passed, revealing at least two more missing volumes, and night had settled thick and heavy against the windows. Finally Iancu collapsed in a chair, slumping with a despair Savedra had never seen in him before.

"I can't believe it," he muttered against his hands. "Not of Lord Varis."

Savedra could hardly believe it herself. Varis respected little, certainly, but of the things he did, she would have ranked knowledge and her mother among the very highest.

"I understand this is an unpleasant situation," Savedra said, kneeling beside him, "and I have no desire to make it worse. But please, will you tell me everything you know about Varis's visit? It's important."

He gave her a wan smile and brushed her hair lightly as he had when she was a child. "I shouldn't, but I will. After dinner, though, or the cooks will be even more annoyed with us."

Dinner was duck in pomegranate sauce with tabouli, delicious even cold, but they ate in frowning silence. Even a good bottle of Ombrian siyah did nothing to lighten the mood, though Savedra was enamored enough of the vintage that she took another bottle with them when they retired to Iancu's private study.

"I'm afraid there isn't much I can tell you," the steward said, after activating the room's silence. "Lord Varis came, as I said, in Janus. He was quieter than usual, perhaps, more withdrawn. I thought that had to do with his companion, since she took such care to hide her face."

"Do you have any idea who she was?"

"None, though of course everyone speculated. Some thought she was just a melodramatic actress, while others decided she must be a member of a great house, one who couldn't be seen associating with a Severos. The kitchen staff had a wager going as to whose wife she might be."

"Did you speak with her?"

"Hardly at all. She was never rude, but she rarely spoke, and even more rarely to anyone but Varis. He was . . . solicitous of her privacy."

"But you didn't like her."

"No." He shook his head, pinching the long arch of his nose. "I knew it was foolish even then, but something about her made me uneasy. You think me superstitious, and perhaps that's so, but between her accent and the nature of her studies I thought her a witch from the mountains. Not all magic is as civilized as it is in Erisín."

"And you never heard a name?"

Iancu pinched his nose again, as if against a headache. "He called her *my lady*, and *darling*, but he calls the gardeners *darling*, so that hardly signifies. And once . . ." The lines on his brow deepened in thought, and Savedra was disconcerted by how old it made him look. He ought to be as timeless as the house. "I thought I heard him call her Phaedra once, or say the name. She didn't respond to it, though, so I wasn't certain. And it's hardly an eastern name. I suppose I didn't expect it to be hers."

It was Savedra's turn to frown, turning her wine glass between her palms and searching for answers in the dark ripple. "I've heard that name recently." It was a perfectly normal Selafaïn name, though not one that had been in fashion lately, so where... "Phaedra Severos. She wrote an essay on blood magic. I saw it mentioned in the Phoenix Codex."

"I don't know of any Phaedra Severos," Iancu said. From the steward of Evharis, it was practically a denial of her existence. "When was this essay published?"

She shrugged. "Four sixty something. Before I was born."

"No sense of history," he muttered with a fleeting smile. He set aside his glass and rose, unfolding long limbs from his chair. He removed a copy of the Codex from his great oaken desk and handed it to Savedra. "Where did you see the reference?"

After several moments of flipping and squinting and muttering imprecations, she finally found the footnote she remembered. " 'On The Transfer of Magic and Consciousness via the Sanguine Humor,' by Phaedra Severos. Published by the Arcanost in 463."

Iancu frowned and took the book from her. "How odd. I've never heard of this woman."

"Neither have I," Savedra said, "but I don't know all my cousins. Perhaps she died."

"Death is no reason not to exist," he said. "Certainly not to Evharis."

"She might have married in, or out." Which was still no excuse, as Iancu's glower told her. "There must be records."

"Unless those are missing too."

*   *   *

And so of course they were.

The library's great clepsydra dripped past midnight before Iancu finally located an intact record—the book had been taken to the bindery to be restitched, and that may have saved it. Phaedra Severos was the daughter of Ilisavet and Leonidas Severos, born in Medea in 441. Which meant that her family was a distant and apolitical branch of the Severoi and it was no wonder Savedra had never heard of them, and also that Phaedra had probably been a very talented mage to be publishing articles for the Arcanost at twenty-two. In 464 she married a minor Sarken margrave named Ferenz Darvulesti. Beyond that, she didn't appear to exist.

Could she have been here four months ago, helping Varis steal books? If that were the case, she appeared to have stolen all traces of herself.

CHAPTER 9

Isyllt's bruised skull healed, and the ringing in her ears faded in the next few days—all the better for Kiril and the Arcanost physicians to harangue her about the poor care she took with herself. She reported to Nikos and saw the stolen goods returned quietly to the Alexios crypt. The prince praised her speed and discretion, and rewarded her from his personal coffers. The silver griffins lay in a warded box beside her bed, winking whenever she lifted the lid—not the most she'd ever been paid for her service, but the first time the money hadn't come through Kiril and the royal accountants. She spent the first coin on a box of expensive sweets and had them delivered to Khelséa.

The matter was closed, as far as Nikos and Kiril were concerned. Not that either of them were happy not knowing the hows and whys of the theft, or what else the wayward vrykoloi might have done before Isyllt found them, but silence and discretion were too important to risk with further inquiry and exploration. Isyllt didn't speak of her

desire to investigate Forsythia's death, because she knew
she would be refused. Her oath to the Crown allowed her
the leeway to do her job as she saw fit, but a direct order
from the heir couldn't be easily ignored.

She had other duties besides those of a Crown Investigator, as well. Her loyalty was first and always to Kiril and
the Crown, but she was also an alumna of the Arcanost,
and the regents believed in using their students as long
and as often as they could. So in between any government
work she taught necromancy and entropomancy to small
advanced classes, and picked up stray lectures for the
beginning courses.

On the eighteenth of Hekate she spent the last two
hours of the morning in a frigid lecture room that reeked
of brine and squid. Several dozen squid lay on slabs of
ice all around her, and one unlucky specimen on the dis-
secting table in front of her, next to knives and bowls and
vials. Glass and steel and pale flesh glistened under her
witchlight.

"As I hope you've already learned in lyceum, squid use
their ink to confuse and escape predators. Scribes, cooks,
and alchemists all have different uses for it. In spellcraft,
the ink is a valuable component in charms of illusion,
distraction, and obfuscation." Had she been in a happier
mood, she might have dragged answers out of the students, amusing herself with their wide eyes and stammer-
ing, but her head was still tender and the stink and cold
weren't helping.

"Squid ink can be purchased at any alchemist's, but you
never know when you may need to harvest your own."

Her voice carried to the top of the narrow amphitheater,
over the rough susurrus of a hundred students breathing

and coughing and sniffling, and the rasp of pens and charcoal against paper. Teaching wasn't the worst profession she could imagine; had any other mage but Kiril trained her, it might have been hers. Exorcists and ghost-whisperers were eight for an obol in Erisín, but true entropomancers were rare and much coveted by the Arcanost. It might still become her profession, if she crippled herself doing something stupid. She kept her left hand—ungloved for fine control on the dissection knives—from twitching, but couldn't stop the wry twist of her mouth.

"The squid must be fresh," she said, lifting her forearm-length specimen carefully by the mantle and shaking it so the spotted flesh rippled. Her magic spread through the corpse, lending shape and animation where it would otherwise be limp and gelatinous. One tentacle twitched, groping cold and wet for her fingers, and someone in the upper tier hissed in revulsion; Isyllt didn't try to control that smile. "If the meat has turned pink or smells like a fishmonger's gutter, throw it out." Half the class leaned back in their seats, grimacing, while a few leaned forward. Some days her purpose was to mark those with strong stomachs and curiosities, but today she wasn't hunting baby spies.

"There are two places from which to extract ink—the main sac in the body, and smaller deposits behind the eyes. To reach the primary sac, pull the tentacles and head away from the body cavity—the intestines will come with them. You're looking for a narrow silvery bag." The squid came apart in her hands, easier for her than it would for the students. With the tip of a knife, she teased the brighter piece out of the gelid white guts and held it up.

Movement at the top of the room caught her eye. There

were always stragglers slipping in late, and students from the University or Lyceum trying to sneak glimpses of sorcery—rarely finding it as exciting as they hoped—but this thin, dark-clad skulker was familiar. Isyllt didn't comment as Dahlia eased the door shut and slipped into the shadows of the farthest row, or even give the girl a second glance. The school employed runners, most of whom were children, but in theory any urchin shouldn't be able to walk in from the street.

"The ink can be mixed with any number of media, depending on your purpose. Linseed for writing or painting, vinegar for cooking, blood, wine, ashes, grease or oil for unguents, and so forth. For today's purposes, we can simply puncture the sac and squeeze it into a dish." Blue-black ink seeped under her fingernail as she did so, and the pungent ocean-smell of iodine cut through the air.

She had the attention of the whole class, but she still felt Dahlia's gaze, interest sharp as needles on her skin. Whatever reason had brought the girl here, curiosity held her now. Isyllt remembered being in the girl's place all too well, and found herself standing a little straighter and brightening her witchlight.

"Next, the ink behind the eyes. First squeeze the head to remove the beak. Perhaps I could find a volunteer?"

After her demonstration, Isyllt summoned the students down to the floor and set them on a squid of their own. When they were engrossed with the task—or slumped in chairs breathing shallowly and trying not to vomit—she scrubbed her hands on a towel and waited by the lower door for Dahlia to join her. The girl moved soft as a mouse, not taking her eyes off the dissections in progress.

Isyllt studied her torn stockings and tattered gloves out of the corner of her eye and tried not to frown.

"You said to find you if I learned anything about Forsythia," Dahlia murmured, her lips hardly moving. Now she looked at Isyllt, and her wide slate-blue eyes were hard and serious. "Do you still want to know?"

The citizens of Elysia were long used to Vigils nosing around and quickly losing interest in deaths and disappearances. Isyllt imagined that Forsythia's body had already been shipped to a pauper's grave on the edge of the city, to free the slab for someone with family to miss them.

"I do," she said, just as quietly. "Walk with me." The girl lingered for a moment on the threshold, staring almost wistfully at the slabs of ice and dead squid and softly cursing students.

"Do you enjoy dissections?" Isyllt asked as they maneuvered through the halls, already clogging as instructors released their students to lunch.

Dahlia gave her another measuring look. "I enjoy learning how things work," she said. "And what they're good for."

An underclassman stumbled out of their way, wide eyes trained on Isyllt's ring, and held the door for them. She gave him a smile for his attentiveness and nearly laughed as he blanched and scurried away.

The day's chill was pleasant after the bite of refrigeration spells. Brown leaves rattled over the lawns and cobbled walks, and the sun was a pale disk behind a low vault of clouds. Starlings and swallows clustered on the domes and spires, occasionally scattered by an encroaching hawk or raven. Voices rose up all around as students crowded the paths and converged on vendors' carts for their noon meals. A protest gathered across the square.

"Let's find something to eat," Isyllt said, "and you can tell me your news. What do you want?"

Dahlia shot her a sideways glance. "Calamari?"

Isyllt snorted. "You missed the first part of my lecture, about the uses of the ink."

The girl's eyes glinted with a repressed smile. Sandy olive skin and black curls were common enough in Selafai, but her long-lashed blue eyes were striking. "No I didn't. I listened at the door. Illusion. Distraction. Obfuscation." She stumbled a little over the last.

"Confusion," Isyllt supplied, "obscuration. Hiding. Sometimes hiding in plain sight." She licked her ink-stained finger and smeared a faint grey smudge on Dahlia's forehead, like a temple's ashen benediction. Her own look-away charms worked well enough, but to divert attention from two people in a busy place she was glad for the ink's extra focus.

Dahlia let Isyllt take her hand and didn't flinch from the touch of her crippled fingers. After a few steps, it became apparent that the spell was working very well indeed. Some of the more perceptive pedestrians stepped around them, even as their eyes slid past, but more were entirely oblivious, and would have run them over had they not dodged. Dahlia had the grace and slightness of youth, if not a decade and more of practice, and they passed the worst of the crowd without collisions.

Isyllt knew she was showing off, and shook her head at her own folly. From the directions she caught the girl's gaze wending, she was also encouraging a young pickpocket.

She dropped the spell in front of a kiosk at the edge of the quadrant, startling two young men enough to claim their place in line. The vendor hardly blinked, inured to sorcerers' tricks. Isyllt bought two trenchers of fried calamari and dolmathes, and found a seat on a low wall beneath an alder tree.

They ate in silence for a while, punctuated by the crunch of breaded rings. "What information do you have?" Isyllt finally asked, licking spiced salt and lemon off her fingers.

Dahlia looked up from her nearly empty trencher, muscles working along the curve of her jaw. She scrubbed a sheen of oil off her mouth with the back of one hand. "I found someone who knew her. Who knows her name."

A true name, along with the lock of hair now safely tucked into her kit, might be enough to conjure with. "Will your contact talk to me?"

"He will. But he wants to know that you'll *do* something."

The protesters—Rosian and natives both—were yelling about justice and wrongs, about the law's disregard; she didn't appreciate the reminder. Some onlookers shouted encouragement, others heckled and jeered. *Go home,* some called, and the increasingly familiar *cabbage-eaters*.

Isyllt frowned at the grease-stained bread in her hands, breaking off chunks and tossing them across the cobbles. Brown clouds of birds descended on the morsels. "I want to find Forsythia's killer. I want to stop him. But I can't promise you justice."

Dahlia laughed bitterly. "If you did, I'd know you were lying." She devoured her bread in quick, methodical bites and dusted her hands on her skirt. "Meet me at the Briar Patch tonight, after the Evensong bells."

She vanished well enough without sorcery.

The protests in Archlight weren't the only ones. Isyllt passed more crowds on her way through Elysia—angry Rosians demanding attention, and locals trying to ignore them or shout them down. Of Vigils she saw very few.

Civil unrest wasn't enough to scare away the Briar Patch's custom. The tavern was packed, and a wall of noise and heat rolled over Isyllt as she opened the door. Ciaran played elsewhere, replaced onstage by a trio of hennaed women singing bawdy songs and dancing with panto-mimed drunkenness. The crowd knew all the words, or invented new ones with enough conviction that it hardly mattered.

Isyllt slipped in just before the cathedral bells tolled. She wore a plain grey dress and dark cloak instead of her usual leathers, with soft knit gloves to hide her hands. It was a guise that would avoid certain kinds of attention, but might attract others. Luckily the drunks were far more interested in the charms of the performers than in a skinny woman lurking in the corner. Even Isyllt couldn't look away when one dancer teetered on the edge of the stage, pinwheeling her arms and leaning so far forward that only a scrap of lace kept her breasts from spilling out of her bodice. A dozen hands stretched out to steady or grope her, but she twisted away with an almost accidental grace, stumbling into her nearest companion instead and sprawling them both across the boards in a tangle of curls and petticoats.

Amidst the shouts and laughter she heard coughing

and sneezes, sniffles drowned in sleeves and handkerchiefs. Sickness had its seasons, as with everything. Cholera and bronze fever in the warm months, influenza in the
cold. Influenza had claimed the lives of more than one
childhood acquaintance, but she had never loathed and
dreaded it like the summer plagues. From the cholera that
took her mother to the fever that claimed Lychandra and
nearly Kiril with her, illness was the one thing that left
Isyllt helpless and useless—she would face vampires and
murderers over that any day.

A quarter-hour after the Evensong faded, Dahlia
emerged from the kitchens. Catching Isyllt's eye, she
nodded toward the back stairs. Isyllt followed, narrowly
avoiding being soaked with beer when a table toasted too
enthusiastically. Someone groped at her skirt and she was
hard pressed not to break his wrist as she dodged.

Dahlia unlocked a room on the second floor and kindled a lamp on a narrow table. A hard wooden chair and
an equally narrow bed were the only other furniture, all
grey with age. A cheap room for the night, not the sort
of place to bring clients. Isyllt put her back to the unwin-
dowed wall and waited for her contact.

She wasn't particularly surprised when Mekaran
walked in. The peacock wore black tonight, snug leather
trousers and a long silk jacket. His bootheels tapped softly
on the hollow boards, nearly lost in the clamor rising from
below. His face was stark and beautiful under white powder and kohl, and the lamplight glowed in his sunset hair.
He closed the door behind him and turned the lock.

Isyllt raised her eyebrows. "So you could have answered
my questions when I first came round, and saved us all
some time?"

"I don't hand out my friends' names to necromancers, even when they're dead. Especially when they're dead. I've heard enough empty promises from the marigolds. But Dahlia thinks you really mean to help."

"I mean to catch Forsythia's killer, and make sure he doesn't do it again."

"Ilora," he said after a long silence. "Her name was Ilora, though she tried hard enough to forget it. What is it you think you can do with that?"

"Find her ghost, I hope. She didn't linger with her body, nor where we found it. But since she was killed elsewhere, she may not be lost beyond the mirror yet. And if I can find her, perhaps I can find her killer."

He cocked a painted eyebrow. "So it wasn't that demon lover of hers? The vrykolos?"

"No. He didn't know who did it, either."

"Didn't?"

"He's dead now too."

Mekaran's lip curled, then tightened in a frown. "I want to say *good*. But perhaps I shouldn't. Lori cared for him, as repulsive as I thought it."

Isyllt sank onto the edge of the bed. The sheets were clean, but still musty from a succession of too many bodies. "Tell me about her."

The wariness returned. "Why do you care?"

"The more I know, the easier it will be to find her."

He began to pace, lithe as a caged cat. "She was Ilora Lizveteva once. From Gamayun." Grey eyes gleamed as he glanced at Isyllt. "My mother was from Sirin— different provinces, but both sacked by the Ordozh. They met when Lori first came to Erisín. My mother asked me to watch out for her. I tried."

He hesitated, with the pained look of one on the verge of breaking a confidence. Isyllt waited silently, trying not to fidget as the bed frame ground into her sacrum through the narrow mattress.

"Lori was raped on her way to Selafai. Not by the Ordozh, but by other refugees. My mother always told me how the Rosians set great store on virginity. It has power, whether kept or given freely, and hers was stolen in exchange for blood and bruises. I tried to help her, but it marked her deep. When she learned how the flowers give up their old names and take new ones…" He shook his head. "She wanted to be Daffodil, like me—thank the saints someone else was already using it. I don't think I could have stomached that. I tried to talk her out of coming to the Garden at all, but so many of her people—of our people—end up here. The lucky ones, at least, who don't sell themselves in filthy alleys in Harrowgate. And Lori was beautiful—all her scars on the inside. I tried to look after her." He folded his arms across his stomach as if he could ward off his failure.

"You're more than an innkeeper," Isyllt said.

Mekaran unbuttoned one sleeve and rolled it up. Sinew and lean muscle flexed under pale skin. He held out his arm to show her the underside, and the black mark branded there: a rose, with barbed vines twining beneath it. "Do you know what this means?"

She'd never seen the mark before, but anyone from Elysia had heard the stories. "You're a thorn. An enforcer for the Rose Council."

"I thought I could help her. Keep her safe."

Raucous laughter rose to fill the silence.

"Is that enough for you?" Mekaran asked. He straightened his sleeve with precise, exaggerated movements.

"I think so. Thank you." She stood, careful of her elbows in the narrow corner.

Mekaran shifted his hips, planting himself squarely in front of the door. "You're not doing this without me."

Isyllt's lips tightened. "This is an investigation, not a public spectacle." She withheld the word *Crown*, and so kept it from being a lie.

"This is Rose Council business. The Roses don't like it when their flowers are murdered, and they know better than to trust your authorities. And," he said with a narrow smile, "if I understand your sorcery, you'll have better luck with me here. I knew her, after all."

Isyllt snorted, but couldn't dispute the truth of that. "Here?" A wave of her hand encompassed the narrow room, the noise and stink of spilled beer rising through the floorboards. "You want me summoning ghosts in your inn?"

He didn't budge. "You're a professional, aren't you?"

She couldn't argue with that either. "Fine. But you'll not breathe a word of anything we hear to anyone. Not even the Roses. Neither of you," she added, glancing at Dahlia, who had curled into the shadows of the opposite corner. The girl was very good at staying silent and still.

Mekaran nodded slowly. "My oaths don't require me to report all the details. If it will help find Lori's killer."

Isyllt studied the room. She could cast a circle and go for theatrics, but it would be ridiculous given how the floorboards gapped. Instead she shed her cloak, leaving it puddled across the foot of the bed, and removed the exorcist's kit from her skirt pocket. It served just as well for summonings.

"Latch the shutters," she told Dahlia, sinking cross-legged onto the floor between the bed and table, "and douse the lamp." A tiny bit of theatrics never hurt.

Darkness filled the room as the flame died, broken only by the light slivering between the floorboards and through the shutters. It retreated again as she conjured witchlight, settling in the corners thick as tar.

"Sit facing me," Isyllt told Mekaran. "Since you're so eager to be my focus." She opened the kit and drew out the scrap of silk tied around the lock of yellow hair. The cold light didn't flatter Forsythia's shade of blonde.

He sank to the floor, the creases on his brow drawn stark and black. "What do I need to do?"

"Keep still, and hold this." She set the lock of hair on his palm, and his fingers convulsed around it. Next she laid her mirror between them, directly under the floating light.

"Ilora Lizveteva. By flesh and memory I call you, and by the name of your birth."

A shiver answered; the woman's soul wasn't yet lost. But neither did she respond. Isyllt repeated the invocation. This time the shiver was stronger, a wordless denial. Something opposed her, something that smelled of sorcery and cinnamon, rust and copper. Blood, and blood magic.

Despite many superstitions, necromancy and haematurgy had little in common. Blood had just as much to do with life; Isyllt's magic began when the last red pulse slowed and cooled. But any street witch or charmwife knew how powerful blood was in spellcasting. She slipped a scalpel from her kit and stripped her gloves off with her teeth.

The blade traced a cold line down her palm, beside the

scar of the wound that had broken bone and severed tendon. Heat followed a heartbeat later, and crimson raveled across the creases of her palm.

"Ilora Lizveteva, I call you with blood, with flesh and memory and the name of your birth."

She shuddered with the force of the conjury, and still Forsythia resisted. The magic and her recalcitrance were separate—the former weakened while the latter grew.

Isyllt realized her error then, and bit back a disruptive curse. She clenched her bleeding hand and hissed as pain spread up her arm. "Forsythia. With blood and pain and the name of your heart, I call you."

The magic stretched like a wire and snapped. Isyllt's head whipped back with the force of it and Mekaran hissed. The light in the mirror splintered and scattered as the ghost burst through the glass with a wail. Isyllt's ring pulsed bright as a star.

In the echoing silence that followed, Isyllt heard the chaos below still, imagined the cold chill that rushed down a dozen spines simultaneously. Then the song resumed, louder than ever.

Forsythia stood in front of Isyllt, arms folded miserably across her stomach. Her ethereal form shimmered softly, pale and drained of color. Death dulled her brazen hair and turned her low-cut dress a drab shade of grey. Her slender throat was unmarred, but when she spoke it was a ragged whisper.

"What do you want?"

"L—Lori?" The steel had left Mekaran's voice, replaced by grief and fear. "Is it really you?"

The wraith turned, and the brush of her skirts chilled Isyllt's legs to the bone. "Meka?"

Mekaran scrambled to his feet, one hand reaching for his friend. He recoiled before Isyllt could warn him away—the embraces of the dead offered no comfort, only a sepulchral chill. "It's me, Lori." Tears shimmered silver in the ghostlight and left streaks of kohl down his cheeks.

"I told you not to call me that." She twisted away, hair coiling around her face as she tilted her head.

Isyllt pushed herself backward and onto the bed. "Forsythia." Now that she knew its power, the name rang in the air. The ghost turned to her, and her eyes were puddles of shadow threatening to spill down her cheeks.

"Who are you?"

"My name is Isyllt. I'm trying to find the person who killed you."

One white hand flew to her throat, then knotted in the neck of her gown. She shook her head, and her other hand clenched in her skirts. "I can't. I can't."

"You can," Isyllt said. "I have to stop them, and you're the only one who can help me."

Even the dead could be coaxed. Forsythia drifted closer. "I was—I was waiting for Whisper." Her hands kept fretting with her dress, and she lowered her face and hid behind the veil of her hair. "I can't. It's gone."

"You were waiting for Whisper," Isyllt said, low and soft. "In the alley off the Street of Thistles. It was sunset, and the sky glowed. Birds flew past the rooftops." If the witness had been alive, she might have taken her hands and sat her down, but this memory-walk would have to be done without a soothing touch.

"Birds," Forsythia whispered, fingers twitching. "Birds watching me, following me for days. Whisper promised to meet me. We were going to disappear, leave the Garden and the tunnels and find somewhere safe. But he didn't come."

"What happened next?" Isyllt prompted when the silence stretched.

"Someone else came. Another vampire—his hands so cold and strong. I couldn't see, and then he pressed a rag to my face." She shook her head, hugging her shoulders. "It smelled awful, sharp and sickly sweet, and then there was nothing."

"Sweet vitriol," Isyllt muttered. A physician's drug, or a slaver's. "This other vampire—you're sure it wasn't Whisper?"

"Of course! He would never hurt me. And when this one grabbed me, he was taller than Whisper."

"Do you remember anything else?"

The ghost nodded miserably. "I woke again later. I don't know how long. My eyes were still covered."

"What else did you notice?"

"It was cold. The air was stale and I could still smell the stink of the drug. I lay on stone—my leg was numb from it. They were talking. Arguing."

"They?"

"The vampire and a woman."

"What did they say?"

"He said...I was a distraction, and I had to be dealt with. That Whisper was endangering the tunnels with his visits and gifts." Her hand rose to the neck of her dress again, and Isyllt wondered if that was where the ring had been sewn. "She said—" She shook her head again. "I don't know. I was cold and scared and confused, and I couldn't concentrate. I'm not remembering it right."

"You're doing fine." Isyllt stood and took Forsythia's

cold ephemeral hands in hers after all. Her bones ached by the time she eased the dead woman onto the edge of the bed. "Everything you can think of will help me." Behind them, Dahlia scrambled away from the spreading chill. The room was too small for four people, even if one was less substantial than the rest.

"I couldn't concentrate," the woman said again, calmer now. "I felt sick, and I was sure if I moved I would vomit. My head ached. And even worse, my skin crawled like I was covered in insects. Everything felt... wrong. Not only me, but the air, the stones under me. I couldn't even be frightened, it was so terrible. I've never felt anything like it."

Isyllt frowned; she had, only days ago. But she couldn't trust too much in the memories of a woman blind and sick with drugs. "What did the woman say?"

"I don't remember." She sounded regretful now, not defensive. "I was too busy trying not to be sick. But at first I thought she didn't want to kill me. Then she was standing over me and she was angry. *You let them use you,* she said, *and now you'll die for it, and no one will save you or mourn for you. You'll be forgotten.* I was terrified then, and crying, and she knelt and caught my face in her hands. *None of us are innocent,* she said. Her hands were cold and strong as the vampire's, but all I could smell was her perfume— orange and cinnamon. Then they hauled me up. I vomited, and they swore but didn't let go. I was screaming and choking. I tried to fight but they were both too strong."

Forsythia shook now, a deep bone-wracking shudder; Isyllt shook too, from shared horror and chill. Mekaran leaned close, his painted mask cracking with grief, but either fear or sense kept him from interrupting.

"They bent me over a table. Hands on my arms and hands in my hair, and I couldn't tell who held me and who held the knife. The blade was cold for an instant, and then hot—the blood was hot and then cold where it soaked my dress. I couldn't breathe, couldn't scream, couldn't get the stink of blood and bile out of my nose. Everything grew colder and colder—"

As she spoke, the white skin of her throat parted and tenebrous black blood spooled down her chest. Her mouth worked but her voice faded to a wet hiccupping gasp. Panic twisted her face and the darkness in her eyes spilled free as well. The temperature plummeted as terror and pain gave her strength.

The last of her restraint broke and Isyllt pulled the dead woman into her arms, held her as she shook and whispered to her low and fast. "It's all right. It's over. They can't hurt you anymore. You're free of them, and you don't have to wear their shackles." She wrapped a hand over the wound, pressing icy flesh together. Her ring blazed so fiercely the shadow of her bones showed through.

"Rest," she murmured, each breath a frosted plume. "Rest, Forsythia, Ilora. Stay with me. I'll keep you safe. I'll find them, I swear. I'll stop them." Madness, to make vows to the dead, madness and folly, but the woman wept like a child in her lap and the words tumbled past her lips before she could stop them. "I'll stop them."

With one last sob, Forsythia faded. The diamond flared once as a new soul entered, then dimmed. The room was black without its light.

Isyllt's pulse roared in her ears, drowning the song and voices below, dulling the closer sounds of weeping. She tried to move, but her limbs were frozen and useless. She tumbled off the edge of the bed, landed hard on one hand and hip. Her wounded hand—the pain of that cut through pins-and-needles numbness.

Something scratched and chattered in the darkness; glass rattled against wood. A tiny opportunistic spirit trying to slip through an unguarded mirror. Isyllt pressed her bleeding hand to the cold surface and banished it with a word. She fumbled the silk cover over the glass and shoved it back into her kit as the lamp glowed to life again.

Mekaran and Dahlia both wept. The thorn had fallen to his knees, while the girl pressed a fist against her mouth hard enough to split skin.

"What happened?" he asked, stopping before he scrubbed his cheeks. "Where is she?"

"Safe," Isyllt rasped. The cold had stolen her voice. "Resting." Her teeth began to chatter. She stumbled twice as she stood. She needed to rest, to get warm, but she couldn't stay in this narrow coffin of a room any longer. Mekaran called her back as she fumbled with the door, but she only shook her head.

The warmer air of the hall dizzied her, the smells of beer and food and sweat. She tripped on an uneven floorboard, staggered into the wall hard enough to send a sharp shock down her right arm, and fell to her knees in a tangle of skirts.

A worn pair of boots stopped in front of her and a familiar voice spoke her name.

"C—Ciaran?" She could hardly raise her head. The chill in her bones curved her spine into a fetal hunch.

"Saints and shadows," he whispered. "What have you done to yourself this time?"

Footsteps shivered through the floor as Mekaran and

Dahlia followed. Ciaran cut off Mekaran's stammered explanation. "Later. I'll take care of her."

He crouched beside her and wound an arm under hers; his flesh burned. She barely kept her legs from buckling as he hauled her to her feet. "You have to walk," he told her. "My room is another flight up and you're too tall to carry up these stairs."

"I'm not staying."

"You're not leaving—there's rioting outside the Garden. Besides, you'd stay in this hall all night if I dropped you. I'd like to think my bed is the more pleasant option."

She gave up arguing and concentrated on moving her feet. And, when she finally collapsed on to Ciaran's bed and breathed in the musk and spices that lingered in his pillow, she was forced to agree. He piled blankets on top of her and kindled the brazier. Light glowed through cut brass, tracing filigree patterns across the walls and ceiling. Isyllt closed her eyes and curled tighter. Feeling returned to her extremities, but the ice settled thick and deep in her core.

The bed creaked as Ciaran wedged himself between her and the wall and held her close. It wasn't wide enough for two, but that had never stopped them before.

"You push yourself too hard." His beard tickled her neck, but she couldn't pull away. "You'll die if you don't stop this."

"Maybe not even then."

"What do you mean?"

It was not the sort of thing to be spoken of, but she was too numb to care. "You know the old stories of necromancers being beheaded and burned when they die? They aren't just superstition. We have the choice, at the end—or so I'm told. We can let our souls depart for the other side of the mirror, or we can stay. Either as powerful specters, or as the undead." Necrophants, the risen mages were called, and even the Arcanostoi said the word softly or not at all.

This must be what it felt like to die, Isyllt thought, cold and aching and hollow. She couldn't imagine an eternity of this, no matter how powerful it might make her.

Ciaran stilled, his breath rough. Then he squeezed her and kissed her neck. "I prefer living women."

She laughed, and the ice began to crack. As it melted, she began to sob. For Forsythia, for all the dead flowers whom no one mourned, for all the cold and hollow dead. Tears scalded her cheeks and soaked the pillow until, finally warm again, she slept.

She woke later to stuffy heat and the fire died to embers. Blankets tangled around her legs and sweat stuck her dress to her back. She grimaced at the taste of salt thick in her mouth.

Ciaran sat on a chest by the window, rolling a wine bottle between his palms and frowning at the night-black glass. A draft rolled over the cracked-open casement, and the single candle flame danced with it. The earlier ruckus had faded, and from the depth of the silence she guessed it must be the final terce. Release, Selafaïns called this hour, for all the deaths and births that it witnessed. Her mother had called it the wolf's hour. The night smelled faintly of smoke.

"The riots have stopped," Ciaran said, not turning from the window. "The Vigils finally came, after a few shop windows were broken and fires started." He glanced back at her. "Feeling better?"

"Mostly. I think that wine might help the rest."

He uncoiled from his perch and hopped lightly from chest to bed without touching the floor or spilling the bottle. He'd been a wire-thin sneak thief when they'd met fifteen years ago—food and wine and less sneaking had thickened his waist since, and put more flesh over his ribs, but he still had a tumbler's grace.

Isyllt took the offered bottle as he settled beside her. Syrah, thick and sweet and well-fortified; she rolled a mouthful over her tongue to wash away the taste of sleep and tears. She handed it back after another long pull. "Thank you." She trusted him to know she meant for more than the wine.

The liquor brought a flush to her cheeks, which worsened the discomfort of her clinging dress. She rose to undo the laces, kicking the gown away when it puddled around her feet. It reminded her too much of Forsythia's pale fragility. Gooseflesh crawled over her limbs as she moved in front of the draft. She expected Ciaran to flirt or tease, but he stayed quiet, still frowning at his wine. She waited, lifting her hair to let the breeze cool her sticky neck.

"Azarné came to watch me play tonight," he said at last.

"Oh," she said, and marveled at her own wit. "I thought you preferred living women."

His mouth quirked. "I do." Finally he looked at her and set the wine aside. She took the invitation and sat beside him again. "Even ones half-starved and pale as you." He dropped a kiss on her shoulder, but his heart wasn't in it. "But—"

"But she's beautiful anyway," she finished. "Do mice find cats beautiful, before the kill? Or owls?"

"If mice have poets, I think they must. I understand how Forsythia could have been seduced."

Isyllt thought of the lure of Whisper's eyes, the shiver Spider's touch gave her. "Yes." She ran her fingers across Ciaran's shoulders, over the sensitive place at the nape of his neck to watch him shudder. "Will you be safe?"

"Are any of us?" He kissed her shoulder again, lingeringly this time. "This room is warded, though, and I always watch where I walk at night. Will you?"

She pressed her face against his neck to hide her frown, but imagined he felt it anyway. She couldn't turn aside from Forsythia now, and that meant hunting vampires and blood-sorcerers. She laid a hand on his chest. "As safe as I ever am."

Ciaran's chuckle reverberated beneath her palm. "I don't find myself comforted." He eased the straps of her shift off her shoulders and her skin roughened in the wake of his touch.

Her fingers tightened in his hair, baring the line of his throat. "I'll distract you from your discomfort." Her tongue flicked across his collarbone, and his breath caught.

The bed was still too narrow, but that had never stopped them before.

CHAPTER 10

Savedra woke to a soft, insistent tap on the door. She had a moment of disorientation at the unfamiliar bed and the different echo of knuckles on wood. Annoyance chased confusion when she realized the sky beyond the window was still a dull pre-dawn grey. By the time she'd stumbled out of bed and found a robe, she recognized the rhythm of the knock as Ashlin's.

"What is it?" she asked, tugging the door open. Her mouth was dry and sour with last night's wine, her head thick—she should remember to stick to brandy. Her back still ached, and her limbs were as stiff as Ashlin had promised.

Ashlin was already dressed and moving much too quickly. She paced a quick circuit of the room while Savedra shut and relatched the door. "How far is it to the Sarken border?"

"What?" She rubbed her eyes and sank onto the edge of the bed. "I don't know. A day's ride, maybe, or less. Why?"

"Your missing relative married a march-lord, didn't she? So maybe that's where we'll find news of her."

Savedra blinked. "This couldn't have waited till dawn?"

"Not if it's a day's ride. You've had your paper chase, now let's try something more tangible."

She wanted to argue, or simply crawl back into bed, but there was a logic in it, and Ashlin's bright-eyed enthusiasm was beginning to penetrate her wine-fogged wits. "You have a lot of border-riding experience, don't you, *Sorcha*?"

Ashlin grinned. "I may have stolen some Vallish honey in my misspent youth. And I could hardly do that under my own name, could I? It would be indiscreet."

Savedra snorted. "Cahal said you were self-destructive."

Dyed eyebrows quirked. "Did he now? Well, not that destructive, at least. Not so much as to make my father go to war to ransom me. Come on—you might be dressed before noon if you hurry."

In spite of Ashlin's teasing and her own preference for leisurely mornings, Savedra stamped on her riding boots as the sun crested the lowest slopes of the Varagas. Her face stung from harsh alchemical depilatory powder, and her hair was an unhappy tangle of braids and pins without a maid and an hour of combing, but she was dressed.

Iancu awaited them in the kitchen. The lines on his face seemed to have deepened overnight, which tied a hard knot of guilt behind her breastbone. But despite the fatigue shadows, his eyes were sharp with interest. He wore riding clothes as well.

"This may well gain us nothing," he warned, though

the speed with which he packed bread and apples and jerky belied the caution. "But it's worth investigating. We can reach Valcov well before dusk with a steady pace."

They rode wide-chested, sure-footed trail horses with dark liver chestnut hides and striking flaxen manes. Ashlin was smitten with her mare as soon as she mounted, and spent much of the ride crooning to the beast in Celanoran. Cahal rode rear guard, his dark eyes moving constantly and a bow ready at his back.

East of Arachne the hills rose wild. The lower slopes of the Varagas were thick with silver firs and sun-hungry oaks and beeches decked in brilliant autumn copper; beneath the canopy ferns and fungus carpeted the ground, and moss cloaked falls of dead wood. A green twilight held the underbrush, broken by stray shafts of light. Woodpeckers drummed the grey bark of snags, a sharp tattoo to accompany the horses' rhythmic four-beat gait and the dry-bone crunch of leaves. Wind swept the upper branches with a hollow rush, dancing spears of light across the ground and stirring the heavy scent of loam and pine and leaf must with the more immediate pungency of warm horse.

Lovely and scenic, a welcome relief from the city's smells and sounds and narrow streets. It ought to have been, at least. Instead Savedra could only watch the shadows for any flicker of movement. Too early for wolves to grow bold, but there were always bandits, and today her head was full of witches and spirits and things hungry for living blood, despite the reassurance of the wards that lined the road. Sometimes she thought she heard a soft tinkle of bells, and remembered the dancing wood nymphs of Iancu's stories. Not the deadliest of forest spirits by far, but she was just as glad she saw no further sign of them.

The horses navigated the steep trails easily and by early afternoon they were in the highest hills. The chill in the air sharpened, and soon they heard the rush and froth of the Ardoş, which split from the Herodis and flowed into the Zaratan Sea. The river's deep-carven chasm marked the border between Selafai and Sarkany.

The village of Valcov straddled the divide, comfortable in the centuries of peace between its parent nations. Sarkany was more concerned with the Ordozh raiders in the north and Iskar to the south, and Selafai's longest grudge was with Assar across the sea.

Townsfolk eyed them curiously as they rode past the sprawling stone-and-timber wall that enfolded the clustered stone-and-timber buildings. They passed fields of turnips and cabbage and winter wheat, and smelled sheep and goats before they neared the pens. When the wind shifted Savedra caught the greater stench of a tannery and mill smoke; the clatter and rasp of lumber-working echoed in the distance.

The center of town smelled more invitingly of a bakery and cooking from the tavern. They watered the horses and tethered them in front of the inn; Savedra, Ashlin, and Cahal went in while Iancu vanished quietly to search for information. As quietly as a stranger in a small town could ask questions, anyway.

"Try not to steal any honey," Savedra told Ashlin as they entered the tavern.

Her stomach rumbled at the smell of meat and herbs, and she ordered ale and venison pies in badly accented Sarken, pretending not to notice how the conversation in

the low dim-lit room faltered around them. She paid with
a silver griffin and received Sarken pennies in change.
Dull silver glinted amid the copper—a thin, uneven coin
engraved with an owl on one side and crude letters on the
other. She knew it from Iancu's stories, too—a striga, or
witch-coin. If she were a sorceress or a disguised spirit
the silver would burn her fingers or glow at her touch. It
stayed cool and slick, and she caught the tavern keeper's
eye as she sorted it from the rest of the change, thanking
him and tucking it into her inner breast pocket. Courtesy
for offered luck, instead of outrage at the implied insult.
The man had the grace to blush, and was very solicitous
in refilling their mugs afterward.

The pies were filled with meat and berries and thyme,
sharp and bittersweet and rich with iron. They ate quickly,
and Savedra sopped the last of the sauce off the notched
wooden plates. With her stomach quiet, the ache in her
thighs and back became more noticeable—another mug
of ale might have helped, but she had to get back on the
horse eventually.

The light spilling across the threshold changed before
Iancu returned, deepening to a watery honey. The bar-
tender had begun shooting them pointed glances, and
Savedra was about to succumb to a third mug of ale to
placate him when Iancu's shadow fell through the doorway. A young woman waited for him outside, and another
awkward stillness rippled through the room as the patrons
saw her.

"I've found someone to help us," Iancu said, stooping
over the table to speak softly. "Apparently there's only one
woman left in Valcov who can."

They left Cahal behind to watch the horses and

followed the dark-eyed woman. She didn't offer her name or any other conversation as she led them to the far side of town. Her black braids were held back in a kerchief, but beads still rattled as she walked; her embroidered skirts rasped with her purposeful stride. She must have been years younger than Savedra, perhaps no more than twenty, but the villagers stepped aside for her in the street with hasty nods. Was she a witch like Varis's mystery guest?

They stopped at a small house on the outskirts of town, where buildings gave way to fields. Smoke trickled from the chimney and the shutters were open to the breeze. The woman stopped in front of the open door, waving them in and saying something to Iancu that sounded like a warning. Her voice rasped, as with long disuse.

"Her grandmother may help us," Iancu said. "We are bid be solicitous of her poor health."

The house was a single open room, the curtained bed the only privacy it offered. A spinning wheel stood beneath one window, surrounded by brushes and baskets of uncarded wool and a fat butter-colored cat who eyed a coil of yarn. Charms hung from the rafters, strings of leaves and beads and coins that rustled and chimed in the breeze. The room smelled of herbs and wool and camphor. In a much-mended rocking chair beside the hearth sat an old woman.

She was frail and stooped, skin creased and thin over once-strong bones and cheeks sunken with missing teeth. One side of her face drooped like hot wax, and her left arm folded unmoving in her lap. A cane leaned against the wall within reach of her chair.

She studied them with one canny dark eye—the other veiled by its creased-paper lid—while Iancu asked his questions. Savedra knew enough Sarken for courtesies and bad directions, but not enough to follow his low urgent tone. When the woman replied her voice was slurred and slow and even less comprehensible. She dabbed her mouth constantly with a handkerchief to keep from drooling. They spoke for several moments, not quite an argument. The woman tried to shake her head, but it was more a feeble twitch.

"*Vau roc*," Iancu said, several times. Please.

Finally the woman made an angry slashing gesture with her right hand. At first Savedra feared she was throwing them out, but then she began to speak.

"I remember," Iancu translated softly, keeping pace with her muttered Sarken. "I remember Phaedra Darvulia, and sometimes I think remembering is what broke my body and my magic. I would trade these memories for my health, but not even gods make such bargains."

Ashlin sank to her knees and Savedra followed, sitting cross-legged on the creaking floorboards like children.

"It was like a minstrel's story," Iancu continued. "A beautiful girl went riding in the woods and became lost. A handsome hunter rescued her and took her home, and they fell in love. Bells rang in the castle and the village on their wedding day, and bright ribbons flew from the battlements of Carnavas. The women wore flowers in their hair as the bride and groom rode by.

"The girl was a witch, and perhaps a little mad—prone to black moods and wild frenzies—but she and her marchlord husband loved each other, and the village loved her in turn. She often spent the winters in the south with her own people, and the mountains were all the colder without her.

"What happened next no one can say for certain. Raiders came. Some say from the north, some from the east; some say they were demons of the frozen wind. I say they came from the south, but I'm the only one who remembers it so. Wherever they came from, whatever they were, their weapons were sharp enough. When villagers came to the castle days later they found only frozen corpses. The lord lay dead in his hall, stabbed through the heart and his sword in his hand. The servants had been rounded up and slaughtered like sheep. Of the lady there was no sign, but her library and workrooms were destroyed. The villagers searched the woods and riverbanks for her but found no trace, though some claimed to have seen blood on the rocks below the castle ramparts.

"We buried the lord and his people, but the castle became home to ghosts and hungry spirits, more than the village witchwives could dispel. Demon birds circled the towers, and many thought them the lady's pets driven mad by her death. The Sarken king sent no new lord to hold it, and the Selafaïns staked no claim, so villagers circled it with salt and wards and left it to molder in its grief."

She fell silent, mopping her chin and frowning lopsidedly. Her chair creaked and clacked as she rocked, and wood fell in the hearth with a flurry of sparks. Dust motes danced and settled in the slanting light. After a long moment she spoke again, the words even more muffled now by the handkerchief.

"The forgetting came not long after, like a fog over the mountains. The castle stands, and everyone remembers the lord, but no one remembers the name of his wife."

Her gaze, distant with memory, sharpened again as she squinted at Iancu. He nodded to her question, then glanced at Savedra. "She asks if we mean to go there. I assume we do."

Visiting a haunted ruin at twilight didn't seem the best idea, but Savedra nodded anyway. She reached for her purse, but the woman made another dismissive gesture.

"She says that she's done us no favors," Iancu said. "But her granddaughter will show us the trail. And that we should hurry."

"Thank you," Savedra said, scrambling to her feet. The woman only shook her head.

The sun hovered a finger's width over the serrated teeth of the Varagas, already peach-red and swollen. The young witch pointed them toward the road that led to the castle and turned away when their feet were on it, vanishing back into the village.

Valcov lay on a small plateau; past the edge of town the road dropped away and valleys and ridges fell like wrinkled cloth, the tangled skirts of the mountains soaring sharp and cold to their right. Somewhere north and west the Varagas gave way to gentle hills and fields which in turn rolled toward the sea, but from this vantage there was only stone and trees and snow high on the peaks, and the wide crush of sky.

The castle Carnavas brooded on the edge of a cliff, overlooking Valcov from one side and the icy rush of the Ardoş from the other. It would have been a forbidding place in any light, but as dusk crawled from the roots of the mountains, it was all too easy to imagine the specters stirring in empty halls. Dark shapes wheeled against the sky, vanishing into the towers; birds home to roost for the night.

"This is as close as we go tonight," Iancu said. Not even

Ashlin argued. But they stood and stared, shivering as the evening chill chewed through layers of cloth, caught in the ruin's spell. The last of the daylight lined the western sky with apricot.

"Tomorrow," Savedra said. The steadiness of her voice surprised her. But they'd come this far, and they certainly weren't about to ride back to Evharis in the dark.

With a glance between them they turned away, hurrying back to the warmth and walls of the inn.

That night Savedra and Ashlin lay back to back in their shared bed. It was a small inn, and they could forsake luxuries for a night. Iancu and Cahal shared the room across the hall.

"What do you think?" Savedra asked, the words muffled by the pillow. The bedding smelled of down must, and the pungent straw beneath the featherbed.

"It's an interesting puzzle. Your whole family is interesting." The last she said so dryly that Savedra elbowed her in the ribs.

"None of that," the princess said with a laugh. "They'll charge us extra if we have a pillow fight."

Savedra chuckled. She'd never shared a bed with anyone but Nikos, not since she was too old to sleep with her mother or her nurse after a bad dream. Lovers, yes, but not the quiet—or in this case creaking with every shifted arm—warmth of another body. Ashlin had no sisters, and Savedra wondered if she'd ever had to share. After a drowsing moment, she asked.

"My brother used to crawl into bed with me when he was scared, in case monsters snuck into the room," said the princess. "I had more weapons at hand than our nurse."

The bed frame creaked as she rolled over and her breath brushed warm across Savedra's shoulder. "On cold nights my riders and I would sleep like puppies, as many in the tent as would fit. Cahal, by the way, snores like a pig and steals the blankets besides. You smell nicer than any of them. And there was one season—" Her voice broke. "I had a lover."

Savedra had known it, of course, but the words were so soft and rushed, so stripped of all Ashlin's usual prickles and armor, that her breath caught in her throat.

"Only for the autumn. Then I was called back to Yselin, and the betrothal moved forward, and.... Well, you know the rest of that." She sighed. "It was nice while it lasted."

Fabric rustled and Savedra felt a gentle tug on her hair—Ashlin's fingers twining in her braids. The sensation prickled her skin. When Savedra raised her face from the pillow she smelled her: garlic and wine from supper, herbal soap and weapon oil, and under that the sweeter musk of her skin.

"I envy you, you know. The bond, if not the man."

"I'm sorry," she whispered.

Bedding rustled and she imagined Ashlin's shrug. "It's not your fault. I could have run away and become a mercenary. It isn't all bad—I do like Erisinian food." She tugged gently on one braid. "How did you end up with hair like this, anyway? I've seen your parents."

Savedra accepted the graceless change of subject gladly. "My mother likes to blame the Iskari on my father's side of the family." She smiled into the dark, remembering her mother's quiet profanity as yet another delicate sandalwood comb broke in her hair. "My father always reminds her of her own Assari grandmother."

They lay in silence while wind whispered around the eaves and the inn creaked and sighed softly to itself. Finally Ashlin's breath roughened and her hands rested, still tangled in Savedra's hair. By the time Savedra slept, the princess was curled warm against her back.

She woke the next morning huddled in a ball and stinging with gooseflesh. Ashlin stood before the open window, silhouetted against a lead-and-rose sky. She turned when Savedra stirred, grinning like a child. "Get up," she said. "It's snowing."

They left for the castle at daybreak. No one warned them away or tried to stop them, though from the way the innkeeper shook his head he thought the mission was folly. He pressed charms on them as they left—cords strung with beads of wood and tarnished silver—and a small pouch that settled like sand against Savedra's palm. Salt, from the smell, and anise or fennel. She thanked the man in mangled Sarken.

Folly or not, their mission was certainly trespass, and on foreign soil no less. Ashlin might be used to such things, but Savedra's head was crowded with visions of Sarken warlords riding down on them and demanding explanations. The hills were empty, though, save for the usual skitter and scurry of wildlife and birds wheeling overhead.

Snow fell in slow fat flakes that melted when they hit the ground. The sky hung low against the mountains, clouds shredding on their peaks, while sunrise pink and gold cooled to grey. The snow was soft but the wind cut like a razor, mocking Savedra's autumn clothing.

The road became overgrown the closer they rode to the

castle. In better light Savedra saw grey crystals glittering amid dirt and pebbles only a few yards past where they had turned back the night before; the salt of the villagers' wards. She touched the bag of herbs and salt in her coat pocket. Despite the fabled mystic senses of the hijra, all she felt was cloth and rasping grains. Likewise the cord around her neck felt no more powerful than the pearls she wore at court.

At the foot of the steep, tree-choked slope they found a long ruin that must have once been a stable. The roof had collapsed, and all it housed now were weeds. A rabbit burst from cover when they drew too close, vanishing into the undergrowth with a white flash of tail. In the shadows behind the building, stone steps led up the hill.

After scouting the area, they left the horses tethered in the dubious shelter of the stable, unconcernedly cropping grass. The animals' calm was reassuring—beasts, unlike most humans, could sense ghosts or strong spirits.

The stairs were cracked and crooked, flagstones washed away and pushed aside by tree roots. Savedra lost count after seven hundred, and they were no more than halfway up. Leaves and fallen pine needles crunched and skittered with every step, sometimes obscuring broken stones and ankle-turning holes. Before long she could hardly hear the crackle of leaves beneath boots over the wheeze of her breath. Sweat soaked her back and her legs and lungs ached to burning. Even Ashlin was winded, and she took some satisfaction in that.

Near the summit, the path cleared the tangled trees, wrapping around the edge of the cliff for several yards before climbing again. To the left, only a few feet of rocks and weeds and scrubby grass separated their feet from a long drop. Far below the Ardoş snaked around the cliff, and pine-thick hills rose on the other side. Snowflakes swirled and spiraled and vanished into grey haze; Savedra regretted her downward glance immediately. The right-hand view was safer, but still breathtaking in its height. And ahead of them the fortress rose, a towering weight of age-stained stone. After a moment's rest they kept walking, into its shadow.

By the time they reached the final landing, Savedra had no more strength to admire the view. Instead she sat with her back to the hulking gate, laying her head on her knees and waiting for her breath and heart to slow. Her side ached like a knife between her ribs and her racing pulse made her nauseous. Ghosts or demons were welcome to eat her, if it meant she didn't have to get up again.

"Here." Ashlin crouched beside her, passing a water skin and a wedge of oily cheese. "Slowly," she cautioned as Savedra lifted the bag.

When her stomach ceased its seasick roil and the pain in her side faded, she rose to face the castle.

Carnavas was a fortress, not a palace like those in Eri-sín. The hulk that loomed above them was solid, heavy walls and arrow-slit windows, built for defense. Built to last for centuries, but twenty-seven years of neglect had taken their toll all the same. Moss and vines webbed the stones, and saplings pressed against the walls like an invading army.

The portcullis was raised, and unlikely to lower again. Corroded iron spikes bled rust down the narrow walls and the bird nests clogged the lattice. The ground below was crusted grey with droppings. The great ironbound double doors beyond were in no better condition, the wood dry

and splintering. One side stood ajar, a handspan gap leading into shadows. The only sound was the rustle of dry
leaves and the mournful sigh of the wind.

Cahal crouched to study the filthy ground. "No one has
passed this way recently," he said, voice hushed either in
caution or out of respect for the stillness. "And no large
animals."

"That's something, at least. I'd rather not walk into
a bandit nest." Ashlin adjusted her sword, and Savedra
checked her own dagger hanging at her waist.

"If there is anyone inside," Iancu said, "they've likely
heard us coming by now."

"Yes." Ashlin raked a hand through her sweat-stiffened
hair. "No use dithering on the doorstep." She started forward, but Cahal intercepted her with a glare.

"Wait your turn, Captain." His sword rasped free of
its scabbard; the steel gathered pale daylight and cast a
watery shimmer against the wall. He braced his free arm
against the door, and Savedra held her breath.

Wood creaked and groaned, then swung inward with a
shriek of rusted hinges. The sound echoed like a scream.
A flock of birds burst from a nearby tree with a rattle of
branches, croaking disapproval. Savedra flinched, and
Ashlin grimaced. Cahal ducked and crouched behind the
other half of the door, waiting for a response.

None came, and the echoes faded into the sighing wind.
The birds settled in another tree, glaring indignantly at
the clumsy humans.

"Well," Cahal said at last, uncoiling from his crouch.
"Now the ghosts really know we're here."

The old witch's story had filled Savedra's head with
visions of corpse-strewn halls, skeletons clutching rusted

weapons or ghosts wailing and screaming for revenge; the ghosts in her imagination looked suspiciously like stage specters in artfully tattered shrouds and greasepaint. None of that confronted them as they stepped into the narrow courtyard.

The stones were fouled with dead weeds and leaves and bird droppings, and feathers drifted like dark snow in the corners. Vines cocooned the well and the wooden cover was broken and half fallen away. The yard smelled of stone and damp and mildew, shit and the sharper pungency of cat urine. Savedra pinched her nose against a sneeze. The ground *was* littered with bones—they crunched alarmingly as she stepped farther in—but they were tiny fragile things. Mice and fallen birds, not the castle's slain guardians.

Despite the stink and ominous doors and hallways and broken-shuttered windows that stared down at them, an ache spread behind Savedra's breastbone. It must have been a pleasant place once—empty flower boxes hung beneath windows, and rotten trellises climbed the walls, tangled with browned roses. Drifting snow and the slanting morning light lent the yard a ruined, antique beauty. Like yellowed lace, or funeral art.

Something hissed in the shadows and Savedra yelped. Eyes flashed copper-green in the gloom of a doorway and Ashlin's hand closed on her sword hilt. A heartbeat later Cahal laughed at both of them as a scruffy striped cat bolted up a flight of stairs and vanished down a gallery. Ashlin laughed too, but touched her shoulder to Savedra's in mutual reassurance.

They startled a few mice and feral cats as they explored the ground floor, and one sleepy owl, but found no other signs of life or unlife. Signs of the previous inhabitants were all around them, though. Beans spilled out of rotted bags in the pantries, and jars of preserves encased in dust lined the shelves. Dishes still littered the kitchen counters, and drawers held crumbling receipts and recipes and lists of stores. The altar in the narrow chapel was spotted with wax, the candles toppled and chewed by rodents. A few tarnished silver sconces still clung to the walls, while others had fallen to reveal cleaner stone beneath. The icons of whatever saints or gods the Sarkens prayed to were darkened and unrecognizable. Moth-eaten clothes and linens filled chests in the servants' quarters, and hints of lives littered the rooms: a shelf of moldering books; a carven box filled with needles and buttons and an ivory thimble; a pair of shoes heavy with once-bright embroidery, much too fine to be worn for daily chores. Paintings hung in flaking frames, long-faded portraits or hunting scenes.

The second story was much the same—no corpses, no waiting monsters, but memories thick as cobwebs everywhere. No one spoke as they searched the rooms, and Iancu's face grew sadder and more strained with each vanished life they found.

On the next floor a painting watched them as they climbed the stairs. A woman sat in the foreground, white-skinned and sable-haired, with dark eyes and beautiful cheekbones still visible beneath the web of cracks that marred the oils. A man stood behind her chair, one hand on her shoulder. He was tall and lean and well-dressed, but his face was too chipped and shadowed to make out.

Ferenz III Darvulesti, the tiny plaque read, *Margrave of Carnavas, and the Margravine Phaedra*.

"Who are you?" Savedra murmured, raising a hand to

the painting and pulling back before she touched the canvas. The frame was grey with dust, but her hands were worse. Her nose had long since closed off in self-defense.

"Who indeed?" Iancu asked softly, standing beside her. Savedra studied his face for any hint of recognition, but his frown only deepened.

"Here," Cahal called. He kindled a lantern and held it aloft. Their own footprints showed stark against the pale drifting dust, but other, fainter prints were visible beneath it. Like tracks in trampled snow clear beneath a fresh fall. Short, narrow feet—a woman or a small man.

"How old are these?" Savedra asked.

Cahal shrugged, sending orange light swaying across the walls. "Hard to say."

The tracks led down the corridor to a bedroom that must have belonged to the Margrave, and crisscrossed the floor there. Bed hangings pulled free of the great oaken frame, and the lantern cast their shadows like great tattered wings across the walls.

Savedra and Ashlin tugged back the curtains and pried the shutters open. The windows facing the cliffside were wider than those overlooking the path; anyone who could scale the cliff and the walls deserved to take the castle. The panes were glass—warped, leaded diamonds. A great extravagance, no doubt, whenever Carnavas had first been built.

Savedra studied the room and the footprints. They led to all the places one might expect in a bedroom: the bed; the wardrobe; the dresser, whose mirror was shattered and turned toward the wall. The dust blanketing the sagging mattress was disturbed as well, as if someone had curled against the pillow. She touched the dimpled cloth, almost expecting some ghost of warmth there. Her fingertips left shadows behind, and she rubbed the silk-soft grime onto her coat. She brushed against the velvet hangings as she turned, and a panel tore free of the bed frame with a snarl. The cloth fell with a muffled *whump* and a billow of grey. She sneezed until her eyes and nose ran. Her hands were grey as well, and every inch of exposed skin itched.

Behind the carven doors of the wardrobe she found dresses, rotten as the bed curtains, fur and jeweled trim pulling free of fragile cloth. Dark, striking colors, garnet and crimson and deep forest green, the sort the woman in the portrait would have worn well. A tall woman, with a narrow waist and a bosom that Savedra could only envy. Mostly heavy, tight-laced gowns suitable for mountain weather, with a few looser high-waisted designs hung to one side.

"Vedra."

Ashlin's voice, unusually soft, distracted her from inspecting the dressing table. The princess stood in the doorway of one of the adjoining rooms. A bathroom, Savedra had assumed, or perhaps a connecting bedroom if the margrave and margravine hadn't shared a bed.

Instead she peered around Ashlin's shoulder into a nursery. The shutters stood open and daylight poured like weak tea over a table and rocking chair, a clothing chest, and a cradle. The faint draft of the door opening sent motes spiraling through the slanting light.

"They had a child," Savedra said, soft as a whisper.

"No." Again that queer hush in Ashlin's voice. Her hand twitched toward the blanketless cradle, toward the table and the half-knitted cap there, stitches still on the needles. "They were expecting one." Fingers clenched, and her fist fell hard against her thigh.

Savedra's mouth opened, closed again on the princess's name. "Sorcha—" Not very convincing, but it drew a humorless laugh from Ashlin.

"It's nothing."

Savedra caught the other woman's arm as she strode toward the bedroom; her fingers smeared grey on Ashlin's sleeve. "It isn't—"

"It *is*." She twitched her arm free. "Leave it be. It doesn't matter."

Bootheels clacked on stone as she vanished into the hall, leaving Savedra to turn away before Iancu noticed her prickling eyes, or her filthy hands clenching helplessly in her coat pockets. But concern and anger wouldn't let the matter lie. She blinked her eyes dry and followed, leaving Iancu and Cahal exchanging glances in her wake. Ashlin's trail was easy to follow; booted footprints led up the stairs, past the fourth story and up again, to an open trapdoor.

The wind caught at Savedra's clothes and hair as she stepped onto the tower, belled her coat-skirts and tugged at her loose trousers. Her eyes watered in earnest with the force of it, rinsing away lingering grains of dust. Ashlin stood by the crenellations, silhouetted against the pewter-bright sky. Her arms were crossed tight, cupping her elbows with opposite hands.

"I'm sorry," Savedra said after a moment of staring at the princess's back. She crossed the weathered floor to stand beside Ashlin, the span of a wide stone block between them, and peered over the edge. She regretted it before she truly realized the height, the length of the sheer plunge below. The Ardoş unwound like a grey ribbon, something delicate and ornamental, not the murderous icy rush she knew to be the truth. Not, she imagined, that the cold and current would matter by the time you reached them.

She put her back to the terrible view and sucked a calming breath through her nose. Clean air was a blessing after the stifling must below, even if it numbed her fingers and toes. She gathered her scattered thoughts and raised her voice against the wind. "It's not my place—"

That drew Ashlin around like the jerk of a chain. Snowflakes landed on her face and hair, melting to leave cleaner spots in the grime. Her eyes glittered, the green of her irises all the fiercer against bloodshot whites. "Not your place?" She barked a laugh. "To tell me when I'm being a fool, and a termagant besides? If you won't do that for me I don't know who will." Her arms snapped open. "You're my friend, Vedra. You can say whatever you want to me.

"And don't think," she said, softer now, "that I don't know your place, or that I've taken it from you."

Savedra swallowed half a dozen responses, along with a lump in her throat. "If I can tell you not to be a fool, then I'll do that now." She closed the distance between them, till the hem of her coat whipped Ashlin's legs. "I have always known how it had to be with me and Nikos. The only thing I didn't expect was to care for the woman he married."

Ashlin's smile was wry and lopsided. "I'm glad you do, since we're alone on a tower." Her smile twisted and fell away, and she waved the bad joke aside. "I wish you could have had it, though. The throne, the prince. Children." Her hand clenched on her belt buckle till her knuckles blanched. "My father could have married off my brother instead of me, if this is the best I can do at bearing heirs."

Savedra caught the princess's hand and eased it away before she could bruise her fingers on metal. "I'm sorry you're unhappy, but there's no sense in recriminations."

Their fingers twined, cold and grimy, and Ashlin squeezed tight. "It's not that I'm unhappy." Her breath hitched, unraveling on the wind. "It's that—"

Whatever she might have said was lost as black wings passed close enough to ruffle their hair and a raven alit on the merlon opposite them. Talons scraped rock as it regarded them with one dark, mirror-bright eye.

"Lady of Ravens," Ashlin breathed. For all Savedra knew, it was. The bird on the tower was certainly large enough; she hadn't realized ravens grew so big. Another bird wheeled overhead, its shadow staining the stones.

"Maybe we should go down," Savedra said, straining to keep her voice calm. "The last thing I want is bird shit in my hair."

"Good idea." She steered Savedra down the steps first, her hand on her sword until she tugged the trapdoor shut behind them. The hollow thunk chased them down the staircase.

They found Iancu and Cahal in the library, past the bedroom at the end of the hall. They stood in the center of the room, surveying the disarray around them.

Books spilled off shelves and tables, lay open on the floor. A lamp had fallen, shards scattered across the once fine carpet. The hearth still overflowed with ashes and a few scraps of withered paper. It was the first true disarray Savedra had seen, the first sign that the inhabitants hadn't simply vanished amid their daily tasks.

"There's more than one set of footprints," Cahal said, not glancing up from the span of floor he was studying.

"It took me a moment to catch it through the dust. They're nearly the same size."

A woman or a small man. A woman and a small man.

You don't know, she told herself. *You can't be sure it was Varis.* But it was too late for that—wrong or not, she was sure. What had he done here, and why?

Savedra knelt by the hearth and picked delicately through the ashes, trying to find a clue as to what had been burned. The scraps were too old, though, too faded and filthy to be legible. Most crumbled when her fingers brushed them.

"What's missing here?" she asked Iancu, but he wasn't standing beside her anymore. She turned to find him examining the opposite wall, running his hands over a stretch of wall between two decorative panels.

"Here," he murmured. His fingers paused, pressed, and something clicked. One of the panels swung outward with a creak and a silver flurry of shredded cobwebs.

Savedra closed her mouth before any more dust flew in. "Oh."

"Clever," Ashlin said. She shot a sideways glance at Savedra. "Do we have those?"

"The palace has spyholes, but no passages that I know of." She took a step forward, even as the depth of the blackness in the opening prickled her nape. The opening was set high on the wall; an awkward step without a stool. The air that breathed from the black mouth was cool and stale, but a pleasant relief from the stirred dust and ash of the library. "Maybe Nikos will add some." That careless *we* would have given the princess away to anyone paying attention, but it warmed her all the same.

Iancu lit the lamp again. The glow lined the angles

of stone stairs and brushed a low curving ceiling. "Shall we?" he asked.

Savedra caught herself touching the pocket that held the striga coin; she swept her hand in a gesture of invitation instead. "Lead on."

Tight spaces had never bothered her, unlike heights, but the chill closeness of the stairway was still oppressive. Her shoulders brushed the sides and she was glad she wasn't any taller; Iancu stooped like a hunchback.

The panel at the top of the stairs took a moment of fumbling with, but finally opened to a thin wash of daylight. She hadn't realized she'd been hoping till her hopes died—the room was a skeleton, bookshelves and tables picked clean. The old woman had mentioned a workroom, and she supposed this might have been that. But no sign of any sorcery remained now, nor any clues.

This room had the largest window in the castle, a paired casement that swung inward with a screech when Savedra tugged at the latch. Ice stung her face, falling harder now. A rusting balcony lined the outside ledge—nothing that would save anyone from a fall, but wide enough to become yet another home for birds. That was all that Carnavas was home to, it seemed—birds and rats and cats, and if Varis had come here maybe that was all he'd found as well.

A crimson glitter caught her eye amid the filth and feathers that clung to the railing. She stooped, grimacing as she flicked aside debris to retrieve something that gleamed red and gold.

She stumbled back at a raucous croak. The giant raven from the tower—or another just as big—wheeled past, so close she smelled the musk of his feathers. She retreated quickly, shoving the window shut behind her.

"Are all the birds in Sarkany that big?"

She asked it lightly, but Iancu frowned. "No," he said. "And I don't like the look of these."

A sharp crack made them all jump. A black shape vanished from the other side of the window as Savedra looked up. The raven. Another shadow wheeled past, and another. Talons struck the glass again.

"Perhaps we've outstayed our welcome." Iancu said, urging them back into the passage. As the panel swung shut behind them, they heard the sharp whine of splintering glass.

"Definitely time to go," Ashlin said, taking Savedra's arm for the long step back into the library.

Too late. The library windows burst inward with a howl of wind. Savedra threw up her arm to ward off splinters; it saved her life as a giant raven struck her.

Talons closed on her forearm and she screamed. She'd felt the force of a falcon landing on a glove—this was worse. She stumbled and fell to one knee, her other hand rising against the blinding storm of air and feathers. Someone else cried out. Steel sang. She scrambled back, groped for a weapon and found a book. Leather and parchment blocked the striking beak that meant to take her eyes. She couldn't reach her knife.

Bone and feathers crunched. Blood sprayed hot across her face and hands and the buffeting weight was gone. The bitter gamey taste of it filled her mouth as she sucked in a breath.

Ashlin stood over her, sword drawn and bloody, equally splattered with red. Her eyes were black and wild. "Out, out!" Savedra read the shape of the words on her lips—she couldn't hear over the roar of wind and her own heart.

As she scrambled up she glimpsed the fallen bird, cleaved nearly in half by Ashlin's blade, and another across the room that Cahal must have slain. Curtains billowed in the draft, and ash thickened the air. Beyond the splintered glass teeth in the window frame, more winged shadows circled. Her boots skidded in moisture as she ran; she didn't know whose blood it was.

She felt the door slam shut behind them. After the brightness of sky the dim hall blinded her. When her vision adjusted she saw Cahal and Iancu leaning against the door. Both men were tousled and grime-streaked but seemed unharmed.

"Are you all right?"

Savedra hadn't realized she'd fallen to her knees until Ashlin crouched beside her. She looked down, and regretted it as pain followed her glance. Her right sleeve was shredded and quickly soaking with blood. Her left hand was merely scratched, but stung like a fiercer wound.

"Shit." Ashlin glanced down the length of the hall and swore again. "Everything here is filthy."

"Here." Iancu stripped off his coat, baring clean linen beneath. With a slit of his dagger and three sharp tugs, he ripped free one sleeve and passed it to the princess.

"There are bandages in the packs with the horses," she said, crouching next to Savedra. "This will do till we reach them." She tore the ruined sleeve away. Savedra closed her eyes against the sight of blood welling from deep claw wounds, and when she opened them again the princess was knotting the makeshift dressing. A drop of red splashed white cloth.

Not all the blood on Ashlin's face came from the birds. A talon had gouged a furrow down her temple and onto the curve of her cheekbone. Rivulets of crimson tracked her cheek, feathering across her skin and dripping off her chin.

"What about you?"

"It's nothing." She snorted a laugh at Savedra's expression. "This time I mean it. Just a scrape. I'll clean it when we get out of here."

"What now?" Cahal asked. Iancu resumed his place against the door so the lieutenant could wipe and sheathe his sword. Nothing struck the wood, but Savedra heard shuffling behind it.

"We get the hell out of here," Ashlin said. "I'm not spending the night in this place."

"There are more of them outside!"

"We have to chance it. Unless you want to stay."

"No," Savedra said instantly. "All right."

More ravens wheeled over the courtyard, rasping voices echoing. A few dove as Savedra and the others raced for the gate, but no blows landed.

"They're driving us off," Cahal said as they paused in the shelter of the gate arch.

"They certainly are. And they can keep the place."

Raucous shrieks followed them halfway down the mountain, finally dying away. Pain and fatigue gave way to fugue, and Savedra could remember nothing until Ashlin hoisted her into the saddle. She caught the pommel right-handed out of instinct and cried out as injured muscles flexed. Sweat soaked her, stinging in a dozen scrapes and scratches and chilling quickly now that she was still.

When they passed the salt circle they dared stop. Ashlin stripped away Savedra's blood-soaked bandages and rinsed the wound, first with water and then with whiskey.

Savedra sobbed at the latter. Ashlin's hands shook by the time she wound the fresh bandages, and Cahal had to tie them off. He cleaned Ashlin's wound too, eliciting an angry hiss. His ministrations left one side of her face clean, the other a half-mask of filth.

"We can stay the night in Valcov," Iancu said. "Get you looked at by a physician."

Savedra shook her head; her eyes ached with the threat of tears. "I want to go home." It was foolish and childish, and she winced at the sound of the words. She waited for the others to talk sense into her, but instead they exchanged calculating glances.

"It will mean riding at night," Iancu said at last, "but I admit I find the idea appealing."

"Let's go then," Ashlin said. "The sooner we get under cover the happier I'll be."

Savedra glanced back as they urged the horses on, and saw winged shadows circling the towers of Carnavas.

It must have been a harrowing ride back to Evharis, but Savedra didn't recall much of it. She had confused flashes of clinging to the saddle, and later slumping over her horse's neck, and finally of Iancu carrying her up the steps into a confusion of light and warmth and concerned voices. She regained her senses inopportunely, as the physician appeared to clean and stitch her wound. Ashlin pressed a glass of brandy into her hand, and the world dulled once more.

It wasn't till well past midnight, after an awkward one-armed bath that nearly lulled her into sleep and drowning, that she remembered the jewel she'd found in Carnavas. She picked up her ruined coat, meaning to drop the filthy thing in a rubbish bin, and something small and glittering fell out of the pocket and rattled across the floor.

Savedra crouched to retrieve it from the shadows under the bed. She'd drunk several glasses of medicinal brandy during the stitching, and the movement nearly toppled her.

A ring. A woman's ring, a brilliant pigeon's blood ruby in a delicate gold band. The setting was clogged with grime, the stone dull with it, but there was no mistaking its beauty or its worth. Such a ring would be costly anywhere, but in Sclafai it would only grace the hand of a mage.

Was it hers? The mysterious missing Severos sorceress?

She staggered off her knees at a knock on the door, and the ring vanished into the pocket of her robe.

Ashlin entered before Savedra reached the door. The princess was freshly bathed as well, her hair and shirt both damp and clinging to her skin. She went straight for the brandy and poured herself a tall glass. From the smell of her skin, it wasn't her first either. The talon scratches on her face had scabbed dark and angry red.

"Are you all right?" Savedra asked, after watching the princess pace several circuits across the rug.

"I lied," Ashlin said, jerking to a halt. She set down her half-empty glass and brandy splashed against her fingers. Her cheeks were flushed, eyes shining. "I don't envy you. I envy Nikos."

Savedra opened her mouth and closed it again. "What do you mean?"

Ashlin closed the space between them. The heat of her skin was a furnace, and the smell of brandy clinging to her reminded Savedra how much she'd drunk herself. It also reminded her that she wasn't wearing anything beneath her robe; her good hand clenched at the collar.

"I watched you come to harm, and I couldn't bear it." She cupped Savedra's cheek with one calloused hand. "It's you I want, Vedra." She took the last step, pressing the length of their bodies together. The princess was hard and lean against her, lips soft and demanding.

"I don't like girls," Savedra whispered when she could breathe again. But there was no denying the attraction, not with the sharp beat of her pulse, the heat and hardness of her traitorous flesh. She tried to pull away, but a bedpost trapped her.

Ashlin's laugh caught in her throat. "Neither do I. But I like you." She shifted her hips and Savedra gasped. Lips and tongue traced the line of her throat.

"Nikos will never forgive me," Savedra whispered, even as she arched into the touch. Pins and combs fell away beneath Ashlin's insistent fingers and the damp cloud of her hair enveloped both their faces.

"He will. He loves you. It's me he won't forgive, and I hardly care." Teeth scraped her earlobe. "I want *you*, Vedra."

A turn and gentle push and the edge of the bed met the back of Savedra's knees. She sat, and Ashlin's knee pressed between hers. With a scramble and shrug Ashlin cast her shirt aside and crawled forward, forcing Savedra back against the featherbed.

Curiosity and envy made Savedra raise her face to her breasts, but the shudder and moan that answered her only made the pressure at the base of her spine build all the more. "This is madness," she murmured against clean soap-scented skin. A nipple brushed her mouth, taut and creased. "Not to mention adultery and treason."

Ashlin pulled away, and she nearly whimpered with pain and relief, but the princess only stripped away her trousers, and then Savedra's robe. The sour-sweet musk of her was alien but not unpleasant. Savedra slid a hand along the silken skin of her inner thigh, driven by curiosity and the insidious desire to feel Ashlin shudder again. This much she could trespass—

Ashlin knelt above her, one hand teasing her nipple rings while the other closed around her erection, calluses scraping tender skin. Savedra opened her mouth for a denial, a refusal, but all that came out was a groan. Not like this, she wanted to say, memories of the Black Orchid and the hijras' temple house thick as opium smoke in her mind. But Ashlin was already taking her inside, all warmth and wet and rhythmic pressure, and she could only sob.

It was quick and awkward and drunken, and Ashlin swore in Celanoran when she came. It was enough to make Savedra laugh, which in turn became a breathless shuddering gasp as her own climax took her. She was crying, and both of them were slick with sweat and tears and fluids.

"I'm sorry, *ma chrí*," Ashlin said when their trembling stilled, holding her close and stroking her sticky hair. She was soft and pliable now, all the hardness of bone and muscle melted away. "I'm sorry. I didn't mean to hurt you."

"You didn't—"

She wiped away tears with her thumb. "Didn't I? I shouldn't have pressed."

"We can't do this again." It might have sounded more convincing had her face not been pressed against Ashlin's collarbone, her hand cupping her hip. "What are we going to do?"

"I don't know," Ashlin whispered into her hair. "I don't know."

They lay together in silence, until pain and fatigue and brandy rolled over Savedra like a wave, and sucked her down into the dark.

She dreams of black wings.

Wings spread wide to catch the wind, the dying sun warm on her back. Wings folded tight against night's chill, pressed close to her mate in their nest. Wings shredding cold fog with every stroke, moisture beading on iridescent feathers. A dozen birds, a dozen images, all of them her.

The air is cold, but the last of the sunlight soaks her feathers. She has flown far and farther still, and the setting sun calls her to roost, to tuck her head and sleep, but her mistress's will overrides those instincts. The light fades and she flies on.

By the time she reaches the human camp she is merely a darker shadow in the night, blotting the stars as she passes. The humans take no notice—the air is foul with their dust and smoke, their mammal sweat and waste, thick enough to clog even her dull nose. Death rolls off them in a cloud, visible to her carrion sympathy and the alien magic with which her mistress has infused her.

The latter sense leads her to her quarry, one tent among the hundreds sprouting like fungi from the field. A man sleeps within, his fire banked but heat still glowing from the coals. Gaunt-cheeked and sunken-eyed, hands gnarled and scarred. He twitches with restless dreams.

Another raven, still her. Now she glides above narrow alleys, searching the harsh stone streets below for prey. She is no owl meant for night flying, not made to fall ghost-silent from the sky. But it isn't mice she hunts tonight, and humans are deaf and dull, blind to the skies above them. The one she follows now never looks up, though it twitches rabbit-wary at every sound. Pale, this one, and underfed, as are all those her mistress hunts. She doesn't understand it—the streets are full of plumper quarry, slower and easy to catch. But hers is not to question, merely to stalk as she is bidden and wait for the scraps her mistress will share.

Another image—

Savedra woke dizzy and lost, hands clenched in the covers to stop her spiraling fall. Her wounded arm throbbed, and the taste of blood sickened her.

The images began to fracture. She had seen Mathiros, and a strange woman on a foggy street, and a dozen other things besides, but they were already unraveling like smoke through her fingers.

She rolled over, groping for warmth to reassure her, but found only cold sheets and rumpled covers. Evharis, she remembered, as the unfamiliar surroundings sank in. Ashlin.

She lay awake until dawn, sick and dizzy with dreams, and with the enormity of what they had done.

CHAPTER 11

Kiril heard crying before he opened the library door. Phaedra had come once more uninvited, but his annoyance at her intrusions faded at the sound of tears. No, he corrected himself as his hand closed on the handle, not tears—no wet sniffles or hiccupping sobs, but a high mournful keen. The dead couldn't truly weep.

She lay in a heap beside the hearth, perilously close to the unscreened fire. Books and parchment scattered around her, torn and crumpled pages drifting like snow. Kiril locked the door, hands tightening at the sight of mangled books. He held back a curse as he crouched beside her, gathering her hair and skirts away from the fireplace. Even in the shadows and red light he recognized the books: her books, her work that hadn't been destroyed at her death. Some he'd taken during the careful sack of Carnavas and others he'd stolen from the Arcanost later. Murder he could stomach, but the loss of knowledge sickened him.

"What's wrong?" he asked, gentling his voice. Phaedra rocked and moaned in his arms, face contorted in the firelight.

A cold draft and movement in the shadows made him glance over his shoulder, already tensing to deal with some new intruder. All his dark-sharpened eyes found were an open casement and a bird perched on a chair beside it. A raven, huge and glossy. It mantled, oilslick rainbows rippling across its wings, but remained on the chair-back. A quick touch found his wards intact; her pets could pass through them as easily as she did. His nape prickled at the thought.

Phaedra's keening died and she gulped air she didn't need. Awkwardly, he cradled her to his chest and stood, carrying her to a chair. His back and knees screamed, but she was lighter than a living woman, dry of so many of life's fluids. He left her curled against the cushions and bent to retrieve what he could of the books. A few scraps of paper curled and fell to ash in the hearth, but most of her violence had been to rip out pages. Many of those he thought he could salvage, or at least rewrite. He shoved the survivors into his desk and lit a lamp. The raven regarded him with one black eye, its gaze canny for even a clever bird.

"What happened?" he asked again, risking a stretch past the bird to close the window.

"Someone was snooping around the castle." She rubbed her face though she had no tears to wipe away. "Pawing through our things."

That made him stiffen. No need to ask which castle, or who else she meant by *our*. "Who?"

"I don't know. No one the birds had seen before. They fled west, so I imagine they weren't Sarken."

"Fled from what?"

She sat up, trying to smooth her tangled hair. "My birds drove them off. I should have burned it, should have razed the stones to the ground."

He drew a breath. Let it out again. "Mightn't it be wiser not to draw attention to the castle? To you?"

"It's difficult to draw attention to my past these days." She gave up on her hair and tugged her gown straight instead. Wine-red velvet today, a modern style. Varis's work, no doubt. "You wrought that very well indeed. But not, apparently, well enough. We've had enough invasion, enough destruction and callous looting. The bones of Carnavas belong to my family now, and they may guard their treasures as they see fit." Her wild rage cooled, settling into an angry chill.

"Be as that may, a little discretion would be wise. You won't find revenge as a pile of salted ashes. Varis and I have no desire for that fate either."

"No. No, Varis doesn't deserve that. He was always so kind to me."

"He worshiped you in university," Kiril said, weary enough for unhappy truths to spill. *And you repay him by making him a party to treason.* But that was unfair— Varis had begun this. Phaedra's magic had kept her from true death, but Varis had found her and nursed her back to sanity and kindled in her the desire for revenge.

Phaedra blinked. "He never said anything."

Kiril nearly laughed. *You never see what's right in front of you.* Isyllt had told him that years ago, her voice heavy with exasperation and resignation. And he, to prove her point, still hadn't realized what she was speaking of. If he had—

Kiril sank into a chair across from Phaedra and rubbed his temples against a growing pressure there. His eyes felt as though they'd been scraped out with a spoon and shoved back into his sockets. "Of course he didn't," he said, forcing his thoughts to different history. "He has a heart, you know, under all that velvet gaud. And he's never handed it away for the breaking."

Which was why their own affair had been so brief. Or perhaps Varis had simply been unable to love someone already sworn to the Alexioi. Whatever the reason, he had broken with Kiril publicly and melodramatically before he left for Iskar, before Kiril had to do the leaving. It had been a kindness, just as his leaving Isyllt had been; that never seemed to make it easier for anyone.

The raven croaked and Phaedra stood, shaking out her wrinkled skirts as she crossed the room. "I know, darling," she murmured, stroking its cheek with one knuckle. "Such a long way you've flown for me. And I'll ask another journey of you still." She slipped a knife from a skirt pocket and nicked the soft brown skin of her wrist. Blood welled, slow and dark and heavy. The bird bobbed its head to the wound, drinking till the edge of its beak glistened crimson.

The creation of familiars was an old practice, but Phaedra's birds were closer to her than that. She had been them, and they her, until she had found a new body to claim. Kiril could scarcely imagine what that had been like—it was a wonder she had any remnants of sanity left.

Phaedra glanced up to find Kiril watching. Her eyebrows rose. "Care for a taste?"

"And become one of your pets as well? No thank you."

"I don't think you would," she said after a thoughtful pause. "Not easily, at least, or from such a small amount."

"But it would start the process. The spread of your power and will and consciousness into me. I did read your articles when you were at the Arcanost, you know."

She smiled. "Then you know how much a taste could benefit you. Haematurgy can heal as well as harm, unlike your necromancy. My power can make you strong again." She wiped a bead of blood off her wrist with one finger, and raised the finger to his lips.

He caught her arm before she touched him, staring at the slick crimson stain seeping along the whorls of her fingertip. "The cost is not one I feel like paying today." Even with the headaches, the weariness and aching joints, the tender, bruised feeling that still accompanied any use of magic? No, he told himself firmly. Even so, her offer wasn't worth it.

"But some day. You will." She swayed against him and he held her carefully away.

"We'll see." He removed his hand and stepped back.

She smiled again, then licked her finger clean and turned back to her bird. After a few more coos and caresses she opened the window, through which it vanished with a flurry of black wings. When she sat her movements were unusually heavy—almost clumsy.

"Are you all right?" Kiril asked. As much as her demon grace unnerved him, its absence was more unsettling.

"Weak," she admitted. "Tired. I had thought to postpone it, but I need to hunt tonight."

"Hunt?"

"Living blood regenerates. Dead blood doesn't. I need a living source every so often, and I didn't imagine you wanted to bleed for me."

"So you hunt, like a vrykola. With them?" Her silence

was answer enough. Her quiet journeys into the underground had intrigued him when they were at the Arcanost together. Without her work, he would never have formed his own fragile ties to the catacombs. But now her renewed involvement brought only trouble, and his unease hadn't faded. Varis's schemes were dangerous enough—who knew what plots the vrykoloi whispered in her ear?

"Do you stalk the slums like they do," he asked, his voice inflectionless, "taking those who won't be missed, or whose families have no recourse to search for them?"

"You wanted me to be discreet. Would you rather I stalk the Octagon Court?"

"I didn't realize you were making such a habit of murder."

She flinched, then stiffened. "Will you play games of conscience with me, spymaster? How many other women disappeared because of you? How many other murders did you clean up for him?"

"None. None like you, that is." Dozens of murders for king and country, hundreds, but never any so personal. And thank the saints for that—he didn't think he could have done it more than once, not for any love or loyalty. "You...He was mad for you, as I'd never seen. Whatever alchemy was between you was a powerful one." Kiril shook his head. "But you're quite right—I have no place to be your conscience." He rose, simultaneously annoyed and amused that he was ever the one retreating from his own home. "Do what you must. But try not to leave any more bodies in plain sight."

He felt Phaedra leave the house not long after. But then, she never really left him anymore. He sat awake well past the final terce, turning a glass of whiskey between his palms and turning memories over in his head. He took them out every so often to keep them polished—he was the only one who carried them now, and he felt he shouldn't lose them. The sight of Phaedra's bird triggered his last memory of her as she had been. The one that should have been the end of it.

No one could survive the fall, no matter how powerful a mage. Phaedra certainly hasn't. Kiril hopes and fears that the river might have claimed the body, denying them confirmation but sparing them the sight, but they receive no such mercy.

She sprawls on the rocks beside the ice-edged water, close enough to soak her skirts. Grey and crimson splatters freeze on stone, clot and crust in the unbound darkness of her hair. Her limbs are broken twigs, neck grotesquely twisted. Birds take flight in a rush of black wings as Kiril and Mathiros approach. They made short work of her; her hands are already picked to the bone, eyes and tongue gone, lips ripped free to bare a white rictus of teeth. They even took her glittering rings, and lesser gems and gold thread from her girdle.

The sight of her bare hands gives Kiril a moment's unease, but no trace of life or unlife lingers in her shattered corpse, no hint of a ghost.

"Leave her for the beasts," Mathiros mutters, his voice raw and hollow.

At another time, Kiril would have shot him a pointed glare. Now he doesn't want to look his liege in the face. "That would be unwise, Highness," he says instead.

Mathiros grunts and nods. "Do as you see fit, then."

He turns and strides back to the path, boot heels ringing on the stones.

When the prince is gone, Kiril kneels beside the body. He might have closed her eyes, but the lids are ruined, and straightening her limbs is out of the question. Instead he calls spellfire. It licks cold and silent around his fingers, flaring brighter when he touches Phaedra's frozen gore-stiff gown, running and pooling as if the damp fabric were soaked in oil. The blue-white flames grow only colder as they burn, but cloth and flesh char and crumble all the same, till all that remains is greasy ash and a few blackened nubs of bone.

The ashes freeze Kiril's hands to aching as he scatters them into the river.

CHAPTER 12

A pleasant side effect of necromancy was that Isyllt's magic warded off any foreign life that tried to take root in her flesh, from plagues like the bronze fever to the little coughs and colds that spread through the streets every day. But even that required a modicum of strength and self-preservation.

Which was how Isyllt found herself bedridden and feverish for days after she summoned Forsythia, coughing and sneezing and choking on phlegm. Her former disregard of the influenza quickly vanished, leaving her weak and aching and wishing for death. She might have asked the landlord's daughter to put her out of her misery when the girl came with soup and ginger tisane, but if so her request was ignored.

The fever brought dreams. Strange, dark dreams, full of wings and towers and the smell of cinnamon. And blood, always blood, oceans and messes of it. Slit throats and torn veins and the thick black vomit of fever victims.

More than once she woke gasping in the dark, the taste of copper in her mouth, certain that the slickness on her skin was more than sweat.

On the seventh day she woke to afternoon sunlight and the feeling that she'd been beaten with truncheons and dragged behind a carriage. Her eyes were crusted with grit, and the taste in her mouth didn't bear contemplating. Despite a head stuffed with snot and dirty rags, she knew someone else was in the apartment. She croaked a question that even she didn't understand.

A rattle of dishes answered from the other room, followed by soft footsteps. The smell of something full of salt and garlic cut through the clinging reek of sweat and sickness, and Isyllt flopped back on her clammy pillows with a sigh.

"For a powerful sorceress, you whine a lot when you're sick."

She started, sticky eyes opening again. The voice, and the shadow that fell across the bed, belonged not to the landlady's daughter but to Dahlia.

"What are you doing here?"

"The girl downstairs let me in. I told her I worked with you, but mostly I think she was tired of listening to you moan."

Isyllt snorted and propped herself up on the pillows. The bedding stank, and her nose had cleared enough to remind her of it. Her scalp and back and breasts itched with dried sweat. Only sweat. Though from the ache tightening beneath her navel, her courses would begin soon. "You can make yourself useful, then. Is that lunch?"

Dahlia handed her a tray of bread and soup; the garlic and ginger in the broth were enough to sting her sinuses.

"You're lucky," the girl said. "People are dying of the influenza."

"They always do. The young and the old, the weak and the starving."

"It's worse this year—the fever is worse. I heard a man in Harrowgate died vomiting blood two days ago."

That made Isyllt flinch. Her spoon shook, spilling broth back into the bowl. She sopped bread instead and forced herself to chew and swallow. It burned the back of her throat, but she felt more alive after a few mouthfuls.

"So you work with me now?" she asked, trying to put aside thoughts of plague.

Dahlia shrugged, perching on the edge of a chair. Her eyes flickered around the room; Isyllt hoped she wasn't casing it. "I convinced Meka to help you. And you might need more help, looking for Forsythia's killer." She lowered her voice at the words, and Isyllt didn't blame her. The memory of Forsythia's sobs was enough to steal warmth from the room.

"I might," she mumbled around a mouthful of bread. Isyllt didn't insult the girl by mentioning the danger. She'd come back after witnessing an unpleasant summoning, and risked a sickbed; that didn't speak of cowardice or squeamishness. She swallowed and studied Dahlia more closely. "You want more than a few weeks employment, don't you?"

The girl's jaw tightened. "I'm not asking for anything besides what my time is worth. Forsythia was kind to me—I want to see her avenged."

But Isyllt had seen the desire in her at the Arcanost. And she had come back now, when any fool knew that necromancers weren't safe or pleasant company. "Shiver or spark?" she asked.

Blue eyes flickered and met hers. "Shiver." Her chin rose with the word.

Sparks, as those with the talent for projective magic were often called, were accepted at the Arcanost no matter how poor or connectionless, if only because an untrained pyromancer was a threat to everyone around them. Shivers—those who could sense magic or hear spirits—were eight for an obol, and without something else to recommend them would go untrained, or find work as hedge magicians or ghost-whisperers. Or go mad from voices they couldn't stop.

Isyllt shrugged, setting the tray and empty bowl aside. "That doesn't mean you can't learn to do more. A well-trained sorcerer can do a little of almost anything."

"Can you?"

She snorted again and shoved back the covers. "I'm too well-trained. Overspecialized. I'm so steeped in death and decay that my magic isn't good for much else. But I can teach you theory. If you want to learn."

Dahlia watched her, eyes narrow and wary. Isyllt remembered that chariness. Was her need to learn worth the possibility of hurt and betrayal? She looked away before the girl was pressed to answer, concentrated on getting out of bed. The room had grown while she was ill, or at least the wardrobe seemed much farther away than she remembered. "Are you an orphan?"

Dahlia shrugged. "I don't know who my father was, or where he might be. My mother is alive, but all she cares about these days is opium. Since I wasn't going to steal to help her buy it, I left home."

"She named you Dahlia."

Another shrug, this one almost fierce. "It was her name

when I was conceived. The Rose Council took it away later, before I was born, when her habit started interfering with her work. She said it would save me time choosing one when I grew up." Her mouth twisted, pinched white.

"Charming," Isyllt muttered. She made it to the wardrobe, leaning heavily on the carved oaken doors. "You don't have to keep it."

"Why not? She was right, after all. I'll be back in a few years, no matter what else I do."

The bitter resignation in her voice distracted Isyllt from clean clothes. "It's hardly that bad. Even if you don't want to study magic, there are plenty of trades that will let you work off apprentice fees. The temples, if nothing else—"

Dahlia laughed, sharp and startled. "You don't know, do you?" When Isyllt raised expectant brows she laughed harder. "I'm androgyne. Not a boy or a girl. I'll be hijra when I turn sixteen."

Isyllt blinked, closed her mouth on whatever words had died unspoken on her tongue. She had seen skirts and a lanky adolescent prettiness and given it no more thought. But now, studying the length and weight of bone, the shape of her face, she supposed Dahlia would make an equally pretty boy. She had glimpsed the veiled and marked hijra and heard the normal rumors, but knew next to nothing of the truth.

"And that leaves you with no choice but to be a prostitute?"

Dahlia raised her hands. "It's what they do."

"The Pallakis Savedra doesn't. If we're being charitable, anyway."

The girl—Isyllt would be hard-pressed to change that

thought now—snorted. "She's the prince's mistress, and one of the Eight besides. She doesn't have to do much of anything. Some of us need money. Food. A place to be." A hint of wistfulness threaded the last.

Isyllt tried to quash an upswell of sympathy. There was only so much she could do. But she could offer something, at least.

"You have a few years to decide, at least. I'll hire you as an assistant until I catch this killer, and my offer of instruction stands. Are you interested?"

Dahlia chewed her lip, twisting her hands in her skirts. "All right," she said at last. "For Syth. I'll help you."

"Good." Isyllt smiled and gathered an armful of clothes. "For your first job, you can run me a bath."

"I'm sorry," Savedra said, not for the first time. She lay propped in her own bed, into which the court physician had scolded her after inspecting her stitches and changing the dressing on her arm. A bottle of opium laced wine sat on the table beside her, as yet unopened—she needed her wits more than a surcease of pain at the moment.

Nikos and Ashlin had traded their normal places. He paced the length of the carpet at the foot of the bed, and she leaned against the doorframe, arms folded tight. Savedra couldn't bring herself to look at either of them. "I never should have put the princess at risk," she said to her lap, to her scabby white-knuckled hands. "It was foolish and thoughtless and—"

"I take my own risks, thank you," Ashlin snapped. The talon scratches were stark and red on her cheek and brow. She was pale, despite her unabated temper, eyes shadowed. "None of this is your fault."

She meant more than demon birds, but Savedra couldn't accept the absolution. She carried a store of little secrets daily, like a child's cache of treasures, but this one was too big, too heavy.

Distant voices rose to fill the silence, the sound of shears and wheels and rakes. In addition to the looming solstice celebration, the palace staff now had an extra strain. A rider had passed Savedra and Ashlin on the road back from Evharis, and they had seen the dust of a marching army blurring the sky behind them. The king would be home soon.

Nikos stopped his circuit and lifted a hand before either of them could speak again. "There's no point in recriminations. I'm only happy neither of you was harmed worse. What exactly did you find, anyway? The secret history of the vrykoloi?"

He joked, but Savedra's mouth pinched too tight to smile. She caught herself fidgeting with the edge of her bandage and dragged her hand away. Ashlin stayed quiet, waiting for her to speak. Something blossomed behind her breastbone, so hot and sharp she wanted to cry. Saints help her. She'd dared one foolish love; she wasn't sure she could survive another.

"Please," she said at last. She couldn't lie, not to him, but neither could she lay the inadequate story bare. "Let me keep this for a time. It's…a family mystery. Let me look for answers before I share it." Her hands twisted in her lap, till her stitches itched and throbbed. "Forgive me."

"Vedra. Love." Three swift strides brought Nikos to her bedside. He cupped a hand against her cheek, tilting her head up. "You've done nothing that needs forgiveness. Keep your secrets. I trust you."

She was her mother's daughter. She didn't flinch. That felt as damning as any lie. "Thank you," she whispered. From the corner of her eye she saw Ashlin flinch for both of them, turning her face to the wall.

No, this wasn't a secret any of them could survive.

Despite her promises of rest to the physicians, Savedra was out of bed within the hour. Her maid frowned and *tsk*ed, but helped her bathe and dress and pin up her hair. She needed armor as well as wits to face her family.

Fog drifted heavy through the streets, and even with her cloak and the shelter of a carriage, she was chilled through by the time she reached Phoenix House. The last light of evening glowed behind the rooftops, tinting the grey haze with sepia and rose. The maid directed her to her mother's study, where Nadesda and Sevastian sat with the remains of a quiet supper and letters sprawled on a table between them. Sevastian's sleeves were rolled up, his shirt open at the throat, and Nadesda wore a dressing gown and her hair unpinned, sable coils unraveling across her shoulders. The quiet domesticity caught in Savedra's throat.

Her father rose to embrace her, his beard tickling her cheek with his kiss. "You look exhausted. I thought you were going to Evharis for your nerves." A teasing smile accompanied the last.

She tried to smile back, but it felt more like a grimace. "Hello, Father. I'm sorry, but I need to speak with the archa." The rudeness of it made her throat ache, but she didn't have the strength for a pleasant visit tonight.

Sevastian's brow creased but he nodded. "Of course." He caught his jacket off the back of his chair.

"Father, I am sorry—"

He smiled ruefully and laid a warm hand on her shoulder as he passed. "I knew she would be archa when I married her. One grows accustomed."

When the door clicked shut, Savedra knelt before her mother's chair and winced; she'd bruised a knee somewhere during the flight from Carnavas.

"Vedra, what on earth are you doing?"

"I won't beg a mother's indulgence, but as a daughter of this house I crave a boon, Archa."

Nadesda's eyebrows rose. "What boon is that?"

"Three questions, answered honestly."

Her mother studied her for a moment, the ghost of a frown tightening her lips. "Very well. Three honest answers you may have." She rose and crossed the room, elegant as ever in her robe and bare feet, and touched the charm of silence on her wide mahogany desk. "Well?" she said, when the distant noises of the house had faded to nothing.

Savedra chewed the tip of her tongue and tried to organize her thoughts. "Who was Phaedra Severos? Darvulesti was the name she married into."

Nadesda frowned. "I don't know," she said at last. "I feel I should. A distant cousin, perhaps? Someone I met at Evharis?" She shrugged. "I'm sorry. But we do have family records, if you need to know."

Savedra's fingers clenched in frustration; the motion made her wounded arm burn. She smoothed her skirt before wrinkles set in the heavy silk. "You'd think so, wouldn't you?" she muttered.

"Is that your second question?"

She snorted. "No. What do you know about Varis's schemes?"

Her mother's frown deepened. "I'm sure he has some, but he hasn't taken me into his confidences. He's been keeping things from me, I know. He never could lie to me, not since we were children."

Savedra sighed, but as she drew breath to speak Nadesda raised her hand. "No," she said slowly. "It's true that he hasn't told me anything, but I am the archa of this house. I know more than that. Are you certain *you* want to?"

She nodded, jaw too tight for speech.

"He's been to Sanctuary." Her mouth quirked disdainfully on the name. "Talking to the sort of people one finds there. He wants the Alexioi off the throne, and I think he's finally prepared to take steps."

The words settled in her stomach like stones. For a moment Savedra thought she would retch. "Why? Why would he? I thought—" Her voice cracked. "I thought he loved me." Stupid, stupid and childish. Her face twisted with the need to cry, but her eyes stayed dry. "And why Varis? When has he ever cared for politics?"

That was more than three questions, but Nadesda didn't bother reminding her. "Oh, Vedra. He's always cared. And he'd do it because he loves you, don't you see? No," she said before Savedra could protest. "You don't. You can't. What do you know about Varis's scandals?"

"Who can keep track of them?" she snapped. "He mocks the Arcanost, questions their teachings, insults half the Octagon Court and seduces the rest. He wears the most awful virulent colors imaginable and brings demimonde opera singers to court. What does any of that have to do with Nikos, or me?"

"Those are the ones everyone sees. Those are his

armor. But there was another, once, before you were born. Before he was born, even." Savedra caught herself leaning forward as Nadesda's calm earnestness dulled the edges of her anger and frustration. "Alena Severos and King Nikolaos were lovers."

That set Savedra back on her heels, which she regretted when her knees creaked. "Before she married Tselios?"

"Yes, and before the king married Korina, though after the betrothal. Oh, it was never announced, but everyone marked how they shared too many glances and too little conversation, tried not to touch one another in public but always seemed to end up alone together."

Varis had always been clear that "Uncle Tselios" was only his mother's husband, but had never even hinted that he knew who his real father was. "You mean—"

"Exactly. Nikolaos shipped her off to a mountain estate when she became pregnant, and bribed Tselios to cover it up. So Tselios ended up with a royal favor and a royal bastard in his pocket to pull out whenever he needed."

"But what happened? Why did I never know?"

"Because Nikolaos was smarter than Tselios, and never let rumors build. And when Mathiros was born the two children looked nothing alike. And Tselios was a petty tyrant, and Alena and Varis both hated him. She tried to escape at least twice—once back to Nikolaos, poor deluded thing, and once away from all of them—but he caught her both times. After the second try, he started poisoning her to keep her weak and biddable."

Savedra didn't realize she'd pressed a hand to her mouth until she tried to take a breath. "How did you find out?"

"Varis found the poison years later and told me. I was

his only ally with Alena so weak. It was her brandy that was poisoned, which only made it worse. And by the time we stopped it, it was too late for her health."

"What did you do?"

Nadesda's smile was chilling. "We poisoned Tselios. And we stood over him as he choked and vomited his life out. He had plenty of enemies, and we were only children. No one accused either of us." Her smile faded. "Alena died less than a year later, and Varis came to Erisín. He wanted...I don't know what. Justice for his mother, recognition from Nikolaos. Anything. But the king paid no attention to him at all. There was no use in causing a scene—no one remembered by then. No one cared. And then he was sent to Iskar, and by the time he returned Nikolaos was dead. So there was never a chance for more."

She leaned back in her chair, shoulders slumping. "And now he sees you, another mistress to an Alexios forced aside by a royal marriage. Nikos may not be anything like his grandfather, but that hardly matters to Varis."

Savedra didn't cry. She'd trained herself out of the habit too well. But her eyes ached like bruises as she looked up at her mother. "Does it matter to you?"

"Oh, darling." Nadesda knelt beside her, holding her close and pressing Savedra's face to her soft shoulder. "Darling, you can't go on like this—it's tearing you apart."

"You're right," she whispered against Nadesda's collarbone, inhaling the comforting scent of perfume and warm skin. More right than she knew. "But what else is there? And that doesn't answer my question."

Nadesda drew away, pulling Savedra up as she stood.

"Your happiness does matter to me. And I do think Nikos would be a better king than his father, at least in peace. But the people who most want Mathiros off the throne don't want to simply replace him with his son."

"What can I do?"

"I don't know. What will you do?" Her mother's dark eyes were serious now.

"If I expose Varis it will only bring trouble down on the whole house. Don't think I don't know that." She didn't glance at the window, at the lightless bulk of Sphinx House. She didn't need to. "I am a Severos, Mother, no matter where my other loyalties lie. But I can't let him assassinate anyone. I'll talk to him. Maybe I can make him understand."

"Maybe you can." The sadness in her voice belied the words. "Saints be with you, then."

Varis's housekeeper didn't want to admit Savedra, but wasn't prepared to deny a member of the family. Since his carriage was visible around the back and lights burned in the upstairs windows, she could hardly claim he was out visiting. She stammered something about the lord being busy, but Savedra broke in with her brightest smile.

"It's all right. I won't stay long. I'm sure he won't mind. I can see myself up." She turned toward the sweeping marble stair before the woman could argue.

Savedra tried to marshal her thoughts as she climbed. What could she say to him? Surely she could sway him. He'd been her doting uncle all her life, and Nikos couldn't be held accountable for his grandfather's sins. And Ashlin—Her throat tightened at the thought of the princess. Ashlin didn't deserve to suffer for a political marriage she didn't even want, but it was rankest naïveté to think that would stop anyone who desired her out of the way.

The library door stood open a crack, spilling a bright sliver of gold across the hall. The hinges didn't squeak as she laid a careful hand on the wood. But her greeting died unspoken as she looked inside.

A woman stood on a stool in the center of the room, surrounded by lamps. A tailor crouched at her feet adjusting her hem, his mouth glittering with silver pins. A beautiful woman, to judge by the figure wrapped in white silk, but her face was veiled, dark hair carefully pinned up.

Savedra froze in the doorway, pulse quickening in her throat. In her turmoil over Nikos and Ashlin, she had almost forgotten Phaedra. Or whoever Varis's mysterious book-stealing friend truly was. She nearly fled to regroup, but her toes scuffed on the edge of a carpet and Varis turned.

"Vedra." For the first time she could remember, he didn't look happy to see her. He covered it quickly, though, pulling on a smile and bowing over her hand. "Hello, darling. You've caught me at a rather inopportune moment, I'm afraid. Which is what happens when one doesn't announce oneself. Or knock."

"Inopportune? Like the time Mother walked in on you with the twin contortionists?" Her smile ached as she held it in place.

"Acrobats. They were acrobats. And not, I might add, doing anything unusually acrobatic at the time. Your mother likes to exaggerate that story more than it deserves. She didn't knock either, as I recall. Besides, I'd much rather be walked in on doing something worthy of gossip. This hardly qualifies."

"Mysterious women are always worthy of gossip." She curtsied toward the woman on the stool. "Forgive me for interrupting."

The woman waved a hand dismissively, earning a *tsk* from the tailor. "Not at all. Few things are more boring than standing still for hours at a time. And now I'm curious about these acrobats."

Her voice pricked the nape of Savedra's neck, soft and husky and oddly familiar. But not, as she'd imagined from Iancu's description, Sarken; this woman's native tongue was Selafaïn. The words were casual, the woman's face not quite turned her way, but she felt the weight of her stare like a hand. Her arm throbbed beneath her sleeve. Did they know?

"Is there something I can do for you?" Varis asked.

"I only wanted to say hello. You've looked tired lately—" She shrugged, artless concern. That at least was true. For an unannounced evening visit to find anyone else unbuttoned and disheveled was normal; for Varis it was alarming. Beneath his open collar she glimpsed the edge of a dark and ugly bruise, and her blood chilled. She'd seen a similar mark on Isyllt Iskaldur, when the necromancer had delivered her report to Nikos. A vampire bite.

"I have, haven't I?" He ran a hand over his scalp and sighed, surreptitiously tugging his shirt closed at the neck. "Even debauchery can be exhausting sometimes. The parties multiply so this time of year, and the planning and invitations and costumes..." He gestured toward the tailor.

"I understand. I'll leave you to it, and to your guest." She smiled at the woman, but found no hint of an answering expression behind the veil. "We should have lunch sometime. You can come to the palace and scandalize everyone."

His smile looked like a grimace. "Yes. We should do that." He leaned in to kiss her cheek, his lips soft and cool. "I appreciate you thinking of your decrepit old uncle." His hand settled on her back, steering her toward the door so lightly and unobtrusively that she hardly noticed it.

"Buying dresses for other men's wives?" she asked as they started down the stairs.

"Someone has to. I can't bear another season of the Hadrians setting fashions."

He took her arm, and released it again when she flinched. "What's wrong?"

"Oh, it's nothing. A bit of clumsiness, is all."

Neither her tone nor face faltered, but Varis blanched. His eyes darkened and splotches of color bloomed in his cheeks. "That lie, my dear, is as old as the hills, and unworthy of both of us. Did he hurt you?"

She drew back from his cold rage, tongue slow with confusion. "Did who—No!" Realization made her stomach lurch. "No, of course not!" She forced her voice low when she wanted to shriek. "Nikos has never hurt me. He never would. How can you think that?"

"I've seen how the Alexioi treat their pets." Anger made him a stranger.

"He is not his grandfather." And so much for saving that particular secret.

Varis's face twisted, finally settled back into his usual sardonic half-smile. "Indeed. Nor his father either, I suppose. That doesn't seem to have helped you, does it?"

"He does the best by me that he can. We have both of

us always understood how it would be." Unbidden, the memory of Ashlin's skin surfaced. She hoped her stinging blush could be taken for anger. "If you act against him— or the princess—you act against me. Please, Uncle. Don't make us enemies for the sake of a man decades dead."

He turned away, folding his arms across his chest. "I act for the living and the dead. And I have more cause than you can pry out of your mother."

"Then tell me! Make me understand this."

She caught the glitter of his eyes as they rolled upward. Toward the library. "I can't," he said softly, and the wrath drained out of him like water. "I don't want to hurt you, Savedra."

Her jaw tightened. "You already have."

He lifted his chin, as chilly and urbane as ever. "Then you'll forgive me or you won't, darling. That's up to you. Perhaps when this is over I can explain it to you."

Her spine straightened in response, and her voice cooled to match. "I hope you can. I hope I can forgive you when I hear it."

She turned away, sweeping down the rest of the stairs and snatching her cloak off the peg before the miserable housekeeper could reach it. She didn't turn back, but out of the corner of her eye she saw him, frozen pale and motionless as marble. If he called to her, it was lost beneath the shutting of the door.

Safely enclosed in her waiting carriage, she let her face crumple, pinching her nose against the building pressure in her sinuses. She wanted to scream, but restrained herself for the driver's sake.

She couldn't fall apart yet. And she couldn't do this alone. Her mother wouldn't endanger the house, and

Nikos couldn't allow anything to threaten the throne. Ashlin might help her, but Savedra couldn't risk the princess again. Captain Denaris was loyal to the throne—

No. She sat up straighter. She didn't need a soldier or a courtier; she needed a sorcerer.

Savedra yanked open the panel that connected the interior to the driver's seat. "Take me to Archlight."

"What happened to your hand?" Dahlia asked later, as Isyllt measured mint and tarragon for tisane.

"A knife, with a would-be assassin on the other end." Her fingers flexed at the memory, bone and tendon aching around their pins. The fresh scars on her throat were obvious; she'd been careful not to show the bruise on her thigh when she got out of the bath. Ciaran must have noticed it, but had chosen not to comment.

"What happened to the assassin?"

Isyllt frowned at the teakettle. "I don't know. I never found her again, only her masters." She stroked the band of her ring with her right thumb—that had been the only time she'd ever been parted from her diamond, and she meant to keep it that way.

"It would sound better if you'd killed her."

"It would, wouldn't it?" She set the kettle on the stove, shivering at the heat pulsing from the tiles. A previous, more culinary-minded tenant had installed the expensive green-glazed cooker; Isyllt had promised herself one if she ever moved into a house of her own.

"What about your wrist? Was that the same assassin?"

Burn scars ringed her left wrist, ridged and glossy tissue in the shape of a man's hand. "No, someone else. He isn't dead either." She smiled a little at that memory, though there had been no humor in it at the time. "We're friends now, actually."

Dahlia snorted. "Do you have any stories where someone dies?"

"Oh, a few. We'll save those for later."

While the water heated, Isyllt found a spare mirror in the clutter of her workroom, and instructed Dahlia on its use. She also passed along the lecture on the cost and quality of the glass that the Arcanost glassmakers gave her every time she broke one. Next she found a knife—nothing as large or elaborate as her kukri, but a sharp blade all the same, and one spelled to wound demon-flesh.

By then the water was boiling, and even puttering around the apartment had winded her. She poured herself and Dahlia steaming tisane and returned to the sitting room to catch her breath.

Dahlia studied the blade a moment before sheathing it. She handled it competently, which was no surprise. "What do we do now?"

"Someone used Forsythia as a blood sacrifice." It was the first time she'd spoken the thought aloud. She didn't like the shape of the words in her mouth. "So we're hunting haematurges."

"Blood sorcerers." Dahlia didn't try to hide her dismay.

"It isn't entirely like the penny dreadfuls," Isyllt said. She remembered all the spook stories children in the city knew, about sorcerers who prowled the streets looking for victims, and what they did with them. Whether or not the murderous mages belonged to the Arcanost depended on the neighborhood, and the storyteller. "Haematurgy is an approved study at the Arcanost. But like necromancy, its reputation is...spotted. And maybe deservedly so.

The more blood you have to work with, the more you can do. And after a certain volume it's hard to find willing donors. The stories about Evanescera Ley and Arkady Tezda are exaggerated, but there's truth at the core. The same applies to all the stories about the vrykoloi."

"Blood sorcerers *and* vampires. And you're going to hunt them."

"*We're* going to hunt them." She met Dahlia's eyes over her cup, waiting for a flinch. It never came.

"What first, then?"

"First we track rumors. I can't imagine Forsythia was the first person they've killed. Even if no one's whispering about blood magic yet, there will still be people missing, or found with slit throats. Between Ciaran and my friend Khelséa, we ought to find anything worth hearing."

"You're friends with a marigold?" For someone so young, Dahlia could fit a remarkable amount of skepticism in raised eyebrows.

"I am. And with Arcanostoi and guttersnipes and even a demon or two. Does that bother you?"

Dahlia shrugged. "Not as long as you're paying me."

Isyllt snorted, but pushed herself up and shuffled to the bedroom and her coffer. Coins clinked as she counted them. "These are for your time," she said, handing over two silver griffins, "a decad of it. And these"—she counted out another griffin and a half in owls and obols and copper pennies—"are to get yourself something to wear. If you're going to tell people you work for me, I'd rather you were wearing decent shoes."

Dahlia rolled her eyes. The money vanished into several different pockets; nothing jingled when she was done.

The ward on the staircase shivered softly in Isyllt's

head and she straightened, locking the moneybox again with a touch. Her magic didn't know the person on the stair, nor was the light knock that followed familiar.

A cloaked woman stood in the hallway, her face hidden by backlighting and the shadow of her cowl. Isyllt shifted and light fell past her, and she couldn't stop a blink of surprise. Savedra Severos was not someone she expected to turn up unannounced on her doorstep. Or at all.

"Lady Severos." Her title as royal concubine was more properly *Pallakis*, but Isyllt supposed she might get tired of being defined that way.

"Good evening, Lady Iskaldur." Her voice was always arresting—not masculine, but rich and husky; according to Ciaran, more contralto roles had been written into operas and musicals since she'd taken up residence in the Gallery of Pearls. Tonight it was rough with fatigue or emotion. "Am I disturbing you?"

"Of course not." Which of course one would always say to someone with the prince's ear, but the curiosity of the visit more than made up for the late hour. "Come in."

"Thank you. I'm sorry to come so late unannounced." Blue silk flashed as she drew back her hood. Her heavy hair was held up in a lattice of pins and ribbons, but stray curls slipped free at her temples. She looked as tired as she sounded; the violet on her eyelids wasn't paint, and her skin was too pale under the flush of cold. She moved jerkily as she crossed the threshold, as if nervous or pained, and Isyllt caught her backward glance.

Isyllt held out a hand for Savedra's cloak even as she sent a questing tendril of magic down the stairs; if anyone had followed her, they lurked farther away than she could sense. "We keep odd hours in Archlight. It's no trouble." Cloth settled heavy over her arm; the velvet was damp from the night, but the silk lining was warm and smelled of perfume—sandalwood and vetiver and bitter orange. The scent lingered as Isyllt hung up the cloak.

Savedra was dressed plainly for the palace, but even so she would stand out on any street in Archlight. Her gown was blue figured silk, a duskier shade than her cloak, slim-lined and high-collared. The pearls at her throat were black, their iridescent darkness broken by the indigo sparkle of iolites. The thought of those pearls scattered on the cobbles made Isyllt's jaw tighten.

"Do you have a coach waiting, Lady?"

"I sent the driver away. I didn't want to attract attention."

"You'll attract another sort if you walk here at night. It's hardly Oldtown," she said to Savedra's quirked brow, "but students have bills and bare cupboards too, not to mention drunken stupidity. I'll see you safely away when you leave."

"Of course." She shook her head. "I'm eight shades of fool lately, it seems. Thank you."

"You needed to speak to me?"

"Yes, if you have the time." Hazel eyes flickered toward Dahlia, who was doing a poor job of not staring.

"Of course. My assistant was just leaving." She steered Dahlia aside.

"You're getting rid of me." A statement, not an accusation.

"I am, and I'll do it again before this is over. But I do need you to find Ciaran and ask after any rumors that might help us. And make sure no one was following our guest."

Dahlia nodded slowly and turned toward the door, curtsying awkwardly to Savedra as she passed.

"Sit," Isyllt said when the door was latched again. Her furniture looked even shabbier beside Savedra, and she was conscious of her worn and comfortable clothes and her hair drying in rattails over her shoulders. "What can I do for you? Would you like something to drink?"

Savedra sat with studied grace, skirts pooling artfully. That grace and her natural beauty distracted from the artifice she wore as elegantly as the pearls. There was very little to remind one that she hadn't been born a woman—the strength of chin, perhaps, the length of the manicured hands that folded now in her lap. Her shoulders were thin enough, and the cut of her dress flattered narrow hips and a flat chest.

"I wouldn't mind some of that tisane," she said. "I could use something calming. I find myself with a mystery," she continued after Isyllt set the kettle on to warm again. "One I can't take to my family or to Nikos. I'd hoped to beg your services as an investigator."

Isyllt frowned. "I'm a Crown Investigator, and oathsworn as such. I can't involve myself in personal matters in the Octagon Court." Only personal matters outside it.

"This isn't—" Her lips pursed and she tried again. "My loyalty is to Nikos, and by extension to the Princess." At that she glanced aside. "So I do support the Crown. But my family thrives on secrets, and any number of them might be damaging if brought to the wrong attention. I'm afraid that a member of my family is keeping dangerous secrets, but I won't risk the well-being of the whole House by taking them before the throne."

Her gaze focused on Isyllt's neck, where her shirt left

the bite uncovered. It was healing well, but still mottled and scabbed and ugly. Savedra's eyes sagged closed, but she straightened quickly. "And I think my family problem overlaps with your vampires, though I'm not sure how. Please. At least hear the story. I don't know where else to go."

The whistle of the kettle forestalled an answer. Isyllt rose and poured more tisane. She set a cup beside Savedra's chair; the woman's hands shook too badly to give it to her. It was the trembling that decided her.

"Tell me. I'll keep your secrets if I'm able."

Their cups cooled untouched while Savedra spoke. Missing records, mysterious references, forgotten relatives, ruined castles and demon birds. It should have sounded like a rehearsal for a particularly melodramatic opera, but no actor Isyllt knew could feign the strained catch in Savedra's voice.

"Wait," she said when Savedra reached the birds, practicality breaking through her absorption in the story. "These creatures wounded you?"

Savedra shrugged. "It wasn't that bad. More frightening than anything else." Her right arm twitched—looking closer, Isyllt saw a bulge beneath her sleeve that was probably bandages.

Saints preserve her from clueless anixeroi. "Demon wounds are always that bad. Let me see."

Buttons lined the sleeve from wrist to elbow. Isyllt unfastened them one by one while Savedra tried not to flinch, until she could see the bandage that wrapped the woman's forearm. Savedra shuddered like a fly-stung horse as cold tendrils of magic probed the wound.

As far as damage to the flesh went, it wasn't so bad. No

poison in the blood, and she still had use of the arm. But sure enough, traces lingered, black and crimson to unfocused *otherwise* eyes. And something else, a faint shadow working through her veins—not septicemia, but a magical taint. Isyllt abandoned courtesy and pressed further, sending her magic chasing through Savedra's flesh till she found the point of origin—a blood-colored shadow on her mouth.

"You ate something tainted, or drank it." She let go and Savedra flinched back against the chair, her lips bruised with chill.

"I didn't— Oh, Black Mother." She scrubbed a hand across her mouth. "Blood. When the bird was killed, its blood sprayed on me. I still remember the taste."

"Saints. Have you noticed any effects?"

"Dreams. Bad dreams." She shook her head. "*Strange* dreams. Oh! I nearly forgot." She fumbled in her pocket and produced a small bundle of silk. "I found this in Carnavas. I thought it must have belonged to a mage."

Not again, Isyllt thought with a grimace as she unwrapped the ring. Not a sapphire this time, but a ruby, set in a delicate white gold band. A more decorative stone than hers, cushion-cut and brilliantly faceted beneath a layer of dirt. The purpose of a necromancer's diamond was not beauty—hence the dulling cabochon shape.

"It was a mage's, all right." The stone throbbed in her hand. "Have you touched it?"

"Not since I first picked it up."

The inside of the silk handkerchief was smeared with grime. Isyllt resisted the urge to clean the stone to study its hue.

"Is it...occupied?" Savedra asked.

"Only diamonds hold ghosts and spirits. Rubies and sapphires and emeralds hold spells instead, or raw power. This one definitely has power." Power that tasted of rust and sweet scabs in her head, like cinnamon and marrow. Blood magic.

She closed the cloth around it again, before magpie greed made her careless. "I think," she said to Savedra, "that I'll be able to help you. I'm hunting a haematurge. Maybe the same one you are." Savedra slumped in her chair, tension-sharp angles softening. "Also, I can probably remove the magical taint from you. But if I don't, it will be easier to track her."

The woman shuddered. "Leave it, then," she said after a moment.

Isyllt nodded approval. "Were you followed here? You looked nervous when you arrived."

Savedra's chin rose as she frowned. "I don't know. I didn't see anyone, but my nerves have been bad since I left Carnavas. I dream of birds stalking women through the streets." She fussed with her buttons, managing one or two before giving up. "I think I saw her tonight, this mysterious Margravine Phaedra. She was at my uncle's house."

Isyllt's hands tingled as they tightened on her chair. "Did she see you?"

"Yes. Do you think I'm in danger?"

"I don't know. I hope not, but we can't assume that."

"No, of course not." Her mouth twisted. "It's always best to assume you're in danger. I have survived the palace this long, after all. What shall we do?"

"I can try to scry her. The ring and the taint in your blood will make powerful foci." Isyllt pushed herself out of her chair. "Follow me."

They cleared a space in the center of Isyllt's workroom and unrolled a map of the city across the bare boards. The corners she pinned with stray mugs and books—not exactly glamorous spellcasting, but she was still too tired for flash and frills.

"What do you need from me?" Savedra asked.

"Stand there—" she pointed to the far end of the parchment, "—and concentrate on Phaedra, anything you know about her." The ruby ring she laid in the center of the map to serve as a marker.

Isyllt took her place opposite Savedra and closed her eyes. Her right hand clenched till the band of her ring cut into her flesh. Phaedra Severos. She turned the name over in her mind, weighing and tasting it. A pity she didn't have a face to accompany it, but the ruby should be focus enough.

Her nape prickled as her focus sharpened. Metal scraped and rattled as the ruby ring began to shake. *Where are you, Phaedra?*

A wall of fog rushed to meet her, dark and red and cloying. The smell of blood and cinnamon filled her nose, coated her tongue, crawled down her throat to choke her. Counter-magic, an obfuscation to thwart prying eyes. Isyllt tried to gather her power, but she couldn't breathe, couldn't concentrate. As her vision washed from red to black, she felt a woman's presence beside her, felt her amusement. Then she fell, an endless dizzying spiral, down and down and down—

"Isyllt!"

Savedra's face appeared close to hers, eyes dark with panic. The floor was cold and hard beneath her.

"What happened?" She wanted to spit out the lingering reek of blood.

"You fell." Savedra caught her shoulder and helped her sit up. "The ring started to move, then everything washed red for a heartbeat and you fell."

"She's taken precautions," Isyllt said. The taste of copper dripped into her mouth. She scrubbed a hand across her face and it came away scarlet and sticky—her nose was bleeding. "I can't break her wards." And, more quietly, "She's powerful."

Fog coiled thick and blue in the streets when Isyllt escorted Savedra out to find a carriage, bleeding orange at lamplight's touch. Mist swallowed the sky, swallowed everything past a few yards in every direction, but Isyllt knew they weren't alone in the night. The city lay still and hushed, but the toll of the night bells echoed all around, shivering in Isyllt's bones.

Savedra jumped at the first peal, then giggled. "Nerves. It still feels like someone's watching."

"I think we're safe from prying eyes for the moment," Isyllt lied, giving her a lopsided smile.

They found a carriage two streets over, and Isyllt tipped the driver well to make sure Savedra reached the palace safely. Not that the man could do much if a sorceress attacked, but it made her feel a little better.

"I'll contact you as soon as I learn anything more," she said as she helped Savedra into the cab. "Please be discreet."

Savedra's glare conveyed a wealth of *don't teach your grandmother to suck eggs,* reminding Isyllt again that she was a scion of the Eight, and a skilled courtier besides. She covered Isyllt's hand with her own grey-gloved one, though, and that spoke only gratitude. "I'll do the same," she said as the door closed. "Thank you."

When the carriage was out of sight, Isyllt slipped into the nearest fog-shrouded alley. A moment later her ring chilled as death breathed over her.

"What are you doing here?"

"Waiting for you," Spider said from behind her. "Keeping an eye on you—I hear of sickness and death in the city."

"Some might call that pursuance. The law frowns on it."

This time she followed him more easily as he moved in front of her. Either she was growing used to it or feeding made him slow. His skin was no less pale, but stolen heat suffused his flesh. He stroked her cheek with one long hand. "Some might call it affection."

A drop of blood glistened black at the corner of his mouth. Isyllt wiped it away with her thumb. "Another willing donor?"

"Do you really want to know?"

His scent filled her nose through the smell of fog and wet stone, and she wanted to lean into it. But she wasn't tired and lonely tonight; tonight she was working. She caught his wrist and pulled his hand away. After a heartbeat he acquiesced, flesh becoming pliable.

"I hope you don't leave the bodies lying in the street for constables to trip over." She scrubbed her hands on her trousers when she let go.

Fangs flashed with his smile. "There's always the river for that."

"Yes." Isyllt thought of the cathedral-cavern beneath the river, of the offerings there. She had dreamed of it too, during the fever, dreamed of finding the swollen corpses of people she knew floating in black water. When she was younger she had dreamed of watching the Vigils pull the corpses of her friends from the slime-slick river gates.

Thinking of the corpse-gates set another thought burning in her brain, bright enough that she nearly jumped. "Yes, there is."

"I thought we might talk tonight," Spider said. The fog softened the sharp angles of his face, dulled the preternatural glitter of his eyes. Or maybe that was only his glamour trying to draw her close.

She forced a smile. "I've been ill for nearly a decad, and I have work to do in the morning. Some other night. You can buy me another drink."

His mouth curled, close-lipped and very nearly human. "Whenever you wish." He pressed a cool kiss on her knuckles and faded into the mist.

Isyllt had no intention of sleeping, though she prowled her apartment for a time with the lights dimmed. When she couldn't take the inaction any longer she changed clothes and put her hair up properly and slipped into the street again. This time she felt no prickle of awareness, no death chill. She knew it would make no difference if Spider were still about, but she took the long way through Archlight's steep and winding streets nonetheless, twisting and doubling back on her way to Kiril's house.

The odds of him sleeping at this hour were just as good as her own. Sure enough, she found a light burning in his bedroom window. She didn't bother to knock, simply laid a hand on the door and let the wards recognize her.

She waited shivering on the doorstep for several moments, till she began to suspect that he'd fallen asleep with the light on. Finally he opened the door, fully dressed and frowning.

"I know it's an unholy hour," she said lightly, "but you

needn't look that unhappy to see me." She meant it as a jest, not a jibe, but he didn't smile. "What's the matter?"

"A long night." He stepped aside slowly, as if reluctant to admit her. He didn't offer to take her coat. She tried to pretend the ache in her chest was only the aftermath of her illness. "For you as well, I take it."

The front of the house was nearly as cold as the night outside, and had an air of disuse about it—less the smell of dust as a lack of the usual polish. That in itself wasn't unusual, but combined with his drawn face and distance it wedged another splinter of worry under her heart. And she knew voicing any concern would only cause him to pull further away.

"An *interesting* night," she said, keeping her fears away from her face and voice. She doubted she succeeded entirely—after fifteen years she couldn't lie to him any better than he could to her. "There's more to this case than tomb-robbing vampires."

Kiril stilled. "The case that the prince and I suggested you let lie?"

She didn't cross her arms defensively, but it was a near thing. "I'm not satisfied with what I've found."

"Some mysteries bring no satisfaction with the solving."

"Even so."

"I could order you to stop."

She nodded, and now her arms did cross, slow and deliberate. "You could."

He smiled tiredly. "So stubborn. I can't imagine where you learned such a thing. Why defy me on this?"

She shrugged. "I promised to find Forsythia's killer."

He didn't wince, but she saw his discomfort. "Promises to the dead rarely bring satisfaction either."

Her composure cracked and she swayed forward, forcing a traitorous hand back to her side. "What's wrong?
Tell me and I can help you."

An unfamiliar scent filled her nose as she drew close.
Not the usual amalgam of spices that clung to Kiril's skin,
but orange and cinnamon and almond, delicately blended.
A woman's perfume.

Jealousy was an ugly, irrational thing, but that didn't
keep its claws out of her chest. Even uglier was the memory that followed hard on its heels, the echo of Forsythia's
hollow voice: *All I could smell was her perfume—orange
and spices.*

Coincidence, she prayed. *It has to be coincidence.* But
she knew it had no obligation to be anything of the sort.

Kiril missed the instant's horror on her face by turning
away. "I can't," he said. "I'm sorry. I can only ask you to
please leave this case alone. For everyone's sake."

"I can't do that. Will you bind me?" He could, as her
master and the keeper of her oaths. It was not an option
that either of them had ever voiced before.

He winced, but she took no pleasure in the strike.
"No."

"Then I suppose we've run out of conversation."

"Isyllt—" She turned, one hand on the doorknob. His
eyes were black holes in his seamed face, and he looked
frailer than she'd ever seen. Shrunken. "I am sorry."

"So am I."

She closed the door softly behind her and fled into
the fog.

As she closed the door of her suite behind her, Savedra
knew she wasn't alone. Her knife was in her hand before

she could think, her already taut nerves singing and her pulse hard and fierce in her throat.

"It's only me," Ashlin said. A match scraped and wept sparks as she kindled a lamp. "Remind me never to sneak up behind you."

"I would be very embarrassed to kill you." She dropped the blade on a table; she'd only cut herself if she tried to resheathe it.

"What's wrong?"

"A trying night."

"Are you all right?"

"As well as can be expected." She reached for the buttons on the back of her neck and hissed as her wounded arm twisted. She'd forgotten about it during her talk with Isyllt, but now it burned and itched abominably.

"Here," Ashlin said, moving to help. "I let the house-keepers draft your maid for decorating. I promised you wouldn't mind."

Savedra sighed. Mathiros's imminent return had the staff strained and rushing about their work. She hadn't realized how peaceful the palace had been without him. She had seen masters far more critical and harsh than the king, but he was always brusque without Lychandra to soften him, and no one wanted to be nearby when his temper snapped.

In her brooding she forgot where she was and whom she was with until Ashlin began removing the pins from her hair. "Don't," she said, stepping away. She clutched her gown to her chest in a ridiculous display of modesty.

"I'm sorry. I didn't mean—" The princess turned, throwing up her hands. "Gods, this is so ridiculous."

Savedra laughed humorlessly. "It is." She unclenched

her fingers and the gown crumpled at her feet. She wanted to kick it aside, but draped it over a chair instead. "What are we going to do?"

Ashlin sat heavily on the foot of the bed, slouching elbows to knees. "What can we do?"

"Pretend it never happened?"

That drew the princess's head up with a jerk. "Is that what you want?"

She ought to lie; it would be easier. "I don't know. I have the choice of hurting you or hurting Nikos."

"You love him. I understand."

"I love you too. But I never expected this."

It was Ashlin's turn to laugh. "Neither did I. I only wanted a friend. I've never had many. Which is my own fault, for being a prickly sharp-tongued bitch. Then I met you, and you should have hated me but you didn't, and you were clever and funny and beautiful and I was so bleeding *grateful*—" She shook her head. "I never imagined it would turn into something more, but now it has and I don't know what to do. I've seen things like this before. I know how ugly they can turn. If— If you want me to go—"

Savedra wanted to scream, to laugh until she wept; her mother and Thea Jsutien between them couldn't have concocted so clever a scheme. All it would take was a bit of jealousy and heartache to undermine the already strained marriage and send Ashlin home to Celanor, leaving Nikos embarrassed and obliged to remarry. And he still couldn't marry her. What would the Jsutiens offer, she wondered madly, if she sent Nikos to Ginevra after all?

It felt like she moved through water as she crossed the room and cupped Ashlin's cheek in one hand, like trying to run in a dream. "I don't want you to leave. But I don't

want you to be miserable if you stay, either." The softness of the princess's skin sent a shiver up the length of
her arm. Even dyed, her hair was finer than Nikos's, the
freshly trimmed tips prickly.

Ashlin turned her head and pressed a chaste kiss on
Savedra's palm, and then a lingering one on the hollow of
her wrist. "I'm not drunk enough for this."

Savedra laughed breathlessly, though it wasn't funny.
Wine, she'd learned, was usually how the princess nerved
herself for marital obligations. She thought of her parents
together, their easy affection and quiet, obvious devotion,
and felt a pang of grief that something so simple should
elude so many.

She might have argued that it was that grief that made
her tilt Ashlin's head back and kiss her. Grief and lingering horror, the need to feel warm and safe again. She
might have said that, but it would have been a lie.

This time was slower, tentative and exploratory and still
awkward. The fit of their bodies was strange and unnerving, but an improvement over Savedra's clumsy and adolescent encounter with a girl from Arachne twelve years
ago. That had been the last time she'd lain with a woman,
until Evharis.

"I don't usually worry about pregnancy," Savedra said
after a long silence, "but we have to." Pragmatism dulled
the pleasant tingle in her limbs, but she couldn't ignore it.

"There is the possibility that I'm barren," Ashlin said,
not quite meeting her eyes. "And wouldn't that be irony fit
for an opera. I could have joined a mercenary company
after all, and spared everyone grief." She squeezed Savedra's hand as she said it.

"It could also be Nikos." It felt like a betrayal to say the words aloud, but he had acknowledged the chance himself after the second miscarriage. In the dark, in fact, in a scene much like this. She swallowed a bitter laugh. "It's not as though I've borne him any bastards to say otherwise."

They lay quietly for a while, with the weight of secrets and costs like a blade between them.

"You should go," Savedra said at last, because some-one had to.

"I should." The shadows hid the princess's face, but the hurt in her voice was clear. Savedra held herself still and silent while Ashlin dressed, though she ached to reach for her, to call her back.

"I'm sorry," she said at last, as Ashlin turned to the door.

"So am I," the princess whispered. Then she was gone.

Savedra wanted to press her face against the pillow and cry herself to sleep. But she was too much her mother's daughter for that. Instead she rose and opened the win-dows to the damp and frigid night, then turned to the bot-tle of brandy on her dressing table. The first glass went down her throat in a single searing gulp. The second she carefully dashed across the soiled sheets. She changed the linens herself, awkwardly hauling a fresh set across the wide bed. When that was done she ran herself a bath and scrubbed away the scent of Ashlin's skin. Next, wet and shivering in the drafty room, she opened the doors of her shrine and lit a stick of incense to Saint Sarai.

By then dawn was a pale blue wash against her win-dows, and she ached to the bone with fatigue. She sealed the room again and crawled into her cold bed. The scent of smoke and sandalwood and brandy chased her into the dark, and haunted her through alien dreams.

CHAPTER 13

The dawn chimes found Isyllt in Inkstone, climbing the broad steps of the Justiciary. The hour of tenderness, the first terce was called, but the only tenderness she felt was her bruised and sleepless eyes. White marble soared above her, painted rose and gold with sunrise—fluted columns holding aloft the pediment and its statues. Meant to be historical figures, but everyone looked the same carved in stone; she preferred the gargoyles crouching on the Sepulcher across the square.

At the top of the stairs Isyllt met a young constable fumbling with her keys. Smaller police stations around the city stayed open all night to collect rowdy drunks and careless criminals, but the central office closed with the evensong bells like any respectable bureaucracy. The girl did a hasty double take when she saw Isyllt.

The front room was tall and broad, lit by high narrow windows and many lamps, which the young Vigil moved to light. The space was meant to intimidate more than welcome; past it desks lined the walls, and doors and halls led to the offices of senior Vigils. Other Vigils began to trickle in, muttering and joking and lighting braziers for tea. Isyllt couldn't imagine having to face so much garish orange at the start of every day.

She must have looked worse than she realized—the young constable brought her the first cup of tea, and was so solicitous that Isyllt wanted to bite her. She smiled instead, though it made her face ache, and took the tea and offered chair and settled to wait for Khelséa. She was staring, she knew—at the ceiling, the Vigils, the leaves swirling at the bottom of her cup. All her thoughts were dark, ugly things with cutting edges. Better to think on nothing and let the noise of the Justiciary wash over her.

The noise was little better: accusations, reports of theft, reports of people missing, tearful demands for aid. No one came to the police with pleasant tidings, after all. Many of those who came asking for help were Rosian; many of them left unsatisfied. Isyllt had an abundance of sympathy at the moment, so much so that she very nearly flung her teacup down and screamed.

Khelséa's arrival saved her an embarrassing scene. Isyllt hadn't seen the inspector since she left St. Alia's, though they'd exchanged notes and Khelséa had assured her she was well. Watching her now, Isyllt knew it for a lie. Pain carved lines around her eyes and mouth and a notch between her brows, aging her years in only days. She walked slowly, deliberately, glancing from side to side as though she feared attack, and every so often she touched a chair or table as she passed, surreptitiously steadying herself.

"You said you were fine," Isyllt said in greeting, lifting her eyebrows.

"I am. I will be," she amended. "The physicians said it will be at least another decad until my ear heals. The pain I can handle, and even the poor hearing, but I keep losing my balance." She tilted her head as she spoke, turning her good ear to Isyllt and keeping her eyes on her deaf side.

"What did you tell the other Vigils?"

"A fast infection. I've had to endure everyone's advice and grandmothers' hedge-magic remedies ever since."

"But only out of one ear," Isyllt said helpfully. It earned her a laugh and a slap on the arm.

"What about you? You're not looking so well-rested yourself."

"I'm—" She shook her head with a snort. "I'm not fine. But I'm working, and I've learned something. We need to talk."

"All right." Khelséa redid her top two coat buttons. "You can buy me breakfast, then."

They ate griddle cakes and mulled cider at the Black Holly tea shop across the plaza, and Isyllt explained about Forsythia's murder and the haematurge.

"She's done this before. She may have done it again since. There will be other bodies for us to find. More young women, probably."

Khelséa snorted, mopping up cream and preserves with a bite of cake. "Do you know how many young women end up in the river with their throats slit? And hardly any of them are fit to autopsy by the time we haul them out. How will you tell the difference?"

"Thaumaturgical residue. I know the taste of her magic now. Look for victims like Forsythia—throats slit left-handed, no other wounds. She may be mad and murderous, but it doesn't sound like she tortures them. She has a vampire working with her, but he didn't feed on Forsythia first."

She lowered her voice as a pair of women wandered past, though they were too engrossed in an account of someone else's romantic pursuits to pay any attention. Perfume trailed after them, peach and citrus and honey-sweetness.

Citrus. Isyllt set her mug of cider down without drinking. She'd smelled that bitter orange note before—first on Savedra, and only a few hours ago on Kiril. And if that was the same perfume Forsythia had smelled—

"Where does the fashionable perfume come from this season?" she asked Khelséa.

The woman blinked. "Kebechet at the Black Phoenix. I bought Gemma a vial of her oils last month. Her shop is in Panchrest Court. Why?" she asked as Isyllt reached for her purse.

"I've smelled her perfume. If I can trace it..." She counted out coins. "Search the morgues—I'll meet you when I'm finished."

Khelséa's eyebrows arched. "I get wet corpses and you get perfume?"

"I bought you breakfast, didn't I?"

"You'll buy me a month of breakfasts for this."

"I'll start a new expense account." Which, of course, she couldn't, not since Kiril had ruled the investigation closed. She kept her good hand from clenching, brushed it quickly against Khelséa's dark fingers instead. "Thank you." She turned before the inspector could respond, bolting for the nearest carriage.

*   *   *

The Black Phoenix was a fashionable shop in an equally fashionable block of the alchemists' street. The Arcanost frequently bemoaned the baseness of commercial alchemy, but it clearly paid better than academia. Vials of ivory and colored glass gleamed in the rising light, and the rugs and hangings were Iskari, and costly. Even so early in the day shoppers drifted through the shop, young and well dressed, likely scions of the Eight, twittering like mourning doves as they browsed.

The air was surprisingly clear, considering the hundreds of bottles and vials and jars of ingredients Isyllt counted, but as she or the other shoppers moved she caught whiffs of scent: herbs and spices, flowers and resins and a dozen other notes she couldn't identify. Delicate scents and harsh ones, cloying and tangy, some that made her mouth water and some that made her fight a sneeze.

A clerk followed the mourning doves, opening vials and dabbing scent on proffered wrists. He cast a solicitous glance at Isyllt but she shook her head; he wasn't the one who could help her. After several moments, a curtain stirred in the back and the proprietress emerged.

Kebechet—the name of an Assari saint, and unlikely her true one—was a tall woman with a fierce hooked nose. Her hair was a black storm down her back, shot through with the glitter of jeweled pins and combs. Despite the chill, her shawl slipped off her shoulders, baring an ample corseted bosom. Rumor held that she was a bastard Severoi who had taken the family device for her own. Isyllt had never heard a member of the house confirm or deny it.

She exchanged pleasantries with the doves, and commended or corrected their choice of scents. When they departed, her black eyes trained immediately on Isyllt.

"Good morning, necromancer. Looking for a scent? Or perhaps a healing oil—something to help you sleep?"

"Is it that obvious? No," she amended, "don't answer that. I'm following a scent and it's led me here."

"Then I hope it was a pleasant one, and not some of that trash they peddle down the street."

"Quite pleasant. Neroli and almond and cinnamon, I think."

"Ah." Kohl-lined eyes gleamed. "Yes, neroli is a popular note this year."

"Do you remember this particular scent?"

"It isn't one of my standards. I make a lot of personal blends." She shrugged one bronze shoulder and her shawl slipped another inch.

"And I'm sure you remember all of them," Isyllt said with a smile, "or have notes. I need to know who you made it for."

Kebechet stilled, flawless and poised as a statue. "That would be a breach of trust. Not all of my customers come to me publicly."

"I respect that, but this is a murder investigation."

"Ah." She turned to the clerk, who was polishing a counter with great concentration. "Kadri, would you be a dear and fetch us some tea, and maybe some cardamom cakes? There's no hurry."

The boy left, a flush darkening his copper-brown cheeks, and Kebechet latched the door behind him. "You think one of my customers is a murderer?"

"Someone wearing one of your blends slit a woman's throat for blood magic. Most likely more than one woman's."

The perfumist swallowed. "All right." She flipped the

sign in the window. "I'll help you if I can. We can sit down in the back." She led Isyllt through the curtain, past a cluttered workroom and into a cramped but pleasant sitting room beside an equally cramped kitchen.

"Do you remember who you made that perfume for?" Isyllt asked as she sat. Her shoulders wanted to slump with fatigue, but Kebechet's perfect corseted posture kept her back straight.

"Neroli and almond and cinnamon? Varis Severos. But," she added quickly, "I'm hard pressed to imagine Varis killing anyone, especially for magic. He won't even bind spirits."

"He may have had nothing to do with it," Isyllt lied calmly, "but the perfume passed from him to the person who did. Did he say if it was for someone?"

"It must have been—he could never have worn something like that. He often gives perfume to his...friends, nearly always personal blends. He has a wonderful nose for combining scents. I remember that one because he brought me a sample, an old bottle with only a few drops left, and asked me to recreate it. Not my work originally, but still quite nice. The cinnamon was much stronger than is popular now—it burns the skin, you know, and no one wants welts on their cleavage."

"Did he say who it was for?"

The perfumist shook her head. "No. Not even an oblique sort of hint—I hear a lot of those."

"Thank you. I appreciate your assistance." She started to rise, and froze with her hands braced on the arms of the chair. "Do you still have the old perfume bottle?"

Kebechet blinked. "I may." She led Isyllt into the work room, and sorted through the clutter scattered across tables and piled into cabinets. "Here." She pulled a cut glass bottle from the back of a shelf and held it out. A thin skin of oil rolled across the bottom. "Will this help you?"

"It might." Isyllt wrapped the bottle carefully in a silk handkerchief before stowing it in her coat pocket. In any proper investigation, she would have enough evidence to go to Varis and demand answers, with the weight of Kiril's and the Crown's authority behind her. She clenched her teeth in frustration with Kiril and his secrets. "Thank you."

Kebechet shrugged gracefully. "Anything to help the Crown. Can I interest you in a perfume, while you're here?"

Isyllt was hardly in the mood to shop, but she knew the value of a healthy bribe. "I do have a ball to attend . . . ."

Isyllt did know how many dead bodies turned up in the river each decad, at least on average. Part of her job was keeping track of the number and natures of deaths in Erisín, so she would recognize oddities.

That knowledge couldn't prepare her for the line of corpses waiting for them in the Sepulcher.

The smell rose from the stairwell: putrescence, rich and layered, more than any incense could drown. Neither sweet nor sour and both at once, choking and viscid. It rolled over Isyllt's skin, coiled in her nostrils and pressed against her tightened lips. And beneath the stages of rot, a fainter metallic bitterness that she associated with the Dis. Her right hand clenched against the burning chill of her ring.

Dahlia, whom Isyllt had collected from the Briar Patch, pressed a hand over her mouth and turned grey.

"Can you stand it?" Isyllt asked, breathing shallowly. Opening her mouth was a mistake. She had probably smelled worse at some point, but she couldn't remember when.

The girl shot her a glance of pure vitriol. "This is why no one likes necromancers."

"One of many reasons. Come on."

Fifteen bodies lay on slabs in the vaulted chamber, swollen, mottled flesh illuminated with the brutal efficiency of witchlight. The oldest was at the limit of its preservation spells, no more than a day from deliquescence. The freshest was still damp. The river cared for no one's vanity, but from the ribbons tangled in the corpse's long ash-brown hair, Isyllt imagined the bloated, peeling shape on the table had once been a pretty girl. The body of a small bronze-black crab clung to the hair above one ear like a ghastly fascinator. The tiny necrophages clustered on the bars of the corpse-gates, where food was plentiful. More than one of the corpses here had likely been eaten hollow before the Vigils pulled it out.

Several of the bodies Isyllt was able to dismiss quickly. Two had traces of white foam in their mouths and nostrils, evidence that they'd been alive when they went into the water. The third had been stabbed multiple times in the chest and stomach—angry, vicious wounds, but not meant to exsanguinate. Swelling stretched the gashes, baring layers of skin and flesh and white-marbled fat. The macerated skin had begun to slough from the corpse's hands. The oldest was so far gone that even Isyllt wasn't willing to inspect it closely.

Of the remainders, four bore slit throats, and three of those carried telltale traces of cinnamon. Isyllt wondered if she would ever enjoy pastries or spiced tea again.

Three women dead since Forsythia, and saints only knew how many others they hadn't found.

They left the Sepulcher by the afternoon bells, as the light began to thicken and slant.

"We can search for more tomorrow." Isyllt said, scrubbing a hand over her face. She regretted it as soon as she did—the smell of corpses clung to her. Dahlia and Khelséa were still ashen, and she doubted she looked any better; no one suggested food.

The bells began to ring only a moment after she spoke. Not the stately melody of the hour, but a wild and enthusiastic tintinnabulation. All down the street people paused mid-stride, stuck their heads out of shop doors, turned to their neighbors for confirmation. Isyllt knew they wouldn't be doing much investigating tomorrow: The army was coming home.

A young man burst from a doorway and bolted down the sidewalk, nearly trampling them. Isyllt swore as she tugged Dahlia out of the way. The rough plaster wall gouged her shoulder blades, and paper crinkled and tore. The parchment fluttered free when she moved and Isyllt caught it absently. An advertisement for the latest opera, or whatever had been the latest a decad ago; the paper was warped with moisture, the ink faded and smeared.

"Looks like I'll be containing crowds tomorrow," Khelséa said with a grimace. "Maybe I'll claim another ear infection. What will you do?"

"I don't know." The paper crumpled in her fist. "More importantly, what will *she* do?"

An idea welled in the back of her mind, and her frown eased. She opened her fingers and smoothed the flier.

"Expensive perfumes are meant to be worn," she said slowly, tumbling the idea end over end. "Especially ones from the most fashionable perfumery in the city. This witch of ours may hide her face, but she also buys scent and has dresses fitted. Where can a veiled woman go and attract the right sort of attention?"

She dangled the paper in front of the others' faces and watched their eyes widen.

Khelséa argued, but it was Ciaran whom Isyllt asked to accompany her. Being seen with a Vigil wasn't the sort of attention she wanted tonight—not to mention the opera would be wasted on someone deaf in one ear.

He arrived at her door at Evensong, resplendent in black velvet and crimson silk, his hair loose and shining over his shoulders. Finer clothes than she'd thought he owned, but what Ciaran didn't have he always knew how to acquire. Not a perfect complement to her dove grey and opals, but hardly an eyesore.

"I didn't think you liked the opera," he said, leaning against the doorway while she pinned up her hair. Her shoulder was still mottled yellow and green, but at least the weather let her wear a scarf.

"I don't, particularly, but this is business." She much preferred spoken theater, or even the musicals that flourished in the demimonde orpheums. Hours of constant song wore on her.

Ciaran sighed. "Of course it is. You couldn't simply want to go out for the joy of it."

She almost made a joke about the joy of expense accounts and bit her tongue. Her hand tightened on a hair stick and she took a deep breath. A crease formed between her reflection's eyebrows. She still looked tired and wan, and hadn't the skill with cosmetics to hide it. No powder could conceal the stark shadows below her collarbones—flesh she could ill afford to lose had melted away while she was bedridden. The iridescent fire of the opals at her throat and ears cheered her, though, and no one expected a necromancer to be plump and rosy with health. She forced a smile, held it in place till it fit, then pulled the black silk covering over the mirror and turned to find her gloves.

"What's playing tonight, anyway?"

Ciaran gave a sigh for her ignorance. "*Astrophel and Satis*. Thierselis's version."

"Damn. I prefer the Kharybdea."

"Of course you do. It's one of the reasons I'm so fond of you." He crossed the room to stand behind her, dropping a light kiss just below her ear. "Is that a new perfume?"

The Orpheum Tharymis rose above the rooftops of Lyre, its marble columns and domes gilded by hundreds of lanterns. Musicians and dancers chased each other through elaborate friezes, and owl-winged gargoyles brooded dramatically over the doorways; golden light glazed the rain-damp street below. Vendors thronged the pavement beneath the broad steps, offering flowers and refreshments and forged programs for cheaper than one could find inside. Ribbons of scent twisted with the breeze— wine and cider, garlic and sugar and bruising blossoms.

The Tharymis was the oldest and grandest orpheum in the city, though many would argue that the Magdalen— or the Garden's Rhodon—had the better productions. Had it been an opening night, even Isyllt's diamond wouldn't have been enough to secure tickets. As it was, most of the other attendees looked through her and Ciaran without the aid of an obfuscation charm.

Witchlights blazed in crystal chandeliers overhead, gleaming on brass and marble and polished wood, burnished the blue velvet seats and curtains. The tiny bowls that lined the aisles were witchlit as well. Beeswax candles burned in wall sconces—easier to light and douse, and less likely to catch someone's cloak or skirts alight.

Isyllt had managed mediocre seats on the ground floor—good enough if one truly wanted to watch the performance, but beneath the notice of the balconies and private boxes. She sent Ciaran for refreshments and tried to watch the Severos box without getting a crick in her neck. Eventually a page rapped at the door with drinks for two, but of the occupants she saw nothing but a pale hand emerging to take the tray. If Varis was there, perhaps his mysterious companion was as well.

Ciaran returned with wine as the witchlights began to pulse and dim. The cacophony of a hundred conversations faded to a gentle susurrus, and finally died as the first notes drifted from the orchestra pit.

The midnight-blue curtains opened, revealing the stage dressed as a city street and the chorus gowned in old-fashioned demimonde finery. They introduced the heroine Astrophel, a poor lacemaker who loved beyond her reach, and the object of her affection, the witch Satis, who lived in her dusty tower with only ghosts and one jealous servant, nursing her magic and grief for a long-lost love. Astrophel was played as always by the season's up-and-coming soprano, a girl the program identified as Anika Sirota. A Rosian name, and she had the milk-and-roses complexion and shining golden hair to match. Satis was a role for aging contraltos, when they weren't cast as mad queens or vengeful mothers. Isyllt had seen Zahara Noïs in a dozen roles over the years—a tall, rawboned woman whose white-streaked auburn mane was visible from the highest seats. The audience shivered whenever she sang one of Satis's mad arias.

Isyllt finished her wine long before Astrophel charmed her way past Satis's doorstep for the first time. Her fingers tightened around her empty cup when they sang their first duet. Sirota's voice rang with passion, with pain and longing beyond an ingénue's years. When the two women sank into an embrace behind a scrim and the curtain fell for intermission, applause shook the orpheum to its bones.

Isyllt kept an eye on the Severos box during the break, and saw Varis come and go. She didn't follow, but drank more wine and let the din of the crowd wash over her. Sirota was the darling of the season, she quickly learned— the daughter of refugees, lifted from the slums by her talent. Isyllt heard a few snide remarks about her origins, but most of the audience seemed smitten with the girl, and thought her story operatic in itself.

Isyllt didn't appreciate Thiercelis's opera as much as Kharybdea's spoken theater, but *Astrophel and Satis* was powerful in any version, especially with singers as talented as these. Someone in the audience was weeping or cursing at any given moment during the second half of the show, as Satis's ghosts tried to woo her back from her mortal lover, and her jealous assistant and Astrophel's suitor Marius—the same tenor Nikos had commented on in *The Rain Queen*—tried to keep the girl away.

Since it was a tragedy, Astrophel's steadfast devotion might defeat mortal jealousy, but couldn't overcome the hungry dead. The servant locked her in Satis's tower overnight while the sorceress was away, and the ghosts did their work. When Satis returned at dawn, she found Astrophel half dead and more than half mad from the attentions of the specters. Thinking Satis another ghost, she threw herself out of the tower to escape. After the lovers' final duet—for which the production spared no expense for pig's blood—Satis stalked through her house dripping blood, murdering her servant and destroying the ghosts before finally drinking lye and dying alone in her tower, surrounded by crumbling dry flowers. Because it was theater she sang to the end, and Noïs's raw, broken voice sent chills through everyone who heard it. Isyllt found herself clutching her throat; Ciaran didn't laugh— his face was slick with tears.

When the curtain fell on the final flower-strewn stage, the house was silent for a long sniffling moment before the applause rose in a tidal roar. Isyllt stood for the ovation, ignoring glares as she slipped down the aisle and up the stairs before the crowd began to pour toward the doors. Those with boxes tended to wait for the press to die, but she wanted to be sure to catch Varis before he disappeared.

Wine still warmed her blood as she climbed the shell-curved side stair. The downward rush of people caught her before she reached the third story, and she clung tight to the banister as she fought her way up.

Her timing was immaculate; the door to the box opened as she drew near and Varis Severos emerged, as eye-catching as ever. Tonight his coat was a green so dark it was almost black, the high-collared shirt beneath searing verdigris. Gems glittered along the curve of one ear, carnelian and amethyst and brilliant citrine; his rings glittered too, bright with power.

"Lord Varis," she called before she could think better of it, and dipped a shallow curtsy when he turned. She knew him well enough from the Arcanost to strike up conversation, but they were hardly peers. In addition to the gulf in age and wealth, he was a vocal opponent of vinculation, and her magic relied on it.

One eyebrow rose. "Lady Iskaldur." His smile was polite and distant, but his eyes were sharp beneath painted lids. He smelled of lime and lilac, citron and musk. "Imagine seeing you here."

He and Kiril had been lovers once; she hardly ever thought of it, but now the idea made her blush. Was that why Kiril was protecting him now? Was that—*No.* She set it aside, ignoring her stinging cheeks.

"Did you enjoy the performance?" Varis continued. His pale eyes narrowed and she knew he marked her reaction.

"I did. Though their tenor is still only adequate, I'm afraid." Which was perhaps unfair—most singers were only adequate compared to Sirota and Noïs, and the character Marius and his infatuation with Astrophel were meant to pale in comparison.

His response died as the door opened behind him; Isyllt's pulse spiked in her throat.

The woman who emerged wore plum velvet, the sort of dress that would cost a civil servant a month's salary. Silver and jet glittered on her hem and cuffs, and spangled the black silk gauze of her veils. Beneath the gauze her black hair was piled high, a few locks uncoiling over her shoulders.

She laid a gloved hand on Varis's arm, cocking her head inquisitively. She didn't need a face to draw eyes from all over the room—her stance and figure and exquisite taste did that perfectly well. Her perfume was even richer and more conflagrant in person.

"Varis?" The woman's voice was low and pleasant and otherwise unremarkable, but it still sent a chill down Isyllt's neck. "Who is your friend?"

"This is Isyllt Iskaldur, a member of the Arcanost. You'll forgive me, Lady, if I don't introduce my companion."

Isyllt held out a hand. "A pleasure all the same."

The woman took her hand so smoothly the hesitation barely showed. The briefest brush of fingers and the contact ended, leaving Isyllt with a lingering whisper of magic and the taste of cinnamon on her tongue. Her stomach tightened with the memory of corpses.

"Likewise," the woman said, and Isyllt heard her smile. "Kiril has spoken of you."

It was meant to goad and Isyllt knew it. That didn't keep her spine from stiffening or her smile from sharpening. Varis's eyes narrowed and he tucked the woman's hand more firmly against his arm. "We should go, darling. If you'll excuse us..."

"Of course." She stepped aside with a sweep of skirts. "A pleasure to see you again, Lord Varis," she said as they stepped past. "And you, Margravine."

She hadn't meant to say it, not really, but too many dead bodies crowded behind her eyes. The woman's velvet-clad shoulders squared as the dart struck home and Varis nearly stumbled on the deep carpet, and though Isyllt knew it was a foolish risk to antagonize them, the rush of exultation more than paid for it.

Neither Varis nor Phaedra responded, only continued down the stairs with their perfect grace intact. As they reached the final landing Phaedra's veiled head turned, and Isyllt felt her regard like the weight of a hand. She had just made enemies of two powerful sorcerers—one with a penchant for slitting throats, and another who could ruin her career with a few well-placed words. At least, she thought as her stomach contracted, now she *knew*.

"What did you do?" Ciaran asked when she returned to his side.

"Something stupid."

"Have you heard anything?" Isyllt asked Ciaran as they left the orpheum. Claiming a carriage from the mob in front of the theater would require more violence than she was willing to bother with, so they turned down a side street to avoid the press.

"About murders and disappearances and blood mages?" His hand twitched at his side, a warding gesture. "Someone is always going missing in Elysia. I'm not sure yet which might be connected to your case. There's something else, though. About the vrykoloi."

He paused, glancing into the dark mouth of an alley as they passed it. "Speaking of which—"

Her ring chilled and she spun, cursing heavy skirts and the lack of her knife as she shoved Ciaran behind her. A shadow moved in the alley. She hadn't expected an attack this soon—

"No!" Ciaran grabbed her arm as her ring began to spark. An instant later the shadow resolved into a familiar shape. Isyllt swore as she lowered her hand, her pulse sharp and painful with unspent energy.

"I didn't mean to frighten you," Azarné said, pausing on the edge of the light. Her eyes flashed red and gold. "But I thought we should speak. I've learned things about the graverobbers. About Spider."

Isyllt nodded; his name was no surprise. "Yes, we should talk. But"—she didn't glance over her shoulder, only because she knew it was useless—"Spider has been following me lately. I can't guarantee you won't be seen in my company."

Azarné's tiny mouth curled in a sneer. "I'm not afraid of him."

Isyllt turned to Ciaran. "What about you?"

"I've survived being your friend for this long. I hardly see the point in stopping now."

Her hand tightened on his arm before she let go. "All right," she said to Azarné. "Meet me at my apartment and we'll talk."

Isyllt stirred the fire and took her hair down while they waited for Azarné, and put the kettle on. She wanted wine more than tea, but she didn't need any more foolhardiness tonight. She could always spike her cup with whiskey if she had to.

Ciaran paced a restless circuit through the room, and Isyllt rolled her lower lip between her teeth as she watched him. Music or theater always roused him, but this energy was nervous, distracted—he should have been humming or talking, sketching shapes of songs with his hands as he tried to make her understand what he heard.

Her wards shivered as the vrykola drew near, as they did with any stranger's approach, but this shiver became an angry buzz as the magic realized the intruder wasn't human. Isyllt quieted the spell before it could strike and allowed the vampire across her threshold. She was, she thought wryly, making a habit of this lately.

Ciaran stopped his pacing at Azarné's light scratch on the door—Isyllt caught him running a hand through his hair as she rose to answer it. She wanted to laugh, if only to convince herself that his new infatuation didn't hurt. She wanted to laugh even harder at her own double standards.

Isyllt had only ever seen the tiny vrykola in shadows and witchlight. The warm light of the lamps made her metallic bronze skin all the more unnatural, but also showed the stains and tatters of her clothes, the dust and grime that caked her hems and dulled her tangled hair. Did the state of undeath lend itself to ruined, dismal beauty, or did the catacombs simply lack dressmakers who could work in the dark?

Azarné's eyes shone as she glanced around the room, pupils contracting to uncanny pinpricks. She didn't stand beside Ciaran, but her weight and attention shifted toward him.

"Can I get you anything?" Isyllt asked automatically as she poured tea for her and Ciaran, and shook her head at the silliness of the question.

"No," Azarné said slowly. "Thank you." She drifted away from the door, spiraling through the sitting room like a new cat to inspect books and ornaments and furniture. Isyllt sat, cradling her teacup to warm her hands and waiting for the vampire to speak.

"What has Spider told you of his plans?" asked Azarné after another circuit of the room. She paused behind a chair, taloned fingers dimpling the cushioned back.

Isyllt sipped her tea, rolling smoke and tannin over her tongue. "He wants to renew the truce. He wants the freedom of the city. He hasn't told me how he means to accomplish that."

"That's true, but not the half of it. He wants control of the city. He wants to set his demon witch on the throne and rule through her."

Her fingers tightened on her cup. "What do you know about this witch?"

"I remember her from the first time she came below. Years and years ago. Spider courted her then, as well, the way he courts you now."

Isyllt snorted. "Tenebris mentioned another sorceress. Spider said she died."

"Oh, she did." She lifted one delicate hand, grey claws gleaming in the light. "That doesn't always keep you from coming back."

Isyllt's nape prickled. A living sorceress was bad enough—if it was a demon they hunted, undead, the matter was even more serious. The dead hungered, be they ghosts or vampires or necrophants. Phaedra must have a great deal of self-control, or careful handlers. Or there were a great many corpses yet to be found. Isyllt rose and added warmer tea to her cup, following it with a shot of whiskey. She leaned against the counter to drink it, pressing her corset stays into her ribs.

"What are they doing now?"

"I don't know. I've followed them through the tunnels, and seen them on the hunt together, but I don't want to get too close. Spider I don't fear, but I'd rather not face the two of them together. The sorceress has the freedom of daylight, and powerful charms besides. I haven't found their lair.

"That's not all," Azarné continued, as Isyllt reached for the whiskey again. She pulled her hand away and forced it back to her side.

"Of course it isn't. What else?"

"Spider's ideas are attracting attention in the catacombs. The idea of roaming free above"—her lips twisted—"of *hunting* free—appeals to some of us."

"To you?" Across the room, Isyllt saw Ciaran flinch.

The vampire bared her teeth. "I *am* a predator. We can survive on sips and drops, on willing donors, but it will never be the same. We all want the kill." She dropped her head. "But Spider wants more than that. He wants to rule the city."

"Do you want that too?"

Azarné was silent for a long time. So still she could have been a statue. When she moved again it was without her unnerving demon grace. She sank onto the edge of the chair and stared into nothing. Embers popped and fell in the hearth.

"I came to Erisín…years ago, with a delegation from Iskar, part of the Sultan's retinue. I never went home again. Many memories of my life have faded, but I remember the court, the petty cruelties of the seraglio. We hurt each other to pass the time, to pretend we had any power but what the sultan granted us. The nobles did the same, and so much worse. Mortals with authority—and those without—do terrible things every day. So imagine what a true monster would do if given power over others. We already hunt and kill for need and for pleasure, and never mind your truce. If we could do so with impunity it would be a hundred times worse."

Her eyes flashed as she moved, the only warning Isyllt

had. In the next heartbeat the vampire stood before her, so close she could feel the chill seeping from Azarné's flesh. The teacup shattered on the floor, spraying both their skirts with liquid.

"You should stop him," the vrykola whispered, leaning in on her tiptoes. "It will be ugly if you don't."

Nerves scalded her skin. Every instinct warned her to recoil; instead she stepped forward. Porcelain shards crunched and bit beneath her slippers as she glared down at the vampire. "You stop him then, if you know how ugly it will be. It won't be only mortals bleeding for this, I promise you that. Your elders let this happen—they can bloody well do something about it. I can't begrudge Spider his revolution, if the rest of you are this *useless*."

Azarné hissed, pupils widening. Isyllt's hands throbbed with anger and stress. Ciaran whispered the vampire's name.

In an eyeblink she moved to the door. "Perhaps you're right, necromancer. I'll tell Lady Tenebris what you said." And then she was gone, and the latch clicked shut behind her.

PART III

Aubade

CHAPTER 14

On the twenty-seventh of Hekate, the King's army returned to Erisín. They rode through the Dawn Gate at first light, as was traditional for victories. Historically, any action not ending in a rout and hasty flight to the city walls was considered a victory. They flew the tower and crescent moon of Selafai, white on grey, and the crowned griffin on blue of House Alexios. The banners would have snapped but for the night's rain. The rain also turned the haze of dust that trailed them into a sucking mire, and coated the soldiers in mud to the knee.

Despite the weather, helms and mail still gleamed and many of the horses were fresh enough to step proudly and toss their heads. Crowds choked the sidewalks, cheering and tossing hothouse flowers. Orange-coated police lined the barricades, keeping the streets clear and preventing any overly enthusiastic onlookers from rushing the procession, or soldiers' families from demanding news of their missing kin. Those questions would be asked later, away from the public eye.

And behind them, far from the cheers and flowers but toiling through the same mud—and more horse shit— came the refugees.

Savedra didn't stand with Nikos to welcome his father home. Some propriety they wouldn't test. But her station— and sharp elbows—earned her a place at the front of the crowd of courtiers gathered in the breathless cold of the palace courtyard. The prince and princess stood at the front, the king's aged seneschal beside them. Garlands and banners flapped around them, the wind stripping petals from hothouse flowers and scattering them across the stones. The cobbles had been scrubbed till they gleamed, and every stray bit of wood and metal polished. The staff all wore smiles firmly fixed, but Savedra was sure they didn't appreciate the king's timing.

The assembled court heard the approaching hooves before the trumpets sounded, the din of the crowds that followed. Three riders passed the gate at a time—first three of the king's honor guard, then the king himself flanked by two others, and then the final three, all on matching black horses. After them came the generals and officers and any soldiers who had kin in the palace. The others would have gone to the garrison by the western gate in Lastlight.

The honor guard opened their formation, circling their horses to the right until they stood in a line behind the king. Mathiros Alexios was not a tall man. He had been lean and strong in his youth, and age had thickened him but not lessened his strength. His ash-and-iron hair and beard were cropped close as any soldier's—shaggy now, after days on the road—and his skin was brown and seamed after a lifetime of sun and wind. He wore plain leather and mail under his blue cloak, and nothing resembling a crown. He didn't need one—the ferocity of his dark eyes was authority enough. Hard to remember sometimes, amid the scheming and complaints of the Octagon Court, just why the Eight rarely managed to outmaneuver or outvote him in the council. But as his gaze swept the courtyard a hundred heads bent rather than meet his eyes.

He stripped off his leather gauntlets and swung down from the saddle, patting his black mare affectionately. When his boots hit the ground the crowd knelt as one, with a sound like a wave foaming over stone. Only Nikos and Ashlin kept their feet, straight and shining.

Nikos had dressed with restraint for the occasion, though Savedra knew it chafed him—silks and velvets as always, but all in black, broken only by the gold and sapphires of his jewelry. The color wasn't his best, but it flattered in a severe sort of way. In a rare display of camaraderie, Ashlin matched him, lithe and slim in black leathers. The rubies she wore in a bloody spray across her throat were the only mark of her station. Savedra and the princess's maids had tried to strip the dye with harsh rinses, but her hair was still several shades darker than normal, a rich honey-gold, glinting here and there with copper.

"Welcome home, Father," Nikos said, his voice carrying over the stamp and jingle of the horses. He bowed first, deep and formal, then offered a hand to clasp. Savedra had never seen Nikos embrace his father in all the years she'd known them.

Ashlin bowed as well, with a soldier's crispness.

Mathiros's eyes glittered as he took her hand. Despite all the tensions of the marriage and the quarrels among the Alexioi, the king had always been fond of his warrior daughter-in-law. It made the treason she and Savedra had committed all the more dangerous.

When the king had greeted his heirs he raised his seneschal from his knees and gave the man an affectionate slap on the shoulder. Then he raised a hand to the crowd, and the courtiers clambered gratefully off the frozen stones. As she stood, Savedra saw Lord Orfion through the crowd, deep in the shadow of the far wall. His face was impassive as ever, but she caught the tired slump of his shoulders as he turned away.

The council that followed the king's return was a farce.

No, Kiril corrected himself ruefully. The meeting was a necessity, to learn the state of the kingdom before tomorrow's open court. It was to Mathiros's credit that he had summoned his councilors after no more delay than a bath and a meal. It was his own presence in the council chamber that was farcical.

The long room was the same as ever—paneled and polished, the rich carpets faded by decades of feet. Fires burned in hearths on either side, their warmth and glow warring with the grey chill that seeped relentlessly through the half-moon mullioned window at the far end. Chairs creaked as counselors leaned toward or away from the heat; paper rasped and crinkled as they sorted through stacks of briefs and notes. An intimately familiar scene, one he'd sat through countless times. Now it was merely salt in the wound of his betrayal, and he was the only one who felt the sting.

Facing Mathiros was more painful than watching

Phaedra in her stolen flesh. Love betrayed might give rise to hate and bitterness, but the original love could never be entirely erased. Even now he saw in the king echoes of the boy he had sworn to serve, the man he'd followed and supported unflinchingly.

He saw echoes of the old king, too, more than he wanted to. *Strong* was what people had most often called Nikolaos Alexios. *Cold* and *hard* were next, the closest one could come to the truth while still being politic. *Cruel* was a better word still, or perhaps merely uncaring. Nikolaos had taken no joy in harming those around him, but neither had he ever taken their feelings into account.

Kiril was twenty-one when he first met Mathiros, a promising young mage with no family to speak of, clever and quietly ambitious. The sort of agent the old spymaster had looked for—the sort Kiril looked for now. The prince had been ten, already grown scarred and hard in his father's shadow, but not yet dead inside. He turned toward Kiril like a sapling toward the sun.

Kiril had thought to shape the boy into a better king than his father, a better man—for the most part, he succeeded. Mathiros learned a little wisdom and more restraint, smoothed the harsh edges of his temper and acquired a modicum of diplomacy. The country had warmed to their forthright warrior prince, and welcomed—or at least tolerated—a warrior king while expansionist emperors held Assar's Lion Throne. Phaedra's death had nearly cost them everything, but they overcame even that. And when Mathiros found Lychandra, Kiril had almost thought that everything would turn out for the best.

Instead she was, inadvertently, the thing that destroyed them.

Adrastos and the priestess Sophia Petreos were deep in argument over the refugee problem and how it might be solved. Mathiros listened—or feigned listening—nodding and grunting at appropriate intervals, but Kiril doubted his mind was on any of the matters at hand. He hadn't seen the king so tired in years, cheeks sunken beneath his beard and his eyes branded with sleepless circles. Blunt fingers moved restlessly against the table, the papers before him, the arm of his chair. Mathiros didn't startle, but his eyes flickered whenever the shadow of a bird flitted past the window.

Looking closer, Kiril saw the sorcery laid on him, faint as a whisper. Phaedra's arm was long—or her wings swift. Scarcely visible, but he was still glad he was the only mage in the council. His would-be successor—a young man with talent and a surfeit of ambition who Mathiros had chosen over Isyllt—was still in Ashke Ros, and Sophia had reached the rank of high priestess through cunning and connections, not mystical acumen.

Nikos noticed his father's unease, if not the witchery behind it; more than once he tried to catch Kiril's eye, but Kiril busied himself with papers and gave no response. The prince had proved himself more than capable in his father's absence, and Kiril had no quarrel with him, but neither would he lead him on with promises of aid. His service to House Alexios was over and done.

So why are you here, old man?

He knew the answer, much as it pained him. He had come because even now he was waiting for Mathiros to change his mind. To apologize, to make some gesture toward mending their split.

It was as ever a vain hope. The king ignored him as

he had for years. Kiril was no more than a shadow in his chair for all the heed Mathiros paid him. The other counselors had long followed the king's example. Some still came to him in private, of course.

The argument broadened to include the treasurer and Secretary of State, and to encompass the matter of military spending. Kiril kept his face and body still when he wanted to bolt from the room. He shouldn't have come— no matter how this ended, he would get no satisfaction from the outcome.

The city was in too much clamor to venture out that day. Instead Isyllt buried her frustrations by teaching Dahlia the basics of magic theory, though she could give the task only a fraction of the attention it deserved.

When dusk rinsed the sky with violet, she realized what she should have done days ago. Shame stung her cheeks—it was too easy for even a necromancer to forget the dead. She stopped in the middle of a restless circuit.

"Forsythia."

The diamond sparked and the ghost materialized with a pale flicker of witchlight. She turned slowly, inspecting her new surroundings. Her skin and gown were shades of smoke and moonlight, her hair a watery gold; the grain of the paneling was visible through her slender form. Her throat, at least, was unmarred. She fixed her lightless eyes on Isyllt. "Hello, necromancer."

"How are you feeling?"

The ghost gave the question serious consideration. "Better," she said at last. "Clearer. The others have talked to me, explained things."

The other ghosts in the diamond, she meant. Isyllt

nodded. "Good. Do you mind answering some more questions?"

Forsythia smiled wryly; Isyllt wished she could have seen the expression in life. "I have nothing but time, don't I?"

"Sit down." Isyllt nodded toward a chair and turned to fetch incense and the last of a bottle of her favorite Chassut red. She lit sticks of sandalwood and olibanum in a brazier, and poured wine for herself and Forsythia, and after some consideration for Dahlia too. The ghost looked askance at the goblet Isyllt set beside her chair, but her outline was clearer already.

"Did you know what Whisper gave you?" Isyllt asked, sitting in the opposite chair. Dahlia drew closer, crouching unobtrusively on the floor.

"The ring, you mean?" Forsythia fingered the neckline of her gown again. "I knew it was a precious thing, something the likes of us don't come by honestly. I knew better than to wear it or show it to anyone. But it was beautiful, and a gift, so I couldn't bear to part with it." The hollows of her eyes turned to Isyllt. "If I had, would you even be here?"

Isyllt had no answer for that, and sipped her wine to rinse the bitter taste away.

"Have you seen Whisper?" Forsythia asked.

"Yes." The bitterness was inescapable. "He's dead too."

Forsythia made a noise between a choke and a sob, one pale fist pressing against her chest. Grey coils of smoke drifted toward her, into her, solidifying her and filling in details; the ragged lace at the neck of her dress was visible now. "Was it you?"

"No." She didn't see the need to explain more about her

involvement. "He was...half-mad with grief for you. He wanted to find your killer. He was going to tell me why he robbed a royal tomb, but didn't get the chance. Did he tell you?"

"He told me lots of things. He liked to talk, after." She crossed her legs, and Isyllt almost mimicked the gesture. "Most of what he said I didn't understand—he talked about the tunnels, about how strange the city was to him, how he missed the wind and the rain. He brought me other gifts, sometimes, bits of jewelry or ribbons, scraps of lace. I asked him once if he stole them—not from anyone who missed them, he said. I guessed then that they were grave-goods. I suppose it should have repulsed me." She shrugged defensively. "But no one else brought me gifts like that, for the joy of something beautiful."

Dahlia stirred, hugging her knees to her chest. "Was he kind to you?" she asked softly.

"Yes." Forsythia shifted in the chair; the upholstery buttons were no longer visible behind her. "He was a monster—I knew that. But he was always polite. He always *asked*. And he was so cold, so clean. I couldn't stand the stink of men—sweat and beer and onions, foul breath. Sometimes I dreamt their stench soaked into me and I could never scrub it off." Her hands closed in her skirts convulsively. "The blood was nothing compared to that."

She shook herself and sat up straighter. There was color in her cheeks now; she might have passed for a living woman to anyone who didn't know better. "I'm sorry. You asked me about the ring. He talked about a woman—a sorceress, I think. He and his friends worked for her, or with her. He could be...vague. I never wanted to press him— I didn't think it was any of my business. He said—" She frowned in concentration. "He said she would help them change things, to walk in the streets again. And once he said...they had to find her a body. I didn't want to know anything else about that."

Even after Azarné's warning, the reminder chilled her. Why was Kiril protecting a demon? She had freed a demon once herself, a little voice reminded her—but, she argued back, he hadn't been in the habit of murdering women for their blood.

"Did he say her name, or the names of any of his friends?"

Forsythia shook her head. "Not the woman's. He mentioned the other vampires, though—they all had false names, like us flowers. It made me laugh. Myca, I think one was. And Spider. Something like that, anyway."

She knew better than to be angry, but it simmered beneath her breastbone anyway. That he had played her from the start she might forgive—it was, after all, a danger of her work—but the ease with which he'd betrayed his fellow vrykoloi galled.

"Does that help you?" Forsythia asked. Her black eyes robbed her face of expression, but her hands plucked nervously at her sleeves.

"Yes. Thank you."

"You'll find them? The ones who killed me? The ones who killed Whisper?"

"I will." Satisfaction or not, this was a promise she meant to keep.

That night, Kiril sought Phaedra out.

She made her home in ruins, which was sensible in spite of her flair for the theatric. No one trespassed beyond the ironbound wall that guarded the ruined palace, and stray whispers of magic would not be remarked upon. If anyone marked her coming or going, it would be just one more ghost story to scare children in Elysia.

Not all such stories were false; spirits watched him as soon as he set foot beyond the gate. Tiny, hungry things clustered at the edges of the path, dark tangles at the edge of his vision. None were brave enough to challenge him, but had he been weak or injured or merely blind to them they might have dared.

The miasma of the ruin scraped like sharkskin against his senses—where the wind touched him he expected to bleed. The magic was no longer strong enough for that, but the pain and rawness still wore on his nerves. Did Phaedra's madness leave her immune to the effect, he wondered, or exacerbate it?

He followed the scent of her magic to a tower, one of the few structures that hadn't yet succumbed to time and the elements. It bore their marks, however, delicate redents and figures worn soft and faceless, once-white sandstone now stained yellow as bone. Perhaps it was this tower in which Tsetsilya Konstantin had purportedly died. That would appeal to Phaedra. The spirits that lingered here were stronger, fattened on scraps of magic.

She set no guard upon the stairs, but he felt her wards acknowledge him and let him pass. His chest and knees ached by the time he reached the top, which only strengthened his resolve to be done with this.

She had settled in the topmost floor. Scavenged rugs covered cold stone, and books were stacked against the walls. Notes and pens lay scattered across a table beside tangles of jewelry and crumpled playbills. A plum-red gown and matching veils draped a chair, slippers kicked halfway across the room. The glowing brazier was no match for the night's chill.

An adjoining room had become her laboratory. Vials and instruments gleamed by candlelight, and journals and stray parchment covered the tables in drifts. It was here he found her, naked, leaning over a tray of surgical knives. Her nudity and the cold glitter of steel were both disconcerting, but so odd in combination that he didn't know what to make of it.

"Hello, Kiril," she said without looking up. "Would you help me with this?"

He stepped forward, though the calmness in her voice was no safe gauge of her mood. Her hair was piled high and sparkling with garnets, her face flawlessly made-up. He knew certain brothels that would have paid a great deal for the effect, especially with a scalpel in her hand.

"What are you doing?" He decided not to mention the brothels.

She sorted through saws and clamps and blades, finally selecting a long cylindrical boring knife, the sort used to retrieve samples when a full autopsy was unfeasible. "I need a bit of liver, and the angle is bad to do it myself." She held out the knife handle first. "Be a dear and fetch me some?"

He almost asked if she was joking, but there was no humor in her eyes, only the intensity that came over her when she worked. "You're well turned out for surgery."

"I'm going out with Varis. This will only take a moment, and I'd rather do it now before I forget."

"All right." Bemused, he knelt at her right side, trying not to wince as his knees met the floor. The candles were insufficient, so he summoned the white glow of a witch-light. He laid his left hand below her ribs, pressing the skin taut. "Here?" he suggested, tapping the spot between thumb and forefinger. When she nodded he set the tip of the knife in place, skin dimpling under steel. With one last glance to confirm her willingness, he twisted the blade home.

"Does it hurt?" he asked, as she made a soft noise. He twisted the knife again and withdrew it. Anatomy classes would be much more interesting if they all had undead to experiment on, but the legal and ethical concerns would likely tie up the Arcanost for years.

"Only if I let it," she said, wiping away a drop of blood. "It's cold, though."

A sliver of greyish-red meat glistened inside the curve of the blade. Phaedra took the knife from him and tapped the liver into a glass dish. When the cover was in place she sealed it with a touch, and spoke a word of stasis to keep the sample fresh. As fresh as years-dead flesh could ever be.

"Thank you. And since you're here, you can help me dress." She shot a glance over her shoulder as she turned toward the other room. "Why are you here?"

"I'm leaving." The words were harder to voice than he'd imagined. "The city, that is."

"Before the ball? You haven't even seen my dress." Teasing, but her brow creased.

"I can't sit through the final act of this revenge play of yours. They're always tragedies, you know."

Her eyes flashed in the witchlight. "I know tragedy very well."

"Then I leave it to you. My part in this is done."

She turned, gown forgotten. "It doesn't have to be. I could use your help, you know, when I take the throne."

His eyebrows rose. "Really? When did you decide this?"

She shrugged. "We've discussed it for some time now, Spider and I." Her pet vrykolos, the one who'd led Isyllt into danger—Kiril stifled a reply as she continued. "Since we're removing a king to begin with, why not take advantage of the opportunity?"

"Why indeed. What does Varis think of this?"

She glanced away. "I'm sure Varis would be happy to see the Severoi back in power, even if the circumstances were unorthodox."

"Of course."

Her lips pursed in a frown. "You don't approve."

"You hardly need my approval at this stage. As I said, I'm finished."

She closed the distance between them and laid a hand on his chest. "Don't leave. You helped one king—help me. Or better yet, *be* a king. I promised to make you young and strong again, and I can. New life for both of us, and a throne besides. Haven't you dreamed of that?"

He took her hand in his. "I know where my strengths lie. Whose body would you steal for me?" The answer came as soon as he voiced the question. "Nikos, of course. What better way to take the throne? And whose flesh for you?"

"Does it matter? Someone young and beautiful. Would you like to choose?"

Her neediness unsettled him—he would rather see her raging. "It might work, but not for me. I have no desire to rule, and even less to steal someone else's life that way. Nikos has done nothing to earn your enmity."

She sagged against him, cold and soft. "Not enmity—expedience. Isn't that always the way of it?"

He took her by the shoulders and eased her away. "I'm sorry, Phaedra. I can't help you anymore."

"But I can help you. Not a new body, perhaps, but strength I can give you. I promised I would." She pressed close again, too strong for him to move without violence. "You broke yourself for me—I know that. Let me make you whole again."

"I told you, I have no desire to be your pet." The denial came more slowly than it should. He needed to leave, before her madness infected him. Before her promises wore him down.

"You won't be, I swear. Besides—" She smiled up at him through her lashes. "Don't you think you could stop me if I tried?"

"I prefer not to make foolish assumptions," he said dryly, "especially where my freedom is concerned."

"Don't you see, freedom is what I'm offering you? You gave your life in service to a king who abandoned you, and spent your strength helping me. I can give you that back, with no vows to bind you."

He could never trust her. It was madness and foolishness and he had to refuse, but the words didn't come. He was so tired—he couldn't remember the last time he had felt strong, even before Phaedra came. He was so tired of weariness and regret.

She took his hand and led him to the laboratory.

CHAPTER 15

Isyllt's plans of further investigation died the next morning when a city runner knocked on her door an hour past the dawn bells, summoning her to the Arcanost. Nearly half the army had returned with some wound or another, and the hospitals were already straining to treat everyone with influenza. With physicians overwhelmed, mages were called upon to treat the injured.

Cursing and rubbing her eyes, Isyllt dressed and rousted Dahlia from the divan where the girl had spent the night curled like a kitten. "Come on," she said. "This will be educational."

The Arcanost's largest dining hall had been repurposed to hold the wounded. Lamps and braziers lined the room, supplementing the wan light from the high clerestory windows. The space was already thick with the heat of a hundred bodies, and the smell of sweat and vomit and sour blood clung to the walls. Isyllt's nose wrinkled as they stepped inside, and Dahlia grimaced. She couldn't imagine students would want to eat here again soon.

Injuries ranged from missing limbs to trench foot, with a myriad of infections and illnesses in between. Isyllt's magic was useless for true healing, but she could numb wounds better than wine or opium, and set and stitch neatly enough. She had the foresight to tuck her ring into her inner jacket pocket, so patients wouldn't panic at the sight of a necromancer descending on them.

More complicated than sword wounds or septicemia was the Ordozh magic some soldiers had fallen afoul of. The Arcanost knew little of the eastern arts—many were inclined to write them off as hedge magic and superstition. Isyllt had always found hedge magic to be reliable in a limited way, no matter what scorn the Arcanostoi heaped on the practice. Certainly the curses she found now had worked well enough. Some were bloody, others merely debilitating—one lieutenant had been made anathema to horses. None would bear him or endure his presence, not even from the back of a supply cart. Now he suffered from exhaustion and gangrenous feet from trailing the army all the way home.

Not only Selafaïn soldiers came seeking treatment—a few Rosians slipped in as well. The Arcanostoi in charge tried to chase them out, but when Isyllt caught them she made sure they saw her ring and her displeasure. In return, they sent all the wounded refugees to her, and soon she was surrounded. She knew only a handful of Rosian words, none useful for medicine, and most symptoms were described through pantomime.

By noon her lack of breakfast had begun to tell on her, but her appetite was nowhere to be found. By the fourth bell she felt wrung dry and knew she had to eat something no matter how unpleasant the thought was. Dahlia served as a mirror—her smock was smeared with blood and pus and vomit, hair tousled and locked with sweat. Her olive skin was pasty, but her jaw was set and hands steady. Isyllt nearly patted her shoulder, but stopped when she saw the state of her own hands.

"Let's find lunch," she said when the influx of patients finally slowed. Her voice was raw and ugly.

Dahlia made an unhappy face at the idea of food, but began hunting for a clean rag. Filthy linen lay in drifts and swags around them and the nearest bowls of water were pink with blood and clotted and stringy with other waste.

They found clean towels and soap at the far end of the hall, and Isyllt scrubbed her hands till they stung. As she wiped her face for the third time, a conversation on the far side of a doorway caught her attention.

"I'm sorry," said a tired man in black robes, "but this isn't the place for influenza victims. Try St. Alia's, or St. Allakho's." That last told Isyllt about the other half of the conversation—one didn't suggest a charity hospital to those with alternatives.

A woman laughed, harsh and brief. Isyllt moved closer—a Selafaïn woman, dark-haired and olive-skinned under layers of scarves and hoods. A young man sat on a bench behind her, shaking beneath bundled clothes.

"St. Allakho's is full," the woman said. "And so is St. Alia's, even if they were taking charity cases."

The man sighed, running a wide brown hand over his face. Isyllt didn't recognize him, but the jade and agates in his rings marked him as a healer-mage, one of the rare few who chose to focus on magical theory instead of taking the more lucrative path of a physician. "Then you should take him home, keep him warm and dry and make sure he has plenty to drink. Broth and tisanes are best. Burn incense if you wish. We're overwhelmed here too."

"How many houses in Birthgrave do you think are warm?" the woman asked, but she was already turning away, helping her companion to his feet. As he stood, Isyllt saw his face for the first time—sallow with jaundice, the whites of his eyes a fierce yellow. Movement made him cough, deep and wet and tearing.

She took three strides toward them before she realized she was moving. The woman glanced at her, and looked away again when Isyllt didn't speak. As she led her friend down the hall, Isyllt turned to the other mage.

"That isn't—"

He cut her off with a gesture, rings flashing. His dark face was lusterless with fatigue. "It *is* influenza." The words were dull with rote response. "We don't understand the jaundice yet, but the other symptoms match." His voice lowered as he leaned close. "Bronze fever doesn't spread in the winter, and the last thing the city needs right now is a panic."

She couldn't argue with that, though for a moment she wanted to. Her jaw worked once, then closed tightly. "I understand."

Relief flickered in his eyes. "Good. Then if you'll excuse me—" He waved one blunt hand toward the rows of waiting wounded.

"Is that what I looked like when I was sick?" she asked Dahlia when he was gone.

The girl shrugged. "Not quite so bad, but yes."

Isyllt shuddered, chilled through. "Come on," she said. "Let's find something warm to drink."

The royal audience began at noon, and the throne room was packed tight an hour before the bells rang. Savedra stood in an alcove near the dais that afforded her a view of most of the hall and the Malachite Throne as well, if too many taller people didn't crowd in front of her.

The hall was a riot of color—gold and green and creamy marble, the rich blue banners of House Alexios, stained glass windows, and all the people contained within. Members of the Eight stood beside—or at least in the vicinity of—merchants and shop clerks and tradesmen, and a few who might have been beggars, all gathered to petition the king, or hear him, or simply remind themselves that he existed.

Savedra saw her mother at the far end of the hall, surrounded by the heads of other families. The Octagon Court could put aside ancient rivalries for a few hours, if it meant a good view of the proceedings. Ginevra Jsutien stood with her aunt—she caught Savedra's eye across the room and smiled. Savedra smiled back unthinkingly, and bit the inside of her lip as she glanced away. Friendships had been rare since she moved into the palace—why couldn't she find one she could trust?

The third bell tolled the hour, and a moment later horns announced the entrance of the king. The audience knelt as he strode the length of the hall, grim and austere as ever. His eyes were still shadowed and sunken after a day and night's rest. Nikos followed, restored to his peacock splendor in green and saffron. Behind them came a handful of the Royal Guard in formal grey-and-white livery. A colorless reminder that they served the Malachite Throne, not the house that held it.

The issues brought forth by the supplicants were the standard sort: squabbles amongst the Eight, conflicts between merchants, bureaucrats requesting money for city projects. All things Nikos had handled in his father's absence, but having the king's attention for even a few moments was soothing to many.

While Aravinds and Hadrians squabbled over borders and orchards, the crowd shifted beside Savedra. A subtle rearrangement of limbs and body heat, but she tensed, turning before a soft voice spoke.

"Savedra Pallakis. May I speak with you?"

She looked up and up again at the captain of the king's private guard. Mikhael Kurgoth was a lanky, rawboned man, scarred and seamed, with incongruously baby-fine sandy hair. He had led the royal guard for as long as Savedra had lived in the palace. A foreign mercenary made good, his rise to authority had been nearly as unlikely as hers. He could have been a general, but had chosen more than once to remain beside the king.

"Of course, Captain."

His dark eyes narrowed, deepening the creases at the corners. He stood very close amidst the press; beneath the crisp grey linen of his surcoat he smelled of oiled leather and steel and fresh soap. "Will you carry a message for me? I must speak to the prince." His tongue slid across his teeth as if he disliked the taste of the words. "In private."

Curiosity prickled, but Savedra kept her face smooth, her gaze moving over the crowd. "Of course. In the Queen's Solar, perhaps, before the sixth bell?"

"Yes," he said, squinting in consideration. "I'll be there. I needn't mention discretion to you."

"Indeed," she replied dryly. "You needn't."

His mouth quirked. "Your pardon. Thank you, Pallakis."

The next moment he was gone, melting back through the crowd to stand beside the dais once more, just in time for Mathiros to dismiss the quarreling houses and call for the next supplicant.

A trio moved forward, a man and two women. All were fair and dressed in plain wool, their dark coats brightened with embroidery.

"Your Majesty," the first woman said, bowing her head. "I am Irena Ariseva, of Millrind Street. This is my cousin Priska, and Taras Denisov of Lathe Court. We are citizens of Erisín." Her mouth twisted. "Or so we were told."

Mathiros nodded. "Selafai is open to all who would swear fealty."

"And swear we did. Why is it, then, that we are not afforded equal protection by Selafaïn law? By Erisín's Vigils."

"Equal protection belongs to any who have not forfeited it," the king said with a frown. Nikos and Adrastos also looked nonplussed. This complaint wasn't one they had expected. "How has yours been lacking?"

"In the past three months, eight young women have disappeared in Elysia and Little Kiva. Rosian women— our friends, our neighbors, our daughters. Half of them have been found dead, pulled from the river. We can only assume the rest have not been found, but that their fate was the same. With every disappearance we go to the police, and every time we are told that someone will *look into it*." Her mouth twisted on the words.

A wary mutter ran the length of the hall. Mathiros leaned forward, his frown deepening. "And you don't believe the police are investigating?"

The woman laughed. "They find nothing. Not even a pretense of an arrest to placate us. They take our stories and we never hear from them again. What are we to think, Majesty?"

"All citizens of Erisín are due the same justice, no matter where they may have been born. I will make sure the Vigiles Urbani are reminded of this."

It wasn't enough—that was clear from Irena's scowl. But it was also the best she would get from such an audience, and that too was clear. She and her companions bowed and retreated, ceding the floor to more mundane problems. The whispers took longer to fade.

The audience lasted six hours, breaking for refreshments at three. Savedra didn't see the Rosians in the crowd when the fourth bell chimed—gone once their business was addressed, or surreptitiously removed?

A palace page elbowed his way through the press and bowed. "Milady. I have a message from Archa Severos."

Out of the corner of her eye she saw Nadesda still on the far side of the room. "Thank you." She traded the boy the sealed envelope for a silver penny. "Does she expect a reply?"

"She said it was nothing urgent."

Savedra nodded, and the boy bowed again and retreated. As soon as he was gone she inspected the black wax and broke the seal. By Nadesda's standards "nothing urgent" only meant that no one would die in the next hour.

The note was a short one, written in a simple private cipher. *Make sure the princess is especially radiant at the masquerade,* it read. *Her newest friends will be there, with gifts.*

She stifled a scream, smiling instead as if reading a pleasant trifle. Her hand was steady as she tucked the note into her sleeve, but only barely. Friends for enemies was a common substitution, gifts for harm another. The assassin would try again.

She might have gone to her mother and demanded more information, but when she turned she nearly stepped into Ginevra Jsutien.

"Imagine meeting you here." Ginevra wore burgundy brocade today, a tasteful and sober high-necked gown that did nothing to hide her slender curves. Savedra envied the girl her dressmaker—not to mention her figure.

"Will your aunt be happy to see you speaking to me?"

"She's gone to the washroom." Yellow topazes flashed in the darkness of her hair as she tilted her head. "I thought I should ask you about your costume for the solstice ball, considering what happened the last time we wore the same colors."

"Saints, the ball." She'd had the beginnings of a costume since the end of summer, but hadn't been in for fittings in decads.

"I know," Ginevra said, her lips pursing in a charming moue. "I haven't decided on anything either. Luckily my milliner is used to me by now."

Savedra met Ginevra's eyes for an instant; they were of a height. Tall, slender, black-haired—her hands tingled as an idea began to gain strength. "About what happened last time... How would you like to play a game with me?"

"Oh?" The sparkle in her grey eyes belied the lazy disinterest in her voice. "What sort of game?"

"How does your dressmaker feel about challenges?"

Nikos came to her at midnight, kissing her before she could finish a greeting. It had been decads since they spent the night together, and she felt every absent day as he pulled her close. She wanted to protest as he led her to the bed, guilt twisting a knife beneath her sternum, but his fingers were tangled in her laces and her hair, and the scrape of teeth and stubble against her neck replaced guilt with want.

They lay in breathless silence when the bells tolled; the hour of regret. Savedra pressed her face against Nikos's neck and breathed in salt musk and the lingering cedar-and-saffron of his perfume.

"What's wrong?" she finally asked, trailing her fingers down his arm. Gooseflesh prickled in the wake of her touch. "Something Kurgoth said?" She had thought briefly of spying on them, but decided against it. She didn't want to lose the captain's trust so quickly, and she had a costume to plan besides.

"He's worried about Father." He laughed humorlessly, his chest shaking against hers. "And imagine how bad it must be if a man like Kurgoth will speak of it. He's nearly as emotionless as Father himself."

"What's the matter?"

"He says Father is tired, stretched too thin—worse than the usual stress of a campaign. Nightmares. And of course Father won't speak of them."

"Does he think Mathiros will share them with you?"

"He knows better than that. He hoped that I could persuade Kiril to help, but I think that ship has sailed."

"You could command him. He is a sworn agent of the Crown."

"He served my father out of love, and Father squandered that. Besides, Father hasn't seemed inclined to listen to him lately, either. The old man deserves some rest."

Savedra sighed and pulled Nikos closer. "Don't we all?"

CHAPTER 16

Erisín celebrated the longest night of the year with masques and parties. Legend held that the masks were meant to confuse the hungry spirits who crept through the mirrors that night, but in more recent times it was an excuse for excess and indulgence before the Invidiae—the demon days that fell at the dark of the year.

In the palace, celebrants gathered in the White Ballroom. The room was exactly what its name implied, but that couldn't do justice to the brilliance of mirror-polished marble and crystal chandeliers. Alabaster lamps chased the shadows from the corners—those seeking privacy could slip onto the terrace. Only the ceiling broke the flawless pallor, covered with a mural of the courtship of Sarai and Zavarian. Daises had been erected on either end of the hall—one for the musicians, the other for the king's chair of state and the lower seats for the prince and princess. Those chairs were empty now, and the musicians tuned their instruments while the growing crowd mingled and loitered and laid waste to the food and wine.

Isyllt waited near the throne dais, trying to ignore the smell of food. Only long practice kept her still, hands folded placidly when she wanted to fidget and tug at the unfamiliar weight of her new gown.

She usually wore white at the solstice masque—the same dress, in fact, for the past three years, each time with a different mask. She would have resorted to it again tonight, choosing convenience over pride, had Savedra not summoned her with an urgent note and a referral to a milliner. A day and a half she would have spent at the Arcanost or searching for Phaedra had been stolen by fittings, but it was hard to regret the lost hours when she saw the finished gown.

Crimson velvet cinched her waist and fell in sumptuous folds to the floor. The hem and the long points of her sleeves were stitched with tiny beads—brass and silver, jet and seed pearls, all blazing in the lamplight. The cloth-of-silver girdle that circled her hips was also beaded. It was the most extravagant gown she'd ever worn. Savedra had quietly paid the bill, but Isyllt imagined she would have wept at the cost. It wouldn't have deterred her, though, not after she felt the fabric swirl against her legs. It might, she thought with bitter amusement, be the closest to a bridal gown she ever came.

Savedra's idea was a clever one—a shell game to catch an assassin. Unfortunately, one of the cleverest pieces of the costume was also the most annoying. Yards of sheer black gauze veiled her face and hair. She could see through it, but the room was blurred, colors muted, and she was left with the unnerving sensation of a shadow always in the corner of her eye. It also meant that she couldn't eat or drink anything without looking ridiculous. She told herself that the loss of vision meant she shouldn't dull her senses further with wine, but it was cold comfort.

She occupied herself trying to identify costumes and their wearers. Ancient kings and queens were always popular, with little regard for historical accuracy. Every year a bevy of nymphs braved the cold in diaphanous gowns, crowned with flowers either real or wrought of silk and silver. Spirits were plentiful, as were ridiculous imaginings of foreign dress. The artful barbarian furs were probably meant to be Vallish, and the blue paint and leathers must be the Tier Danaan of the western forests. She wondered if her friend Adam, half Tier himself, would be amused or merely scornful. One woman had constructed an elaborate gargoyle costume, complete with curling horns and wings made of real owl feathers. She would be a menace on the dance floor and her wings had already begun to shed, but Isyllt applauded the effort all the same.

The crowd thickened, voices rising in a formless birdlike chatter. The room warmed with each new body, till sweat prickled Isyllt's scalp and rolled down the small of her back. Kebechet was right about the popularity of neroli—the air was thick with bitter oranges, along with sandalwood and attar of roses and other scents. She had nearly abandoned her dignity for a cool glass of wine when the trumpets sounded. Conversation died as Mathiros Alexios entered through the private door beside the dais, and the crowd knelt with a vast rustle of feathers and fabric.

Mathiros wore a simple black domino for the occasion, and a narrow gold circlet. His clothing was black as well,

clean lines free of ornament. Amidst the pomp and gran-
deur, the effect was striking. More than one gaze lingered
appreciatively as he climbed the dais steps.

Nikos and Ashlin followed a moment behind, and a
wave of giggles threatened the respectful silence; Isyllt
was glad her veils muffled her snort of amusement. The
prince had come as his namesake bird, dressed in brilliant
peacock blue with a skirt of feathers trailing behind him.
His mask was white and black and blue, glittering with
sequins and paste gems. Ashlin, a peahen to match, wore
simple leathers in dull brown, except for a green leather
gorget. Even Mathiros seemed amused as they walked in.

Isyllt tensed for an instant, waiting for trouble, but the
prince and princess reached their chairs and stood waiting for Mathiros's sign. When he gave it they sat—for
Nikos this involved the delicate operation of sweeping his
tailfeathers out of the way—the crowd rose, and the musicians began the soft notes of a minuet. A hundred voices
lifted in laughter and conversation, and so began the festivities on the longest night of the year.

Savedra slunk into the ballroom after the first dance had
begun, if one could slink weighed down by pounds of
beads and velvet. From the dais she caught a flash of gems
as Nikos glanced her way. She smiled, though he couldn't
see it—or see how sad and strained it was. Captain
Denaris watched her too, white-and-grey livery blending
into the wall beside the throne. Captain Kurgoth loomed
beside her.

The dais was guarded by the best and soldiers watched
all the doors, but assassins had breached palace security before. A knife in the dark was different than a pub-

lic murder, of course. Did the man expect to survive the attempt? Was the reward worth the risk? How much was Ashlin's life worth, exactly? She ought to ask Varis.

The crowd shifted and she glimpsed Isyllt on the far side, vivid as a bloodstain on white sheets. The sight was uncanny, like a reflection out of place in a mirror. The Vallish had a word for such a glimpse of oneself—*vardöger*, they called the spectral double. The idea had been brought to Erisín in several plays and operas. None of them, now that she thought of it, ended well.

The costume was too hot for the press of the hall, but there was no other way—she and Isyllt might be much the same height and build, but no amount of cosmetics would turn Isyllt's skin a convincing brown, or her own stark white.

She caught a few glances cast at her and her sister-bride, a few giggles and whispers hidden behind hands. Always an embarrassment to find one's costume duplicated, and amazing to see it duplicated so perfectly.

The Severoi were already in attendance, mostly clustered around Nadesda in a small circle of chairs against one wall. Savedra ignored them, preferring to save her anonymity for the moment. Varis must be here as well, but she hadn't spotted him yet. She saw Konstantins as well, and Aravinds and Hadrians, each drawn into their own familial knots. Most Alexioi concerned themselves with their estates in Medea; Mathiros was scrupulous about not favoring his own house over others. Savedra often thought he held all the Octagon Court in equal contempt.

The Jsutiens made a fashionably tardy entrance, timing their arrival with the end of the second dance. Thea was dressed as some historical empress or another, a tasteful costume for an older, stouter woman, while still costing more than many courtiers' summer homes. Her husband, a notoriously handsome younger man, wore a cloth-of-gold turban and flowing silks, so Thea was probably meant to be the Iskari dowager empress Kârekin—Kârekin before consumption killed her, apparently, since she'd forgone the usual dramatic blood-spotted handkerchiefs.

And then came Ginevra, a pillar of crimson and black veils, and the giggles and whispers became murmurs.

In Selafai, brides wore red—the color of life and life's blood, virgin's blood, the blood of childbed, blood co-mingled in children. A color of fertility and fruitful unions. Veils had mostly gone out of fashion, and those who wore them usually chose gold or silver, or more crimson if their complexions could stand it. Black veils had been made famous decades earlier by the playwright Kharybdea, who chose the color for Aristomache in the tragedy that bore her name, the priestess of Astara who broke her vows for love of the prince Sarapion, only to be betrayed and abandoned on their wedding night after he had stolen her temple's greatest treasure. She killed herself on Astara's altar and haunted Sarapion in revenge, driving him to madness and finally death. It took a woman of morbid or vicious humor to dress as Aristomache for a masque; that three had done so tonight would surely be called an ill omen.

Savedra and Isyllt slid through the crowd, and Save-dra had the pleasure of seeing Thea stumble as she saw her niece mirrored not once but twice. She shot a sharp glance at Ginevra; Savedra couldn't follow the movement of her lips from so far away. Ginevra, however, showed no sign of surprise or dismay, merely glided into the ballroom and turned unerringly toward a pair of her friends, Aravind nymphs. Savedra, succumbing to a moment's spite, curtsied deeply to Thea.

To Ginevra it was a game, a way to annoy her aunt and confound the palace gossips. And, she'd added slyly, a way to sneak a dance with Nikos. For Savedra it was a way to confound assassins. Ashlin herself couldn't take part, but now anyone who wished her harm had to guess who was standing next to her at any given moment—Savedra, a necromancer, or the niece of the woman who wanted the princess dead.

The crowd shifted again, turning away from the mystery of the three Aristomaches as the prince and princess rose from their chairs. The third dance was traditional for royal couples, and the musicians began an intricate vals as Nikos and Ashlin bowed to one another.

Nikos managed not to trip on his ridiculous train; Ashlin avoided stray plumes with her usual grace. Toward the end of the dance a feather worked free of the skirt and drifted across the tiles. Savedra thought two giggling nymphs would come to blows over it.

Another lively tune followed, and couples crowded the floor. Ashlin returned to her chair with a glass of wine, but Nikos stayed on the floor, making a show of searching for a partner.

"This might be the most fun I've had at a masque in years," Ginevra whispered, leaning close. Their veils rasped against each other and Savedra smelled warm skin and Ginevra's subtle perfume. "Aunt Thea is livid, and doesn't know who she should be angry with. My friends can't tell if this is an insult or flattery or some bizarre coincidence. Eventually, though, I'm going to steal a plate of those cakes and hide in the garden to eat them. Veils aren't very practical. Oh, who's our triplet?"

"I'm not sure I should say." Gauze hid her smile, but she couldn't keep the amusement from her voice.

"Does she know who I am?"

"You walked in with Thea and House Hydra. I imagine everyone's figured it out."

Ginevra's veil rippled with her soft huff. "That doesn't seem fair."

"You'll have to deduce her identity, then."

They broke off as Nikos bowed to them both. "I shouldn't trust vengeful women, but I can't resist. Will one of you mysterious ladies honor me with a dance?"

He held out his hand to Savedra, and even if it was only a lucky guess it still warmed her. But true to her word, Ginevra cut in, bumping Savedra aside with a soft hip and laying her hand in the prince's. He looked from one to the other in exaggerated confusion, but acquiesced as Ginevra tugged him toward the floor.

Savedra wanted to laugh, but that would break character. Instead she raised her chin and turned away in a satisfying hiss of skirts. Ginevra would have to have fun for all of them, since she and Isyllt couldn't afford to.

Dancing was a pleasure Isyllt rarely found time to indulge. By the time Savedra relieved her of her post by the princess's chair, she was ready to press any hapless passerby into service as a partner. On her way to do so, she nearly collided with an Assari ifrit in a blazing crown of feathers and sequins. She murmured an apology and began to turn away when she recognized Khelséa.

"What are you doing here?" she asked.

Khelséa did a double take and grinned. "The Vigils always get a few invitations for diplomacy's sake. I made sure I got my hands on one."

"Nice dress."

"Isn't it?" She spread her arms and spun, flaring tattered layers of red and gold and orange skirts and trailing sleeves. The orange was nearly the same shade as her uniform, but the low-cut and tight-laced bodice drew a different sort of attention. Her hair was unbraided for once, hanging in shining coils down her back. "Gemma made it. Yours is lovely too, but why are there three of you?"

"Assassin bait."

"Charming." The inspector drained her wine cup and set it on a passing servant's tray. "Excellent timing, though. I thought I would have to dance with a stranger." She claimed Isyllt's arm and led her to the floor.

"Isn't Gemma with you?"

"She's attending Solstice services. Her sister is a priestess of Erishal."

"Ah." The priesthood quietly disapproved of secular necromancy; Isyllt was certain that it was because the priests had far less fun.

The dance was a wild one, with couples circling the floor and trading partners at a hectic pace. Isyllt was breathing heavily by the second measure.

A familiar note caught her attention amid the miasma of sweat and wine and perfume—cinnamon. Isyllt stiffened, cursing the blur of the veil as she scanned the room. The dance swept her on and she lost the scent.

Another circuit and she caught it again. There—a woman in white lingered by a pillar, a lace shroud pooling around her feet. An equally cumbersome length of veil hid her face. No inch of skin was visible, but the gown made up for that by clinging to every curve between her neck and thighs; she would have to unstitch it to take it off again. Isyllt felt the woman's answering stare through two layers of fabric. Then she was out of sight again.

Isyllt's hands clenched Khelséa's when they came together again. "She's here," she said, her voice harsh and ragged.

"Who?"

"The haematurge. Phaedra Severos."

Khelséa's full lips tightened. "What should we do?"

"I don't know." She forced her aching hands to loosen. "If I confront her here all our secrets will be spilled, and I don't have the support of the Crown. I don't even know what she wants."

"I doubt it will be pleasant, whatever it is."

The dance ended and Isyllt scanned the crowd, but found no trace of Phaedra. She whispered a warning in Savedra's ear, then succumbed to heat and thirst and claimed a glass of wine and plate of food, retreating to the shadows of the terrace with them. She wouldn't be much use to anyone if she passed out.

Couples lingered on the balcony, and on the steps leading to one of the palace's many gardens. Most had found the darkest shadows for privacy, and all politely ignored each other. Isyllt claimed a far corner and set her plate and cup on the railing. The night air was a shock as she pulled aside her veil; her cheeks burned and her breath escaped in a shimmering cloud. Her skin crawled with gooseflesh and sweat-damp fabric chilled instantly. She drained half her wine in one swallow.

Below, the lawn glittered with frost, hedges pale and spectral through drifting haze. Blue and white lanterns swayed in the breeze. Dark trails marked the grass, evidence of lovers trysting in the garden. Isyllt wasn't sure any amount of lust was worth freezing one's toes, or other delicate parts.

"We need to talk, little witch."

Witchfire crackled around her fingers as she spun, bruising her back on the stone balustrade and knocking her precariously balanced plate into the bushes. Someone giggled in the shadows below the railing.

"Softly," Spider said, raising a hand. He wore a hooded cloak—anyone who glimpsed his face would tell themselves it was a mask. "You don't want to cause a scene."

"What are you doing here?" She let her fire die, drawing shadow and silence more tightly around them. "The palace is warded."

His smile was mocking. "Mortal wards are so rarely as strong as you like to think them. I'm here to admire the festivities. And to see you."

She took another sip of wine and set the cup safely away from stray elbows. "To pledge your affection again?"

"To warn you." He moved closer, till she could have wrapped herself in his cloak; his nearness did nothing to lessen the cold. "You're meddling in something you shouldn't. I don't want to see you hurt."

"See my throat slit for a sacrifice, you mean? It was you, wasn't it? You snatched Forsythia off the street, held her while Phaedra bled her dry. And then killed your friend Whisper to throw me off the trail."

"I did what was necessary. I think you understand such things."

"Yes." Her smile was cold and sharp. "I understand. But I don't murder random strangers for my magic."

"No, only for your Crown." His lip curled on the word. "Anyway, Forsythia wasn't random. Whisper's affection for her distracted him, clouded his judgment. The others, however—" He shrugged. "We are hunters of opportunity."

He sounded so reasonable. And, Isyllt supposed, he was. She would never ask a wolf to justify which deer it killed. But neither had a wolf ever been a deer.

"I, on the other hand, hunt and kill with purpose. And part of my purpose is to protect this city from demons and murderers."

Spider's lip curled, baring fangs. "You kill where you're bid. I'm sorry," he said quickly, lifting a hand again. "I didn't come to quarrel. I mean it, you know, when I say I don't want to hurt you. Changes are coming soon, and you could benefit from them."

"Changes. You mean a coup. I swore an oath to the Crown, Spider."

"It isn't your Crown that we would remove, only the man who wears it. We aren't the only ones who wish to see someone else on the throne. But the others would merely replace him with some different mortal politician, and what would that change?"

"Whereas you would replace him with a demon. That will certainly make me sleep soundly at night."

"You're hardly squeamish about the undead, necromancer."

"Spider. You've lied to me, stalked me, tried to seduce me. With," she acknowledged with a wry tilt of her head, "some success. Why don't you tell me what the hell it is you really want?"

"I already told you—I want the vrykoloi free of the sewers, not hunted or ignored. Your mages treat spirits as a commodity to be used and demons as abominations to be destroyed, and I want to see that end."

"I'm not without sympathy," Isyllt said slowly, "but the fear is bred too deep into mortals. Change will take decades. Centuries."

"Not if we take the throne."

"The city wouldn't stand for it. The country wouldn't. You're powerful, but so is the Arcanost, and the living outnumber the undead."

"They wouldn't know what had happened until we wanted them to. Phaedra has walked this city for months now unnoticed—humans excel at turning a blind eye to unsettling things."

She stared into the sulfurous light of his eyes for a moment. He was a monster, both literally and as men judged such—a liar, a schemer, a murderer and manipulator, callous and cold. Small wonder, then, that she wanted to lean her head against his chest and let him comfort her. Already her magic quested toward him unbidden. Death loved a killer.

Isyllt drew a deep breath, closed her eyes and opened them again. "Not so blind as that. It will turn ugly and people will die—mortal and demon alike. It's madness, and I won't help you."

He studied her, eyes glittering in the depths of his hood. "Then I can only tell you to stay out of our way. I'm fond of you, but Phaedra has no such weakness."

She felt his glamour like a fog across her mind—she tried to fight, but by the time her vision cleared she shivered alone on the balcony.

*   *   *

Kiril resisted Phaedra's entreaties to stay, but in the end couldn't refuse to attend the Solstice ball. Only two days' delay, he told himself. A chance to say a few discreet good-byes. He didn't believe for a moment it would be so simple, but his newfound strength made it easier to ignore misgivings.

Phaedra's magic worked. Unpleasant at first, both the consumption of blood the spell required and the lowering of his defenses, but after the initial nausea and dizziness faded he found his pulse strengthening, his breath coming easier than it had in years. All the little aches and scars he had grown accustomed to over the years faded from his awareness—no creaking knees, no aching wrists, no cold in his bones. Even the fatigue that had been his constant companion receded. It was dangerous, this demon gift, but his magic sparked inside him again, as it hadn't in months, and for the moment he was willing to overlook the cost.

Three days ago the simple obfuscation he wore as he crossed the room would have pained him; now it was as simple as a breath, as it should be.

He found Varis lingering alone in a corner, which was unusual. Even more unusual was his costume—he wore plain black scholar's robes, with none of his customary glitter or gaud. A mask of bronze-painted leather hung against his chest, and a small bronze-bound book hung from a chain around his waist. Mnemos, the saint of scholars and of memory.

He arched an eyebrow at Kiril's own black robes. "You're not even trying."

"I could say the same of you."

"It's a costume, darling. I'm not supposed to be myself."

"Where are all your paramours and hangers-on?"

"I'm in seclusion tonight. Keeping up with them grows so tiring." He said it with a disdainful flick of his wrist, but the fatigue was real—Kiril saw it in his hollowed cheeks and fragile eyes.

"What's wrong?"

Varis began another dismissive excuse, but Kiril was already looking closer, *otherwise*. The sparkling violet and gold of Varis's magic had dulled, and the more ordinary colors beneath had paled as well. Not a shadow in the heart such as a mage might see in Kiril's own aura, nor the darkness in the lungs that showed in consumptives—this was a thinning of the blood itself.

He stretched out a hand, ignoring Varis's feeble attempt to block him, and turned down the other man's high collar. The bruise was violent against his pallor, purple blotching to green at the edges, the punctures in the center scabbed. An identical long-faded mark shadowed the other side of his neck.

"There are others, aren't there?"

"I'd be happy to show you. We could find a coat closet—it would be like old times."

Kiril's frown deepened. "How long?"

"Months now. It's...worth the pain." His eyes darkened, color rising beneath his powder. "Are you going to criticize my taste in vices? That's always so tiresome."

"It's Spider, isn't it?" The defiant tilt of Varis's chin was answer enough. "Of course it is. Is that how they've won your support of their mad scheme?"

"What scheme? Besides the one you've been so instrumental in."

Kiril shook his head, newly absent fatigue returning. Reality could never be ignored for long. "Phaedra and Spider are planning to take the throne. How I don't know, and I doubt they know for certain either. Phaedra thinks it will be a matter of stealing the right body. Any others she can bind to her with blood. Perhaps she's right—I've seen more ridiculous plans succeed."

Varis was too pale to blanch, but his lips thinned and a muscle worked in his jaw. He had always been the most vocal of the Arcanostoi against vinculation—the binding of spirits. He had seen firsthand what it was to have choices stolen, to be trapped in service. Kiril didn't think he was hypocrite enough to condemn the practice against spirits and condone it for humans.

"I know you loved her once," he said, softer than he had intended. "But if you cleave to her now it will destroy you."

Varis turned to him, naked of his armor. "I loved you once too," he said. "I survived that."

"You left. And that's what you should do now."

A flash of red caught his eye. Across the room Isyllt threaded her way through the crowd, dark and burning in black and crimson. Even veiled he would know her anywhere.

Varis followed the direction of Kiril's gaze, and his armor reassembled itself piece by chilly piece. "Spoken like a man who should take his own advice," he drawled. His smile was nearly a sneer, but his eyes were sad. "Go, then. It's love that kills us all, in the end."

Of all the dangers Isyllt had anticipated that night, encountering Kiril wasn't one of them. In retrospect that was

foolish, since he always attended the masque, but she had
tried to put him out of her thoughts after their last meeting. When she saw him crossing the room toward her, she
wanted to turn on her heel and flee. Instead she stood her
ground, shoulders tightening.

"The color becomes you," he said after a brittle pause.
He smiled wryly, acknowledging all the unpleasant asso-
ciations that went with the compliment.

"You look well yourself." She didn't mean to say it,
but it was true. He stood straighter, walked without the
pained motions she'd grown used to. His silver domino
brought out the white in his beard and made his eyes all
the blacker.

"Will you dance with me?" he asked.

A knife wound would have hurt less. Even when they
were together they had hardly ever danced. But she wouldn't
flinch from the pain, not here in front of all the court.

"Of course, my lord." She placed her hand in his and
let him lead her to the dance floor. Only the very edge—
neither of them liked to be the center of attention.

The dance was a slow and stately one, with little
thought needed for the steps. She might have wished otherwise. Anything to dull the awareness of his hand on her
hip, their fingers laced together. He wore his black diamond on his left hand and the stones shivered when their
rings touched, even through her glove.

"I'm sorry," he said after several measures of silence.
His mouth twisted. "It's not easy for me to say this."

Her crippled hand twitched against his shoulder. "If
this is about my investigation—"

"No. At least, not entirely."

She fell silent again.

"I've done many things that I've come to regret," he said at last. "I don't want you to be one of them. I've treated you poorly—both during this investigation and over the past three years. Will you forgive me?"

She swallowed. She tried to cling to her anger, to wear it like a shield, but it cracked before the sincerity in his voice. "I trust you've had reasons for what you've done during this case. As for the past... You've done nothing that needs forgiveness. Not to me."

"I've hurt you. I've made decisions for you that I had no right to make." He waited, eyes dark and solemn.

"I forgive you," she said. Then her voice and composure cracked. "Of course I forgive you. I love you, you idiot." She missed a step and they both stopped, leaving other couples to maneuver around them.

"I know." He cupped her cheek, gauze slithering against their skin, his voice rough with something not quite pain or wonder. "I've never understood it, but I know."

"We ought to step outside," she said as flatly as she could manage, "or I may make a scene."

That drew a startled chuckle. "I could never abide scenes." He led her toward the terrace door; glances from the crowd followed them. She scanned the darkness, stretched out questing tendrils, but found no trace of Spider or anything else inhuman, nothing but a drunken couple groping each other below the terrace.

She turned back to Kiril and stripped aside her veil. "What are you playing at, Kiril?"

"Not playing," he said softly. "Not with you." He touched the edge of her veil—carefully avoiding her skin, but she felt the warmth of his hand through the gauze. She couldn't stop her sharp indrawn breath.

"You are—" It took her a moment to gather her thoughts. The bottom had fallen out of her stomach and she couldn't let it take her wits with it. "You're protecting a demon and a blood sorceress!" she whispered. "Don't you dare deny it." This wasn't the place for such conversations, but she couldn't leave the matter unspoken any longer.

He laughed, but humor died quickly. "No, I won't deny it."

"Why?"

A silence settled around them, heavy as a shroud. "Phaedra has a vendetta against Mathiros. She is... justified. I can't stand in her way."

"You're oathsworn to the Crown."

"Not anymore."

Her hands tingled with shock. "You mean—"

"I'm forsworn. For months now." His mouth quirked. "You thought I was merely growing old and feeble. That may be true, but it also took all my strength to break the geas. I'm only now recovering."

"Why doesn't Mathiros know?"

Kiril shrugged. "The mage who took my oaths died peacefully in his sleep years ago. A more paranoid king would have had me swear them anew, but Mathiros trusted me." His lips thinned, eloquent bitterness. "Had he even a shiver, he might have felt the vow break, but he's anixeros to the bone."

"By telling me this you've broken mine."

He chuckled. "No, my dear. I'll know when that truly happens. I have, though, put you in a dangerous position. Which was what I've been trying to avoid." His eyebrows rose. "Do you mean you would choose me over your vows?"

"I swore an oath to the Crown, but I meant it to you. All my service was only ever to you. You idiot."

Her voice broke and she nearly began to cry. She mastered the urge with a sharp pinch to the bridge of her nose and a scowl. "What are we going to do?"

Before he could answer, they heard the screams.

Something wasn't right. Savedra had no mystical sensitivity of which she was aware, but she had learned to trust her instincts after years in the palace, and beneath the weight of sweat and hair and gauze her neck was prickling. Everyone on the dais was where they should be, guests laughing and chattering while the musicians rested. She could find nothing amiss as she scanned the room. Neither could she find Isyllt.

The musicians began again, a stately slow vals this time. A heartbeat later a murmur swept the room. Savedra didn't understand the cause until movement on the dais caught her eye: Mathiros had risen, and descended the stairs. She thought he meant to leave the room, which would be rude but not unprecedented. Instead he walked toward the dance floor, the crowd parting around him. He moved slowly, stiffly, like a man steeling himself to something, and his face was pale beneath his mask.

The courtiers fell away, their obeisance and shocked looks unheeded, till only a woman in white stood before Mathiros. Savedra's stomach twisted and chilled—she recognized Phaedra from Isyllt's warning, and from her own glimpse of that white dress being fitted in Varis's library. She caught Nikos's shocked expression before he schooled his face.

She didn't need to hear the whispers hidden by hands

and fans to know what they said; the king had not danced with anyone in three years. But he offered his hand to this ghost now, and she took it, and together they claimed the floor. They moved in silence, never breaking the form of the dance. From the set of Mathiros's mouth, he might have taken a mortal wound, and remained standing by will alone.

The dance ended and the music died, the musicians waiting for a cue, a clue as to the king's will. The woman curtsied and stepped back, somehow vanishing into a crowd that gave her as much space as possible. She might have melted into the stones for all Savedra could tell. Mathiros stared after her, one hand clenching at his side. The courtiers waited, breathless, not knowing what they had witnessed.

Not knowing the woman in white was a witch and a murderer.

Finally Mathiros shook himself and turned away. When he sank back into his chair, the musicians stumbled into the beginning of a pavane.

A moment later Mathiros stood again. The crowd had no time to bow before he strode from the dais and out the private royal exit. Glowering, Kurgoth followed at his heels. Murmurs rippled across the room, then died as Nikos gestured for the musicians to continue.

After several moments Nikos leaned toward Ashlin, gesturing Savedra onto the dais as well. "I don't like this," he said. "I'm going to see what's wrong. Charm the guests while I'm gone, won't you?"

He rose gracefully, bowing over Ashlin's hand and pressing a kiss on her knuckles. He also plucked her a feather from his tail, earning a laugh. He gave the crowd a jaunty wave as he rose; *everything is fine,* it said, *carry on.* Savedra wondered if anyone believed it.

"Charm them, he says," Ashlin muttered. As the music died she rose, smiling as though someone had a knife to her back. "Play something livelier, won't you?" she called, her voice carrying across the hall. "I've been sitting far too long."

Immediately a dozen courtiers knelt before the dais, imploring her for a dance. Savedra recognized an Aravind, a Hadrian, and a member of the Iskari ambassador's staff—the rest were strangers, or too well masked.

A man dressed as a circus acrobat twisted out of the crowd, vaulting over the kneeling Hadrian to land before the princess. He bowed toward the startled laughter and whistles from the crowd, then bent his knee to Ashlin. Laughing, she stepped down to take his hand.

Too late, Savedra saw the flash of steel. She shouted, lunging forward; gauze and velvet tangled her and it felt like trying to run in a nightmare.

Ashlin flung herself back as the assassin struck. Someone in the crowd screamed, then another. The blade scored a line across her stomach, thwarted by leather. Savedra fumbled for the knife on her calf, her movements slow as cold honey. Ashlin was faster; she drew a blade from her vambrace and regained her balance, rocking on the balls of her feet.

"Yes," she said, baring her teeth in a grin. "That's better. Give me a proper fight." The man shifted toward the terrace doors and Ashlin moved to block his escape. Savedra had watched her in a dozen practice combats, but had never seen her eyes shine with bloodlust like this.

Captain Denaris appeared at Savedra's side, sword in

hand. The crowd shouted in confusion and alarm, those closest to the fight stumbling back while those in the rear pressed forward. "Idiots," Denaris muttered, and Savedra didn't know if she meant the spectators or the participants. Either way, she was inclined to agree. A red shadow paused at the terrace doors; Isyllt had returned.

Ashlin feinted and lunged, and her blade sliced across the man's chest. Savedra waited for him to stumble, waited for blood. Instead the torn cloth gapped, exposing leather armor.

Another strike, and this time his blade cut through Ashlin's sleeve. She hissed and blood darkened the leather just below her shoulder. The sight curdled Savedra's stomach and ended her paralysis.

She leapt down the stairs, ripping off her veils; pins scattered across marble tiles. Lunging forward, she cast the gauze like a net over the assassin's head. He kicked, knocking her feet from under her and sprawling her across the stones, dazed and breathless. But he also cursed as the veil tangled in his mask and blurred his vision, and one hand rose to claw it free. It was all Ashlin needed. Her blade flashed under his guard, sinking home in the soft flesh of his throat. Blood spurted as she pulled back, blossoming like roses on white stone.

"Alive!" Denaris wailed. "Why does no one ever leave them alive?"

Silence crushed the room as the man's boots scuffed the tiles and fell still. The smell of blood and piss filled the air and Savedra's stomach churned. Someone in the crowd wept softly. Ashlin knelt beside the dead man and wiped her blade clean on his shirt. Her hand was steady as she sheathed it again.

"I beg your pardon," she said, bowing toward the dumb-struck crowd. "I didn't mean to interrupt the dancing."

Those in front knelt first, and it rippled like a wave till all the room was on its knees. The cheer started at the back and rushed forward. And now, Savedra thought, warmth spreading through her chest, now she had won them.

Ashlin turned to her then and held out her hands. Savedra let herself be drawn up, not bothering to hide her trembling. She didn't have to be the strong one now. But when Ashlin kissed her cheek, chaste as a sister, she nearly sobbed.

"Thank you," the princess said, strong enough to carry. "I won't forget everything you've done for us."

That drew another cheer, and Savedra's face burned.

As the applause died and Ashlin released her, Savedra noticed something: despite all the noise, neither Mathiros nor Nikos had returned to see what had happened.

Then they heard the shouting.

Ashlin and Savedra moved as one, bolting through the royal door and down the corridor. Footsteps followed: Isyllt and Lord Orfion—that explained Isyllt's distraction. Captain Denaris shouted orders in the ballroom, keeping the guests contained.

They reached one of the small withdrawing rooms and found Kurgoth and Nikos pummeling the closed door. Buried under the thump of flesh on wood Savedra heard voices—Mathiros and a woman.

"The door is locked," Kurgoth growled. "Witched shut."

"Stand back," Isyllt said, shaking Lord Orfion's hand off her arm. "It won't be for long." She laid both hands on the polished wood, feverish color burning in her cheeks.

"You won't thwart me this time, bitch," she murmured as her eyes closed in concentration.

Savedra felt...something. Something cold and wrong. Before she realized it she was pushing Ashlin back, keeping herself between the princess and Isyllt's magic.

The sorceress's lips pulled back from her teeth and her face drained white. Savedra's jaw slackened as Isyllt's fine kid gloves cracked and peeled and fell from her hands in black flakes. Her diamond blazed and sparked. The wood greyed and splintered at her touch, spiderwebs crazing the varnish. Tarnish blossomed on knob and hinges.

"There." Isyllt stumbled back, chest heaving. "Kick it down."

Kurgoth complied, drawing back and slamming one heavy boot onto the wood beside the lock. The door split, spraying splinters as rotting slabs crashed to the floor.

Mathiros sprawled on a divan and the woman in white leaned over him. Her veil was gone, but black hair shrouded her face. One long hand held his jaw, the other braced against the back of the chair.

"You'll remember me," she hissed. She let go of Mathiros as Kurgoth charged her, but didn't look up. Instead her hand shot out, fingers spread and clawed. He stumbled and slowed, but kept moving. Finally she turned to him, catching his wrist in one hand and pressing the other to his chest. The man gasped, choked; a crimson bubble burst on his lips. Phaedra shoved and he flew backward, slamming into a sideboard and collapsing amid the shards of a shattered decanter.

"No!" shouted Lord Orfion, as Isyllt and Phaedra faced each other across the room. Isyllt's diamond crackled with witchlight and Phaedra's rubies glowed sullen scarlet. They ignored him, rings flaring bright and brighter still. Neither woman moved, but Isyllt hissed in pain and Phaedra gasped. Then a wall of white light blazed between them and both stumbled back.

"I said no," Kiril said, deathly calm.

"You won't stop me again," Phaedra said. A shadow that smelled of rust and cinnamon filled the room; Nikos cursed and Ashlin's hand tightened on Savedra's arm like a vise.

Heartbeats later the shadow passed, revealing the garden door open to the night, and Phaedra vanished.

"Father!" Nikos knelt beside Mathiros. The king was grey and trembling, his coat unbuttoned. "Are you all right?"

"I— She was—" Mathiros scrubbed a hand over his face.

Kurgoth moaned and stirred, and Ashlin turned to help him. Blood streaked his face, but he seemed to have stopped coughing it up. Isyllt's nose was bleeding as well; she wiped at it absently and scowled. The look she shot Kiril was cold and harsh.

"Father," Nikos said, helping Mathiros to his feet, "I saw her. It was—"

"You saw nothing!" Mathiros snarled, jerking away. "An assassin. A demon." His eyes narrowed, training on Ashlin and her bleeding arm. "What's happened?"

She flexed her shoulder absently and winced. "An assassin in the ballroom. Not a demon, though—he died easily enough."

He nodded. "Mikhael, are you hurt?"

The captain spat blood on the expensive carpet. "I'm standing."

"Good enough. Find me Adrastos. I want the palace sealed and searched immediately. Kiril—" He had the grace to look abashed, at least.

Kiril tugged his mask off. "I am at your disposal, Majesty."

"Help Adrastos, then. I want to know where these bastards came from."

"Of course." His eyes sagged shut as he turned away, and Savedra fought to keep the naked sympathy from her face.

And with that Mathiros, Kurgoth, and Kiril all left the room, leaving the others standing in the draft. Ashlin, ever practical, closed and latched the garden door.

Nikos sat down hard on the chair his father had vacated. He was the one trembling now, his face ashen. Savedra abandoned propriety and went to him, clasping his shaking hand between hers.

"What is it?"

"I saw her," he whispered, his voice scraped dry and hoarse. "I saw her face. It was my mother."

CHAPTER 17

The Solstice ball was meant to last throughout the longest night. But while none of the guests had expected to see their beds before dawn, this wasn't how they'd imagined the party would end.

Savedra helped calm the guests now sequestered in the ballroom while Isyllt and the palace mages questioned them: Had anyone spoken to the assassin, or the woman in white? Had anyone seen them arrive? No one had, of course, though several courtiers began to second-guess themselves and others developed acute cases of hindsight.

"I knew something was wrong with her from the moment I saw her," said an Aravind matron, fanning herself excessively. "My aunt is a mage, you know, and I have a bit of a shiver myself. But no one else paid her any mind...."

Nikos handled the whole thing gracefully, sending for more refreshments, issuing polite orders and reassurances, and never letting Ashlin out of arm's reach. The princess clearly wanted to snap at him, but the courtiers were already responding to his concern. If she'd known the good a public assassination attempt would do, Savedra thought wryly, she could have saved herself long hours skulking in gardens.

Mathiros led the search patrol himself, despite arguments from Nikos, Kurgoth, and Adrastos. It looked very brave, of course, but Savedra could feel the court clinging tighter to Nikos in the absence of his father.

Good, she thought, and resisted the urge to smirk at Thea Jsutien.

Tempers and nerves began to fray when a young dandy from House Hadrian stopped complaining about his headache and began to shake and cough instead. Within the hour he was limp and feverish, propped in a corner while his erstwhile bosom companions edged away and breathed through handkerchiefs. Soon half the hall was arguing for fresh air, or braziers for warmth, or incense to keep the illness at bay—the other half demanded to leave, or to call their personal physicians. No one wanted to say *influenza*, which was an illness for the poor or unlucky, but everyone knew the signs.

During an especially loud argument over the virtues of incense versus fresh-sliced onions to ward off the ill vapors, Isyllt appeared at Savedra's side.

"We won't get anything useful from them now," she muttered, "not even silence. I need your help."

Savedra followed her down the side hall, and eventually onto a porch leading into the gardens. "Where are we going?" she asked. "And can I fetch a cloak first?"

"To the temple, and no. We need to be there and out

again before we're noticed." By lantern-light Isyllt's face was grim and pale. "I kept your secrets—now I need you to keep one for me."

Savedra nodded and followed Isyllt across the lawn, tucking her hands beneath her folded arms.

Isyllt held onto her as they entered the temple; the sleepy acolyte didn't look up as they started down the black mouth of the stairs. Savedra wanted to question, to protest, but wasn't sure how far a whisper would carry—the slither of their skirts over timeworn stone was unnerving enough. She tested each step carefully and tried not to imagine all the things that might be waiting for them at the bottom.

At the foot of the steps Isyllt conjured a light, which Savedra took as a sign that they were safe to speak.

"Where are we going?" she asked, and winced at the broken weight of silence.

"The Alexios crypt." A muscle worked in Isyllt's square jaw. The light turned her eyes into cold mirrors. Savedra withheld the rest of her questions, at least until they reached the door.

"Do you have a key?" she ventured then.

"Always." She laid a hand on the lock plate, and Savedra's nape prickled with the same sensation she'd felt earlier.

"What is that?"

"Entropomancy. The essence of death and decay." Isyllt's voice cracked. "I don't like to use it. It hurts."

It also worked. She set her shoulder against the door and pushed, and it scraped inward. Savedra touched the ruin of the lock and her fingers came away red with rust.

Isyllt turned her attention to the queen's coffin and

Savedra's stomach twisted. "I thought Nikos said the seal on the sarcophagus was intact." Her skin crawled, ears straining for the sound of footsteps. Mathiros would send them to the headsman for this.

"It is." Isyllt's eyes met hers across the carven lid, cold and pale as the marble. "Whatever we find here, swear to me you won't speak of it until I do."

"All right. I swear."

Isyllt laid her hands on the queen's stone breast and frowned. She stood like that for long moments. Finally blue sparks crackled from her fingers and she straightened. "Help me move the lid."

Savedra thought she would be sick. She fought it down, forcing herself to take the last steps across the room and set her hands on the coffin.

On the count of three she and Isyllt pushed. Muscles corded and her still-healing arm burned fiercely from the effort. Stone gave way with a terrible scrape, inch by inch until the head of the sarcophagus was open. Wan and sweating, Isyllt summoned the light closer, filling the interior with its opalescent glow.

Empty.

False dawn lit the sky when Isyllt finally left the palace, chasing the Hounds into the west; the Dragon's breath did nothing against the cold. The palace guards had found nothing, and had finally released the guests. Dancing away the longest night was one thing, but no one wanted to face the dawn of the demon days.

Isyllt imagined she would be seeing all too much of the demons this year.

Kiril joined her in front of the palace gates as she

waited through the line of angry and frightened courtiers. More of them had already begun to cough and sniffle, which might merely be chill and fatigue, or the influenza's touch.

She didn't look at him for several moments, though she didn't pull away from the line of warmth he offered, either. A scream coiled in her throat and she feared to let it loose.

"Let me see you home," he said.

"Afraid your blood witch will come for me?"

"Yes."

The honesty of it knocked the acerbity out of her. She let him help her into a carriage, and didn't speak again. The things she had to say couldn't be spoken in the open. She wasn't sure she could speak them at all.

When they stepped onto the frost-rimed stones of Calderon Court, she knew she had to try. "Come inside."

She didn't take his cloak when she shot the bolt behind them, or offer tea. Familiar ritual was no comfort now, and he knew where she kept the cups. She went straight to that cupboard and poured herself a shot of ouzo. Its anise-and-coriander fire numbed her throat enough to let the words free.

"I checked the wards on the queen's coffin, when first we investigated the stolen jewels. They were intact, as strong as if they'd just been cast. Too strong, though of course I never thought of it. You opened the coffin, stole her body for a demon, and sealed it again."

"You see why I didn't want you investigating this." His humor was fleeting. "Yes. That was the act that broke my oath, and my power. Listening to conspirators is one thing—that was more than Mathiros would ever forgive."

She poured herself another shot and downed it. "Why? What possibly justifies such a violation?"

Kiril sighed, and moved past her to pour himself a drink. Cradling it, he sank into a chair. "Had you ever heard of Phaedra Severos, before you found that girl's body?"

She shook her head, sitting opposite him.

"You should have. You would have, if not for Mathiros and me. She was a powerful mage and a brilliant scholar. The things she could do with haematurgy were a marvel." He sipped his drink, grimacing as he always did at the taste. "She was also mad. Not like she is now, but bad enough—she spent days in frenzies of research, creating wondrous things, only to burn her notes in black despair because nothing she wrought was as flawless as it should be. She went from mania to despair without warning. And more rarely and worse yet, she fell into a sort of fierce nihilism, like a phoenix who meant to take the whole world with her when she burned. That fire, I think, is what drew Mathiros."

"They were lovers?"

Kiril knocked back the rest of his drink. "There was nothing of love between them, no matter how loosely one defines the term. But yes. She was already married. I met her husband once, before all that began. He reminded me of Mathiros, actually, but older and wiser and far calmer. Ferenz weathered Phaedra's moods like a mountain. Mathiros couldn't offer that—he was little more than a boy when they met, cocky with his rank and the strength of youth. He wanted her because she was beautiful, and because—" He stared into the bottom of his empty glass. "Because he has always been searching for that fire that will consume him, ever since he was a child. And in each other, they found the means to destroy themselves.

"I couldn't stop it. I was already Mathiros's closest advisor, but nothing would keep him from Phaedra. It was ugly and brutal—not the brutality of fists, though possibly that too, but of words and heart. And eventually it went too far. Perhaps he struck her, or merely said the wrong hurtful thing. Whatever it was, she responded with magic, and drew his blood. And then it was treason.

"That might have been the end of it. She fled the palace and returned to Sarkany, and without her presence to goad him I think I could have calmed him. But the palace maids thought Phaedra was pregnant, and the rumor reached Mathiros. I silenced it, but too late." His mouth was a grim line, and Isyllt didn't ask what measures he'd taken for that silence.

"Now we had a royal bastard to deal with, who would be raised by a Severos blood mage and a Sarken noble. The possibilities were…unpleasant. Mathiros was determined to deal with it, and I couldn't dissuade him from doing so personally. We rode to Carnavas in all the stealth my magic and lies could give us. I still hoped that we could solve this reasonably." His smile was humorless. "The folly of youth.

"It began with discussion, but quickly degenerated. Mathiros and Ferenz fought, while I pursued Phaedra to her tower. Then Ferenz fell, and all the fight went out of her. She threw herself off the tower." His eyes closed, fingers tightening on the arm of the chair.

"But she didn't die," Isyllt said. "Not permanently." Her jaw ached from the effort of keeping her teeth from chattering. She hadn't lit a fire, and the room was nearly as cold as the dawn.

"No. Though I didn't know that at the time. And so we were left with a castle full of corpses and the makings of an international incident."

"What did you do?"

"I killed all the castle servants, to start, and used their deaths to cover our tracks at Carnavas. But that did nothing about the city full of people who knew and would miss Phaedra. Hushing up a bastard is one thing, but murdering a scion of a great house would mean open revolt from the Octagon Court. So I erased her."

Isyllt swallowed, her throat gone dry. Erasing a moment's memory was one thing, but a lifetime— "How?"

"With more murder, of course." His voice was harsher than the winter outside. "I carried the souls I collected to the labyrinth beneath Erishal's cathedral and offered them to her, along with three years of my life. She took my offering—she does so enjoy watching secular mages prostrate themselves. And slowly everyone who had ever known Phaedra began to forget her. The physical evidence—her papers and research—I stole from the Arcanost, so no one would be reminded."

"Does that mean Mathiros?"

Kiril nodded. "Also has no memory of her. He couldn't remember, or he would have spent the rest of his life a butcher. I took the burden from him to give him another chance. When he found Lychandra, I thought it had worked."

"But you bore the burden."

"I did. Phaedra was due that much. But I wasn't alone, it turned out. Varis loved her, and was in Iskar when she died, beyond Erishal's reach. He searched for years, and finally found her."

"How did she survive?"

"She had learned how to transfer consciousness—soul—through blood. She kept a flock of familiar birds who had been drinking her blood for years, who served as her eyes and ears. They stole her rings off her corpse, and between blood and foci, she lived on in them."

"A demon."

"Yes. But her magic was stronger than the chain of flesh is to most demons. Eventually she grew strong again, more herself, and arranged for a mortal to drink the blood of her birds. Her consciousness grew again in a human body, and she began to regain her strength. I imagine being a flock of birds for years was...taxing. This was the demon Varis found, who he brought back to Erisín, and to me."

It was a great law of magic: the combination of spirit and flesh that created a demon could only happen once. To find it so easily overthrown knocked the wind from her lungs. She forced her mind away from the implications and back to the story at hand.

"She didn't try to kill you?"

"What would be the point?" He laughed harshly. "Mathiros had already cast me aside. And she knew her murder had never been my goal. All her rage is for him."

"And he doesn't remember why." She remembered Phaedra's fury in the palace—*You'll remember me*—and Mathiros's confusion.

"Yes. I should have struck her down when she came to me, or gone straight to Mathiros with the news. But I couldn't do that to her again. Not after—"

Not after everything.

They sat in cold and silence for a moment, while the blue light of dawn rose behind the curtains. She didn't say *that's horrible*, because he knew it was. She didn't say *how could you?* because she knew how he could. She didn't say *I'm sorry*, because that didn't help anything.

"She's due her revenge," Isyllt said at last. "I grant you that. But what about Forsythia, and all the others she and Spider have killed? Don't they deserve the same?"

"Justice for all?" His eyebrows rose. "Have you become an altruist?"

She laughed. "I've become what you made me." She rose, unsteady as liquor and fatigue surged through her limbs. "What are we going to do?"

"We?" He rose to meet her. "You would still stand by me?"

"You've done terrible things. I can't say that I wouldn't have done the same. I was made for terrible things, wasn't I?"

"I may have made you a killer, but your strength and cleverness are your own. Don't throw yourself away for me."

A muscle worked in her jaw. "I thought you were done making decisions for me."

He touched the disheveled wreck of her veil again, then cupped her cheek, skin to skin. She leaned into the touch. He lowered his mouth to hers.

Her left hand tightened against the nape of his neck; her right tangled in his robes. The taste of ouzo on both their tongues slowly melted into the familiar warmth that was his alone.

When they drew apart her pulse beat hard and fast in her lips and the ocean-rush of blood in her ears deafened her. Her eyes were closed, but she felt his sharp intake of breath. He still wanted her, and that dizzied her more than liquor ever could.

She took his hand and led him to the bedroom. He didn't argue.

CHAPTER 18

The demon days were meant to be spent indoors, either at home with family or in a cathedral for prayer and meditation. No one ventured out between dusk and dawn for fear of the Invidiae, the jealous demon sisters who gave the dead days their name—most didn't venture out at all. So when Thea Jsutien arrived before noon demanding to speak with her, Savedra was at a loss.

Her equally disgruntled maid dragged her out of bed and helped her scrub off the remnants of last night's cosmetics. On any other day she would have made Thea wait, and wielded her wardrobe like a weapon. Today, slow and aching with fatigue and bruises from her fall, she very nearly left her rooms in a robe with her hair in snake-tangles around her face.

Instead she found a plain black dress and let Marjana comb her hair and braid it and knot it at the nape of her neck. She wore no jewelry, not even her pearls—jewels and fine things were said to attract the Invidiae, a legend she had no desire to test. And if Thea had come to her here, she hardly needed to remind the woman of her station.

Marjana had left the archa waiting in the gallery's solar, which offered an excellent view of the frost-decked gardens. It offered the garden's chill as well—fire in every hearth was another luxury to be avoided; tea and cakes were right out. Savedra's breath fogged the air as she sighed.

Thea had dressed simply as well. Savedra had never thought to see such a thing, but the woman could have been any merchant-wife in plain brown wool, her greying hair coiled neatly. She was of an age with Savedra's mother, but today she looked much older.

"Good morning, Your Grace," Savedra said. "What can I do for you?"

Thea's shadowed eyes narrowed. Deep lines framed her tight-set lips. "What have you done with my niece?" Her voice was dry and strained.

"What?" Her wits were too dull for fencing.

"You heard me. Where is Ginevra?"

Savedra's mouth opened and closed again. She sat gracelessly. "I take it the answer is not House Hydra, then?"

Thea scowled. "She wasn't with us when we left the palace last night. She never came home. Do you mean to tell me you aren't responsible?"

"I certainly don't have her bound in the back of my wardrobe." Now she forced her sticky mind to work—when had she last seen Ginevra? At the ball, of course, but when? A glimpse of red across the room, or had that been Isyllt—

"I don't know what you meant by those costumes—"

"Those costumes were as much Ginevra's idea as mine," Savedra said. "And making people disappear seems more your style than mine, don't you think? I don't know what's happened to her, nor do I wish her harm. She managed not to grow into a scheming bitch, despite your best efforts." Saying what she felt was much too pleasant; she couldn't make a habit of it.

"Her mother's blood. Talia has always been too trusting. And look what good it's done her now."

Savedra didn't bother to hide her frown. It might be a trick. If Ginevra's chances for the throne worsened, she doubted Thea would scruple to use the girl in some other way. But if it wasn't…

"I may not wish Ginevra ill, but why would I help a house that wants me dead?"

Thea's chin rose, firming the soft flesh of her neck. "House Hydra has no quarrel with the Severoi. I may not be fond of the Alexioi, but I want no trouble with Nadesda, and that's what your death would earn me, now isn't it? Not all the houses feel the same, I'm sure, but if someone has tried to kill you, it's no scheme of mine."

Savedra didn't believe her for an instant, but in the end that didn't matter. "Will you ask the king for help?"

Thea sniffed. "I'm sure he has enough to worry him." Of course she wouldn't want the Crown investigating anywhere near House Hydra—who knew what they might turn up? "Do you swear you had nothing to do with Ginevra's disappearance?"

"I swear it."

"Then—" Thea scowled. "Then help me. I want Ginevra home and safe, and for whatever reason she seems to like you. I know you have resources, to have kept your place here so long…"

She wanted to tell Thea to go to hell and crawl back to bed. But if Ginevra was in danger, especially if it had anything to do with their subterfuge last night, she couldn't turn away.

"All right," she said at last. "I'll see what I can find. I'm sure my mother will be glad to help, if it means forming a closer bond with House Hydra."

Thea acknowledged the debt with a frown and a nod, and rose stiffly. "I hope for all our sakes that you find her quickly, then. The turning of the year is no time to have affairs in such disarray."

When Savedra was alone she chafed her frigid hands. Then she stood, shaking out her skirts, and returned to her rooms for a cloak, wondering how she would bribe a coachman to take her out on Indrani.

Isyllt and Kiril lay together, her head on his chest and their legs entwined. The blankets trailed uselessly off the foot of the bed, but Isyllt didn't mind the chill. She didn't dare take her hands off him, for fear he would dissolve like smoke if she did. Beyond the curtains, the cold light of Indrani brightened.

"I only wanted to spare you pain," he whispered, stroking the line of her shoulder blade as if he meant to memorize the shape.

"It doesn't work that way." Her fingers traced the valleys of his ribs and the planes and hollows of his stomach. His skin had softened with the years, flesh and muscle lost beneath, but she still felt the familiar strength in his hands.

"No. I begin to understand that."

Their magic moved as well, tendrils of power teasing and exploring, raising gooseflesh as they ghosted over skin. Neither Ciaran's clever hands nor Spider's poppy-sweet kisses could match the sensation of magic so inextricably intertwined.

"Three years of your life?" she said at last, kissing the stark line of his collarbone between each word.

"That was what she demanded. I didn't have a better offer."

She frowned and raised her head; her hair slid across his chest and tangled both their arms. "But how can she know? Can even a saint see the end of your life, to know where to snip it short?"

"I don't know. It may have been a hollow threat, merely meant to make me miserable. Shadows know it would have been easier if she'd snipped the thread three years ago, instead of leaving me like this."

Isyllt bit his shoulder in response, hard enough to elicit a hiss of pain. "Don't be stupid. She's had her time, then. The rest is yours."

"Mine." He laughed, his chest jerking sharply against her. "Five years I gave to Nikolaos Alexios. Thirty years to Mathiros. Three to Erishal. I can scarcely remember what I did when my time was my own."

"Give it to me, then. I'll make use of it."

He laughed, until she smothered it with a kiss and her hair fell around them like a veil.

"Come away with me," he said later, so softly she barely heard it. Sleep lapped slowly over her, but that drew her awake again. No bells rang on the dead days, but she

guessed from the light that it was near the second terce—
the hour of virtue.

"Where?"

"Anywhere but here. What's left for us in Erisín?"

What was there for her? Twenty-four years of history.
Ciaran and Khelséa and Dahlia, and a handful of other
friends she saw less often. A lot of ghosts. The Arcanost
and her classes. Her favorite shops and taverns and all the
streets she knew as well as her own hands. Her home.

But what kind of home would it be without Kiril?

"It would break my oath." How that oath was still intact
she didn't understand. But there had been no clause in her
vow to serve and uphold about not keeping secrets from
the king. The crafters of the oath had obviously understood the latitude her job often called for.

"You'll suffer for it, true. But you're strong enough to
overcome it."

"And let Phaedra and Spider throw the city into chaos?"

"Is it really our concern anymore? Erisín has endured
worse than a coup."

She couldn't argue that. If it were only Mathiros she
wouldn't lift a hand to save him. Nikos had his own people. But no matter what Spider claimed, it was the city
that would suffer for a revolution.

She didn't realize she'd made a decision till she pulled
away, dragging a sheet closer around her.

"I can't leave. Not like this. I'll resign my position and
go with you when it's over, but I won't let Phaedra and
Spider drag the city into their madness."

Kiril sat up, the covers pooling around the sharp
angles of his hips. The winter chill rushed to fill the space
between them. "Phaedra won't be easy to oppose."

"I promised Forsythia justice. There will never be justice for all, but for this one I can do something." She had never set great store on honor—it was transitory and subjective, and often directly opposed to practicality—but she needed some scrap of self-respect, and knew she wouldn't keep it if her word meant nothing at all.

"Justice at the cost of your own life?"

But that wasn't the true cost. The importance of her own life had always been a fluid thing, to be guarded or gambled on a whim. The price of pursuing justice now would be another chance at spending that life with Kiril.

"Could you do it so easily?" she asked. "Leave everything you've lived for? Or would you only be miserable?" He had said it himself: he didn't know what to do with his own life. She might start over, if she had him. She had always known, in those lonely hours when she dwelled on such things, how easily Kiril had defined her. How easily he could become her world. And she also knew that his love for her was real, but nowhere as broad or as deep as hers.

"I don't know. But I'm willing to try."

"We both make ourselves miserable all too well. I'm not willing to help you."

The silence stretched taut. Finally Kiril rose to collect his scattered clothes. Isyllt watched him dress, and her stomach felt too small.

A knock at the door snapped the strained stillness. Isyllt hadn't realized she was holding her breath till it left in an aching rush. She winced as her feet touched the icy floor, huddling in her worn and faded robe as she went to the door.

Her wards recognized Savedra now, but without them

Isyllt might not have known her on first glance—she'd never seen the other woman without silks or velvet or the luster of pearls.

"I'm sorry," Savedra said. "I didn't mean to wake you."

Isyllt's cheeks warmed. "You didn't. Come in."

Kiril emerged from the bedroom, his clothing rumpled but in place, and now Savedra blushed. "I should go," he said. He nodded politely to Savedra as he passed. "Lady Severos."

Say something, Isyllt thought as she followed him to the door. *Stop him. Don't let it happen this way—* But her tongue was numb, her jaw locked. Her hand twitched as he crossed the threshold. He paused on the first step, his mouth twisting in that sad familiar smile. He caught her hand before it fell back to her side, brushed his thumb softly across her knuckles. Then he turned and faded into the shadows of the stairwell.

"I'm sorry," Savedra said again as Isyllt closed the door. "I didn't know—"

"It's all right. You saved us some argument and awkward farewells. What's wrong?" No one went visiting on the demon days if everything was well.

"Ginevra Jsutien is missing. Her aunt believes she's been abducted."

"Do you believe it?"

"I don't know. Saints know Thea is a liar and a schemer, but I believe she's upset. What if someone thought she was one of us last night?"

Isyllt frowned. "We both had our veils off after the assassin attacked the princess. When did she disappear?"

"I don't know. I can't remember when I last saw her."

"Damn. Who would want her gone?"

"I would, if I were any more ruthless." Savedra's mouth twisted. "Though I find myself liking her. But everyone knows Thea wants Ginevra to be queen when Ashlin is gone, and I imagine there are plenty of factions who oppose that." She rubbed at her injured arm fretfully. "You don't think Phaedra had anything to do with it, do you?"

"I wouldn't put much past her, though so far she's taken victims who wouldn't be missed."

As soon as she said it, memories clicked like puzzle cubes: the protests in Archlight and riots in Elysia; the angry families in the Justiciary demanding answers; all the pale bodies on slabs in the Sepulcher.

"Saints and shadows." She shook her head, impressed by the plan even as her stomach clenched. "They're not random." *Liar,* she thought, remembering Spider shrugging the deaths aside, and laughed.

Savedra's eyebrows rose and she went on. "They're killing refugee girls. And why not—there are enough of them in the slums, easy to snatch. But for every girl that disappears, the Rosian community gets angrier. There's been rioting in Elysia already. It will get worse now that the army is home and the city is even more strained."

"They're antagonizing the Rosians on purpose?"

"They must be. They want the throne—turning the city against Mathiros can only help them. An unloved king is easier to overthrow, for reasons both practical and thaumaturgical. Then they seize the throne and the killings stop."

Savedra rocked back. "But a coup would throw the city into more chaos. They would have to kill Nikos, too, and then the Octagon Court would snarl like dogs over the throne." Her face paled as she spoke. "And why now? The demon days are hardly an auspicious time to do anything."

"They are if you're a demon. Phaedra's power will only increase over the next few days, and the city is at its most vulnerable."

"Shadows. Nikos is in danger."

"Go to him. Warn him and keep him close."

"What are you doing?"

"Going to the Garden. I need to convince Little Kiva not to riot again, and I think I know someone they might listen to."

Carriages were scarce on the dead days, so Isyllt walked to the Garden. There were more people on the streets of Elysia than there should have been, and too many of them scowled and clustered in angry conversation.

The Briar Patch was closed, as was every shop and tavern on Thistle Street, but smoke trickled out of the chimney. Isyllt hammered on the kitchen door; her hand ached before the latch lifted and Mekaran's frowning face appeared in the gap.

"What in the black hells do you want, necromancer?"

"I need your help."

His frown didn't fade, but the door opened. "Your timing is bad. But maybe you can help me in turn." He ushered her inside, into warmth and the comforting smell of garlic and ginger. "Dahlia is sick."

Isyllt's stomach tightened. "The influenza?"

"What else?" His mouth quirked. "I want to blame you for sending her on errands in the cold, but I know that's

ridiculous. There's someone sick in every house, lately."
He wore no paint today, and coppery stubble shadowed
his jaw. His clothes were plain and dark, and even his
hair had begun to fade, cinnamon-brown roots showing
beneath the dye.

"Is it bad?"

He shot her a scalding look. "Bad enough. Can you do
anything for her?"

"I'm no healer. But let me see her, please."

Dahlia's room was a small one above the kitchen,
hardly wider than a closet. Warm enough, at least, between
heat from below and the brazier glowing by the foot of the
bed. The cot was layered in blankets, and Dahlia had bur-
rowed into them. Her hair spread in lank tangles across
the pillow and her cheeks were blotched with fever and an
alarming yellow flush.

"Lady Iskaldur." She coughed as soon as she spoke,
deep and wet. The whites of her eyes were washed yellow;
Isyllt winced at the sight. Bruised lids sank shut a moment
later, and the rasp of the girl's breath deepened.

She remembered the last time she'd sat a sickbed like
this—her friend Ziya caught the influenza when they
were fifteen and living in a freezing tenement attic in
Birthgrave. No money for a physician and only the scant
herbcraft Isyllt had gleaned from her mother to fight the
illness. If Ziya had died that night, Isyllt would have lost
everything.

Instead Kiril had found her, and offered help in
exchange for her apprenticeship.

She didn't realize she was crying till a tear slipped
off her chin and splashed the blanket. "How long has it
been?" she asked, scrubbing her cheeks.

"Two days," Mekaran said from the doorway. "The fever hit yesterday and the jaundice came this morning. What is this plague? I've never seen anything like it."

"Neither have I. The Arcanost swears it's just influenza, but they're lying to prevent a panic." She sank onto the edge of the bed and took Dahlia's clammy hand in hers. The symptoms were an unnatural mix of influenza and the bronze fever. A fever the city hadn't seen since the summer of Lychandra's death....

Isyllt remembered her fevered dreams—blood and more blood, and black wings. She closed her eyes and extended her magic, sending tendrils of power questing through Dahlia. Death answered, a shadow in the girl's lungs, a sickly yellow glow pulsing through her veins and coiling in her liver. Not the sharp echo of a mortal illness, not yet, but the potential was there.

She forced her awareness deeper, clenching her jaw as Dahlia began to shiver at the invasive chill. Dimly she heard Mekaran's indrawn breath, but he had the sense not to interrupt. There. Scarlet ribbons twined the muddy yellow of the plague, shining with a faint porphyry glitter. The taste of cinnamon spread across her tongue.

Phaedra had taken the dead plague as well as the dead queen's flesh, quickened it and melded it with the influenza till she had a new plague that would spread in winter. Isyllt's breath hitched at the ingenuity of it, the skill involved. Silently, she cursed Kiril and Mathiros and all the fates for making this woman her enemy.

Then she gathered herself and launched her magic against Phaedra's. Dahlia shuddered and writhed and Mekaran swore. Death-magic flashed like a scalpel, slicing the ribbons of haematurgy. Crimson unraveled into yellow, and the yellow in turn began to fade. Magic spread the dead fever—if she could break Phaedra's spell, only the natural illness should remain.

She opened her eyes as Mekaran's hand closed on her shoulder; she felt the violence harnessed in his manicured grip. Dahlia had curled into a shivering ball, her breath coming in soft keening gasps. Her lips were bruised blue, as were the tips of the fingers Isyllt still held. Sweat cooled on Isyllt's brow.

"The plague is sorcery. Another attempt to weaken the city." She let go of Dahlia's hand and pulled the covers tightly around the girl's neck. "I broke its hold on her."

Mekaran released her; her shoulder throbbed where his fingers had ground flesh to bone. "You nearly killed her."

She nodded, unclenching her aching jaw. "I'm no healer," she repeated. "But it worked. She's still sick, but the taint is gone. The jaundice should clear soon —if it's anything like the real bronze fever, her urine will be bloody when it passes. Keep her warm and full of soup and tisane—she's strong enough to fight the rest." Or so she prayed.

Mekaran's frown remained, but his shoulders slumped. He added fuel to the brazier before leading Isyllt back to the kitchen.

"What do you need my help for?" he asked as he poured tea. He set a cup in front of Isyllt, followed by a plate of yesterday's bread and honey.

Between sips of tea, she explained about the murdered women, the riots and the growing unrest. "The last thing the city needs during the demon days is rioting. Violence and destruction will draw spirits like a beacon, and only further these demons' plans."

"And this demon witch who made the plague is the one who killed Forsythia."

It wasn't a question, but Isyllt nodded anyway. "Between you and Ciaran I thought you might talk some sense into the instigators. Once we deal with this sorceress they can march on the Justiciary all they please, but not in the next five days."

Mekaran stared at the mug cradled in his broad hands. "I know some of the leaders. I'll talk to them. They're angry, though, and the marigolds who refuse to help them are a likelier target than demons no one has seen. Pray they listen."

Isyllt laughed grimly. Her prayers were spread thin these days, and she knew the sort of answer she was likely to receive.

Nikos wasn't in his chambers, and rather than hunt him through the palace Savedra settled in to wait. His room was cold, the air heavy with ash and incense—he didn't often pray, but the doors of his shrine were open now, the burners streaked with ashes. She hoped the saints were listening.

She knelt in front of the cabinet, letting the scent of sandalwood and myrrh ground her as she gathered her wits. She'd waited too long to tell him and the story had grown too convoluted. A coup she could understand, even Varis's misguided need for revenge on the Alexioi, but demons and stolen corpses—

Footsteps broke the spiral of her thoughts and she straightened her shoulders. The connecting door to Ashlin's suite swung open, and Nikos entered with the princess at his heels. Savedra's carefully planned explanations crumbled in surprise, and she drew back into the shadows to regroup. Neither of them turned in her direction.

"What is it?" Nikos asked when the door was latched behind them. His face was drawn, his voice strained. He inspected a bottle of wine on the sideboard before he poured, and Savedra smiled in approval—she'd insisted he seal all his bottles, and always check them before he drank.

"I'm sorry to trouble you," Ashlin said slowly, waving aside an offered goblet. "I know this isn't a good time for distractions."

"You're my wife," he said with an exasperated laugh. "You're allowed to distract me whenever you wish. Some might even encourage it."

Ashlin didn't so much as smile. Savedra knew she ought to speak before she eavesdropped further, but her tongue was frozen.

"I'm pregnant."

Nikos's mouth opened and closed again. "Are you sure?" Savedra felt as though she'd turned to stone.

"This is the third time. I know the signs."

He drank before he spoke. "Forgive me," he said after a long swallow, "but—"

Her mouth twisted. "But how can that be, when we haven't shared a bed since I lost the last one?"

Savedra's hands ached, clenched white-knuckled in her skirts.

"I would never accuse you . . . ."

"It's true, though. It isn't yours. I'm sorry." She squared her shoulders, a soldier facing discipline. "I didn't mean for it to happen, and I won't dishonor the oaths I swore any further by lying. I know the odds are poor that I'll keep it any longer than the others, but I thought you should know. If you wish to begin divorce proceedings—"

"Slow down, please. You're making my head spin." He set his goblet aside. "Most state marriages last at least five years before public scandal and divorce. But if you're that unhappy . . . ." All of them flinched at the hurt in those last words. More than injured pride, and Savedra's chest ached; he loved Ashlin after all, or something close. "I don't suppose you'd tell me whose it is? As long as it's not my father, I think I could stand to hear anything."

That drew an outraged laugh, but Ashlin sobered quickly. "I'm sorry, but it's not my place to say."

"No," Savedra said slowly, pushing herself off her knees. "But it is mine."

They both startled. Nikos's goblet teetered on the sideboard and fell, spraying wine across the carpet with a metallic thunk; Ashlin groped at her belt for an absent blade. She flushed as Savedra stepped out of the shadows. "Vedra—"

"My place," she went on, cutting her off. "My place, and my child."

Nikos blinked, and his jaw slackened in confusion. It tightened again with the realization that followed. "You can't mean—"

"Yes. I'm the—" Her voice broke. "The father. Forgive me. No, forgive Ashlin. I understand mine is the worse betrayal."

Nikos lurched away from the wall and Savedra tensed for shouting, for rage, even for a blow. But he turned back to the sideboard to fetch a new goblet and pour more wine. His hand shook and garnet-red drops splashed the table.

"It was my fault," Ashlin said. "I pressed the matter, abused my position and Savedra's trust."

"Please." He laughed bitterly and raised his cup. His throat worked as he swallowed. "You said no lies. I know you too well for that."

"I'm no ravished maiden," Savedra said, her voice so dry she hardly recognized it. "Let's place no blame beyond what we've earned."

"Vedra—" His eyes were dangerously liquid. Her composure would shatter if his did. "Is it over, then? Between us?"

She started forward, stopped short as if held by a leash. Her cheeks tingled; her hands shook. "I love you. I love you as I always have. I would never leave you willingly, but what I've done—" She forced the words past her tightening throat. "It's treason."

"You love me." No mockery, no doubt. "Do you love Ashlin, too?"

She saw the princess tense as if for a blow. No assassin could ever wound them all so gracefully. "Yes."

"Well, then." He drained the rest of his cup. "Doubtless my father could be decisive about something like this, but I don't think I can. I need time, and more wine. I trust neither of you have spoken of this to anyone else? Good," he said when they both nodded. "Then please don't. I— Excuse me." With that, he left, easing the door shut behind him so it didn't make a sound.

Ashlin and Savedra stared at each other.

"When did you know?" Savedra managed at last.

"I've worried since we got back from Evharis. The timing was right for a child to catch—which I should have thought of then, but I was too drunk and stupid. And then this morning my breasts began to ache, and I knew."

"And you didn't tell me?"

"I looked for you this morning. I thought of waiting, but that would only have put the burden on you, and been a coward's choice. I'm sorry, Vedra. It seems that all we can do is hurt one another."

She turned back to her rooms and shut the door behind her.

Savedra stood for a moment, stunned and sick, before she remembered the reason she'd needed to talk to Nikos in the first place. With a curse she ran after Ashlin, catching her before she reached the door of her suite.

"Wait! Saints, Ashlin, your timing is impossible." She couldn't look the princess in the eye, but she forced out an explanation of Phaedra and Isyllt's suspicions.

"Blood and iron," Ashlin swore. "No, we can't let him wander off to drink himself stupid now. Where would he go?"

They searched the library, the stables, and the wine cellar with no luck, and Savedra silently cursed the cold and empty halls. Whenever she and Nikos tried to find a moment alone, the palace was crawling with servants, and now it was desolate.

An hour passed before they found a groundskeeper who pointed them toward the palace temple. The memory of the black crypts and the queen's empty coffin sped Savedra's stride, till Ashlin had to jog to keep pace.

His guards waited inside the temple, but directed Ashlin down to the crypt. "His Highness ordered us to leave him," the unhappy sergeant said. And, more reluctantly, "He's been drinking."

Ashlin's smile didn't fool anyone. "I think I can carry him if he's too drunk to walk. Stay here.

"I hate these places," the princess muttered as they descended the stairs. The lantern swayed in her hand, and their shadows capered back and forth. "The dead should be burned and given to the sky, not locked up in vaults like preserves. And you call my people heathens."

After several twists and curves, they saw a glimmer of light ahead. Nikos had set his lantern on the ground outside the Alexios crypt; its glow cast his face in shadow where he sat beside his mother's sarcophagus, legs sprawled in front of him and a bottle of wine in his hand.

"I probably shouldn't be found here," he said, tilting the bottle. "I'd be called morbid and unstable in no time."

Savedra's hands clenched in her skirt. "Nikos—"

He waved the bottle in a silencing motion; wine sloshed black against the glass. "Wait. Listen." He caught the edge of the coffin and pulled himself up; Savedra winced, remembering the scrape of stone as it opened. He took another long pull and set the bottle down.

"Vedra, I love you. I wouldn't give you up for propriety, or my father, or even a political marriage. I don't ever want to give you up."

A painful knot lodged in her throat—before she could swallow it he went on.

"Ashlin. I know this marriage isn't what either of us wanted, but I find myself not half as miserable as I expected. You're clever and strong and competent and only a termagant every other decad or so. I *like* you, and the alliance is a good one. I can't think of any daughter of the Eight that I'd rather be saddled with. You could have forced me to set Savedra aside, and you didn't. And—and so it seems heartless and hypocritical for me to force you to set her aside." He fumbled for the bottle again, and Savedra was too stunned to speak.

Ashlin wasn't. "Do you mean—"

"I mean I don't want to lose either of you. If ... if you bear the child, I'll accept it. I would gladly have a child with Savedra—this is the closest I'll ever come. And—" He looked away, throat working as he swallowed. "And if you don't, we're no worse off than before.

"I just—" His voice dropped to a hoarse whisper. "I just don't want to end up alone and miserable like Father."

Savedra's paralysis broke. She crossed the room in swift strides and took him into her arms. He sobbed once and pressed his face into her neck.

"I won't leave you," she murmured, fingers tangling in his hair. "Not ever." It wasn't something she'd ever promised before—it was the sort of vow fate took too much joy in breaking. She turned and stretched a hand to Ashlin. "And I don't want you to leave, either. Stay with us."

"This is madness," Ashlin said, staring at them. Then her hand rose to clasp Savedra's. "We'll kill one another in months."

They stood that way for a long moment, precariously balanced until Nikos laughed breathlessly and pulled away. "Then I won't have to worry about what will happen if Father finds out. But we should go up, or the guards will think we're already murdering one another." He squeezed Savedra's free hand and knelt to retrieve the wine bottle.

"We have to talk," Savedra said. "Isyllt and I have learned something."

"Not here," he said as they left the crypt. "I've exhausted my morbidity for the day. And what happened to the lock?" he added as the heavy door swung shut behind them.

"This is important—"

Savedra knew they weren't alone a heartbeat before a ghastly white shape flitted out of the darkness. Taloned hands closed on Nikos, tugging him down the corridor. He yelped and the bottle shattered on the floor.

Ashlin's lantern shattered an instant later as the princess lunged after him. The air reeked of wine and smoke and olive oil, and a strange inhuman musk. Savedra snatched up the second lamp and followed, terrible visions flashing through her mind.

Nikos and his assailant had vanished when they reached the next turn, with no trace to show which way they'd gone. The tunnel was silent save for the harsh echoes of their breath, and the voiceless laughter of the fates.

CHAPTER 19

Savedra had dreamt of death, or plague, of ridiculous arguments and of Nikos abandoning her for the unlikeliest members of the court. But never in the worst of her nightmares had she imagined she would have to go before Mathiros and tell him his son had been kidnapped.

The king was closeted with his advisors when they burst into his study, the mood in the room already heavy. Savedra breathed a silent blessing when Ashlin stepped forward to speak. The princess delivered the account like a reporting soldier, leaving out only their conversation before the demon struck. She would have searched the black tunnels herself, but Savedra had insisted they not do so alone.

Adrastos paled at the news. Captain Kurgoth, still wan from his encounter with Phaedra, swore under his breath. Mathiros's hand tightened on the arm of his chair, but his expression didn't change. He looked worse than Savedra had seen him since the queen's death—ashen and sunken-cheeked, eyes dark with lack of sleep.

She ought to speak, tell him all she knew. It was treason not to, and her secrets and slowness had led Nikos into
danger. Or worse. *No*, she told herself fiercely, digging her
nails into her palms. Not worse. Never that. Then Ashlin
stopped speaking and Mathiros began, and her moment's
resolve was lost.

"Mikhael, take men and search the tunnels," the king
ordered immediately. "Adras," Mathiros continued when
the captain saluted and strode from the room. "Bring me
Kiril. No excuses, no delays—find him and bring him
here."

The chancellor nodded, but the crepey flesh of his
throat worked as he swallowed. "As you wish, Majesty."

"Sire," Ashlin said when they were alone, "what can I
do? My sword is yours."

Mathiros tried to smile and managed a grimace. "I'm
glad my son has you. But now I—and Nikos—need you
safe. Stay inside. When I have some news I'll let you
know."

"Of course, Your Majesty." Ashlin couldn't hide her
annoyance at the dismissal, but Mathiros gave no sign of
noticing, only stared into the distance. He hadn't looked
at Savedra since they first entered the room. It would have
angered her, but at the moment she didn't want that black
gaze trained on her. When he didn't speak again the princess gave a shallow bow and turned on her heel.

Ashlin snarled as soon as the door closed behind them.
"I'll be damned if I'll pace my cage and wait for news. We
have to *do* something, Vedra. But what, against demons
and sorcery?"

"We'll find him," Savedra said, and almost laughed.
She'd never thought she would have to reassure the princess

when it came to Nikos. "And against sorcery we need a sorceress."

Isyllt returned home to find a coach waiting outside her door and an unhappy soldier shivering beside it. Dusk was too close to be out on a dead day.

"Lady Iskaldur?" The soldier's Celanoran accent made her name into something musical. "The princess sent me to fetch you to the palace. Will you go?"

His voice was mild, polite, but his posture spoke of trouble and haste, perhaps worse than what they might find being out of doors at nightfall. "Of course," she said, saving her questions, and let him help her into the carriage.

"The princess sends for me?" she asked when they were underway. Purpose and motion were a ward against little spirits—misdirection was their most powerful weapon, luring travelers away from safe paths, tricking them into stopping. If they were set upon by a demon, they would need more protection than the walls of a carriage.

"The princess commands me," the soldier said, pulling his scarf aside to bare a lean, chill-reddened face. "But in fact I believe it's the pallakis Savedra who sends for you. I came because we heathens don't have a healthy fear of your dead days." He grinned, baring a chipped eyetooth. Isyllt smiled back, though the expression felt clumsy and stiff. "Although," the man said, cocking his head, "I don't like the sound of the wind."

"You shouldn't. However much superstition surrounds these days by now, the dangers at night are real. Most of the spirits you'll see tonight are harmless, wildling things and tricksters, but they're still hungry, and enough of them together may try more than tricks."

He touched a charm nestled in the hollow of his throat—a bead painted with a red eye. The sign of Andraste, Celanor's warrior goddess, if Isyllt remembered their legends aright. Saint Andraste, the politic would call her now—only years ago the Celanorans were spirit-worshiping heretics.

The soldier frowned, and she realized he'd said something. "I'm sorry?" she said, pressing her shoulders against the padded seat.

"I asked if you were well, Lady."

"Underslept, is all." Underslept, overextended. All the scars on her heart ripped fresh. But she had no time to indulge in grief. After the New Year, after Erisín was safe and this demon dead and her ashes salted.

The soldier—in fact a lieutenant, and named Cahal—led her not into the palace proper, but to the Gallery of Pearls. She'd never been inside before, and would have paused to study the portraits and busts that lined the broad hall had she not had to hurry to keep pace with her escort.

In Savedra's rooms she also found the princess, and Hekaterin Denaris, the captain of Nikos's private guard. The grim cast of their faces was identical. The air was heavy with sandalwood—incense burned on the altar across the room, shedding smoke in lazy coils.

"Nikos has been taken," Savedra said when the door was safely locked and Cahal guarding the hall. "Snatched from the palace crypts. Whoever grabbed him wasn't human."

"Black Mother." After months of creeping, Phaedra moved quickly enough now. But she had to, if she wished to see all her plans realized in the next four days.

"We have to get him back," Savedra went on. "We have to stop her."

"Does Mathiros know?"

"He does," Ashlin said, "though not the details. But he's closing us out, and I won't sit by helpless." Her hand closed on Savedra's shoulder. "We won't."

Isyllt nodded. "Phaedra has him. And while she's thwarted my attempts to scry her, I might have more luck with the prince."

The casting would have been stronger in Nikos's own quarters, but also more likely to draw attention. So they rolled up the fine carpets and pushed furniture aside till they had space to work. Captain Denaris brought a map of the city, and Savedra found an earring that Nikos had left in her room, a raw emerald caged in gold. Isyllt stationed one woman at each corner of the map—wife, lover, guard, and sworn agent. The earring she set in the center.

Hands clasped, pink and pale, olive and brown. Isyllt took Ashlin's sword-calloused hand in her left, Savedra's soft one in her right, and fixed the prince's image in her mind.

A shiver traced a circuit through the four of them, pricking gooseflesh as the magic rose. Isyllt didn't often practice spellcraft on the demon days—the power sharper, clearer, as if a veil had been drawn away. The cost, of course, was that they shone like a beacon to every spirit for miles around.

The red fog of Phaedra's obfuscation answered at once, choking them with blood and cinnamon. Hands tightened as they shuddered against it, bones grinding through flesh.

"Hold on," Isyllt whispered, gathering her power, imagining a blade to cut away the shroud, cold and clean. She couldn't match Phaedra strength for strength, but it wasn't Phaedra the spell was meant to find. And unlike Phaedra, Nikos wanted to be found. The earring began to rattle against the map, gold and stone scraping across parchment. Isyllt pressed against the weak spot in the fog, felt it give like skin beneath a knife's edge.

She opened her eyes to see the earring spinning across the map, spiraling tighter and tighter till it chose a spot and stayed there, shivering in the lamplight.

Directly over the ruined palace.

Kiril stood in his library as dusk settled against the windows, trying to decide which books he couldn't bear to leave behind, trying to think of nothing beyond that choice. Everything else could be left, or sent for. He couldn't afford to delay for possessions, no matter how dear. He couldn't delay till sunrise, either, not if he truly meant to leave. He didn't relish the thought of traveling during the dead days, but it wouldn't be the first time he'd done so.

Isyllt no longer needed him. She hadn't for a very long time. He couldn't let himself need her.

He had told himself he was rescuing her, fifteen years ago, from misery and poverty and an untimely death. It was likely true, but he had still known all the other dangers he was exposing her to. And if she thrived under them, an orchid blossoming at the threat of death, that did nothing to lessen the cruelty of his choice.

He had also known since the beginning how dangerous she might become, but he hadn't truly appreciated it until the first morning he woke to her weight in his arms. Her magic and cunning made her a weapon without him, but he had honed her and guided her. And turned her to his own heart.

A hammering at the door roused him, sharpening his pulse. His wards showed him the unhappy soldiers gathered on his doorstep. Adrastos Agyros was with them, stooped and huddled in his winter cloak. Kiril's smile felt cold and ugly on his face; Mathiros was finally finished ignoring him.

He might have ignored the summons, but the guards were clearly prepared to break down the door, and violence was unlucky on the demon days. So he descended the stairs and opened the door, smiling benignly as if they delivered an invitation to tea.

Adrastos's frown didn't lessen as they walked to the waiting carriage. He was only ten years Kiril's senior, but time and worry had stooped him and worn his bones fragile as a bird's. A hawk once, now his wrinkled neck and bald head made him a vulture. His eyes were sharp as ever, though.

"What's the matter, Adras?" Kiril asked. The man had never liked him much, having a healthy distrust for sorcery and spies, but they had always respected each other's efficiency.

"Trouble in the palace. I'll let the king explain—he knows more than he's telling me." He was quiet for a moment as the carriage wheels clattered over stone. "You shouldn't have left him."

Kiril's lips thinned in something that was almost a smile. "One might argue that it was he who did the leaving."

"He was a fool. A grieving fool. But we swore to defend him, and I always took that to mean even from himself."

"We all have our limits, Adras. I'm glad you haven't yet found yours."

He tugged a window open and watched the darkened streets flash by. The city was silent, muffled beneath low clouds that promised snow, but its peace was a ruse. He felt the tension, tasted it on the wind, stretched taut and waiting. And in that tension he smelled the conflagrant spice of Phaedra's perfume.

The strain he sensed waiting in the city was manifest in the palace. They passed patrols of soldiers, and worried servants lurked in corners. More than one tried to question Adrastos, but the seneschal waved them away, unflagging as he delivered Kiril to the king.

Mathiros waited in his study, hands laced white-knuckled in front of his face. He didn't stir until the door was shut, and when he did his joints popped loudly. Kiril fought a sympathetic wince; they were neither of them young anymore.

"You summoned me?"

The full weight of Mathiros's black eyes turned on him, burning with rage and revelation. "What did you do, Kiril?" He stood, hands flat on his desk. His sword lay across the paper-strewn surface—still sheathed, but an eloquent promise all the same.

"For months I've had dreams. Black, murderous dreams of a woman I didn't know. I thought I was going mad. Even now I can barely remember her real face. The night of the ball she was screaming at me to remember, and I still didn't understand."

"But you remember now."

"Yes. Why did I ever forget?"

Little point in keeping secrets now, when all their old scars were being ripped open.

"I took the memories from you," Kiril said. "From everyone. It was the only way I could think to keep your secrets. To keep you safe."

Mathiros laughed, cold and harsh. "It didn't work. And now she's taken Lychandra's face to taunt me. She's taken *my son.*"

That drew Kiril's head up. But of course Phaedra wouldn't abandon her plans just because he wasn't there to help her. She was stubborn as Mathiros when she chose to be.

"I'm sorry," Kiril said with a sigh. The honesty of it surprised him. "I'm sorry that Lychandra's memory is tangled in this mess. And I'm sorry for Nikos. It's you Phaedra means to destroy—Nikos merely has the misfortune of being too close."

The king flinched at the sound of her name. "And isn't that an irony, that Nikos and I might ever be too close. How long have you known?"

"Long enough."

"This is treason. I could have you killed."

"It is, and you can certainly try."

Their eyes met, and it was Mathiros who broke. The king had never been one for cowardice, so he must still have a sense of shame. He stepped around the desk, leaving the sword where it lay. "Where is she?"

All Kiril's anger was spent, only the bitter lees remaining. Just as he'd promised Isyllt, there was no satisfaction in any of this. "She lairs in the ruined palace. I imagine she's waiting for you already." He turned, infinitely weary.

"You can't leave," Mathiros said, entreaty threading the words. "Me, perhaps, but not Nikos. This isn't his doing."

He thought of Nikolaos, and of his own father, nearly forgotten after so many years. "Sons should never suffer for their fathers' sins, and yet they always do. I'm sorry for that as well, but I have no service left to offer you. Goodbye, Mathiros."

The door shut behind him, and with its echo he felt the sundering of thirty years. Not even the moment he broke his vows had felt so final.

He wrapped a shadow around him to avoid the inquisitive staff and turned toward the stables. He hesitated for a moment, and nearly laughed at himself. After all his great betrayals, the thought of stealing a horse gave him pause. But he needed to be gone, and that was the fastest way to do so.

It had begun to snow. Fat flakes snagged on his cloak as he crossed the courtyard. The first snow of winter. If it didn't melt, it might last clean and untrampled till the New Year, when children would build forts with it.

Then the wind changed, carrying whispers of rage and blood and distant torches, and he knew the city wouldn't stay clean.

Kiril paused in front of the stables—he'd thought to beat Mathiros there, but others had beaten him in turn. The princess and the pallakis Savedra waited in the courtyard while Captain Denaris gathered horses. Isyllt was with them. Riding after Nikos, through whatever chaos Phaedra had wrought in the city.

Isyllt lifted her head, scenting the night, and glanced unerringly toward him. She stood straight and slender as a blade, and the wind unraveled her braid in black ribbons. Through snow and shifting, torchlit shadows her eyes met his, and he felt the weight of her name on his lips.

She turned from him, the shape of her shoulders a shutting door.

CHAPTER 20

Isyllt had no time to regret walking away from Kiril; as soon as they neared the palace gates she knew something was wrong. A moonless night, but snowlight washed the sky soft and grey as a mourning dove's breast. Except to the east, where clouds seethed red and angry. Something was burning.

"Don't go out there, ladies," called a guard at the gates. "Oldtown is rioting."

"What happened?" Isyllt asked, drawing rein. Her gelding, a compact warmblood, responded easily. These were the same sort of horses the Vigils used, bred to be nimble on city streets, and unflinchingly calm above all else.

"We've only rumors still," another said, "but word is that some opera singer turned up dead, her throat slit. A Rosian girl. Now all of Cab—-Little Kiva is up in arms."

Some opera singer. A Rosian girl. Isyllt remembered Anika Sirota's pale pretty face raised in song, remembered the thunder of applause as the curtains fell. Oh yes, Little Kiva would rise to avenge her death, or to give her a pyre worthy of an opera.

"Shadows take them," Isyllt swore. At the moment, she meant it for the murderers and the vengeful refugees alike.

"Thank you for the warning," Savedra said, steering her black mare closer. "We'll be careful."

The guards looked at one another unhappily, but finally unbarred the gates and let the riders pass.

The city was dark and silent, though Isyllt glimpsed faces peering through shutters as they passed. The closer they grew to Oldtown, the more citizens left their homes to see what was happening. Spirits clustered too, shadows moving across rooftops, iridescent ripples in the air at the corners of Isyllt's vision. Nothing that could challenge her, but she'd lay odds that more than one of the gawkers would come to harm before morning.

Snow caught and melted in her horse's sorrel mane; it had begun to stick to the cobbles and eaves, softening the lines of houses. As they neared the city's heart, the flakes that drifted over them were grey and unmelting—ash.

They passed Vigils and a few brave runners as they rode, and pieced the story together one scrap at a time. Sirota's body had been found at sunset, sprawled on a street outside Little Kiva. The crowd that gathered ran to the nearest police station, only to be turned away because of the day and the hour. Shouting turned to thrown rocks; windows were smashed. It only worsened from there. Most hearths were cold on the dead days, but they still found fire for their torches. Now Oldtown was burning and Vigils and citizens alike were dead, but no one knew how many.

The last runner they met was a boy no older than four-teen, cocky with youth and the urgency of his news, blind to the grinning spirit perched on his shoulder. Skrals, her mother had called such, malicious spirits usually too weak to cause harm. This one bared ephemeral black teeth in a grin, daring Isyllt to challenge it.

She could have destroyed it easily, or banished it beyond the city walls. But Ashlin and Denaris were already urging their horses on, and she had no time. She let a little of the night's chill into her heart, and rode on.

The smell of ash worsened as they neared the city's heart, and the shouts and crashes grew louder. The sorrel flicked his ears but didn't slow. At the end of the street they met a police barricade; torchlight washed the Vigils' orange coats bloody. Constables wheeled at their approach. Isyllt caught the shine of a raised pistol before Captain Denaris rode forward in her white-and-grey uniform.

"What's going on, Sergeant?" asked the captain, finding the coat with the most black bars on the sleeve. Isyllt kept her eyes on the nervous constable.

"The refugees started the riot, but now half of Birth-grave has joined in." The woman spat in the thickening snow. "Those bastards are always looking for a reason to start trouble. Now they're looting and burning anything they come across."

Isyllt's hands ached. Leather creaked, and she realized she was twisting the reins. How often had this woman ever been in Birthgrave? Orangecoats were notoriously rare on those streets, especially when trouble was near. Her horse snorted, unimpressed by her temper, and she forced her shoulders to relax.

"No," said the sergeant in response to something Denaris had said. "This is our jurisdiction, Captain, and we're not opening this barricade. Find another way in. Or better still, go home."

"Is there another way?" Savedra asked, leaning close.

Isyllt shook her head. "It would cost us hours at this rate."

"We don't have hours!"

"Don't worry." She tugged off her right glove. "I'll get us through."

Ghostlight flared brighter than the torches. This the horses didn't like, but she stroked her gelding's neck and he held steady.

"You're correct about jurisdiction, Sergeant." The witchlight's pale glare washed the woman's face sallow and ghastly, and showed her fear very well indeed. "But the royal guard and the Arcanost would both appreciate your assistance in this matter."

The sergeant's resolve folded before Isyllt could press further. "Of c-course, Necromancer." She lifted a hand, but her men were already scurrying to move a section of the barricade.

Isyllt smiled; the cold made her teeth ache. Denaris led her horse through the gap, and Ashlin and Savedra followed. Isyllt's cruelty wasn't entirely spent. "Thank you, Sergeant. We would welcome assistance, if you have anyone to spare."

"I—" The other Vigils shifted backward nervously while their leader stammered. "That is, my men are needed here, to hold the line."

"Of course." She nudged her horse toward the barricade, then paused. "Oh, have you any word of Inspector Shar's cohort?"

The sergeant shook her head. "I think they were among the first to respond, so they may be deeper inside this mess. Beyond that—" She shrugged.

Isyllt nodded and urged her gelding through the gap. The Vigils were replacing the barricade as his tail cleared the opening.

Once Isyllt would have thought the scene inside something from a nightmare, a Mortificant's vision of hell. She'd seen worse since, but not much. Flames licked from rooftop to rooftop, and gouts of smoke shredded in the wind to choke them. Snow was trampled to slush, grey with dirt and ash and sometimes dark with blood. Broken glass glittered vermilion amid the filth.

"Saints!" gasped Savedra, even as Isyllt's ring chilled with a different flavor of death.

Gaunt shapes crouched on a rooftop across from the barricade, eyes blazing by firelight. Razor teeth flashed with their laughter. Vrykoloi, at least four. More than Isyllt had ever seen outside of the catacombs. Spider's young rebels, come to feast in the chaos.

"What are they?" Ashlin asked, her hand on her sword.

"Vampires."

"What do we do?"

"Ride on," Isyllt said, her mouth dry and bitter with smoke. "We have no time, and we're not their prey tonight."

Ashlin's eyes narrowed. "Who is?"

"Anyone without swords or spells." Isyllt set heels to her unhappy horse, leading them deeper into the burning quarter.

They passed tendrils of the mob, shouting and smashing windows and pounding on doors, and smaller clusters of looters. Some families fled burning apartments; others lingered, faces ghostly behind barred windows. Praying, no doubt, that fire and violence passed them by. Victims and instigators both turned to the riders, but Denaris urged them all away. She and Ashlin carried naked blades, the steel not yet stained—boots and warnings and the bulk of their mounts would only protect them so long.

When hands closed on Isyllt's leg and tried to unseat her, she conjured ghostlight, a web of unearthly fire that unfolded around the four riders. Her attackers fell back, crying out as the cold singed them. The horses whickered and drew closer together, away from the web, but their steady canter didn't slow till they reached Desolation Circle and the grey bulk of the Hecatomb wall.

"Isyllt!"

She tugged on the reins, turning to look down at Khelséa's blood-and-ash-smeared face. She let the web fall.

"Are you all right?" Isyllt asked. The inspector's pistol was in her hand, her face dull beneath the mask of grime.

"Oh, splendid. I'm glad you made it to the party." Her eyes glittered in the too-near firelight as she glanced at Denaris and Ashlin and Savedra. "And in such company, too."

"We need inside the palace, Khels."

"Are you looking for the king?"

Ashlin and Savedra swung around in an identical motion. "Is he here?" Ashlin asked, leaning over her horse's neck.

Khelséa nodded. "He came through with three octads of soldiers." Her mouth twisted, the grimace ghastly in the shifting shadows. "They rode warhorses—the crowds didn't have a chance. They broke open the main gate—I think his men are still guarding it."

A frown passed between the four riders.

"We would prefer not to meet the king just yet," Isyllt said. "Is there another way in?"

"Follow me."

Khelséa led them to the walls of the ruined palace, where a handful of her cohort had put their backs to the stone. Beside them was a wagon carrying lumber and sandbags, the makings of a barricade. The cart's horse was nowhere in evidence, severed harness straps hanging uselessly against the ground.

"It's not graceful," Khelséa said, gesturing toward the cart as Isyllt swung down from the saddle, "but you can brace the planks and climb to the top. I'm not so sure about the drop on the other side."

Isyllt stared up at the walls—twenty feet high, at least, granite blocks moss-veined and weathered smooth. The ice and rusty iron that crowned them glittered bloody in the firelight.

"Do we have ropes?" Ashlin asked.

Khelséa shook her head. "Not enough to lower you safely. I wouldn't trust the rock not to slice them, anyway. You can take your chances with the king's guard, but the gate is on the far side of the circle."

"Blood and iron. All right," Ashlin said. "This is the fastest way."

"No!" Savedra's hand closed on the princess's arm. "You can't risk it, not with—"

A weighted glance passed between them. "Hush, *ma chrí*," the princess said softly. "You can't coddle me forever. Besides, I've done this sort of thing before. The trick is to crumple and roll when you land—don't try to keep your feet."

Isyllt and Denaris left them to argue and helped the Vigils brace the lumber against the wall. Between the cart and the boards they had just enough height to reach the top of the wall.

"Nikos won't thank me if I get his wife and mistress killed trying to rescue him," the captain muttered as they hoisted planks.

"They'll kill themselves just as easily without you," Isyllt said.

Denaris went first, scrambling up the makeshift ramp and leaping the last few inches with the grace of a girl a third her age. Isyllt held her breath as the woman's boots scrabbled for purchase on slick stones, but with one good hoist the captain hauled herself up and writhed between the spikes.

They waited when she disappeared over the edge, ears straining against the cacophony of the riots. After a moment with no screams, Ashlin shrugged and started up.

The princess waited at the top to help Savedra, who was hampered by skirts. When Ashlin's fair hair vanished from sight, Isyllt began her own ascent. Splinters caught and broke in her leather gloves, speared through her trousers into her knees. Plays and operas were full of sorcerers who flew on cunning wire contraptions—she would have traded all the souls in her ring for one of those now. Her crippled hand slipped on the top of the wall, but Savedra caught her wrist and tugged while Isyllt wedged her toes into chinks.

They balanced precariously at the top, holding each other as snow danced and spun around them. Isyllt laughed, and the wind whipped the sound away.

"You're as bad as Ashlin," Savedra gasped, steadying herself against a corroded iron spike.

The top of the wall was a yard across; a small mercy in the ice-slick dark. Several spikes had rusted away, leaving only jagged nubs of iron protruding from the stone. Peering over the edge, Isyllt saw Ashlin waving. The ground was a shadowed tangle of snow and briars and saints only knew what else.

"Go on," she told Savedra. "They're waiting."

"You go first." The woman's hair had come free of its pins, tangling around her face in a wild black cloud. Her face was grey as the falling ashes beneath.

"And leave you alone, too scared to jump or climb back down?"

Savedra scowled, but didn't deny it. "I can't do this."

"Oh, yes you can, Pallakis. Your prince is waiting in there, remember?" She swept one arm toward the shadowed white ruin.

"Damn you," Savedra whispered. And, more softly, "Thank you." She edged closer to the drop. "What do I do?"

"Hold on and lower yourself down. Push off and let go, and remember to crumple when you hit the ground."

"Easy for you to say," she muttered, but sank to her knees and backed slowly toward the edge, both hands white-knuckled on the barbs. "Oh, saints—"

She shrieked as she let go, followed by a muffled *whump* from below. Isyllt gave the others a moment to drag her out of the way.

The fall lasted long enough for her to regret every part of this plan. Then the ground met her boots with a jolt, and the shock of landing rippled up her legs and spine and snapped her head back. She rolled, curling her arms around her head as a knot of brambles stopped her. She lay still, winded and throbbing, while black and red spots swam across her eyes. When she had her first breath back she spent it on curses. The taste of copper filled her mouth; she'd bitten her tongue.

"I am never doing that again," Savedra muttered somewhere nearby. Ashlin laughed.

"I'll make an adventurer of you yet," the princess said.

Isyllt sat up, wincing at the rectangular bruise her kit had left on her hip. A heartbeat later she realized the ringing in her ears wasn't from the fall—it was silence.

The noise of the riots ended at the wall; within the stone boundary, a preternatural hush reigned. A red fog drifted over them, spice-sweet and charnel. Isyllt coughed as the smell coated her nose and mouth, mingling with the taste of blood. Savedra gagged, muffling the sound with one hand. A conjured witchlight did nothing to drive back the haze, only stained it porphyry.

"Saints and specters," Denaris gasped, and Isyllt frowned at the strain in her voice. "What is that?"

"Phaedra's magic." She rose to her knees, peering through the red-tinged darkness till she found the captain sitting at the base of the wall. "Meant to disorient anyone who makes it this far. What's wrong?"

The woman snorted. Her face glistened with sweat, and a muscle jumped in her jaw. "My ankle. Broken, I think. I'm too old for tumbling."

"Shadows," Savedra breathed. "What can we do?"

"Go on," she said. "Find the prince and take care of this witch. Then send me some handsome soldiers with a litter, and tell stories of my valor." Her hands shook as she touched her injured leg, belying the words.

Isyllt nodded. "Stay here. Stay quiet. You may see things in the shadows, spirits trying to trick you. Ignore them. Even if they look like your dearest friend." She brushed her hand across the woman's slick brow and whispered a word of obfuscation.

"Keep them safe, necromancer," Denaris whispered, closing her eyes.

Isyllt looked at the seething crimson fog, at the ruins rising from it like a giant's bones. "We're far past safe, Captain."

The silence didn't last. The fog was full of spirits, hissing and chittering and laughing as the three women pressed deeper into the ruin. Voices carried through the haze, some frightened and angry, some tearfully imploring. Isyllt heard Dahlia's voice pleading for help, and Ciaran's, and Khelséa's. From the grim expression Ashlin and Savedra shared, they heard their own loved ones in danger.

They tried to follow paths, but the stones were cracked and overgrown, and turned or ended unexpectedly. Crumbling walls and broken pillars loomed around them, and voices mocked them from the shadows. The fog thickened, till the world drowned in red an armspan all around. The echo of sour magic lessened in the open air, but the pulse of it from the ground still made Isyllt's stomach twist and drove a splinter of pain between her eyes. Amidst all the distractions, she felt someone watching, a familiar whisper at the edge of her awareness. Spider.

"We could be going in circles," Savedra said after they stumbled through a second knot of thorns. Her eyes were liquid, her jaw clenched tight. Ashlin's free hand reached for hers and squeezed.

"Here." Isyllt drew her exorcist's kit from her coat pocket and fumbled a silk-wrapped lump from the leather wallet. Phaedra's ruby glittered as she unfolded it. "Take this. It will seek out its own."

"I'm no mage," Savedra said, eyeing the stone with distrust.

"You don't need to be. All you need to do is wear it and pay attention. You'll feel the pull." Sending anixeroi out in this alone might be murder, but she needed fewer distractions to deal with her stalker. She closed her eyes in concentration as she called another light, fixing this one to the foreign magic in the stone.

"Where are you going?" Ashlin asked.

"We're being followed. I'm going to deal with it."

Savedra twisted the ring onto her left hand. The band dug into her flesh as she made a fist. "I feel it," she whispered. The pink tinge of the new witchlight cast her face flushed and fevered.

"Then go," Isyllt said. "I'll catch up."

As Savedra and the princess vanished into the fog, she hoped that wasn't a lie.

CHAPTER 21

This might not have been the best plan," Ashlin muttered, squinting into the eddying darkness. Her hair shone red in the unnerving light, dark with sweat at the nape. The sheen on her brow could have been blood.

Savedra laughed breathlessly. The ruins had been bad enough with Isyllt beside them; with her gone they were a dozen times worse. She wanted to take the princess's hand again, but knew better than to interfere with someone holding a sword. The ruby shivered on her finger, tugging her deeper into the fog.

Something sharp and cold clawed her ankle, pricking through the soft suede of her boots. Savedra shrieked and kicked. *Brambles,* she prayed as she whirled, *shrubs or rubble*— The ground at her feet was clear.

"What—" began Ashlin, only to shout and jump in turn. "Something grabbed me!"

"Me too." Sharp unseen fingers tugged at her hair and pinched her arm hard enough to bruise. "Shadows!" Each time she saw nothing, but she heard skittering in the fog, and mocking inhuman laughter.

"Keep moving." Ashlin's eyes were wild but her sword held steady. "Isyllt said all they can do is distract us."

"This is more than distraction," Savedra muttered, rubbing her arm.

They didn't dare run, but they stumbled and scrambled as fast as they could. Savedra wept, from pain and fear and frustration, never knowing where the next vicious pinch or bite would come from. She tried to think of Nikos, but soon gave that up for the more immediate concern of not sprawling headlong and being eaten.

The tower appeared so quickly they nearly collided with it. A darker shadow against the sky, till the fog thinned to reveal pale, vine-laced stones. Reliefs had covered the walls once, but time had worn the figures soft and faceless. The ruby sparked with a sullen light as Savedra touched the carven sandstone.

"Here," she gasped. "She's here." She held out a hand to Ashlin; her grin made her face ache. "Come on!"

The door was only a few yards away, a dark hole in the wall. She turned toward it—and walked straight into the shadow that detached from the wall to envelop her.

She screamed, short and shrill, before the blackness filled her mouth and choked her. Cold and clammy and slick as oil, it sank icy hooks into her flesh, a hundred pinpricks that stole her warmth and drained her strength. It coated her tongue, rolling slowly down her throat, and she couldn't breathe, let alone fight—

Someone was shouting. She didn't think it was her. Not Ashlin's panicked cries but a man's voice, over and over, the same command. She didn't understand it, but the darkness must have: It peeled away, and a sudden blaze of violet light blinded her.

She lay on the broken stones, skirt tangled around her legs. Her lungs ached; her throat burned; her skin felt scoured raw.

Ashlin knelt beside her, easing her up and cradling her head against her armored breast. "*Ma chara*," she breathed, stroking Savedra's brow. The moisture that smeared under her touch was thicker than sweat. "*Ma chrí*. It was all over you, on your skin. I couldn't cut you free—"

"I'm all right." She coughed around the words, tasted blood and mucus. Pinpricks of blood glistened black on her hands—more streaked her fingers when she rubbed her face, and her dress clung wetly to her skin. She found no wound—the monster had sucked it from her pores. "What happened?"

"He saved you."

Savedra looked up to see Varis leaning against the wall, pale and cold-flushed and ghastly beneath a cloud of witchlights. His jacket hung open, shirt unbuttoned to reveal the ugly marks on his throat.

"I thought it was the mimikoi toying with me when I heard your voice," he said. "I decided they wouldn't show me the princess." He gave Ashlin a sardonic bow, and his knees buckled as he straightened.

"Uncle!" Savedra fell forward when she tried to stand, and crawled to him across the frozen ground. Her anger was nowhere to be found. "You're hurt."

"Just weak. I didn't expect a banishing." He stood, lifting her unsteadily with him.

"Was that one of Phaedra's pets?" she croaked.

"No. An old horror, a remnant of the Hecatomb. I'm sure her magic fanned its appetite, though."

Her hands tightened on his shoulders and she flinched from the starkness of bone. "She took Nikos."

He nodded, leaning against the wall again. His skin was translucent in the lilac glare, veins dark and ugly. "I know. I tried to stop her." He laughed bitterly. "Saints know I'd see all the Alexioi dead, but not like this."

"What happened?"

"She sent me away. I'm lucky that's all she did. What they intend is madness and worse, but"—he shook his head—"I'm not powerful enough to stop them. If Kiril—" He shut his teeth tight on that thought, and didn't finish it.

"I won't leave Nikos here."

She expected refusal, but he studied her in silence. His knuckles brushed her cheek, soft as a benediction. "If he deserves even a fraction of your devotion, he's a better man than I could ever have been."

She laid her hand over his; blood stuck their skin together. "He's just a man, but I love him. I love you both."

She glanced over her shoulder, where Ashlin stood guard against the night, watching the fog to give them privacy. A path unfolded before her, but it was a dangerous one, and it wasn't only her life she risked. But she couldn't rescue Nikos only to see Varis executed. Sorcery and debt weren't the only ways to bind—her mother had taught her that as well.

"Go with Ashlin," she said. "I need you to keep her safe."

"You can't possibly mean that. After everything I've done."

"The princess is pregnant."

"All the more reason, then—"

The words stuck in her tender throat, but she forced them out. "The child is mine."

That silenced him, and Savedra wanted to laugh as he blinked. "You can't mean—"

"Funny, Uncle, that's exactly what Nikos said. Yes. The Princess and I are lovers. She's carrying my child."

"And Nikos knows?"

"He's accepted the baby as his. Need I be clearer?" she said as he stammered. "A Severos bastard stands to inherit the Malachite Throne."

She had never seen Varis at a loss for words. After several speechless moments he slid down the wall, buried his face in his hands, and began to laugh. The laughter quickly turned to sobs.

Savedra drew Ashlin close. "Go with my uncle, please. He can keep the spirits off you, but he's weak. Take him to Captain Denaris and get them both out of here."

Green eyes narrowed. "Don't try to set me aside."

"I'm trying to keep you safe! Damn it, Ashlin. I may still lose Nikos. Don't make me lose you too."

"I might say the same," Ashlin replied, but her resolve was weakening. "What am I supposed to do if you die?"

"Hold the throne. Keep the heir safe."

"Unfair," she whispered.

"I know. But I'll ask it anyway."

In answer Ashlin caught her shoulders and kissed her, hard enough to split cold-chapped lips. "You owe me," she whispered on a shared breath.

"Lord Varis," she said, turning away. "Vedra means to coddle us both like blown glass. May I escort you back to the wall?"

"It would be a delight and an honor, Your Highness. I shall do my very best to be coddled.

"Congratulations," he said to Savedra, wiping away tears and smudged kohl. "You've managed a scandal to put all mine to shame. I shall run mad with envy." He twisted the orange sapphire off his finger and folded his hands around it, eyes sagging shut. "Here." He took her hand and slipped it onto her right ring finger; it fit snugly—her hands were bigger. "This much protection I can grant you. As long as you don't attack, no one should be able to harm you. I wouldn't test it against Phaedra more than you must, though—her power is doubled in the demon days, and she has fresh blood at hand to spill."

She couldn't ponder the source, or she'd scream. "Thank you."

His eyes were colorless by witchlight, and more serious than she'd ever seen. "I can only try to earn your forgiveness."

"Start by keeping the princess safe." She kissed his cheek, cold skin against colder.

She watched Ashlin and Varis till the fog swallowed them. Then she stepped into the tower's black mouth.

Isyllt didn't have to wait long before she heard Spider's voice.

"Isyllt."

He crouched on a broken pillar, a white-marble grotesque. She was so used to his mocking diminutives that the sound of her name in his mouth startled her. He uncoiled and leapt, landing silently before her. The red haze thinned around him. "I can't let you interfere. You know that."

·Her blade rasped from its sheath. "Haven't you always wanted to know how it would really have ended between us?" The chill in her voice was only bravado—after everything he'd done, the thought of killing him made her stomach ache. But she couldn't face him and Phaedra together. Spellfire licked the edges of her blade.

"I wanted us to be friends." The quiet sadness in his voice made her wonder how many friends he'd had in the catacombs. How many he'd sacrificed to further his plans.

"Spider—" The catch in her voice was real; the lowering of her blade was a feint.

She threw witchlights in his eyes and lunged, swinging the silver kukri. Fabric opened against the edge, and skin below that. He was gone before the stroke bit deeper, his animal hiss echoing in her ears. Isyllt spun, cold fire in her left hand and spelled silver in her right.

Her heartbeat's advantage was already spent. He moved in a white blur and she staggered, a sudden pressure on her jaw warming to pain. Copper washed her tongue again, mingling with the acrid taste of nerves. Her jaw wasn't broken; luck, or had he pulled the blow? She turned the stumble into a crouch, rocking on the balls of her feet as she tried to keep him in sight.

Easier tried than done—he moved silently and weightlessly as any ghost, but much faster. She blocked a blow that would have opened her throat, and it felt like dragging her limbs through honey. She was rewarded with the jolt of blade on bone and Spider's quite audible cursing. He cradled his hand to his chest, black blood seeping between his fingers.

"This is foolish, little witch."

"It certainly is." She flung another blaze of light and lunged again. Her shoulder struck his chest and her knife turned on his ribs, slicing through cloth and skin and desiccated muscle. The smell of musk and anise and bitter earth filled her nose.

Spider snarled, fangs shining inches from her face. He tore the knife from her hand; it clattered across the stones, out of reach. His other hand seized her jaw, redoubling the ache from his last blow.

"I would have let you live," he murmured as he forced her head back. She kicked and clawed, but it was like fighting a statue.

She hadn't wanted to use the cold, not with Phaedra still to face, but she was out of options. She reached for the emptiness inside her—the Arcanost called it entropomancy, but to her it was the nothing, the chill that ran deeper than death.

"Oh, Spider."

Isyllt teetered on the brink of the void; Spider froze, his jaw distending like a snake's as he leaned in for the kill. She knew that voice, like slow-pouring water....

"This is not what we do."

He dropped Isyllt and spun, fangs bared as he faced Tenebris.

The red fog curled away from her. Shadows deepened in its place, spilling ink-black from beneath pillars and arches to cling to her skirts. They twined her arms and nestled in her hair, pressing against her neck like children. Of her face Isyllt could see nothing, save for the angry glitter of her eyes and the gleam of her fangs when she spoke.

"Did you think we would take no notice of your revolution?"

"Why would you?" Spider spat. "You sleep away the years and do nothing while the mortals keep us locked in the darkness."

"We *are* the darkness, little fledgling." Humor and sadness veined her voice, a warmer current amidst the cold tide. "We are darkness and dust. It may be our nature to hunger for warmth and light, but we must extinguish them or be seared. We are hunters, teeth in the night, not shepherds to keep humans for chattel. The kingdoms of men mean nothing to us."

"Rot in your ossuaries, then. I want something more, and I'm not alone."

"Really?" Again the humor, sharper now. "You seem quite alone to me, little one."

Which is why, Isyllt thought, *you don't use allies as scapegoats.* She didn't say it, though—she didn't feel like attracting more of Tenebris's attention.

"I, on the other hand," the vrykola continued, "am not."

A pale shape moved in the shadows and Spider recoiled. "Aphra!"

The elder vrykola was slight and fine-boned. She wore grey velvet, yellowed with age and rotting at the seams. Lace snagged and tattered on the broken flagstones. Her hair was the color of old ivory, her skin dull and grey until the light kissed her—then she glittered like raw marble, a statue brought to life.

"Spider." Her voice was the whisper of dust across cathedral floors, the sound of stone dissolving in the relentless flow of time.

"You're awake."

Isyllt had never heard his voice sound so human, threaded with fear and longing and anger.

"Azarné came to us, told us what you've done." She advanced on him slowly, inexorably, one long grey hand rising. "Oh, child. I thought you would fare better than this."

"I only wanted—" His voice cracked and died. His shoulders slumped, legs wavering as he struggled to stand.

"You wanted the world. And that is no longer ours." She touched his hair, and he fell to his knees as if she'd cut his strings. Black tears tracked his cheeks.

Stone scraped against Isyllt's palms as she crawled forward. She hadn't meant to move, but his weakness and misery were unbearable. He should die fighting—

"Hush, child." Tenebris's icy hands closed on her arms, drawing her gently up. "It's better this way. She is his maker—the unmaking is also hers." Shadow fingers stroked Isyllt's bruised cheek, wiped a drop of blood from her split lip. "I'm sorry he hurt you."

The vampire draped an arm across Isyllt's shoulders, turning her away from Aphra and Spider. He was crying now, low keening sobs. The sound twisted Isyllt's stomach. She tried to look back, but Tenebris held her, wrapped her in shadows like liquid silk.

"It's better if you don't watch."

She was wrong—the wet sounds that followed were worse by themselves, mingled with Spider's soft gasps.

Finally they stopped, and Tenebris drew her shadow-draperies away.

Isyllt turned to see Aphra bending over Spider. Blood shone black on the vrykola's colorless mouth as she straightened, and on the ruin of Spider's throat. His head hung against his chest, his hair a spiderweb shroud.

He was too pale to show the petrification that took the vrykolos in death, but Isyllt watched his limbs tremble and grow still. Her vision blurred, and she scrubbed away a glaze of foolish tears.

Aphra laid a hand on Spider's head again, a final caress. Then she twisted. His spine cracked like crushed gravel and his head fell and shattered on the ground. The rest of him toppled slowly after, disintegrating into a glittering drift of dust.

Aphra turned to Isyllt, fixing her with colorless crystalline eyes. "He did care for you," the vrykola whispered. "As much as he was able." She turned and vanished into the fog before Isyllt could think of anything to say.

Tenebris lifted the shadow of her face toward the sky. "We will return to the catacombs and take our wayward children with us. They won't bother you again, at least tonight. The demon in the tower, though, is not of our doing, and none of our concern. Good luck, necromancer."

And she was gone.

The wind chilled Isyllt's face; she was crying again. She wiped her cheeks and began searching for her knife.

The climb might have lasted a year, but Savedra knew the tower had no more than four or five stories. Spirits crowded the stairs, scuttling and chirping, but didn't touch her. The only light was the spark of her rings, orange and blood red. That glow drew her upward, though her heart pounded to break her ribs and queasy sweat greased her palms. The darkness changed as she climbed, greying with the promise of light.

The door at the top of the stairs stood open, lined in

gentle lamplight. Savedra stood before it, pressing a sweat-and-blood-slick hand against the stitch in her side. She heard nothing from the other side; she heard nothing at all but the sick pounding of her heart. When her pulse slowed and the pain in her ribs dulled, she drew a breath and stepped across the threshold.

She didn't know what a haematurge's lair should look like, but whatever she expected, it wasn't the disrepair she walked into. No blood or filth, but scattered books and rugs and missing furniture, like a half-vacated house. After the frozen night, the warmth of braziers stifled.

Her breath left in a deflated rush. No Nikos, no demons—where were they? Then a red lump in the corner that she'd taken for cushions stirred, and she jumped.

Ginevra lay in a heap against the wall, her hands bound behind her with heavy rope. The crimson dress was black with grime, the hem snagged and bleeding beads. Her lustrous copper skin was dull and ashen, her eyes hollow, but save for a rust-colored smear across her mouth she seemed unharmed.

Bruised eyelids fluttered as Savedra whispered her name. "Vedra." The hope in her smile was terrible. "You came."

Savedra dropped to her knees beside the girl, touching her face with trembling fingers. No fever, at least, and no more chilled than one would expect from sitting on frigid stone. Someone had given her a blanket, but it had slid aside and become trapped under her legs.

"Are you hurt?"

"I don't know. I don't think so. I'm so tired, though—"

"Yes," a voice said behind them. "Better if you rest."

Savedra's nerves snapped and she leapt like a startled

cat. She fetched up crouched against the wall beside Ginevra, her knife flashing in her hand.

Lychandra Alexios stood before her, still gowned in white. Savedra had thought herself prepared, but she moaned at the sight, eyes squeezing shut and the knife falling from numb fingers.

Fabric rustled as Lychandra—*Phaedra*, she told herself, *Phaedra*—knelt beside Ginevra. "Sleep. It's easier that way."

Now Savedra understood why Phaedra's voice had chilled her when they met at Varis's house. Lychandra's throat, Lychandra's lips shaping the words, but the tone and inflection were wrong. She forced herself to look again.

Phaedra smiled, and that too was familiar and all the more terrible for it. "Startling, isn't it? I still catch myself off guard in mirrors. Varis spoke of your cleverness, but I admit I didn't think you'd make it this far. But not unscathed." One cold finger touched Savedra's face, came away pink and sticky.

She held out a long brown hand. Seeing no safer option, Savedra took it, letting the demon draw her to her feet. Her dagger slid from the folds of her skirts and clattered against the floor.

"What are you doing to her?" she asked, looking down at Ginevra.

"Keeping her safe. If she were awake she would only wear herself out with panic." The sorceress hadn't let go of Savedra's hand; she raised it now to study the ruby ring. Identical stones shone on her fingers. Savedra tensed for wrath, but all Phaedra said was, "Wherever did you find this?"

"In Carnavas," she answered, her mouth dry and sticky. "In your workroom." At least Phaedra's demon birds weren't here now—that was something to be thankful for.

"Ah. I always wondered what happened to it." Luminous orange eyes moved from Savedra to Ginevra and back again. "Would you like her?"

Savedra blinked stupidly. "What?"

"This body. I thought at first to wear it myself, but we came up with a better plan." Her gaze softened, the dead woman's face ghastly with sympathy. "I understand what it's like to be trapped in the wrong flesh. Varis explained it to me—the cruel trick of your birth. I could fix it. It's the least I can do for him. I'm not entirely sure how the process would work between two anixeroi," she said, frowning, "but it would be a fascinating experiment."

Savedra's mouth opened and closed again on an unspoken denial. She stared at Ginevra's slender limbs, her smooth cheeks, the rise and fall of her breast. Beautiful and graceful and feminine, even bound and filthy. Everything Savedra had ever wanted to be, everything she was in her dreams until waking returned her to the truth.

"Is it so simple?" she asked. Would the hijra call it miraculous, or abhorrent?

"It's not *simple*," Phaedra said, sculpted brows pulling together in indignation. "It's a delicate and complex thaumaturgical process. It's been my life's work. But it is *possible*."

"It would make me a demon."

"That's a broad, clumsy word that the Arcanost relies on too heavily. But strictly speaking, a demon is created from the merging of flesh—living or dead—and a spirit or a ghost. I'm not sure what you would call the transfer of a living soul into a different living body."

Madness, Savedra would call it. Abomination. Temptation.

Nikos had always said he loved her, not the flesh she wore. Did he really mean that?

"No," she said at last. "I can't."

Phaedra frowned. "You could if you were desperate enough. But never mind. I can certainly find a use for her myself."

"Please. Where is Nikos? I need to see him."

"You came to rescue him? How sweet." Phaedra gestured toward another doorway. "He's here."

The adjoining room looked like a mad sorcerer's laboratory ought—vials and bottles and dishes, books lining the walls and lamps and candles cluttered on tables. In the center of the room on a stone bench lay Nikos. His shirt and jacket were gone, revealing hand-shaped bruises on his shoulders and short, scabbed cuts tracking the vein down one forearm. Savedra's heart clenched, but he still breathed.

"What are you doing to him?"

"Transfusion. I drain his blood—slowly, of course—and replace it with my own. When enough is replaced, I can transfer my mind and my power with it. I balked at first, about wearing a man's flesh, but Spider convinced me that was foolish. It's just another experiment, after all, not to mention the quickest means to our end."

"And what happens to Nikos?"

Phaedra paused. "He'll be consumed. Subsumed. Some memories may linger—I collect more every time I do this." She touched her temple as if they pained her.

"You can't," Savedra said. "Please, you can't. Let him go."

Phaedra's eyes flickered toward her. "Can't I?" she snapped. But her temper died. "Is he anything like his father?"

Savedra shook her head. It took her two tries to manage "No."

"A pity, then." She brushed a stray curl off his brow; his eyes flickered beneath pale lids. "Speaking of his father—" She smiled, and it looked nothing like Lychandra. This was a predator's smile. "I think I hear him coming now."

Isyllt met Mathiros Alexios at the base of the tower, and came perilously close to regicide when he materialized out of the fog beside her.

"Majesty." She lowered her knife. His face was ashen and wild-eyed; scratches dripped blood down his cheek and brow, and more blood glistened on his drawn sword. Demon or mortal she couldn't say.

She thought he might attack her, but his gaze focused. "Iskaldur. What are you doing here?"

"Looking for your son, Majesty, and for the woman responsible."

"Phaedra." A whisper, more to himself than to her. She couldn't keep the surprise from her face. "Yes," he said with a harsh laugh. "I know her name. I remember her." His eyes narrowed. "You know."

No point in dissembling now. "I've heard the story."

Black brows pulled together. "And do you think I deserve whatever fate she has in mind for me?"

"Yes. But she's a madwoman who's already tearing the

city apart, and Nikos doesn't deserve to suffer because you were an idiot. Your Majesty."

Mathiros's scowl broke and he laughed, harsh and raw. "I should have taken you to the Steppes after all. The horselords would like you."

"I'll bear that in mind when this is over." She gestured toward the tower. "Phaedra is up there, somewhere, and likely Nikos too. Shall we go up?"

She expected tricks and traps, but the way was clear. Past the dizzying taint of the stones, she felt power gathering at the top of the stairs.

Phaedra waited for them, still clothed in white and stolen flesh. Not the gown she'd worn to the masque, but a new one of silver-trimmed velvet. Not a practical color for a haematurge. It didn't flatter her complexion, but was striking all the same.

Mathiros stumbled on the last step. "Lychandra—"

"No."

"No." He dragged a hand across his face; blood smeared from his cuts, welled fresh. "No. Phaedra."

Isyllt shuddered at her smile. "Yes. You do remember."

"Phaedra!" Isyllt's hand tightened on her knife as those orange eyes turned to her. "Spider is dead. You've lost your vampires. The palace is warned about you. It's over."

The demon blinked. "Even if that's true, I have the king and the crown prince."

"And me to deal with."

Her lips curled. "I can stop the prince's heart where I stand. But enough threats—go home, necromancer. For Kiril's sake I'll spare you."

"This has nothing to do with any of them," Mathiros said. "This is between us."

Phaedra nodded. "Yes. Come inside."

Mathiros squared his shoulders and stepped into the room. Isyllt, cursing, followed. Magic settled over her, rust-red and sticky, nearly tangible as Phaedra's power grew. It spread in webs throughout the room, winding around the woman who sprawled in the corner—Ginevra Jsutien, and that was one mystery solved.

"Where is Nikos?" Mathiros asked.

"Here." She led them to an adjoining room, where Nikos lay on a stone bench. Savedra knelt beside him, murmuring softly and insistently as she tried to help him up. Her hazel eyes flashed white when she saw Phaedra and the king.

"If I—" Mathiros's throat worked under his beard. "If I surrender to you, will you let Nikos free?"

"I have no desire to harm him," Phaedra said.

"She's lying," Savedra said, her voice cracking. "She means to take his body, make him a puppet to steal the throne. He won't survive that."

Phaedra's eyes narrowed. "Technicalities." Her stance was relaxed, unconcerned, but she crackled with power. Mathiros, on the other hand, had lowered his sword, shoulders hunched and face twisted. Isyllt had never known him to balk at anything, but against his dead wife's face and his son's life in the balance he was shrunken, helpless.

Isyllt sighed. She would have to do this herself.

Kiril rode through the burning city, warded against spirits and men. His diamond ring blazed with the death in the air, but the destruction wasn't as bad as it might have been. The quarter would be decimated, but the Vigils' barricades still held, and the thickening snow damped fires and tempers alike. He sensed newly fledged demons, and passed a few—the shambling dead, mostly, opportunistic spirits worming into fresh corpses, still clumsy and dazzled by incarnation. His stolen horse balked, but responded to soothing words and steady hands.

Soldiers and police gathered at the gates of the old palace. One slab of ironbound oak had been broken down, and tendrils of red mist snaked around splintered boards. The commanding officer recognized him, and the man's face lit with sick relief. All Kiril's attention was for Varis, however, when he saw the other mage leaning against the wall, sharing a wineskin with—of all people—the crown princess.

Kiril handed his reins to a nervous soldier who needed something to occupy him. The crowd parted for him as he joined Varis.

"Still not very good at taking your own advice," Varis said by way of greeting

"No better than you are." He took the proffered skin, letting cheap wine rinse away the taste of char.

"Mathiros is still in there," Varis said, more soberly. "So are Savedra and Isyllt and the prince."

Kiril closed his eyes. There was nothing in those walls for him but grief. Isyllt had made her choice, and not asked for his help. He should have abandoned all of this.

But he was here.

Varis touched his face. They might have kissed, but those days were past. Instead Kiril lowered Varis's hand, squeezing gently before he let go. They were past farewells and benedictions, too, so Kiril turned without a word and stepped into the darkness of the bone palace.

He knew the path despite the deceptive mist, knew the

number of strides to the tower, the number of steps to its peak. His knees didn't ache this time, nor his traitorous heart. He almost laughed—he could think of more pleasant ways to spend his borrowed health. Maybe Isyllt was wrong—maybe they could have been happy somewhere else, had they abandoned all their oaths and duties.

Too late for might-have-beens now.

He heard shouting as he neared the top and quickened his pace. The air was thick with magic, Phaedra's and Isyllt's both, and the metallic scent of fresh blood.

The king and both sorceresses stood in the open first room, stationed in a rough triangle. Blood dripped from Isyllt's nose and coursed from wounds on Mathiros's cheek. Blood smeared the king's sword as well, and Phaedra's gown was rent across her ribs. The wound hadn't slowed her. Through the laboratory door he glimpsed Savedra holding Nikos amidst a wreckage of broken glass and drifting notes.

"Phaedra," he said as she raised her hand for another strike. "No."

"Kiril!" Her face brightened. The same surprised hope lit Isyllt as well, and the sight was like a fist in his stomach. "You came."

"To stop this. I can't let you do this, Phaedra. I'm sorry."

"Oh, Kiril." Her lips pursed in a disappointed moue. "Not again."

Her power hit him like a wave. The weight of it crushed him, while the demon blood in his veins answered her call, burning him from the inside.

She was stronger than the last time they'd faced each other, on another tower so many years ago. Then she had been clever and desperate—now she was a demon, and all the hate and madness that soaked the stones answered her. But Kiril was cannier with time, and knew better than to break himself against her onslaught. Instead he diverted her, twisted the raw red rush of her aside like a stone in a flood, while his defenses co-opted the strength of demon blood and made it his own.

One step at a time he crossed the room, through the bloody tide of magic, and took her in his arms. She swayed against him even as her magic hammered his. Isyllt fought too, flashes of silver-white and bone at the edge of his awareness.

"Let it go, Phaedra," he whispered. Sticky warmth dripped into his beard, and a dozen scars ached as she tried to reopen the wounds. "This will bring you no peace."

She touched his lips. "I would have forgiven you, if you'd only asked."

He readied himself for the last assault he knew would follow.

He didn't expect her to use a knife.

Isyllt shouted as the blade glittered in Phaedra's hand, screamed as it slid home between Kiril's ribs. Her throat ached with the force of it. He stumbled backward, into a wall, and slid slowly to the floor.

Phaedra watched him for a moment, her face grim and sad. Then she turned back to Mathiros. "Where was I?"

Isyllt stood frozen. Phaedra's magic hung in red rags—now was the time to strike. But she could only stare at Kiril and will him to rise, to shake off the wound.

"Isyllt!" Nikos stood in the doorway, braced between the arch and Savedra's supporting shoulder. "Stop her!"

A son's plea. A prince's command. Isyllt jerked toward Phaedra as the sorceress closed on Mathiros. The king dropped his sword, his face slack with despair. Kiril's face was grey as ashes, his hand trembling as he reached for the knife. Blood spread shining across his black coat.

"Stop her," Nikos yelled again.

"No," she whispered, and turned to Kiril.

She took three strides before something inside her snapped like a kithara string and the force of her broken oath crushed her to her knees. Her vision greyed; the air in her lungs thickened and burned. She crawled, dragging useless legs behind her. Nikos was screaming. Mathiros was screaming. She ignored them all and crawled to Kiril's side.

Her magic filled her like shards of glass; it would slice her to the bone if she seized it. But her death-sense remained: As soon as she touched him, she knew the wound was mortal. The blade shuddered with his heartbeat when she touched the hilt. A scalpel, a tiny thing, but it had found its mark.

"What do I do?" she asked, touching his face with trembling fingers. "What can I do?"

"Forgive me." A bubble of blood burst on his lips. "Pull the knife out and let me die swiftly. Or leave it in, and let me spend a few more moments with you. Whichever option seems best to you."

She cradled his head in her lap. Tears and blood dripped off her chin. "I'll kill her," she whispered. "I swear it."

"Don't." His hand groped for hers, clung tight. Already cold, but some strength remained. "No revenge. You see what it does to you. But yes, you should stop her. It would be a mercy." Each word was softer than the last. His dark eyes began to dim.

"You don't have to die," she whispered, lowering her head. Her hair and her tears fell over his face. "Not truly."

"And become a demon? Undead? Could you stand the sight of me?"

She sobbed at the thought. Cold and empty, forever, dead and undying—

"I love you. Always you."

"I knew it would be you—"

The words faded into a long rattling breath and the last spark inside him guttered. Death surrounded them, an owl-winged shadow reaching for Kiril. Isyllt flung herself against it, scrambling for power that sliced and crumbled at her touch.

She followed him into the dark.

The dark would not have her.

Savedra didn't watch Mathiros die.

Nikos tried to intervene but his knees gave way, dragging them both to the floor. She pulled his head against her chest and buried her face in his hair, whispering meaningless sounds to drown the wet noises coming from Phaedra and the king.

When she opened her eyes again, Mathiros hung like an empty husk in Phaedra's hands. Blood coated him, dripping from his fingers to dapple the floor. More slicked Phaedra's hands and mouth. As Savedra watched, the red stains vanished into her skin—the splatters on her white gown remained. When the last drops were gone, the sorceress let him fall. Her face crumpled as she stared at the sunken corpse, exultation fled.

"How does it feel?"

Savedra started, scarcely recognizing Isyllt's voice.

The necromancer still knelt by Kiril, her face a half-mask of blood beneath the shroud of her hair.

"Was it worth it?"

"For a moment," Phaedra said, almost too soft to hear. "For a moment it was. Now ... it doesn't matter now. It's done."

A spark of steel caught Savedra's eye. Ginevra was awake, bound hands groping across the floor for Savedra's knife. If Phaedra noticed the movement, she gave no sign.

"Now what?" Isyllt asked. Her eyes flickered—she noticed, and was trying to keep Phaedra distracted.

The demon stared at her hands, clean of blood. "Now I finish it, I suppose. I don't want to wear this flesh anymore."

"It won't be different in anyone else's," Savedra said, finding her voice at last.

Phaedra turned. "It will, for a time." Behind her, Ginevra had finished sawing through her bonds and chafed her raw wrists, jaw clenched against any sound of pain.

"Mathiros is dead," Isyllt said. "Spider is dead. Kiril is dead." Her voice was too hollow to crack. "You have your revenge, but your plans are ruined."

"Perhaps you're right. I only wanted—" Phaedra shook her head. "I don't know what I wanted. Rest, perhaps." She glanced at Savedra and Nikos. "Keep your prince. The other is all I need."

At last she turned toward Ginevra, in time for the girl to launch herself off the floor, knife in hand.

Clumsy and slow, but Phaedra only gaped as the blade flashed toward her, rocked back as it struck her face. Ginevra fell, wan and sweating, and Phaedra stumbled back, one hand clapped to her cheek.

"You—" She pulled her hand away, and blood glistened on her palm. Mathiros's blood, Savedra supposed. The slice laid her cheek open to the bone; flesh gapped as she spoke. Dark rivulets ran down her chin to stain her bodice.

"Dead flesh doesn't feel pain," she told Ginevra. "I'll be more careful when I'm wearing yours."

Ginevra's grey eyes were dark with pain and hopelessness, but she gave Savedra a fleeting smile.

"I find," she said softly as Phaedra walked toward her, "that I'm tired of being anyone's pawn or plaything." She turned the knife. Savedra's lips moved as she understood, too slow to stop it.

The blade flashed one last time, as Ginevra drove it into the soft flesh beneath her chin.

Savedra screamed as Ginevra fell. Phaedra shrieked in rage. Isyllt breathed a name.

"Forsythia."

A whisper was all the dead needed. Her ring sparked and the ghost appeared beside her, translucent and wild-eyed.

Isyllt reached for her magic as well, for the biting cold that gave her strength, but it fell to ashes at her touch. Her power would return, Kiril had said. She could endure this. But for the moment she was useless.

"What's happening?" Forsythia asked, watching Phaedra kneel in the spreading pool of Ginevra's blood. "Is that—"

"That's her. I need your help to stop her."

Transparent hands knotted in her skirts. "I can't. I can't."

"You can." Isyllt levered herself off Kiril's shoulder, trying not to think of the cooling flesh beneath her. "You're the only one who can. If we don't she'll do this over and over again." She touched Forsythia's shoulder, numbing her fingers to the bone. "I'm too weak to do it alone."

The ghost straightened. "What do you need from me?"

"Possess me." Her jaw wanted to lock on the words. "Wear my flesh. I can't use my magic, but maybe you can." Her voice shook. "It might destroy us both."

Forsythia smiled crookedly, an echo of her mortal beauty. "I'm already dead, aren't I? What do I do?"

Isyllt cupped the dead woman's face in her hands, drawing her close. "Come inside." Her defenses, already shaken and cracked, fell away, leaving her bare.

It was as cold as she'd ever imagined. Colder. Painful, too—shudders wracked her, muscles cramping and contracting, pulling her into a fetal ball. Fingernails cracked as she clawed the stones.

The pain ended, but the cold remained. With it came a fierce strength and hunger. All her aches and scrapes and fatigue faded away; she was strong again. Alive. Colors dizzied her, the texture of stone and cloth and the weight of her hair against her neck overwhelming in their intensity.

Focus, she whispered, before Forsythia grew drunk on sensation. *We have to stop her before she recovers.*

"Phaedra." She felt her lips and tongue shape the sound, but control wasn't hers. Dried salt and blood and mucus cracked and flaked as she moved. The air reeked like a slaughterhouse.

The sorceress rose, blood sticking her gown to her

knees. Her hair fell in stormwrack swags around her ruined face. Her eyes burned.

"I'm sorry for Kiril," she said as Isyllt tried to stand. "I never wanted that."

"I'm sorry too." She—they—gained their feet, and took a halting marionette step. In time she-and-Forsythia would be as strong and graceful as Phaedra, but they didn't have that time. Was this how it always felt? The boundaries of host and possessor slowly blurring? Too slowly— she couldn't teach Forsythia how to use the magic she'd studied for decades in only a moment.

"You can't stop me," Phaedra said. "You know that, don't you? You can barely stand."

Another awkward step, then another, and they were close enough to touch. Had Phaedra struck her, Isyllt would have been doomed, but she only watched, her demon gaze dimming with grief.

She cupped Isyllt's cheek. "You loved him."

"More than anything."

"I know what it's like to lose that much, to live with the loss." She leaned her forehead against Isyllt's, cold breath drifting over both their faces. "I can take the pain. It would be a mercy."

"Yes," Isyllt whispered. "Mercy." She had no anger left, no strength, but she could do that much.

There. She tugged Forsythia's attention to the cold place she carried beneath her heart. *That's where the nothing lives. Release it.*

She pressed her cheek to Phaedra's ruined one; the woman's hair tickled her lips. "Take everything."

Phaedra cradled her face in cold hands and magic crawled over them. Isyllt expected pain, but none came, even as beads of blood welled from her pores—that was a relief, at least. The blood rolled toward Phaedra, sinking into her skin.

The empty place opened and the nothing poured out with her blood. Forsythia didn't have the knowledge to control it, and Isyllt didn't have the strength. They didn't need to. Phaedra drank it down.

She realized her mistake a moment later. She pulled away, but Isyllt caught her hands and held her. The world dulled around the edges, but she had a demon's strength.

Phaedra rallied her magic, but it unraveled beneath the tide of entropy. Brown skin bruised and bled as the sorcery that kept it fresh dissolved. Stolen flesh sank, shriveled, cracked.

Isyllt knew she had to stop or the nothing would take her too, but she was too cold, too tired, and the emptiness soothed her with promises of dark and quiet. Phaedra's wrists snapped in her grip, disintegrating like snow and ashes. With nothing to lean on, Isyllt fell.

As she crumpled, she heard Forsythia whisper farewell.

CHAPTER 22

It was warm in the darkness, warm and still and soothing, save for the occasional interruption of voices and hands. Isyllt would have floated there forever, but nothing so peaceful could ever last. Black gave way to red, and then to brilliant gold as her crusted eyes cracked open. Tears blinded her and she tried to sink into the dark again. The voices returned, calling her out. A warm hand brushed her brow and she flinched.

"She's waking up."

"Isyllt?"

Her mouth was dry and chapped, sour with thirst and sleep. Her tongue peeled free from the roof of her mouth, but the only sound she could manage was a croak.

"Water," someone called. Wet cloth swabbed her lips. Tepid moisture leaked between her lips, the sweetest she'd ever tasted. "Careful," the voice said, and the rim of a cup touched her lower lip, clicked against her teeth as she tried to move. Water sloshed down her chin and across her chest, just enough spilling into her mouth to make her choke. The cup vanished and she nearly sobbed; she'd never been so thirsty.

A shadow moved in front of the blinding light and she had a heartbeat's impression of a small room, and walls that rippled dizzyingly. The walls became curtains with another glimpse, the light a lantern hanging from the ceiling.

St. Alia's. It had been a long time since she'd woken up in a hospital bed.

"What happened?" It took two tries to shape the sounds properly.

"You did something stupid."

She tried to laugh at Khelséa's dry voice, but it turned into a rasping cough, which gave way in turn to tears.

"Careful," the inspector said, "or they'll make me leave. Ciaran won't be back for an hour."

Isyllt wiped her eyes, alarmed at the heaviness of her limbs. The halo around the lamp slowly faded till she could make out Khelséa and the rest of the room. "He's been already?"

"We've taken turns watching you, he and Dahlia and I."

She tried to sit up and quickly abandoned the idea. "How long have I been here?"

"The better part of a decad. It's the fourth of Ganymedos."

"Saints." Then she noticed the white armband on Khelséa's orange coat. The woman's skin was dull with fatigue, cheeks hollow and circles carved beneath her eyes. "The riots?"

"Burnt out, with half of Elysia. The city is calming,

slowly. The king went to Little Kiva himself, to talk to the people and see the damage."

That gave her a start, till she realized that "the king" meant Nikos now.

"Is he—"

"He seems well. Exhausted. Grieving. No one understands what happened in the ruins, though, except you and him and the pallakis." Khelséa held out the cup and Isyllt took another greedy sip of water. "She was here too, the pallakis Savedra. She didn't stay long, but she was grateful that you were alive."

A nurse came soon to shoo Khelséa away, bringing lukewarm beef broth. Isyllt would have eaten the wooden bowl for last drops of salt and liquid. Her hands were shockingly white, veins stark blue through transparent skin. Her nails were blue as well, and she shivered despite the weight of blankets and glowing brazier.

Ciaran came soon after. He joked and teased and flattered her, but she saw her reflection in his dark eyes and knew she looked like death. Maybe she was.

She flinched away when he reached for her hand, remembering Phaedra's skin cracking, Kiril's heart slowing beneath her touch. She was death—she could never let herself forget that.

The nurses chased Ciaran off in turn and doused the light above Isyllt's bed. She lay in the darkness surrounded by the breath of her fellow patients, their coughs and snores and whispered prayers. She was wrung dry, but tired of sleeping.

She stirred from a doze when the bells tolled a lonely hour. Eyes closed, she touched her ring, picking at the layer of grime that crusted the curve of the diamond. She could feel the difference in the stone already, the lightness. She tried anyway.

"Forsythia."

There was no answer. She remembered a whispered goodbye. She hadn't said one of her own.

She cried herself to sleep.

Two days later, she went before the king.

Nikos wore mourning white, which didn't suit him, and no jewelry but his nose ring and sapphire signet. He'd cut his hair; for the first time Isyllt saw his father in the bones of his face.

"Lady Iskaldur." They met again in his study, but no tea or informality this time, no clutter on his desk. The room was nearly bare—he would move to the king's suites soon. "I'm glad you're well."

"Likewise, Your Hi—Your Majesty."

His mouth twisted. "Awkward, isn't it? No one quite has it memorized yet. Least of all me."

"What happened, Your Majesty?"

"Phaedra...disintegrated. I was a bit cloudy at the time, but Savedra tells me it was spectacular. You passed out. We thought you were dead too, but when we came back with the guards you were breathing."

"And—" Her throat closed. "And Kiril?"

His hand twitched against the desk. "We didn't find his body. We searched, but there were spirits everywhere, and the riots—I'm sorry. He'll have a tomb in the royal crypts for his service."

She closed her eyes, too tired to care if he saw her pain. He didn't know—that was obvious from his helpless misery—about Kiril's betrayal or just what the missing corpse might mean. It would be a mercy if he never knew. "I understand. Thank you."

Silence stretched for a time. "Savedra tells me how you helped her," he said at last. "Before and after I was captured. Thank you. And thank you for stopping Phaedra. But..." He couldn't meet her eyes.

"But I forswore myself," she said softly.

Nikos nodded. "I would have done the same, I think, had it been Vedra hurt. But you broke your oath." *You let my father die,* said the catch in his voice. "It's—" Again he stopped short. This time, she imagined, the unspoken word was *treason.* "Not something that can be known. I can't ask you to return to my employ."

He was right, of course. That didn't stop her cheeks from stinging, or help the hollow sensation in the pit of her stomach. "I understand, Your Majesty."

"You'll be compensated for your service, of course." His hands curled against polished wood. "I am sorry."

"So am I," she whispered. She straightened her shoulders. "Thank you, Your Majesty. Is that all you need of me?"

"Yes." He stood, awkwardly, and she did the same. "Thank you for all your service, Lady Iskaldur."

She bowed farewell. There was nothing else to say.

Savedra Severos met her in the halls. Mourning white suited her no better this time than it had when the queen died. She wrung her hands when she saw Isyllt, then forced them to her sides.

"I'm sorry," she said, voice rough. "Nikos told me— and after all you did—I'm sorry."

"It's all right." Savedra flinched from her smile; she knew how ghastly she looked. "I understand the need. One can hardly make a habit of forgiving traitors."

Savedra flinched again, and color rose in her cheeks. "Even so. Oh, here." She tugged at her left hand, and Isyllt swallowed as she recognized the ruby glitter. "I don't need this anymore." Her right hand glittered too, a magnificent orange sapphire that Isyllt had last seen on Lord Varis.

"You can keep it," she said, not reaching for the offered jewel. "You should. She was your relative."

"I don't want it! Please. It's a mage stone."

Isyllt lifted a reluctant hand. The ring was warm from Savedra's skin. No echo of magic stirred as she closed her fingers around it.

"Thank you."

"If there's anything you need," the pallakis whispered.

"There's nothing." Too harsh—she tried to smile. "But thank you all the same."

She had inherited all of Kiril's estate that did not revert to the Crown. The thought of walking through his house, of touching his books and his clothes, made her gag. She knew that would fade; she still regretted parting with mementos of her mother, though the sight of them had brought only pain at the time. But for the moment she couldn't leave her apartment without seeing streets they'd walked together, shops they'd visited.

Staying in was no better—she heard his footstep on her stairs as she tried to sleep, felt the touch of phantom magic at her wards. Once she leapt from bed and flung open the door, but the hall was cold and empty.

Khelséa visited her, bringing food every time. Ciaran came with wine and flowers. Isyllt invited them in each time, but had no heart for pleasant conversation, or the pretense of it. She wasn't entirely sure she had a heart at all.

On the seventh night, she opened the door to find Varis Severos on her doorstep. He wore white as well; it suited him better than it did Savedra.

"I imagine I'm not someone you most want to see right now," he said, "but may I come in?"

"Of course," she said after a pause, stepping aside. "Would you like tea, or wine?"

He grimaced. "Do you have anything stronger?"

She poured them both ouzo while he claimed a chair, and prodded the fire to life before she sat in turn. "How can I help you, my lord?"

He didn't speak for a long moment, watching the embers fall instead. Behind him, city lights blurred through the windowpane. Finally he emptied his glass in one neat swallow.

"You know they never found Kiril's body," he said at last.

She couldn't stop a wince. "I know."

"That's because I took it from the tower."

That broke through her fugue. Ouzo splashed her fingers as she startled, chilling as it evaporated. She drained the glass before she could spill the rest. "What?" She coughed on the fumes. "Why?"

"Because I know the choice that death brings for the likes of you. And I believe in the freedom to make such choices."

Her lips peeled back from her teeth, and she wanted to say something vitriolic about his choices and their consequences. She couldn't find the right words.

"Why are you telling me this?"

"Because if you're anything like him, you'll find out eventually." He smiled wryly. "And I know you are. I left him in a safe place, warded from opportunistic spirits. I returned after the demon days, and he was gone."

She had understood the possibility since Nikos had told her of the missing body, but it wasn't any easier to hear again. Her left hand clenched till her scars ached.

"I thought you should know," Varis said after a long silence. "Now, while you have time to think on it. I know how much you meant to each other."

"Yes." Her lips shaped the word but no sound followed. She drew a breath and tried again. "Thank you, my lord."

"I'm sorry," he said. The pain in his voice made her flinch. She preferred him glib and mocking. "So very sorry."

"Yes, well." She rose, less gracefully than she might have wished, and led him to the door. "We knew the risks when we took the job."

She didn't answer the door for the next two days. She wept, raged, flung books and muffled her sobs and curses in pillows. Her magic was still burned to the root, or she might have wrought worse destruction.

The second night she sat down in the ruin of her bedroom and knew she couldn't stay. Kiril had asked if she could stand to see him as a demon. She knew she could. Even now her hands ached at the thought of touching him. If he came to her now, cold and lifeless, she would run to him as she always had. Nothing, it seemed, could burn her need for him so deep that it wouldn't grow back.

She couldn't go on like this, not with the wounds so fresh.

*   *   *

Dahlia came the following day, when Isyllt had stopped crying long enough to clean up some of the wreckage. She wouldn't have answered that knock either, but the latch clicked anyway.

"I took your spare key when you were sick," the girl said, lingering in the doorway. "I thought it might be useful."

Isyllt snorted. "I suppose I'm lucky you didn't steal the dishes while I was in St. Alia's. Though the glasses might have fared better if you had." She nudged a shattered wine stem with one toe and set the broom aside.

"I would have come sooner," Dahlia said, closing the door behind her, "but I needed to think." Her face was still sallow, thinner than it had been two decads ago. The effect aged her, made the androgyne clearer in her bones.

Isyllt waited, leaning against the cupboard.

"I want to be your apprentice," the girl said in a rush. "If you'll still have me. I don't want to—to end up like my mother, or Forsythia, or any of those other girls. I want..." Her hands traced shapes in the air as she searched for words.

"Choices?" Isyllt suggested.

"Yes."

She laughed softly; it made her chest ache. "I understand. And I would teach you, though I won't be fit to anytime soon, nor fit company, but—"

Dahlia's face was already closing. She raised her eyebrows as her jaw tightened. "But?"

Isyllt sighed. "I'm leaving Erisín."

"Oh. Why?"

Her mouth twisted. "I'm running away. There are

ghosts here I can't face. Decisions I can't make. I need distance."

"Oh." Dahlia folded her arms across her chest. "I could go with you," she said quietly.

Isyllt frowned, running her tongue over her teeth as she tasted the idea. "I suppose you could." It was a bad idea; that was probably why she found herself considering it. "People have the habit of dying in my company."

Dahlia laughed, as scathingly as only an adolescent could manage. "People have a habit of dying in Oldtown, too. I'd like to see something different before my turn comes."

Coward, she named herself, to take a child into danger because she didn't want to go alone.

She met Dahlia's eyes, already narrowed against the threat of rejection. Not quite a child, and no stranger to risk. Old enough to make her own decisions, perhaps.

Isyllt knew exactly how well making those decisions for her would go.

"Something different." She pressed her tongue against her teeth thoughtfully. "I think we can manage that."

ACKNOWLEDGMENTS

I could never have finished this book without the help and support of so many people. These include but aren't limited to: Elizabeth Bear, Jodi Meadows, Jaime Lee Moyer, Leah Bobet, Celia Marsh, Liz Bourke, and everyone in the drowwzoo chat, for endless brainstorming and commiserations; the Partners in Climb, for moral support and getting me out of the house on a regular basis, and for never dropping me on my head; all my blog readers who listen to me bitch and look interested and sympathetic; my fabulous agent Jenn Jackson and equally fabulous editor DongWon Song, and everyone at Orbit.

Thank you!

DRAMATIS PERSONAE

Adrastos Agyros – the king's seneschal

Anika Sirota – an ingénue

Aphra – an elder vampire, Spider's maker

Ashlin Idaran Alexios – crown princess of Selafai, wife of Nikos Alexios

Azarné Vaykush – a vampire

Cahal – a lieutenant in Ashlin's retinue

Ciaran – a musician and friend of Isyllt

Dahlia – an urchin

Ferenz Darvulesti – a Sarken margrave, Phaedra's husband

Forsythia – a prostitute

Ginevra Jsutien – a courtier, heir of House Jsutien

Hekatarin Denaris – captain of the prince's guard

Iancu Sala – steward of House Severos

Isyllt Iskaldur – necromancer and Crown Investigator

Kebechet – a perfumist, proprietor of the Black Phoenix

Khelséa Shar – police inspector

Kirilos Orfion – sorcerer and spymaster, Isyllt's mentor

Mathiros Alexios – king of Selafai, Nikos's father

Mekaran Narkissos – owner of the Briar Patch

Mikhael Kurgoth – captain of the king's guard

Nadesda Severos – archa of House Severos, Savedra's mother

Nikos Alexios – crown prince of Selafai

Phaedra Severos Darvulia – a sorceress

Savedra Severos – Nikos's mistress

Sevastian Severos – Savedra's father, Nadesda's husband

Spider – a vampire and rabble-rouser

Tenebris – an elder vampire

Thea Jsutien – archa of House Jsutien, Ginevra's aunt

Varis Severos – sorcerer and member of the Arcanost, Savedra's uncle

Whisper – a vampire, Forsythia's lover

Various other citizens, courtiers, vampires, and redshirts

APPENDIX I

Calendars and Time

Selafai and the Assari Empire both use 365-day calendars, divided into twelve 30-day months. Months are in turn divided into ten-day decads. The extra five days are considered dead days, or demon days, and not counted on calendars. No business is conducted on these days, and births and deaths are recorded on the first day of the next month; many women choose to induce labor in the preceding days rather than risk an ill-omened child.

The Assari calendar reckons years *Sal Emperaturi*, from the combining of the kingdoms Khem and Deshra by Queen Assar. The year begins with the flooding of the rivers Ash and Nilufer. Months are Sebek, Kebeshet, Anuket, Tauret, Hathor, Selket, Nebethet, Seker, Reharakes, Khensu, Imhetep, and Sekhmet. Days of the decad (called a *mudat* in Assari) are Ahit, Ithanit, Talath, Arbat, Khamsat, Sitath, Sabath, Tamanit, Tisath, and Ashrat.

In 727 SE, the Assari Empire invaded the western kingdom of Elissar. Elissar's royal house, led by Embria Selaphaïs, escaped across the sea and settled on the northern continent. Six years later, the refugees founded the kingdom of Selafai, and capital New Tanaïs. They established a new calendar, reckoned *Ab urbe condita* but otherwise styled after the Assari. Selafaïn years end with the winter solstice, beginning again after the five dead days, six months and five days after the Assari New Year. Selafaïn months are Ganymedos, Narkissos, Apollon, Sephone, Io, Janus, Merkare, Sirius, Kybelis, Pallas, Lamia, and Hekate. Days of the decad are Kalliope, Klio, Erata, Euterpis, Melpomene, Polyhymnis, Terpsichora, Thalis, Uranis, and Mnemosin.

Selafaïns measure 24-hour days beginning at sunrise. Time is marked in eight three-hour increments known as terces. The day begins with the first terce, dawn, also called the hour of tenderness. The second is morning, the hour of virtue; then noon, the hour of reason; afternoon, the hour of patience; evening, the hour of restraint; night, the hour of comfort (also known as the hour of pleasure or of excess); midnight, the hour of regret; and predawn, the hour of release.

APPENDIX II

The Octagon Court

The Octagon Court refers to both the district in Erisín that houses Selafai's eight noble houses and the governing body formed by the houses' archons. Both were established in 134 AUC, after the capitol was moved from New Tanaïs to Erisín. The Council of Eight gathers in Erisín twice a year, usually near the vernal and autumnal equinoxes, to discuss policy and meet with the king. A three-fourths majority of the Eight can override royal policy. The last time such a majority was reached was in the reign of Ioris Severos, who promptly ignored the consensus; the Octagon Court in turn removed him from the throne, bloodily.

The Eight:

House Alexios is the youngest of the Eight. Isola Alexios was a general at the time of the Hecatomb, and used her military influence to wedge her family into the gap left by the fall of House Korinthes. The Alexioi have traditionally been a martial family; following in Isola's tradition, Typhos Alexios was a general before he led the coup against Ioris Severos and claimed the throne for himself. Their family estate is in Nemea, and their crest is a rampant griffin, gold on blue.

House Severos came to power just after the founding of the Octagon Court, replacing House Kylix. It has long been thought that the illness that decimated the Kylices was very convenient. Their 106-year hold on the Malachite Throne was the longest unbroken reign of any house. Notable among their monarchs were Darius II, the sorcerer-king who stood with the Arcanostoi against the demon plague of 353 and brokered a truce with the vrykoloi, giving the vampires control of Erisín's underground. Ioris Severos was also notable for being mad, or at least so venal and self-centered that the Octagon Court reached a majority to remove him. Severoi lands are in the northeast, bordering Ashke Ros and Sarkany. Their crest is a silver phoenix on black.

House Jsutien is a founding member not only of the Octagon Court but of the kingdom. In the sixth year of her reign, Pandora Jsutien oversaw the removal of the throne from New Tanaïs to Erisín. Her daughter Naomi was instead famous—to the chagrin of her family—for filling the newly renovated palace with scores of her lovers. Despite her excesses, the Jsutiens held the throne until Kallisto I died childless in 215, passing rulership to her Petreos husband and his kin. Years of thwarted ambitions to reclaim the throne have stung Jsutien pride. Recently they have allied themselves with House Aravind, increasing their wealth with southern trade. Their crest is a bronze hydra on crimson.

House Konstantin is an old house whose Selafaïn blood has been thinned by foreign marriages. Their family holdings border Vallorn and Veresh, and they have many alliances among the northern peoples. They had strong ties to House Korinthes, but haven't been close to any ruling family since the Hecatomb. Their presence in Erisín has been slight in recent years, but other houses eye their mountain stronghold with suspicion, and wonder when the Konstantins will appear on Erisín's doorstep with a barbarian army in tow. Their crest is a grey wolf on white.

House Aravind retains the closest ties to the old blood of the Sindhi, the people who ruled the Sindhaïn Archipelago and southern coast before the coming of Embria Selaphaïs. Their southern holdings are rich in trade but weak in strength of arms. They have long been considered one of the least ambitious houses, but in recent history they have begun to ally themselves with the Jsutiens. Their crest is a green serpent on scarlet.

House Hadrian was once a military power to rival the Alexioi. Lately, however, their wealth has come from agriculture, and fewer of their scions rise to military prominence. They have grown to be seen as a sleepy, provincial family, and younger members flock to Erisín for lives of fashion and debt. Their crest is an orange lion on white.

House Petreos held the Malachite Throne for thirteen years, the shortest time of any house. Iodith Petreos inherited the throne at her father's death, and ruled for ten years—she is most remembered for establishing the Vigiles Urbani, and for dying in a suspicious accident in 228, allowing House Korinthes to take the throne. The Petreoi hoped for a return to power when Nikolaos Alexios married Korina Petreos, but the marriage was loveless, and Mathiros Alexios favored his mother's family no more than his father's. It is widely supposed that Korina's ties to a Mortificant cult did nothing to help her relations with her husband and son; Sophia Petreos, the current high priestess of Erishal, tries to distance her house from such cults. The house's crest is a cockatrice, vermilion on brown.

House Ctesiphon was another house present for the founding of Selafai. Though their star has risen several times, they have never held the throne. They are currently nearing the end of a thirty-year exile after their archon Kraetos attempted to assassinate Nikolaos Alexios. Their crest is a crouching sphinx, grey on indigo.

The Fallen House:

House Korinthes is not the only house to have fallen from glory, but is certainly the most notorious. Beginning with the rumors surrounding Iodith Petreos's death and ending with the Hecatomb, their 73-year reign is generally considered a shadow on Selafaïn history. Demos I was a ruthless ruler, as was his daughter Damia. Demos II was a burgeoning tyrant when Tsetsilya Konstantin's death triggered the destruction of the palace and the devastation of Erisín. Historians often speculate what sort of king Ioanis might have been, but most are just as glad not to know. Their crest was a winged boar, red on black.

extras

www.orbitbooks.net

about the author

Amanda Downum was born in Virginia and has since spent time in Indonesia, Micronesia, Missouri, and Arizona. In 1990 she was sucked into the gravity well of Texas and has not yet escaped. She graduated from the University of North Texas with a degree in English literature, and has spent the last ten years working in a succession of libraries and bookstores; she is very fond of alphabetizing. She currently lives near Austin in a house with a spooky attic, which she shares with her long-suffering husband and fluctuating numbers of animals and half-finished novels. She spends her spare time making jewelry and falling off perfectly good rocks. To learn more about the author, visit www.amandadownum.com.

Find out more about Amanda Downum and other Orbit authors by registering for the free monthly newsletter at www.orbitbooks.net

if you enjoyed
THE BONE PALACE

look out for

THE HUNDRED
THOUSAND
KINGDOMS

by
N. K. Jemison

I

Grandfather

I AM NOT AS I ONCE WAS. They have done this to me, broken me open and torn out my heart. I do not know who I am anymore.

I must try to remember.

* * *

My people tell stories of the night I was born. They say my mother crossed her legs in the middle of labor and fought with all her strength not to release me into the world. I was born anyhow, of course; nature cannot be denied. Yet it does not surprise me that she tried.

* * *

My mother was an heiress of the Arameri. There was a ball for the lesser nobility—the sort of thing that happens once a decade as a backhanded sop to their self-esteem. My father dared ask my mother to dance; she deigned to consent. I have often wondered what he said and did that night to make her fall in love with him so powerfully, for she eventually abdicated her position to be with him. It is the stuff of great tales, yes? Very romantic. In the tales, such a couple lives happily ever after. The tales do not say what happens when the most powerful family in the world is offended in the process.

* * *

But I forget myself. Who was I, again? Ah, yes.

My name is Yeine. In my people's way I am Yeine dau she Kinneth tai wer Somem kanna Darre, which means that I am the daughter of Kinneth, and that my tribe within the Darre people is called Somem. Tribes mean little to us these days, though before the Gods' War they were more important.

I am nineteen years old. I also am, or was, the chieftain of my people, called *ennu*. In the Arameri way, which is the way of the Amn race from whom they originated, I am the Baroness Yeine Darr.

One month after my mother died, I received a message from my grandfather Dekarta Arameri, inviting me to visit the family seat. Because one does not refuse an invitation from the Arameri, I set forth. It took the better part of three months to travel from the High North continent to Senm, across the Repentance Sea. Despite Darr's relative poverty, I traveled in style the whole way, first by palanquin and ocean vessel, and finally by chauffeured horse-coach. This was not my choice. The Darre Warriors' Council, which rather desperately hoped that I might restore us to the Arameri's good graces, thought that this extravagance would help. It is well known that Amn respect displays of wealth.

Thus arrayed, I arrived at my destination on the cusp of the winter solstice. And as the driver stopped the coach on a hill outside the city, ostensibly to water the horses but more likely because he was a local and liked to watch foreigners gawk, I got my first glimpse of the Hundred Thousand Kingdoms' heart.

There is a rose that is famous in High North. (This is not a digression.) It is called the altarskirt rose. Not only do its petals unfold in a radiance of pearled white, but frequently it grows an incomplete secondary flower about the base of its stem. In its most prized from, the altarskirt grows a layer of overlarge petals that drape the ground. The two bloom in tandem, seedbearing head and skirt, glory above and below.

This was the city called Sky. On the ground, sprawling over a small mountain or an oversize hill: a circle of high walls, mounting tiers of buildings, all resplendent in white, per Arameri decree. Above the city, smaller but brighter, the pearl of its tiers occasionally obscured by scuds of cloud, was the palace—also called Sky, and perhaps more deserving of the name. I knew the column was there, the impossibly thin column that supported such a massive structure, but from that distance I couldn't see it. Palace floated above city, linked in spirit, both so unearthly in their beauty that I held my breath at the sight.

The altarskirt rose is priceless because of the difficulty of producing it. The most famous lines are heavily inbred; it originated as a deformity that some savvy breeder deemed useful. The primary flower's scent, sweet to us, is apparently repugnant to insects; these roses must be pollinated by hand. The secondary flower saps nutrients crucial for the plant's fertility. Seeds are rare, and for every one that grows into a perfect altarskirt, ten others become plants that must be destroyed for their hideousness.

* * *

At the gates of Sky (the palace) I was turned away, though not for the reasons I'd expected. My grandfather was not present, it seemed. He had left instructions in the event of my arrival.

Sky is the Arameri's home; business is never done there. This is because, officially, they do not rule the world. The Nobles' Consortium does, with the benevolent assistance of the Order of Itempas. The Consortium meets in the Salon, a huge, stately building—white-walled, of course—that sits among a cluster of official buildings at the foot of the palace. It is very impressive, and would be more so if it did not sit squarely in Sky's elegant shadow.

I went inside and announced myself to the Consortium staff, whereupon they all looked very surprised, though politely so. One of them—a very junior aide, I gathered—was dispatched to escort me to the central chamber, where the day's session was well under way.

As a lesser noble, I had always been welcome to attend a Consortium gathering, but there had never seemed any point. Besides the expense and months of travel time required to attend, Darr was simply too small, poor, and ill-favored to have any clout, even without my mother's abdication adding to our collective stain. Most of High North is regarded as a backwater, and only the largest nations there have enough prestige or money to make their voices heard among our noble peers. So I was not surprised to find that the seat reserved for me on the Consortium floor—in a shadowed area, behind a pillar—was currently occupied by an excess delegate from one of the Senmcontinent nations. It would be terribly rude, the aide stammered anxiously, to dislodge this man, who was elderly and had bad knees. Perhaps I would not mind standing? Since I had just spent many long hours cramped in a carriage, I was happy to agree.